Great Crossing

Judalon de Bornay

Published by Judalon de Bornay, 2021.

GREAT CROSSING

First edition. May 25, 2021.

Copyright © 2021 Judalon de Bornay.

ISBN: 979-8201308827

Written by Judalon de Bornay.

Table of Contents

to my husband

The Johnson Family of Great Crossing, Kentucky

Robert "Robin" Johnson, born 1745,
married **Jemima Suggett**, born 1753.
Their children were:
Betsey: born 1772, married John Payne
James: born 1774, married Nancy Payne
William H.: born 1775, married Betsy Payne
Sallie: born 1778, married William Ward
Richard Mentor: born 1780, married Julia Chinn
Benjamin: born 1784, married Matilda Williams
Robert: born 1786, died War of 1812
John Telemachus: born 1788, married Sophia Lewis
Joel: born 1790, married Verlinda Offutt
George W., born 1792, died 1810
Henry: born 1794, married Elizabeth Flournoy

Chapter 1
Inauguration
March 4, 1837. Washington, DC

A pity the sun chose today to shine for the first time in months. A shame he couldn't use the freezing rain as an excuse to cut short his time in the Senate. He did not want to leave the warmth of his bed for an upstart ray of sunlight. He needed the stillness of his grief more than the trouble of his inauguration. Let a man bereaved of wife and daughter remain in the shadows where all good vice-presidents belong.

Thirty years ago, he thought he was everything, and Washington behaved as hopelessly naïve, as maddening in its optimism as he had. And by 1814 that second war with the King had left his body and this town in ruins. In the quarter century since the war, he'd used his battle scars to good effect. But the town had taken a turn toward faithless ignorance and aimed its terrifying, deliberate cruelty towards too many, including himself. It happened without anyone in particular getting the blame, and it happened in that slippery, small-town fashion: a look cast with the lighting of a cigar, a word murmured after a sip of floral tea.

At night, unable to sleep, he fancied the wind full of the cries of good boys like he'd once been, as they threw over their good intentions in order to survive just one more election. And when he walked each morning to the Senate and turned his head toward the sky, he could almost see the impossible promises and muttered threats lift into the air to join the mists rising off the Potomac.

In a few hours, he would swear an oath of office. And what would that be? To uphold the past two terms of promises and threats from his old friend Jackson. Marty got picked for the top instead of him, and it was a sore that would never heal, but they both accepted the fact that their mentor's hands would still hold the reins.

He thought of the wreckage left in Jackson's wake and his stomach clenched with the sure knowledge every whipping boy learns the hard way: he would pay the price, not Marty. The new president had little in common with the old. Marty played the indoor games, while he and Jackson earned fame the hard way as Indian killers. The president's expulsion of the Civilized Tribes stank of cruelty, and Marty planned on finishing the order. But who would get the blame? He would, because he'd killed too many Indians twenty and some odd years ago while Marty'd stayed indoors. Because of that damned reputation, his penance—the Indian Academy back home—might very well be put to the torch.

He and Jackson shared another fame that he thought had made the president more his brother than Marty's. They had shared the exquisite torment of ridicule from the press and the public because of their wives. And his ambition for the White House–knowing Julia and their daughters would never be allowed to cross its threshold–made him pander to such childish policies as letting Peg O'Neale tear up Jackson's Cabinet.

A sudden screech of wind through the chimney agreed with his thoughts. Bitter cold, despite the sun, would punish old Jackson and Marty both, as they made their victory ride down Pennsylvania Avenue. It would punish him as well, making his battle scars constrict and his hands rigid as old leather. At least *his* swearing-in would be in the Senate chamber by a nicely stoked fire. That would serve as a bit of consolation for playing second fiddle.

The thought encouraged him enough to throw off the covers, careful not to ruffle Lydia in her sleep. He sat on the edge of the mattress for a minute, waiting for some sign of feeling in his toes and stared at the painting over the fireplace mantel. It depicted an old castle fortress, clinging to a sea cliff. How Julia had feared it, as if one day she'd pass by and find the castle fallen into the waves below. Her superstitious notion that it portrayed their lives had led him to give way to his own superstition after her death. Each morning he stared at it reverently and prayed the briefest moment.

Don't be too disappointed. I almost made it.

You would have made it had you left my girl where she belonged.

Not Julia's sweet consolation; not Adi's teasing assurance. He heard his mother. With a sigh, he crawled back under the covers, but closing his eyes did not close off the memories or the regrets.

It was no use; he sat upright again and stared once more at the painting. As he watched, the sunbeam that had roused him expanded and lapped gently at the castle ruins. Suddenly, millions of dust bits entrapped within the beam turned brilliant, taking on a life of their own. He felt a familiar warmth embrace him, a pressure on the bed by his thigh.

It's our first morning, isn't it? He asked. The pressure moved up his scarred arm.

They had shared breakfast for the first time as man and wife in a humble widow's kitchen where the sun lit up Julia's face and made her sparkle like a jewel.

Richard stared in wonder at the shimmering air until his chin trembled and he could bear the memories no longer. Then he put his head in his hands and wept.

Chapter 2
First Run

October 10, 1794. Johnson Farm at the Great Crossing, Kentucky

Richard wondered if the war with Spain had already started. The jostle and clatter beneath his window sounded like some kind of battle. He shook his head clear of sleep and found himself alone, without any little brothers clinging to him. A norther' must have blown in because the air in his room pinched the skin on the back of his hands and wouldn't let up. He kicked his legs free of blankets, walked over to the window and cracked it open just a sliver as he took quick aim at the chamber pot.

Their overseer stood next to his father and nodded. A jumble of talk from his big brothers and sister grew louder: James cursed Spain and the blockade and Will cursed President Washington, getting a sharp rebuke from Ma for his trouble. Above them all was Sallie's laughter.

Why hadn't Pa gotten him up an hour ago? Richard panicked as he pulled on his clothes. Ma must've won out at the last minute. He'd overheard his parents arguing the day before. Even though it felt shamefully good to be the sole object of their fury toward each other, his rising anger against his mother unsettled him. The moment he stepped into the upstairs landing, he sighed with relief to see his travel pack gone.

5

He peeked into the next room and found where Benj and Joel had migrated. All five of his little brothers lay curled against each other for warmth, their quilts a heap on the floor. God bless Robert, John T, Benj, Joel and George, he whispered. Ma always said you had to say every single name in a God Bless prayer, otherwise it didn't count.

Richard's thick wool socks made him slip on the oak floors and he tensed every muscle in his body to keep from falling. By the time he made it downstairs, he felt like he'd already traveled a mile over solid ice. The stable boy, Jacob, had left Richard's boots propped against the entry hall bench and they shined with a fresh layer of grease—bear, from the smell of it. Such a thick coating meant Pa expected a downpour.

A cold current trickled toward him from the back door and he heard the Singin' Sisters humming as they got breakfast plated up. It smelled. Since their cook died having a baby, they'd been stuck with the old twin servants and their cooking testified to why they'd been replaced. Ma needed to do something soon. They'd need a first-rate cook for Sallie's wedding. She couldn't marry the high and mighty William Ward with a shabby table. Even he knew that.

Richard heard their laundry girl, Lucy, giggling somewhere down the hall. Sure enough, Jacob came grinning from the pantry, loaded down with two big lunch baskets. He started to tease them but stopped when he heard his mother's voice coming from the end of the porch.

"I want Richard here with me, Robin Johnson!" Richard knew Pa was in for it. When his parents got in the thick of things, calling each other Robin Johnson and Jemima Suggett gave everybody a clear sign to stay away.

"A boy should be with his mother on his birthday!" She changed to a whisper so the servants wouldn't hear, but he could feel his mother's anger with every raspy syllable all the same. Sometimes he wished she'd just yell. What difference did it make being an example of Christian virtue when everybody didn't hear as much as feel his mother's wrath? It came off her like heat from the frying pan.

His father made the mistake of chuckling. Richard couldn't see his mother's face, but he knew it had changed color.

"His *birthday*? You've got five little boys to treat like babies. Age of fourteen's about time to let this one grow up."

Thanks, Pa. About time, alright.

His mother said nothing, a bad sign.

"I don't understand you, Jem. You never had a problem with James or Will making a Louisville run, and they were a lot younger when they went along. Even with all this talk of war, it was more dangerous back then."

"They were different. They had to grow up fighting for their lives. Richard's got no memory of the fort or the fires or nearly dying of starvation. He's the first to grow up during our easy times."

On the other end of the porch, Richard heard Sallie, Will and James laughing. They didn't seem much like survivors of anything special, except Ma's strap, maybe. He strained to hear his parents and held his breath.

"Call it motherly intuition or a warning from God. Something." She spoke softly now, no longer in that annoying whisper-hiss, and he heard her clearly. "I have a feeling something terrible is about to happen. He's so different from the other children, Robin. He looks at everything so strange, and I blame you. Stuffin' his head full of Merlin. Percival. Quixote." She'd gone back to hissing.

Richard's chest tightened with that new feeling of irritation at his mother. He loved those stories the way none of his brothers ever did. They filled the hours when he followed Pa around the Crossing. Just yesterday Pa used Don Quixote to explain how somebody as low-down as Aldonza could be the lady Dulcinea. But with every argument he overheard between his parents, he couldn't help thinking that even treating a lady like a lady must be near impossible. Ma was a fine Baptist woman, but she could try the patience of a saint, and Pa was no saint.

"If this were just another business trip, I might bend a little. But this is politics. He *is* different, Jem, and I've got just as strong a feeling as you have that it'll change his life. He's the one who's got the chance." His father's voice sounded urgent, hopeful. Chance for what, Richard wanted to ask out loud.

"You really think they will see it in him?"

See what, Richard wanted to scream, now. The strange and secret understanding between his parents let them leave out too many words.

His mother sighed. "Alright then. Watch out for him. He is in danger, and I don't know if it's from the riffraff on the barges, or something when you get to Louisville. But don't let him out of your sight. Promise me."

Richard heard them kiss. Scrapping one minute, kissing the next. He would never understand them. He backed away from the door and stepped into the dining room just as they walked in.

"Eat up, boy," his mother ordered, giving him an annoying pat on the back. He ate as much as he could stand, which wasn't much.

When he rose from the table, she came and stood next to him, his four extra inches forcing her to look up at his face. It made him uneasy to think they had drifted apart over the past few months. In his eagerness to be on his own, he hadn't stayed close enough to her to notice this change in his size. He'd spent years measuring himself next to her—first her knee, then her waist, then her shoulder. Now it seemed she'd always been small, almost insignificant.

"Stay close to your father and mind your manners at the conference. They're important men, and powerful. They may remember you in future." She spoke in soft staccatos, a blend of old Virginia genteel and Kentucky hard-boiled. She offered her cheek, and he obliged with a light kiss and a respectful hug, which her bulging stomach made difficult.

"Take good care of my little brother, Ma." He stepped away from her.

"Which one?" she asked with a laugh.

He gave her a sober smile. "The one that's coming, of course."

His parents exchanged a look, and he hoped that, whatever it was they expected of him, he'd be able to give it.

RICHARD LEANED OVER the boat rail, the mild hissing of the Ohio River not nearly loud enough to drown out the lecture Mr. Marshall was giving Pa. Their families went way back to the days when Great Crossing was a fort called Bryant Station. The man talked like the devil, but at least he'd left behind his sons, Lewis and Humphrey, who really were devils. They were Richard's age or thereabouts. He would have thrown one, or both, into the river by now.

Mr. Marshall's words didn't seem to bother Pa, who puffed at a cigar, staring off at the Kentucky side of the river as if the man were reciting the *Iliad*.

"And another thing I want to know is, what are we going to do about Washington's pig-headed proclamation? We got us a mob in Louisville that don't cotton to being told their meetings are unlawful assembly. I've heard him referred to on more than one occasion as King George, so just what kind of resolutions against Spain can we make that'll get his approval?"

Marshall noticed how much of his own cigar had turned to ash, cleared his throat and tapped away the wasted two inches of his smoke.

"Just the kind that'll make sure no more Kentucky boys set fire to Spanish forts or shoot another soldier. This is a quarrel between

Spain and France, and we cannot get between them. We don't have money for a war with anybody. Simple as that."

Richard took a step closer to the men. Just the word 'war' gave him a mixture of thrill and fear.

"So, we have to keep our heads cool while we're surrounded by a bunch of hotheads? I tell you frankly, Johnson, if we don't get those barges moving again down to New Orleans, we're going to have civil war. And I can't say as I blame our boys. It's hard to stand behind the president when he gives the impression of callous disregard for our western way of life."

"Well, if it's any comfort to you, Marshall, the president's letter gives us his blessing and his prayers. He's counting on us to calm our boys down long enough to get things squared with the diplomats. And we all know how long it takes those fellas." Robin chuckled.

Marshall did not respond with any humor. "Easy for you to say. You shipped east. You aren't sitting on a year's worth of hemp or cotton or tobacco growing mold in some dockside warehouse. I'm just giving you fair warning that these men aren't in the mood to listen to somebody who looks like they've got a deal with the devil, an' sealed with a letter from the almighty president."

"YOU UNDERSTAND A LITTLE better what's at stake, Richard?" Pa nodded toward the bulging warehouses ahead of them as their keelboat docked at Louisville. A slow, chilling wind ruffled the Ohio and knocked about the rows of empty barges in their moorings. Marshall and others hurried by, saluting and exchanging somber words. The town had the feel of a funeral attended by a dead man's worst enemies.

They had no trouble finding a couple of Irish boys to tote their bags. Richard swallowed hard when he saw their thin jackets and rags wrapped over remnants of what once had been shoes. He stepped onto the road just as a boy plodded by, struggling with a cage full of spitting cats.

"Have to keep those river rats killed off," Pa told him. "All those grain sacks are easy pickings." He shook his head in disbelief after taking in the waste. "I can understand now why they want to burn out the Spaniards."

Richard pictured their people back home in the fields of hemp and cotton, toiling at the mill and the rope walk. What if everything had been lost because his father had chosen the Mississippi run instead of going up Lake Erie way? He felt something new to him, a kind of godly sorrow, as he passed the people congregating by the warehouses. Their families faced ruination. "How'd you know which way to ship this year, Pa?"

"Reading the journals from back east, something you should start doing instead of reading so many stories." Richard glanced at his father as they walked briskly toward the center of town. He could not believe things had gotten so bad Pa would consider abandoning their books. Homer, Milton, Cervantes gave them not just stories but secret passageways between their minds, maybe even their souls.

"That revolution in France has gotten everybody stirred up, including Spain, and it got me to thinking that we should sell to Americans instead of foreigners."

"Smart thinking, Pa. I hope I'll be able to figure things out like you do."

"If I were smarter, more people would have followed my example."

"Do you think they're jealous? The way Mr. Marshall talked..."

"Maybe. Anybody lucky enough to have all we've got has to make other people envious. I've learned, and you may as well learn it too, people are going to think what they want, and you will have little power to change their minds."

They neared Hill Street, where the fragrance of damp chestnut leaves cleared their heads of the smell of rot along the river. Richard looked down, conscious of the Irish boys' eyes on his boots. He felt ashamed of the contrast between them.

Pa nodded in the direction of a large red brick house across the street. "Our inn looks nice. Your future brother-in-law told me about it."

"Colonel Ward's not right for Sallie. He's too old," Richard blurted.

Pa laughed. "Now why would a young lady of seventeen want to marry a boy her own age? Believe me, son, older men make the best husbands. Besides, who else in our neck of the woods could afford to take care of your sister?"

Richard frowned. "Money isn't everything," he muttered, giving a shy glance at the ragamuffins coming to a halt beside him.

"Thanks, boys. Drop those things on the porch. We'll take them in." Pa gave them each a coin.

Richard looked down again at his slick boots. "Wait," he mumbled before the two stepped off the porch. He fumbled in his jacket to find the hidden pocket where he'd squirreled away his spending money and dropped the coins into two of the dirtiest hands he had ever seen.

The next morning, Richard and his father bundled themselves against the north wind. Richard said nothing about his fourteenth birthday as they walked toward the meeting hall. It made him feel like a man to let it pass unrecognized. He repented of being harsh in his thoughts about his mother, knowing she was thinking of him right about now. They stepped into the Democratic Society meeting, already warm from the well-established fire at the end of the room. The crowd of angry men gave off a different kind of heat, however. He strained to hear his father over the noise.

"Listen to everyone, even if at first they seem like fools. Reserve judgment. And Richard, keep the thoughts in your own head quiet. That's the hardest part."

Richard noticed how his father stuck to the President's commission, determined to get resolutions, not arguments, from the delegates, but nothing came of the first day. He sensed, however, that something extraordinary was happening within himself. His pages of notes, made in lightning-fast scribbles only he could interpret, seemed to impress the men sharing their table.

When Richard returned to the inn with his father, two other delegates accompanied them, intent on drafting a first report for Washington. Julien Leclerc brought his cheerful twelve-year old son, Alphonse. John Henderson, an enormous man, carried a wicker basket of victuals suitable to his size. The aromas rising from the food bin made Richard's mouth water.

As they walked, he noticed Alphonse take a surreptitious peek under one of the flaps, but checkered napkins kept everything well hidden. The inn's food was passable—an improvement over the Singing Sisters—but Mr. Henderson's basket left room for only one question in Richard's mind: was there anything in there for him?

"Now my friends," Mr. Henderson grinned, ballooning his jowls against his cravat, "I want to introduce you to one of the jewels of Louisville." Their small party huddled round a wobbly tea table in a corner of the inn's dining hall. Rain had begun to tap against the window panes; a chill scurried down Richard's back. He scooted his chair nearer the fireplace, and saw Alphonse do the same. They both had trouble disguising the wolf pup hunger in their eyes.

"Hmm?" Mr. Henderson raised his eyebrows knowingly as he spread open the napkins, revealing delicate breads in impossible twisted shapes; bite-sized morsels of meat encrusted with peppers and spices Richard had never smelled before. The pies and cakes also came in sizes just right for him to pop into his mouth.

Chapter 3
Fire
October 1794. Louisville, Kentucky

Richard sat near the fireplace in Edward Chinn's house. He took in the high ceiling, panels and rails that made the large room expand upward and outward at the same time. The variety of paintings, sculpture, human-size vases and tiny figurines distracted him from the papers his father wanted him to see. He heard the words of the Bible in his head counsel against love of Mammon, but he knew he could love God and Mammon if this were the Mammon.

Before their introduction, Mr. Henderson explained how all of Chinn's wealth had vanished not only because of the Spanish blockade, but because of the arrest of his business partners by the revolutionaries in France. Yet, for a sick man who had lost everything, Richard thought he saw a gleam of hope in Mr. Chinn's eyes. Pa had just given him thousands of dollars.

He'd lost track of the names on the transfer of ownership papers Pa and Mr. Chinn had been exchanging for the last two hours. He remembered the fancy name of Jasper. He was a butler and would be Sallie's best wedding present. Pa took a liking to Jamie the coachman, along with a carriage and its matching horses. Pa had papers for a gold-skinned young wheelwright Jamie described as "indispensable". His name was Sandy, like his color. Richard overheard Mr. Chinn tell

Pa he'd give him a bargain on the cook's sister and daughter, adding with a shrug, "Why break up the family?"

Richard grew alarmed, however, when his father added enough furniture and artwork to fill two supply wagons. Which he also purchased, with horse teams.

Mr. Chinn called Jasper to him without looking up from the paperwork. "Fetch Henrietta and the child."

Jasper entered the kitchen, headed toward a plate of leftover muffins and popped one into his mouth. "Farmers. Big place back east next to Georgetown," he informed Henrietta.

Where's that?" she asked as she scalded the breakfast dishes.

"Not too far from Lexington. Horse country." He dashed off the crumbs spoiling his perfect waistcoat then rubbed his gloved fingertips clean.

"Jasper, we live in Kentucky. What isn't horse country?"

He laughed quietly. "Long way from here and best of all, any Chinns. You ready to meet the new master?"

"Ready as I'll ever be. What's he like?"

"Nothing like the Chinns."

"Where's Julia?" She changed her apron and covered her hair with a clean white cap.

"Playing with Delia and Caroline. I'll get her. He's taking Milly, too," he said as he left.

Henrietta leaned against the pantry door, choked back a sob and said a little prayer of thanks.

As she walked through the entry hall, she heard Jasper whisper, "Run catch up with your mama." Julia grabbed her hand, and they stepped into the drawing room together. Henrietta curtsied and signaled to Julia to do the same. The little girl held out her apron instead of her skirt as she bent her knees but kept her head up and stared wide-eyed at the new master's son.

"This is Henrietta," Mr. Chinn mumbled. "Master Johnson and his son, Master Richard," he added in her direction.

Richard forced himself to break off staring at the woman and child standing before him by glancing over at Pa, who quickly averted his eyes to the floor. The cook was tall, fair-skinned, with a shape like Aphrodite observable even through her thick, coarse gown. The child looked like Mr. Chinn's daughters. Was it his imagination, or was Chinn squirming a bit in his chair?

Pa cleared away the catch in his throat with a cough that echoed off the high ceiling, and managed to ask, "What's the little girl's name and age?"

Henrietta answered in a deep, soft voice, "Mas Chinn—the oldest one, that is—named her Julia, for her being born on Independence Day. Four years ago."

Edward Chinn mumbled, "These are my grandfather's people. We inherited them along with this house at his death last year."

"And your sister?" Pa asked in an unnaturally strained voice.

"Milly, sir, and she is thirteen."

As the grownups talked about duties and expectations, Richard turned his eyes to the child and stared back at her. She slipped away from her mother to come closer to him.

"Fire," she whispered, and pointed a tiny finger at him.

Richard looked wonderingly at Julia's pale, delicate face. She looked like Mr. Chinn. He felt blood rush to his cheeks when he realized it might be the truth. She was gangly like a newborn foal, a sure sign she'd be tall like her mother. Chinn was tall, too. Julia stood inches from his face now; he found her wide-eyed stare irresistible. Her gray-green eyes made him think of a kitten Sallie once loved. What a shame Ma wasn't going to have a little girl.

"Nothing like a fire on a damp and chilly day. Your hands cold?" Richard nodded toward the cheerful blaze in the fireplace.

Julia tilted her head, puzzled, and brought her hand inches from his hair. "Fire," she whispered.

"Oh!" Richard laughed and gave a tuft of his thick hair a yank. "When I was a baby, some Indians tried to burn me in my cradle, and my sister threw a bucket of water on me. She says my hair turned red, so I'll never forget she saved my life and I owe her everything!"

Julia moved even closer and blew at his hair. Richard felt a little gooseflesh rise on his scalp. "Her name's Betsey. She was very brave," he said in mock seriousness. "Are you brave, too?" He lowered his head and shook it back and forth, tickling her hand with his head of fire. To his delight, she let out a squeal of laughter.

Richard broke off his play with Julia when he heard his father's voice turn unfamiliar in its coldness. "At Great Crossing, families stay together unless someone runs. If any of you tries, you'll be sold in opposite directions. Do I make myself clear?"

Richard turned his attention to Henrietta. She was the most beautiful creature he had ever seen. Just looking at her made him aware of parts of himself he didn't want to think about.

She answered firmly, "You don't have to be concerned on our account, Mas Johnson." Pa gave her a peculiar look Richard didn't understand.

They set out midday, caravan style. Jamie led out in the carriage with Richard and his father. Jasper drove the first supply wagon with Henrietta and Julia on board. Milly quivered with joy as she climbed next to Sandy in the last wagon. The sky cleared, the winds calmed, and the roads looked dry. Robin gave God the glory.

"Chinn was right, Jamie is a masterful coachman. You can't read a journal in every carriage," Robin said. Richard brought his eyes back inside the coach, feeling guilty for stealing so many glances at their new cook. She had wrapped a blanket around herself and her child and joined Jasper on the wagon seat. Truth be told, he had noticed Pa peeking a time or two at her from behind his newspaper.

Richard had to force himself to read about Washington's rough second term in the hope of casting Henrietta—and Satan—out of his mind, but his mind would not cooperate. With his eyes still on the paper, he asked, "Was it Seneca or Heraclitus who said, 'War is the father of all things, making some...'"

"'Free men and others slaves.' Seneca." Robin lowered his paper. "You are about to ask me some unanswerable question. You know, you're a lot harder on your pa than your older brothers and sisters."

"It's only that I was thinkin' how right now there's just the threat of war."

"It wasn't just a threat for Mister Chinn," Robin interrupted. "Even though he's thousands of miles from France and Spain, his life has been ruined by their quarrel."

"I was just thinking, though. That little girl, Julia? If her mother weren't a slave, she'd be one of...us." Richard's color rose to his cheeks, but he could not restrain himself. "Henrietta's like no woman I've ever seen, so I can understand Mr. Chinn giving in to temptation. But how can he sell his own daughter?"

Robin cleared his throat, yet still struggled to speak. "Son, little Julia's his aunt."

Raised on Virginia genealogies, Richard needed only a moment to understand: the old man had forced himself on Henrietta. "Mr. Chinn's grandfather," he shuddered. "How could he? She's like...Dulcinea."

"Some masters forget their duty. It's called unrighteous dominion. Lording your manly power over a servant's something only weak men do. And ungodly men, because mixing blood is just Satan's way of making men more like animals."

Richard nodded his head and turned back to his own journal. Pa had made it clear the subject was done. But he saw nothing animal in Henrietta. Goddess, maybe. Somebody somewhere along the line mixed that blood to perfection.

PERHAPS IT WAS BECAUSE of the maternal instincts blasting through Miz Johnson as she nursed her newborn son. Perhaps it was the longing to replace her daughter after the wedding. Whatever the reason, Henrietta's new mistress made a fierce bond with Julia, and within weeks the two became inseparable. Joel, one of the passel of little Johnson boys, called Julia his sister. Strangers assumed Julia was Miz Johnson's own child, which came as a revelation to Henrietta how backward Great Crossing was. It hurt all the same.

Henrietta's extraordinary cooking kept her caught in that unbreakable cycle well known to slaves: the more she pleased her masters, the more they expected. At Great Crossing, she prepared meals in large quantities of hardy food instead of the delicate plates she had perfected in Louisville. The Chinn's elegant kitchen had been a haven where Julia, Delia and Caroline could play at making little tarts and cakes. Here, she could not allow Julia near the cookhouse. Hot metal, boiling water and searing oil made life dangerous even for adults; she had to remind herself a dozen times a day what a comfort and a blessing it was that Julia had Miz Johnson's favor.

She could not let her jealousy show, even when Julia cried because she could not sleep near the new mistress and baby Henry. But her own mothering time had been reduced to the hours of sleep, the only chance they had to be together, and she guarded it selfishly. At least she could watch Julia grow, even if she could only measure her against the length of their cot.

Henrietta thought this was a safer place than most. The Singin' Sisters told her they'd come with the Johnson clan from Virginia on a fervent Baptist mission. Young Lucy said the women hadn't had problems since Mas Robin whipped an immigrant mill hand near to death for getting on one of his girls. And Miz Johnson kept her husband happy. Scared, too. They'd all laughed when Lucy added that little tidbit of truth.

Still, Henrietta stayed out of sight as much as possible. Something—she hated to call it a spark—passed between her and Mas Johnson when they met. She avoided him like the devil. If she got on Miz Johnson's wrong side, it would ruin any chance for Julia to have a bearable captivity. She wore baggy shifts to hide her body and made Milly do the same. Too many of the Johnsons and their people were of the male variety, and that was never a good thing, even among so-called good Christians. No one in Louisville had been called a better Christian than her former master.

She thanked God old Chinn was dead. The thought of him still brought on the shakes, but she knew she was more fortunate than others. He had been a widower those last six years when he made too much use of her, so she had not endured the wrath of a jealous wife the way many servant women must.

Jasper once told her young Mas Edward's father was Milly's, that he'd beaten Mama when Milly turned out to be too dark for his fancy. She remembered when old man Henderson bought Mama and carted her away, with Mama praying, "Lord Jesus, keep my girls together." By some miracle, that prayer had been answered.

Henrietta never did find out for certain who her father was, but there was no denying Edward Chinn's daughters and Julia looked cut from the same cloth. In her nightmares, which were still too frequent, the old man himself was not only Julia's father, but her very own as well.

Chapter 4
Distractions
July 1, 1804. Great Crossing

"There's a new seamstress in town, Mama," Betsey opened, a first volley in today's skirmish with her mother.

"Since when has a seamstress been of any interest to you?" Jemima retorted.

It was true. Betsey had enough skill to stitch tree bark into breeches. Given a piece of fine fabric, she could make a gown even the angels would envy. The blessing frock they were lavishing their skill upon was for Sallie's baby. All that was beside the point, now.

"Since my hands have gotten too full of children to make anything for myself, that's when." Betsey tried to keep her voice light. She knew that seven babies in fourteen years did not impress her mother. Sallie sprawled on the divan. She had given birth to only five children, and was nursing her most recent accomplishment, baby Malvina. Breasts were all the rage in fashion that season, and she enjoyed the extra attention her décolletage received thanks to the baby. She had agreed before this visit to keep her mouth shut and let Betsey, the one with tact, do all the talking. They were here not to sew but to remake their mother.

Jemima remained quiet, so Betsey continued carefully. "You know, Mama, Frankfort is run by a new group of ladies who don't know anything about Papa's influence in the old days."

Sallie stifled a laugh. Betsey shot her a warning look. "Jimmy and Dickie have an opportunity to make real careers in politics this year, and John's turned heads now that he's a general. I think we owe it to them to exert more influence. But all the styles are so new..."

Jemima looked up from her needlework with a stare that paralyzed her daughter. "Julia, take the boys to the spring and fetch us some water," she requested calmly.

"Can I bring you anything else, Miz Jemima?" Julia asked.

"No thank you, dear. No need to hurry. And shut the door, please." Betsey's little boys, Willie and Newt, along with Sallie's four-year-old, Junius, toddled after Julia like ducklings.

"Am I to assume you're going to bring up the gossip about my husband, Mama?" Betsey hated how false her voice sounded; it betrayed her. And her mother's politeness to Julia irritated her to distraction, even though she long ago begrudgingly accepted that the child was more than just a servant. It outraged her that in ten years Julia had never felt the leather strap that had terrorized all the real Johnson children.

"Sallie, have I said a word about John, or gossip?" Sallie opened her mouth, but nothing came from her throat except a tight, high-pitched noise. Betsey glared at her younger sister: *thank you for nothing*.

"But since you have brought it up, yes, I would very much like to have a talk with you girls. Neither of you is a fool. Grow backbones. Betsey, tell John you know what he's up to, and he needs to stop it, all of it, including the servant girls. You pay attention too, Sallie. I warned you about that husband of yours. He's getting a bad reputation over certain business dealings, and I wasn't surprised to hear about the wrong kind of dealings with women as well. And you'd best be keeping all your servant girls out of his sight."

"Mother!" Sallie jerked the baby away from her; Malvina shrieked with rage. Betsey turned as red as the baby and looked to her sister for help. Although Sallie was six years her junior, she had none of Betsey's reticence when it came to butting heads with Jemima. "How dare you make insinuations about John and Will? We've got twelve children between the two of us, and I think that's more than enough proof that they aren't philandering."

"A rooster can never have too many hens. And both of you, I'm afraid, are stuck with two of the cockiest in the roost."

The sisters exchanged a look of helplessness. Nothing stopped their mother once she started an attack with a homespun proverb.

"It doesn't matter that you have no proof, or that you have no names, because I do, and for your sakes, I'm not telling. And besides, those are particulars that most women waste time on. You don't have any more time to waste. We have to think about the family's reputation and fast before this election gets going. Jimmy is a possibility as far as Frankfort goes, but I've got my heart set on Richard going to Washington someday. Your husbands cannot be distractions. You need to take better care of them."

"I do the best I can," Betsey muttered. Her mind shouted, John's a general. Jimmy's your oldest son and should be getting all this attention. But it's Richard. Not even Dickie anymore, but *Richard*. Like he's some English king!

"I mean, very good care of them. Sallie, I'm not so concerned about, because she doesn't mind it so much."

Betsey stared at Sallie. Even Sallie's mouth dropped. "I'm exhausted already, Mother!" Betsey exclaimed.

"Believe me, you will lose more sleep worrying about his other women than if you lose sleep attending to him in the way he needs to be. And if you haven't got enough servants to watch the children so you can have more leisure, I will send you home with some of mine."

They heard Julia and the boys coming down the hall. Betsey and Sallie forced their faces into masks of calm as the children ran into the room. Jemima put on her placid smile, nodded at Julia to set the water near her, then asked her daughters sweetly if the new seamstress might be willing to call on her.

"I will send her a note requesting that she come tomorrow. Or perhaps the day after," Betsey answered in the same tone, although shocked that her mother returned so meekly to the original topic.

"One day's as good as the next, since we don't have one go by without some crisis. And you are right, my dear; your father's bound to win this time. So why shouldn't the next lieutenant governor's wife have a new gown?"

Betsey struggled to disguise her confusion. Was this her reward for submitting to humiliation over John? When she said nothing, her mother took it as a signal to continue.

"Do you know if she's fast? I do hope she will be able to get it over with quickly."

"It's not a tooth-pulling, Mother," Sallie tossed out.

The little laugh she added had a hint of rage to it, Betsey was glad to detect. Why hadn't they guessed? That getting Mother to update her wardrobe by twenty years only took reforming their marital relations!

Sallie continued, barely controlling her anger. "Julia, take Malvina to Milly for a changing before we go. And tell my Thomas to get our buggy ready." Free of the baby, she splashed water onto her napkin and roughly wiped the beads of sweat off the faces of her little boy and nephews.

"Mama, I cannot understand why you spoil that girl." Betsey ignored the glare from her sister that all but screamed, *No! We got what we came for! Don't ruin it over Julia!*

Jemima answered with a high-pitched tone of hurt. "What else can I do? Turn her out to the fields? Or put her with the riffraff at the mill? She's always been my little helper, and I don't want her anywhere else."

"Mama, she's not 'little' anymore. And I don't think it's wise to have her associate with John T and Joel or even little George. She's so..."

"What, Betsey? So pretty, like her mother? Afraid she'll be a distraction to your brothers?"

"No, Mama," Betsey snapped. Sallie's smirk infuriated her. It was exactly what they both believed, and the reason why they kept their husbands away from Great Crossing. It took no imagination to picture any man with one of those accursed Chinn girls.

"I have more peace concerning her than I do any of my children," Jemima replied. "And do you know why? She's as devoted to the Lord as I am. Add to that the fact that your father's put the fear of God in every man a hundred miles of this place."

Betsey heard Sallie mutter through her teeth, "It's not men a hundred miles away we're worried about." Since their mother ignored Sallie's retort, Betsey gave free reign to her indignation. "No matter how devoted to the Lord or you she is, she's at an age when girls like her can't help themselves. The only question will be when the time comes, will the baby be black, or white?"

Jemima sat motionless, never a good sign. Her voice quivered when she finally spoke. "How dare you be so crass in my presence?"

Before Sallie could stop her, Betsey shot back, "And your advice to me wasn't?"

They turned at the sound of Julia's footsteps on the hall floor, then stared at the silhouette of the girl and baby.

Betsey looked down at her sewing. "White, it appears," she murmured.

Georgetown, Kentucky

Suzanne Bayton wished the tiny quarters she rented had a tree for shade. She sat upright on a small, padded chair and finished the hem on a customer's Independence Day frock. Her own gown was of the lightest gauze she dared be seen in, but a rivulet of sweat ran down her spine all the same. Answering the knock at her door came as a welcome break.

A young man with skin like dark velvet stood before her. "Jacob Chase, Miss. I come from over at Great Crossing. Miss Betsey—Miz Payne—sent me to you with this." He smiled and handed over a note of fine paper.

Suzanne remembered the woman. Last week, they had met at the home of Martha Scott, her only customer of any importance. Mrs. Payne was tall, haughty, and pretty enough to arouse envy in Mrs. Scott's circle of friends. The note invited her to come to Great Crossing tomorrow, 'if you are free to create a new wardrobe for myself and my mother, Mrs. Robert Johnson.'

Entire new wardrobes? "Mr. Chase," she managed to utter.

"Just Jacob, ma'am," he corrected her with a chuckle.

"Can you return for me tomorrow morning, in a small wagon?"

"Got just the thing," he assured her. She sat to write her acceptance, hoping to convey sophistication instead of desperation. When she finished, she sprang from her chair and handed him the note with a trembling hand.

Jacob was sure he heard her scream as he mounted his horse.

"WHERE ARE WE NOW, JACOB?" Suzanne asked. Hemp leaves the size of a man's back overhung the narrow cart road, giving welcome shade from the morning sun.

"Most everything the past half-mile's been Mas Robin's. It gets real pretty once we get into the woods and cross the Little Elkhorn. Lots of springs, too."

This endless stretch of greenery, the smells of dirt, grass and horse lather lifted Suzanne's spirits higher than they had been in weeks. Too many hot, miserable days had gone by since she'd seen the outside of her shop. Her eyes ached from strain, but she had finished her orders for the Independence Day celebration by working late into last night. How she hoped Mrs. Johnson wasn't the demanding, hurrying kind.

Up ahead, a droning sound accompanied by unfamiliar cracks and pops shattered her self-pitying thoughts. The cart lurched over a low pile of ragged hemp stalks and rattled into a wide clearing filled with dozens of laborers. A few raised their heads in greeting, fewer yet offered a smile. Most continued to sing wearily, keeping rhythm with their reaching, bending, lifting.

Within seconds, Suzanne felt the blow of the full sun on her back. Her parasol offered very little protection; she knew her dress would be soaked in minutes, all chance of making a good impression on Mrs. Johnson ruined.

To protect the children darting between the hemp piles, Jacob slowed his wagon to a crawl. Suzanne watched the workers, her eyes particularly drawn to a dark-skinned girl of a size rarely found in women. She lifted bundle upon bundle of hemp stalks off the shoulders of men and women passing below her, stacking the crop into a wagon with daunting efficiency. The muscles in her shoulders and back rivaled those of a man. Rags crisscrossed her forearms and hands, meager protection against the brutal hemp as red welts and bloody scratches on her skin proved. Suzanne averted her eyes, looked at her hands gripping the parasol handle. Hands gloved in delicate crochet. "God forgive me," she whispered.

"Heph!" Jacob called out to the muscled woman. "Don't let that Sandy-man outload you!" 'Heph' did not stop her work, just smirked and wagged her head toward a man heaving his enormous frame into a wagon bed. He was the color of wet sand with freckles large enough for Suzanne to see some twenty feet away.

"You keep lookin' at my Hephzibah like that, I'll have to break you like a hemp stalk, you lazy house boy!" Sandy shook a huge bundle of hemp over his head and grinned like a madman at Suzanne's astonished face.

"You got yourself a fine woman, Sandy!" Jacob hollered over his shoulder as they rolled past. "And a fine place out here, safe from ol' Miz Johnson runnin' you ragged like she does me!"

The clearing ended abruptly as Jacob drove the cart into the woodlands. Much-welcomed shade prompted Suzanne to discard the parasol and sigh with relief. She glanced at her driver. He appeared unaffected by the heat, Sandy's ravings, or her presence. Before her confidence waned, she blurted, "Don't you mind being a slave?" Once the words escaped, all she could do was quickly apologize for her rudeness.

"No apologies needed, ma'am." After a long minute, Jacob clucked at the nag; the wagon rolled a little faster. "It's not so much mindin' as it is bein.' A few of us have earned enough freedom money for ourselves. Just not enough for a whole family. Can't do that in a lifetime."

"I am sorry," Suzanne said feebly. "How I hope and pray all this will change."

When Jacob turned to look at her, she noticed his faint smile held a touch of pity. "Hear that?" He asked, happy to change the subject.

"The river!" Suzanne exclaimed, eager to see. Fast-flowing water slapped at rocks and pilings, churning up the smell of fish and algae. Soon they clambered over the bridge, and within moments, Jacob had turned off the narrow road from the river onto a long drive. Far down at the end, she could make out a rambling whitewashed house surrounded by a dozen barns and sheds, pastures filled with grazing livestock, and massive rock fences. How many slaves had broken their backs stacking and straightening those slabs of rock, she wondered?

As they neared the house, she saw that it sat on a foundation of the same silver-gray stone. The grounds appeared to be uninhabited although she smelled a bitter stench coming from the same direction as sounds from hammers, shouts, and mill wheels.

"See where that black smoke curls up? Tar kettles at the rope walk. Whole village over there. The Johnsons, they got a great big family. They got stores and mills, all kinds of smithies workin.' That's where most of our people labor, get switched out to the fields for punishment. But I don't know which is worse. Some riffraff like the Irish work a month or two, but they move on. Pullin' hemp into ship rope's too hard a work except for my kind."

Suddenly a wind blew off the stretch of open land behind the house, making Suzanne hold onto her bonnet strings with both hands. The smell of tar disappeared, replaced with the sweet scent of trampled grass and horses. "That's the Great Crossing back there." Jacob moved his free hand in a long arc from side to side. She followed it as he waved across a huge swathe of meadow that stretched for miles to her left and right.

"What crosses there?" she asked, awed at the perfect evenness of the land, as if a great flatiron had smoothed away every crease and unwanted fold.

Jacob chuckled. "Just Johnsons and their people and animals, now. But in the old days, herds of buffalo, millions of 'em, ran down this stretch to get to the river."

A small boy ran toward them from behind a nearby barn, three hound puppies on his heels. "Daddy!" he shouted, setting the pups to yapping. The pack trotted alongside until Jacob reined the horse to a stop.

"Simon! Get on up here and hand me down some of these packages," Jacob called over the dogs' ruckus. As Simon scrambled into the wagon bed, father and son exchanged grins.

"He's a fine boy," Suzanne said.

Jacob's eyebrow twitched as he offered her a weak smile. "My reason for staying," he whispered as he handed her down from the wagon bench. Immediately, she turned and reached for a parcel jutting from the wagon. A mild voice with a piercing quality stopped her. "Jacob and Simon will take care of that."

Suzanne turned; she saw a solid woman of perhaps fifty years, middling in size, but with a strong presence. "Jemima Johnson," the woman said, extending her hand. Streaks of warm silver mixed with chestnut peeked from an old-fashioned cap. Her dark hazel eyes gave off enough warmth to offset the sternness in her jaw. She wore a colonial style skirt of green and white stripes, and a bodice with leg of mutton sleeves. Suzanne could not help but pity her, but there was a rigidity to her bearing that inspired fear, as well.

Behind the woman stood a tall, pretty girl in an equally old-fashioned dress whom Mrs. Johnson introduced as Julia. Suzanne instantly pitied her more. She had seen so many of these last-born daughters, expected by the entire family to sacrifice their lives so the others could do as they pleased once their parents turned feeble.

"How do you do, Mrs. Johnson. I am Suzanne Bayton, at your service." They stepped onto the porch and the welcome relief of its shade.

"Any relation to the Peytons of Charlotte, Virginia?"

Suzanne had grown accustomed to people misunderstanding her name. "I'm afraid not. My family was Huguenot, named Baton. They settled in New York a hundred or so years ago, but when the French became so unpopular with the last president, we changed it a bit. Bayton. With a 'B.'"

"Ah! I see. Well, I have no love for John Adams. You may be interested to know my husband helped draft the Kentucky Resolutions to help the French."

"They did help, indeed. Your husband must be a great man," Suzanne offered as she entered the cool foyer. The Johnson house lacked appeal from the outside, but the interior compensated for that disappointment with its wealth of art and antiques of extraordinary craft. She noticed the reflection of her dress and feet on the polished wood floor as they walked through the rooms. "Your house is beautiful. It feels strong."

The respectful tone in the young woman's voice pleased Jemima. "We built it ourselves, with our oldest five children, along with our people." She led Suzanne into a large drawing room. "Its foundation and walls are built to last. Like our family." Jemima paused. "Do you have family, Miss Bayton?"

Suzanne hoped the woman was not as menacing as that tone of voice. Steeling herself, she answered, "No longer. My parents are gone, and I am the only one of their children to survive." Her hands stayed busy uncovering drawings and design books. Julia smiled shyly at her and helped her unpack and arrange the items on a large side table. "I have several illustrations for you. A design that you admire is always a good place to start. I can make any changes you would like."

"You are quite sure of your craft, aren't you?" Jemima quickly stepped over to the table and began turning over the pictures.

"My grandmother and my mother were artists with a needle. All I can hope is that my skill will manage to keep their art alive."

"Very honorable. My daughter could not praise you highly enough." After a minute turning over the illustrations, Jemima looked up, creasing her brow. "I fear these Grecian monstrosities will not do your reputation any good, however."

"Are those the French plates? Jacob must have packed them by accident." Ashamed that she could so easily put a slave in jeopardy to save face, she murmured, "No, I must have. They are monstrous, aren't they? I keep them more for a reminder of what not to do." Julia smiled when Suzanne made a face at the grapes and tassels dangling from shoulder and bosom.

"Well, I like these," Jemima pronounced, pulling towards her several sketches of modest day frocks and no-frills evening gowns. "These look refined, instead of ridiculous, and more to my taste."

"Thank you, Mrs. Johnson. These are my designs."

Jemima took a seat on a highbacked chair, raised her chin, looked the seamstress over. "Then let's get started. My needs are simple—two plain dresses for making calls, and something of good material for the governor's ball. My daughter will be another matter. Julia, please close the curtains, except for this one." Suzanne turned to see an enormous oak outside the window where Mrs. Johnson pointed. The tree blocked the view but allowed enough light for her to work.

"I also want you to make something smart, but very simple, for my girl. She'll be accompanying me to Frankfort after the election. Show me what you can do by starting with her."

"Thank you, Miz Jemima, with all my heart," Julia exclaimed.

Suzanne's own heart jumped to her throat. The child was not a daughter, but a servant! Perhaps an Irish girl taken in to work off a debt? No, that couldn't be right, not here. This wasn't New York, or even Ohio. The image of Jacob's giant friend in the clearing came to her. Julia was a fair-skinned slave.

Julia's complexion was paler than her own. The girl's honey curls were streaked with light gold, her green eyes far more subtle than Suzanne's eyes of smoky gray. She struggled to hide her indignation as she thought of some "master" abusing his power over this poor girl's mother.

She had no choice but to shake it off and set to work; she had nothing to rely on except her craft, she bitterly reminded herself. Pulling a drawing from her folio, she offered something she used for the maids of a New York merchant to the scrutiny of Mrs. Johnson. "This perhaps? It is in the latest style from the Continent, without the pretense."

"Yes, that will do nicely. Let's start the muslin, shall we?" Mrs. Johnson smiled and gave Julia a kindly pat on the arm. The gesture seemed monstrous to Suzanne. Julia, now clad only in a thin summer shift, fetched a stool without being asked.

"Thank you, Julia. You are practically a foot higher than I!" Suzanne stepped onto the stool. She began to drape and fold the length of muslin from the tall girl's shoulders.

"How old are you?" Suzanne asked in hopes of relaxing them both.

"Fourteen tomorrow, Miss."

An Independence Day baby! Suzanne hated irony. It always struck a cruel note, but few as cruel as this. She worked rapidly, fingers pressing the muslin into tiny pleats, snipping and pinning.

"You are fortunate to be so tall." When the girl managed a hint of a smile, Suzanne added, "I'm envious." Julia looked down at Suzanne as if ashamed of every inch. "To be on the safe side, I'm adding growth pleats to the skirt, and perhaps an extra dart in the front of the bodice."

Julia crimsoned at the suggestion.

They heard a commotion outside. Julia shimmied out of the muslin and yanked her old dress over her head.

"My daughter and her children, no doubt." Suzanne sensed tension in Mrs. Johnson's voice; when Mrs. Payne entered the room and made no effort to hide a grimace thrown Julia's direction, Suzanne understood why: the woman was jealous of Julia. The true mother and daughter tolerated each other. But even Suzanne had to admit that between Mrs. Johnson and her slave was a bond that felt more like family affection.

WHEN JACOB AND SIMON loaded the wagon late that afternoon, Suzanne clutched her purse tightly until she could feel the outline of the gold coins, partial payment for a dozen garments and the realistic hope of getting her business established. How many coins would it take to free Jacob and his family? Neither she nor Jacob could hope of earning such a sum. Was there any consolation in knowing you were so valuable? *Not the mindin', just the bein'.*

As the wagon moved away from the Johnson home, Suzanne pictured herself working by candlelight, nights on end, to fill this order. She pictured Hephzibah working in the glaring sun, days on end, with no hope of anything better except the rope walk, whatever that was. And Julia, who could pass under the nose of any bounty hunter in the state, but instead stood attendance to fulfill the whims of her mistress.

Throughout their afternoon together, she sensed how Mrs. Johnson and her daughter barely concealed their contempt for her as a working woman and a northerner. Somehow, she managed to keep her dignity despite the tension that had quickly grown between them.

Oh, Papa, why did you have to die here? Why did you have to ruin everything for me back home?

This storm of desperate thoughts gave way to a man on horseback, a powerful rider in complete command of his mount. She turned to watch him, always drawn to anyone with the talent to ride well. But, when he reined his horse and trotted toward the wagon, she had to whip her head around quickly, keeping her gaze aimed at the river road ahead. How she hoped he hadn't noticed her staring.

"Mas Richard!" Jacob called out.

"Jacob Chase, you scoundrel. Taking off with another pretty woman?"

"No sir, I'd need your Pegasus to do that right," he answered casually.

Suzanne glanced quickly at the man, then back at Jacob. The two were grinning at each other! "Mas Richard" appeared delighted to see Jacob. She would never get used to the paradox of slave-master relations. How she hated those two words, always coupled together. Julia's face popped into her mind, and she grew incensed, turning her neck and cheeks a deep rose color.

The horseman caught her eye and held it long enough for her to observe him tip his hat and rise in his saddle. He must have mistaken her color as a blush, not a fit of anger, because he apologized for his comment.

"I am the scoundrel, Miss. Do forgive me. Richard Mentor Johnson, at your service," he said, then waited for her reply.

His face, now inches from hers, startled her for its warmth. He was so close she could feel his breath on her sleeve, see the fiery color of his hair, the yellow and turquoise flecks in his hazel eyes. They gave him a fierceness, like a wildcat. She cleared her throat. "Miss Bayton, Suzanne Bayton," she croaked.

"I apologize for letting Pegasus kick up such a dust storm," he said without breaking his gaze at her. "A Virginia Payton?"

"No, I...Mrs. Johnson asked the same question." She looked away from his face, which had gone from threatening to broad and pleasant when he smiled at her. She concentrated on the stripes of clouds in the sunset, straining to regain her composure. "It's been an honor meeting you, Mr. Johnson, but I really must get home."

"It'll be dark in less than an hour. I can't leave Jacob at the mercy of curfew enforcers. I hope it won't be an imposition if I accompany you to..."

"The Academy Quarter." Feeling protective of Jacob, Suzanne welcomed Mr. Johnson's company. Curfew enforcers sounded terrifying. The road to Georgetown was too dusty and rutted for conversation, however.

When they reached the level streets in town, the wagon and horseman slowed to a walk. As they halted in front of her small building, Mr. Johnson leaned toward her from his saddle. "I'll be delivering the Independence Day oration at the Crossing tomorrow. I'd be honored if you would attend."

"I have no transportation, Mr. Johnson. But I do wish you well in your speech." She fumbled in her bag for the latch key, self-consciously clanking her new coins together and trying to ignore the effect Mrs. Johnson's son was having on her.

Jacob jumped down from the wagon and started to unload without a word or a look in her direction. Richard dismounted and extended his hand to help Suzanne climb down from the seat. His fingers were warm from gripping the reins. She struggled to gather her skirts with her free hand.

"Permit me?" Richard asked. In a swift motion he lifted her from the wagon and placed her on the walk. She let out a gasp as he pressed her against him. His size overwhelmed her. He was not much taller than young Julia, but his massive chest and shoulders reminded her of a wrestler in New York. One of her father's only sure bets.

"I seem to be doing nothing but apologizing to you this evening, Miss Bayton. Please understand I'm accustomed to my enormous family. I have no end of little brothers, nieces and nephews. We're a very physical lot, I'm afraid."

She held the key at last in her shaking fingers and decided it best to reassure him instead of making him sorrier. "You've so much the advantage over me, Mr. Johnson. All my family is gone. I am, I suppose, far too used to being alone."

He said nothing after this revelation, but bit his lip instead and muttered, "Allow me," and entered the place ahead of her. Jacob, undeterred by the dark, stacked the first armload of Suzanne's books and cloth on her cutting table, exactly where he had gathered them hours earlier.

"Thank you, Jacob," Suzanne smiled openly at him, but quickly turned away when she noticed Mr. Johnson raise an eyebrow in the man's direction. Upon lighting a candle, the small dimensions of her shop became all too apparent.

"You needn't worry for my safety, Mr. Johnson, although it is kind of you. I have the best of neighbors. As you can see, we live so near, I daresay a sigh could be heard as easily as a scream."

Richard did not laugh at her dark humor but looked over the room as if expecting to find a hidden intruder. "I suppose you'll be safe enough." He added to her surprise, "You are such a tiny thing. This place suits you."

Suzanne watched from the doorway as Jacob turned around the wagon and Mr. Johnson mounted his horse. He stared down at her for a moment then in a tone of quiet command said, "Tomorrow, eight o'clock. Jacob will be here for you. You must hear my speech, although it may not go well for me. I won't sleep knowing you are all alone here."

As she broke away from his gaze, she glanced at Jacob, waiting patiently atop the wagon seat, his head shaking back and forth before he offered her a quizzical little smile.

SUZANNE STEPPED OUT of the wagon, and Jacob drove off in a hurry, mumbling about hell to pay if those dishes didn't get brought up. Walking down the hill toward the gathering, she swallowed back her elation at seeing her dresses in the crowd. A podium had been set up on the knoll where the unfinished Baptist church rose.

She could understand why this spot was chosen for the Independence Day celebration. The view of the great buffalo crossing took her breath away. The speaker could be heard for a mile. But the noise of squealing babies and shushing mothers and clanging dishes could be heard just as far.

Mr. Richard Johnson's voice carried over it all. He had to be proud of that voice, the way its resonance fell agreeably on the ear. It had the effect of making her heart race just as it had last night when he rode away. She heard the words "warms and animates the bosom of the rising generation and pervades the different ranks of people". She looked down at her feet in embarrassment after noticing the grin on his face as he spotted her. All around her were young women gazing up at him, ready to swoon at his feet.

Think about his slaves. Julia. Jacob. Little Simon. They aren't part of the 'different ranks of people.'

But distracting her mind with his faults did no good. Her heart still pounded. She wanted to gaze at him in absurd adoration as well.

After his speech came a rousing musical number by the Baptist youth, followed by a prayer, which droned on too long even for devout and grateful patriots. The aromas drifting from the tables added to her agony. Suzanne glanced up and noticed others eyeing the food, too. Finally, the reverend released them to graze on the well-blessed piles of meat, biscuits, berries and cakes. A Baptist matron gave her a worn smile and a chipped plate loaded with more than Suzanne could eat in a week.

He meandered toward her, shaking hands and fielding compliments. Even before he reached her, he produced a large handkerchief and spread it over a nearby tree stump, motioning her to sit. Something like roots rose from beneath the stump and grabbed hold of her ankles.

She couldn't move; she couldn't even breathe. His breeches were a fine quality gabardine. Should she tell him so? No! He was telling her how lovely she looked in her white dress with the patriotic touch of the blue sash and red bonnet. She lifted her gaze to his massive chest covered in a hideous vest of scarlet sateen.

"We both appear to dress for holidays!" she blurted.

Ignoring that, he went on, "Last night, I had some idea of what a perfect little creature you were." His voice was low, intimate. "But in broad daylight you are even lovelier. Exquisite, I'd say." He scanned her eyes and mouth.

"Petite, as we say in French." Suzanne struggled against his charm, knowing his flirtation excessive and probably brought on by the success of his speech. But oh! How she wanted more. She mustered an inadequate change of subject. "Thank you for sending Jacob. He's good with horses, isn't he?"

"You know something about horses?" His face lit up like a boy's.

"A little. My father and uncle were trainers, and excellent jockeys. I came with them to Lexington two years ago."

"I take it things did not go well? Last night you mentioned your family..."

"They failed to take into account great stables not only own the horses but the jockeys as well. Why hire when you have talented slaves for riders? They fell on hard times. Consumption finally took

Papa. My uncle tried to carry on, but he finally succumbed last winter."

"Consumption as well?"

"No. Despair."

Richard looked away. A long minute passed before he turned back and looked into her eyes. "You have suffered, Miss Bayton, far more than a young woman should endure. How did you come to live in Georgetown? I would think Lexington more suited to someone of your talent."

"Lexington had too many sad memories. I remembered our passing through Georgetown, how lovely it was, what with the new academy."

"I must tell you my father considers Rittenhouse his greatest achievement. I can't help but agree if it brought you here. But, forgive me if it's too painful if I ask, why did you not return to your home?"

"There was nothing left. It's a familiar story. Horses and gambling go hand in hand, don't they? Bad men out to destroy foolish men like my father. They made it impossible for me to go back. I don't know if you've ever seen debtors' prisons, but I have too little strength for such a fate." Suzanne stopped, tried to bite into a strawberry but found she no longer had an appetite.

She did not want to see a look of pity on his face. Some spell of intimacy had bound her to him too quickly, and she needed to break it. "All of this food! The decorations! It's beyond anything I've seen, even for Christmas!"

"I take it you come from a more Puritan part of our nation?"

"I was born and raised in New York, which has little in common with New England these days. But the notion of having slaves for the workforce has gone out of fashion there, so we keep our celebrations rather modest."

"Why, on the contrary, Miss Bayton. New York had more slaves counted in the last census than Kentucky."

"It has ten times the population of Kentucky as well. And we've started gradual emancipation. In twenty years, New York will have nothing but free citizens." Suzanne noticed the people nearby, studying their plates, eating in silence. Couldn't the ground swallow her up and transport her back where women argued openly, and nobody thought less of them for it?

"You have no sympathy with our peculiar institution, I take it?"

His smile dazzled her, the glee in his eyes infuriated her. "I find it distressing. Isn't it a bit ironic to speak of freedom as you've just done, surrounded by people who have no control over their own lives?"

"But wouldn't you agree that heathens who live in ignorance of Christ's grace, in filth and superstition, have even less control of their lives?"

Suzanne set down her plate, only too aware that she and Mr. Johnson were now a source of entertainment, a continuation of his speech. For a moment, she waivered until she remembered how easily she had used Jacob as a scapegoat the day before. "I agree that only someone ignorant of Christ's grace would keep another human being in chains. But once a Christian teaches an ignorant person the gospel, they become brothers in the eyes of God. That makes them equals."

Instead of taking offense, his eyes took on a glow of warmth that puzzled her. "What chains do you see here, mademoiselle?"

Suzanne forced her voice to become nearly a whisper. "The invisible kind. Forged from threats, and either suffering or witnessing the carrying out of those threats."

He shook his head back and forth like an agitated preacher. "You must consider that we here take our responsibility as stewards over these childlike people very seriously. Who could threaten or harm a soul as sweet as Jacob, for instance? You see, Miss Bayton, we believe we have been called upon as tools in God's hands to be their rulers so they can be blessed with food and shelter, and honest labor. And remember, a servant receives no worse discipline than we would give to one of our own children should they be wayward."

His words came smoothly. Were they lines from a speech he had memorized, perhaps given a dozen times? Suzanne hated his words but desired him. It confused and strangely emboldened her. "You have heard of Rousseau?"

She noticed a touch of condescension in the smile he gave her as he quoted, "'Man is born free and everywhere he is in chains.'"

"But most people omit what comes next," Suzanne quickly followed, "'One thinks himself the master of others and still remains a greater slave than they.' I have heard your arguments before, Mr. Johnson. There is desperate poverty in New York, worse than the ragamuffins up and down the Ohio River. But at least, they have freedom to choose their own destiny."

His mouth twitched as he prepared to interrupt her, but she would not permit him. "You have the gift of rhetoric, whereas I have little skill in expressing myself. I believe you are a gentleman, so you will permit me to remain unconvinced that any person should be deprived of freedom."

He removed his hat. "I bow to the lovely lady's convictions."

The gesture with his hat broke the spell on those around them, who began to murmur. Suzanne caught a "Well, I never." Raising her voice a notch, she said, "Thank you for inviting me. I am sincere when I say that your speech was inspiring."

Richard followed her cue. "Allow me to say that I am always zealous to debate an intelligent woman. It is the curse—or blessing—of being a member of my family."

With that, he placed her hand on his arm and led her away. She watched a slave boy carry off her plate, devouring her untouched slice of ham as he ran. It broke her heart.

"You've met my mother and my eldest sister. Permit me to introduce to you my other sister. She's what you might call a character, but I am very partial to her."

Suzanne quickly became aware that his words were for the benefit of eavesdroppers. As they walked, his voice relaxed and took on the quiet intimacy of earlier. "Now I must warn you. Don't get your hopes up with Sallie. Her husband has business in New Orleans and never fails to bring her back the latest fashions."

"New Orleans?" She savored the name. "I envy her already."

Jemima sipped a glass of cool tea as she sat in the shade of an oak. She looked on as her boys Henry, George and Joel chased her grandchildren toward Richard. Who is that delicate, perfectly outfitted doll, she wondered?

Oh no, Richard. No.

The little ones squealed with joy as Richard dropped Suzanne's arm and scooped them one at a time into the air. "We have a guest, Mother," he hollered over the ruckus.

Jemima forced a smile. "Miss Bayton."

"Mrs. Johnson," Suzanne replied with a deep nod of her red bonnet.

"My youngest brothers and those nephews I mentioned..." Richard rattled off their names as the smaller ones climbed on his legs or tussled with his arms.

"Go find the races and win me some prizes!" Sallie commanded the little ones. She grabbed Richard and planted a generous kiss on his cheek, knocking him into Suzanne.

"Miss Bayton, this is Mrs. William Ward. My Sallie," he grinned, pulling his sister to him. His other hand grazed the seamstress's back.

"Glad to meet you, Miss Bayton. I've heard you aren't one of those stultifying Virginia Paytons. Saved by the letter B," she said in her mother's direction. "Speaking of B's, Betsey, look who's here. Your protégée!"

Betsey came, stone-faced, to greet them, complimented Richard on his oration, then pulled the seamstress away, leading her to a bench under the oak. She looked over her shoulder with a glare at her sister and brother.

Jemima called out to Julia, "Bring my parasol, dear." Since baby Malvina dozed in Julia's arms, Richard plucked up the parasol himself, twirling it over his shoulder like a demoiselle. He sauntered over to his mother, opened the sunshade before handing it to Julia, and clumsily took Malvina in his own arms. The baby whimpered.

"Dickie, you are worse than George or Henry," Sallie fussed as she took her daughter.

Jemima placed her girl at an angle to block the sun—and the view of Suzanne.

"You would have made a first-rate general, Ma. Julia, mind you cover your head, as well!" He touched the tip of the parasol with his finger and watched the shade move over her kerchief. "Much better. No freckles on our birthday girl!" He flicked her nose with his finger and stepped back in mock surprise. "Mother, our girl is nearly as tall as I am! You're going to need a shorter parasol holder."

Julia lowered her head and turned pink.

"Do go now, Richard. People are waiting to congratulate you," Jemima said crossly, waving him away.

He accommodated her by taking a few steps toward the oak tree where he could catch Suzanne's eye. "Miss Bayton, I leave you to the formidable ladies of my family. Jacob is at your disposal. I do hope we shall meet again sometime."

"Jacob, my foot," Sallie rolled her eyes in Richard's direction. "You shall ride home with me." Sallie ignored Betsey's narrow-lipped glare of disapproval. "I'm dying to see an actual atelier, Miss Bayton. My brother says yours is quite charming."

Jemima tried to ignore them. Her eyes followed Richard as he meandered through the crowd. He snubbed Aurelia Scott, Nancy Mitchell and a number of other girls.

I know what you're up to, Richard. You are a fool, and I will not let you get away with it.

Chapter 5
No Contest
October 1804. Georgetown, Kentucky

"I know you shy away from strangers, but Richard needs you to help me influence these women. And it wouldn't hurt you to have a new customer or two. At least for a few more months. Until you're married."

Suzanne blushed, but knew it didn't fool Sallie, who had easily guessed her hopes weeks ago.

"Make it look more Grecian, Pet." Sallie pointed to the drapery swathing the buffet tables. Suzanne apologized to Jasper with a look and a shrug; he already had the room arranged to perfection.

When Jasper left, Sallie whispered, "And I forbid you to discuss you-know-what. Everybody knows your opinion, and none of these women are going to change theirs. It will only scare away business. And don't give away any of your trade secrets. These penny-pinchers will cajole every one of your ideas if you let them then boast how they thought it up all by themselves!"

"I'll be good, I promise!" Suzanne smiled as she watched her party-frenzied friend dash out of the room. Although she was two years older than Sallie, she found comfort in playing the role of younger sister, even answering to the nickname "Pet," which Sallie had abbreviated from petite. Suzanne relished it. She hadn't felt part of a family in a long, long time.

In the four months since Independence Day, Suzanne had lost count of the teas and garden parties the Wards had held to promote Richard's election. But today's luncheon was in Robin Johnson's honor. His bid for lieutenant governor looked secure, at least in Scott County, but Sallie thought he needed to impress the younger men. The old ones had been dying off and with them their votes, an obvious fact he seemed to be ignoring.

Suzanne's heart hammered as she waited for Richard's parents to arrive. She knelt at the corner of the table and pinched the folds of the fabric into place. Would his mother wear the dark green dress and jacket she finished for her last week? She hoped Julia would come today in her new little outfit. *I could dress her like a princess. I could steal her away to New York, and no one would ever know she was a...*

"Guess what?"

Suzanne jumped at the sound of Richard's voice, bumping the table and rattling china.

"What on earth has Sallie got you doing now?" Richard pulled her to her feet, lifting her mid-air. "My little hummingbird. I swear Malvina outweighs you!" He planted a kiss on her mouth before she could speak. "You were deep in thought. Didn't you hear me come in?"

"No! I have to confess I was devising a plan to sneak Julia out of the state."

"I've no objection. And you wouldn't have to sneak her out. If Mother didn't have such a hold on her soul, she could walk right out in broad daylight. But you didn't answer my question so let me start over: "Guess what? I'm going to Frankfort!""

"Well of course you are, Richard, I have every confidence you'll win this elec..."

"That devil Marshall and sap Flournoy dropped out of the running. I'm uncontested. So—"

"By the time you're thirty, you'll be a Senator," Sallie interrupted. "I am so happy for you, and for me, too. Afraid I was going to have to shoot them both just to make sure my parties hadn't been wasted on you!" She kissed Richard's cheek. "Mama's here. She looks marvelous, thanks to you, Pet. At least ten years younger."

Richard extended his arm to Suzanne. She looked at him, and the fear was unmistakable. "You're my girl, darlin.' Father likes you. Don't let Mother think you're afraid."

Sallie took her other arm. "Three against one are better odds," she added, and they stepped through the wide dining room doors into the drawing room.

Aurelia Scott, age twenty, stood in the parlor between her parents and Richard's. Suzanne knew that everyone in the Johnson clan except Sallie had chosen Aurelia to be Richard's wife. She cleared her throat to prevent a laugh escaping when Richard drew a 'T' on her arm with his finger. After the last encounter with the Scotts, he told her, "I'd rather breed hummingbirds than turkeys."

Aurelia wore a lemon-yellow gown that drained the color from her pale face and blue eyes, adding twenty pounds to her already full form. It complemented the girl's black hair, however. She was a big girl and quite beautiful. It's not her fault she's rich, young and marriageable, Suzanne thought, and promised herself to chide Richard about calling her a turkey.

Mrs. Johnson wore the gown exactly as Suzanne advised she should. The shoulder detail on the jacket drew the eye away from her stomach, distended by years of childbearing. Both the silver and dark auburn in her hair contrasted pleasingly with the green dress.

But the most beautiful girl in the room wore a dove gray gown trimmed in black velvet. Her organdy apron was starched and pressed with great pride. Little strands of honey-colored hair fell from the tight coil of her chignon. She nodded somberly at Suzanne when their eyes met, but the smile was missing. And it was unmistakable: when Julia looked at Richard, she colored to a most attractive pink, and bit her lip to hold back tears.

November 1804. Great Crossing

"She isn't even American!" Jemima hissed.

"I think a hundred years in a country is long enough for a family to prove they're loyal Americans," Richard retorted, not bothering to hide his sarcasm.

"The French do not give up their ways no matter how long they live here. I will not have my grandchildren brought up by someone who scorns tradition and thinks our religious morals of no importance."

"Mother, Suzanne is Protestant like we are. And if you question her morals, then you question mine, and we are both above reproach. You should apologize."

"I will not! And I will not tolerate this behavior towards me. Just because you're going to Frankfort tomorrow doesn't give you the right to belittle me. Don't you understand? We're talking about making you a future president, not some backwoods justice of the peace. If you do not marry well, and I mean very well, all our hopes are ruined."

"Well, how can Suzanne's hopes, or mine, compare with that?" He added softly, "She is utterly alone, except for me."

"That is no more than misplaced gallantry on your part. I wish you'd gotten more of my common sense. But you're a dreamer like your father. And what does he say?"

"A lovely, hard-working girl with a good head on her shoulders," Richard mumbled. He felt defeated. Suzanne was so much more than the drudge his father saw or the trollope his mother evoked.

"You've only known her five months, Richard. Five months! There are dozens of girls of wealth from the best families you have known your whole life. And we didn't give you the Blue Spring property to waste on a northern girl who knows nothing of our people and our ways. I cannot bring myself to give my blessing. It would be impossible for me to stand by and watch you make the biggest mistake of your life. Forgive me, but I know I'm right."

Jemima waved her hand toward the end of the long, dark room. Richard followed the movement and saw Julia rise from a corner chair with a basket of mending in her arms. He was disgusted with himself for having so little presence of mind not to have seen her. As she walked by, she pressed a finger to her lips to reassure him no one would know of this argument.

"Julia, my lamb, fetch my pince-nez from my bed table."

How curious, Richard thought, that Mother never hides anything from Julia.

"Yes, Miz Jemima, fast as I can. Good evening, Mas Richard."

Her voice had an unfamiliar sound to it. Soft, deep. And why did he feel a sense of panic now at being truly alone with his mother? They sat in silence for a long minute, weary warriors between battles.

Someone knocked softly on the door. "Yes," Jemima called. "Come in!"

Lucy carried in a tray. "Julia thought you'd like a little something." She poured tea and arranged shortbread on little plates. Next to Jemima's cup rested her pince-nez. Richard felt an unexpected pang of disappointment that Julia had not delivered them herself.

"Thank you, Lucy. Come back in ten minutes to clear up, will you?"

Richard admired his mother's gentleness with their people, but it contrasted sharply with her domination over him and his brothers and sisters. She was proud that all the house servants had been baptized; she treated them as respectfully as her temperament allowed. But he and most of his brothers declined baptism, much to his parents' embarrassment. He related more to Percival than Saint Peter, but neither seemed of much help right now. His test of faith was how to honor his mother because he sorely needed a wife. *His* choice of wife.

"I thought a ghost had risen out of that chair while ago. Don't you ever let Julia out in the sunshine? It can't be good for her to be so cooped up."

"Now you sound like my new doctor, Theobald. Always fussing about Julia's health as if I am not in the same room. But let me tell you, son, she does get out with me, on my ministering rounds." Jemima's voice brightened. "She's driving my buggy!"

"Mother, that's too dangerous, for you and her." He shot her a critical look over his cup. Doubtless, old age was affecting her judgment.

"Nonsense! I need a driver. Your father keeps Jacob too busy, and I don't trust any of the young bucks. Your brothers have too much schoolwork. Besides, you see how tall a girl she is. Strong too, and quick. She picks up everything I tell her. Not only can she set bones, she's got a way with her mother's burn salves. She's clearing up all the blisters at the rope walk and the tar kettles!"

"You can't take her to the rope walk!" He brought down his cup, sloshing tea over the delicate sweets. "Ministrations be hanged, the riffraff working with our people over there are a hundred times more dangerous to Julia than boiling tar!"

"What has gotten into you? Julia this and Julia that! Never you worry about a man troubling her. Your brothers protect her like a sister. Besides, I can't do anything much with these crippled-up hands of mine. She's become my hands *and* feet, and now my eyes. I tell you, when I'm gone, there's no one I'd trust more with running the Crossing than my girl. None of my own children have put their hearts into learning the place the way she has."

Richard was as fond of Julia as anyone, but his mother's words were wildly out of proportion. He devoured the tea-sogged shortbread instead of arguing that Julia was property, could only do what she was told. She'd have rounded on him that his seamstress had put ideas in his head. At least one thing was clear: praising Julia was safe territory, even if defending her virtue wasn't.

"So, you've taught her to write and cipher, I hear. You're finally considering having an official housekeeper?"

"Perhaps. I have my own plans. You're not here often enough, but have you heard her play the pianoforte? She's mastered the hymns, a little Mozart and Handel, and I have a few Scottish tunes..."

His mother continued rattling on. He thought about Joel, who acted like a lovesick puppy around Julia. John T showed a few of the same signs, too. No matter, the girl had no freedom. She slept at the foot of Mother's bed at night; sat, walked, and rode alongside her all day long. But he knew how tempting it was to be young and ready to experiment a little with a stolen kiss or two from a...

"No, I don't think I could ever part with her as long as I live," Jemima's voice broke through his thoughts. "I am that fond of her."

"We all are, Mother," Richard answered absently. "Don't upset yourself with any fears of our neglecting her."

When Julia returned, he paid careful attention to her for the first time since she thought his hair was fire. The memory made him chuckle, and he studied her approvingly. His admiration turned to mild annoyance within a few minutes, however, as she fluttered. It reminded him of a votary paying homage to a queen on her throne. When had his stalwart pioneer mother become so dependent on pillows, foot stools and lap robes?

Julia showed by her actions to be a creature without guile. Not only did she fuss over his mother in a way no one else would, she comforted her with what appeared to be genuine kindness. As good a woman as his mother was, she was not easy to love, yet Julia appeared to love her.

He studied the girl's physical appearance. Really, only fourteen? More like twenty. She had become quite lovely, though she lacked Henrietta's stunning beauty. Julia had too much of the Chinn haughtiness to her features. She could easily be mistaken by a stranger as his orphaned cousin from Virginia, but never his slave. Perhaps he could obtain her, free her, to please Suzanne.

"I'll be leaving now, Mother. I've said my farewells to Father and the boys. They're not night owls like we are," he offered her a conciliatory smile.

"You can't keep me company another hour?" Her reproachful tone told him she wanted to distract him from his "northern trollope".

"I have a great deal to get in order at Blue Spring before morning." He stretched and stepped over to her chair. "But I do expect to see you and Father at the Governor's Ball in a month."

She sighed. Robin had taken his election loss hard. "Yes, I suppose we must be gracious and attend, or tongues will wag. Who will you be inviting?" she asked blankly, working on her embroidery.

He froze in alarm. But, instead of bringing up Suzanne again, he bent and kissed her. The scent of chamomile lingered on her skin. "Think of me kindly while I'm in the Capitol," he added.

"Help him out, Julia," was his mother's reply.

Julia followed him to the foyer. As she glided him into his greatcoat, he brought his head close to hers, his voice only a shade above a whisper. "Julia dear, have you noticed anything peculiar about my mother lately? Trouble bringing people's names to mind, anything like that?"

Julia's skin quivered when Richard's breath touched her ear. He brought the candle close to their faces, and she saw the golden flecks in his eyes. She wanted to look away but there was no room.

A thought hit her with an awakening force: *I am grown. I am a full-grown woman.*

The proof was in the fact that she stood as tall as the man in front of her. She did not lower her eyes. In the parlor while ago, they exchanged a look and talked to each other without words, the way Lucy and Jacob, and Mas Robin and Miz Jemima did.

She hesitated, feeling for the first time a traitor's heart beating within her. "Yes," she began. "She forgot I was in the room with you."

His look emboldened her; she spoke more rapidly. "Some days I have to fetch her spectacles a hundred times or tell her she's already given Mama orders for the meals. And she distrusts everybody, like she does your Miss Suzanne."

A wave of disgust washed through her and she finally looked down. "I think I've said enough. I feel like I'm tattling."

"No, you've done well telling me. I've had my worries for some time now."

He leaned against the wall making the candle sputter, spilling hot wax onto his fingers and the palm of his hand. He bolted straight up, switched the candlestick to his other hand, and cursed as he shook his hand. Julia swiftly brought his hand to her tongue and licked the wax to cool it, then peeled it off. She blew on the red spots that flared on his skin.

"I feel like a scalded kitten!" he laughed softly and raised the candle in his good hand to get another look at her face. It was filled with concern and free of embarrassment.

"Oh, no, I didn't mean to treat you like a baby. It's just I've learned to act fast when the little ones do that so they don't scream." Reluctantly, she let go of his hand.

"Maybe I'll scream next time," he teased her in his old tone. "You do have a soothing touch," he added in a less familiar voice. He chucked her under the chin in his usual gesture. "Has anyone ever told you what a treasure you are to our family?"

"This is my home," she whispered.

"Nobody is more devoted to my mother than you."

"She's better to me than I deserve," she answered, looking directly into his eyes.

"I doubt that!" he grinned. "But keep a look out for a girl you can train. Lucy's girl, Katy? She might do."

He glanced at the spots on his left hand as he picked up his hat and riding crop. He recalled the feel of her mouth on his skin and forced himself to shake it off. "Run along. Mother will be wondering why I've kept you." He opened the door then turned back toward her. "Oh, and Julia? Practice your script and ciphers faithfully, every day. Would you do that for me?"

She nodded, a bit bewildered, and waited in the doorway as Jacob led Pegasus from the stable toward their master. "Safe journey to you," she called out.

Had he noticed? She had not called him Mas Richard, not once. She closed the door, clinging to the crunching sound his boots made as he walked on the gravel drive. As she made her way back to the parlor, she rolled the bits of candle wax stuck to her fingers into a little ball. The taste of his skin lingered on her tongue. Soap and lavender water, tea and shortbread crumbs. Her heart began to beat frantically. A strange sick feeling took hold of her.

"What kept you, child?" Jemima demanded. The candle began to gurgle—the one he had held in his hand. She gave the struggling flame a little puff and felt a kind of power as it vanished.

"He made inquiries about your health, Miz Jemima, that's all. He's afraid you aren't well, for some reason."

"I declare, if a woman doesn't agree with a man, he insists she's either crazy or unwell. I assume he wants you to put in a good word for Miss Bayton?"

"No, ma'am. He made no mention of her at all," Julia answered. She stepped over to the window and watched Jacob hold Pegasus steady while Richard settled into the saddle.

"Julia, I do believe you are the only person these days that I can completely trust. Just between us chickens, what do you think of her?"

"I have to agree with you, I don't think she's the girl for him." She lingered over closing the drapes and got a final glimpse of Richard as he rode away.

THE LIGHT OF DAY MADE the argument with his mother—and the even more troubling lust for her girl—as distant as another lifetime. He needed this detour back to Georgetown before riding to Frankfort. He saluted his father's beloved Rittenhouse Academy on his way to Suzanne's.

He found her rumpled and disheveled by lack of sleep. "You've worked through the night!" he chided her, pulling her to him and kissing her. He knew this was how she would look every morning when they awoke, and thought she was at her most beautiful. Certainly, her most desirable.

"I woke up at midnight with a foolish notion, and it wouldn't leave me. So, I made you this, for autumn!" She shook out a vest of fine gold corduroy. She snipped a thread off the last button. "It's already pressed. I moved the buttons over. I always forget how broad your chest is. But this is right." She spread it over him.

He longed for her as he removed his coat and put the vest on. She smoothed it over him, picking off tiny pieces of thread, but stopped when he put his arms around her, and pressed her cheek against the fabric. "I can hear your heart," she said as she always did when he held her. Her ear fit exactly over it when they stood together.

Neither spoke. Minutes passed in silence. He felt his shirt grow wet. She was crying without a sound, and when he bent to kiss the part of her hair, she shook with sobs.

"You are gone from me, my love, and I cannot bear it."

He had never seen his strong, independent girl weep. The barrier was down. It was the moment he had waited for. "I have a suggestion, then. Marry me. My inheritance comes when I turn twenty-five, and Blue Spring will be signed completely over to me. Think about this: we will be inseparable this time next year."

Suzanne tightened her grip around him and nodded her head yes. She kissed his chest. He pulled her chin up, bent and kissed her slowly, feeling her muscles unloose until she relied entirely on his arms to hold her up.

When they untangled, she fussed over the wet spots on his vest and shirt. He unbuttoned the vest, flapped it to get it dry, and noticed a dark spot on the inside. She had appliquéd a hummingbird on the lining that lay over his heart.

"Lawzoo moose." His terrible French always made her laugh.

"*L'oiseau mouche, mon amour*," she corrected him, although she did not laugh.

Chapter 6
Defeat
December 1804. Georgetown, Kentucky

Suzanne had lost her power to hope. Every day, a hundred times a day, she relived the morning Richard left her. It replaced the memory of lowering her father's body into a common grave, of the sight of her uncle's body in the stable. Richard's love had been her salvation when despair had nearly destroyed her. Now it seemed that love was no longer hers.

The shop door opened; she heard Sallie's quick steps. Suzanne came across the little room to meet her.

"You've been crying, Pet. Richard?" Sallie led her friend behind a stack of fabric in case anyone should enter the shop.

"One letter all week. Not even a letter, really." She pulled a small page from her pocket and handed it to Sallie, who tossed her muff and cape on the floor at their feet. Suzanne cringed at this mistreatment of such beautiful things but was too miserable to pick them up.

Sallie embraced her after reading the brief letter. "No wonder you're sick at heart. You might as well be a stranger."

Suzanne's fear overcame her, and she sobbed like a forsaken child. "He wrote me every day at first, but for two weeks I've received nothing but these." She took a few steps to her little writing desk and gave Sallie three notes. "And I have to tell you—forgive me, it's about your mother..."

"No need to apologize. You do realize Mama has lost her mind?" She pulled a face and Suzanne laughed a little, despite her misery.

"She made me stand by her desk to pay me for the final fitting on her ball gown. She had a letter from Richard opened flat so anybody could read it. And I saw Aurelia's name, something about the ball, and your mother making arrangements for her to come."

"Had to have been deliberate. How could she have been that cruel?" Sallie pulled her friend toward the little settee.

"I was so upset my hand shook when I put the coins in my purse. Then she called Julia over to fetch me some tea and cakes because I appeared ill. And she told me I needed to take better care of myself, or however would I manage to take care of a family?"

"Well, there is some truth to that. You work far too hard."

"Not now. I used to hear the bell on my door every half hour. Now I'm fortunate if I have one customer a day. Not a soul ordered anything for Christmas holidays."

"That's because you're in Baptist country. Christmas isn't a grand affair around here." Sallie waited a moment. "If you're short of funds, I can..."

"No, Sallie, don't say it. I have enough to manage a while longer. But if Richard—you know of our engagement, but no one else does, and so he has no..." She stopped, remembering her father often told her to keep her predictions of failure to herself.

"If I had my way, you'd have been married months ago. Your gowns are superb, even that little outfit you made for Julia. You're as good as any in New Orleans, William says so. It's a shame my provincial brother can't marry you and let you set up shop in Frankfort."

"Oh, he'd die of shame! Sallie, is that the problem? He's ashamed of me? You know he's already head of an important committee. He's meeting influential people, wondering how I could possibly fit in."

"That's nonsense. He was always so proud to be with you. Why should that change just because he's on some stuffed shirt committee? If I were a man, I'd have gobbled you up ages ago!"

Suzanne laughed despite her tears and finally put away her soaked handkerchief. She studied her friend for a moment. The physical resemblance between Sallie and Richard was remarkable. Their features radiated strength, their vitality drew people to them. No wonder she needed Sallie's presence so desperately.

"I think we both know who is at the heart of this," Sallie sighed. "The thing that's so troubling is why my brother is putting up with her at your expense. My guess is, she's threatened to take away Blue Spring. But try to put your mind at ease. I promise I'll take care of everything."

May 1805. Near Fort St. Louis, Indian Territory

S uzanne stood on the deck of the keelboat, trying to glimpse a star, any star, in the murky sky. Occasionally a rip in the clouds revealed a ray of moonlight but mended itself quickly, leaving her in darkness again. The Mississippi, fat with spring rains, sloshed beneath her. The little ship seemed giddy with the prospect of making an effortless trip. She felt like stone and fought the impulse to toss herself into the black water.

I am twenty-eight. I feel fifty. I failed as miserably at making a new life as Papa did.

She thought of the thousands of people like them who got churned up and spat out like the wake on the river. Kentucky took her father, her uncle and all their dreams. Now it had taken her heart.

Each memory of Richard lived so brightly in her mind that she could conjure it up and feel exactly as she had that first moment. She saw herself sweeping up her empty shop. A scrap of silk fluttered up from the broom, part of the hummingbird on Richard's vest. She felt the heat from the fire as she burned each of his letters, remembered how the papers curled up and turned to ash. They became nothing, like she had become to him.

Richard's mother had won out, obligating him to live her plan of his life. It had more appeal to him than the one they had shared so briefly. She wanted to hate them both, along with all the people in Georgetown who abandoned her under pressure from Betsey.

She wanted to hate even the ones loyal to Sallie who paid her for tutoring their daughters in French, needlework, and sketching because they were too cowardly to be seen in one of her dresses. But all she could do was muster enough strength to fight off the night pressing down on her.

At least Sallie remained loyal, suggesting and paying for this escape, for that was all Suzanne was doing. Running away. Sallie said it would be worth it to be among people of taste and culture who would appreciate her talent.

Despite my talent, I am considered low class. Not good enough for the likes of some dowdy farm woman! She gripped the handrail and sucked in the river's smell in an effort to keep away the tears. It would be a new life in New Orleans.

Richard and I planned to take our honeymoon in New Orleans.

Was there no place for her thoughts to turn without coming back to him?

The boat deck came in to view in a dazzling burst of moonlight. The grimy planks and cabin walls became drenched in mother of pearl. She gazed up at the moon and let the tears flow. For whatever reason, she had her love for beauty. She had gratitude for life. She had hope for the future.

"Thank you, God, for giving me your moonlight," she said softly, then disappeared through the narrow opening that dropped down into the women's quarters.

Alphonse Leclerc lit a superb cigar. He had been amused by the tiny person staring so intently at the water and the sky. He walked the length of the keel boat to where she had been standing.

He leaned over the boat rail to see what all the fuss was about. He saw nothing but the filthy river. Over his head passed clouds that obscured the moon completely. Ah well! He had a way with women, and no doubt he would be able to charm a story out of this woman. Life could not stay this boring for long.

Chapter 7
Election
January 1807. Great Crossing

Julia wanted to die. Richard had won his election to the United States Congress, and before moving to Washington, he was going to New Orleans. She had not seen him in over a year, not since his break with the family after Miss Suzanne took off. Now it would be months before he returned. Miss Sallie talked Jemima into giving him tonight's farewell party so they could all make up and show off for their rich friends.

Julia stole a furtive glance at her reflection in the window. Her best gown, the gray, fit snugly, even with the growth pleats let out, and she had to use a demi-handkerchief to cover her bosom. In her imagination, her mother and she wore blue silk, their golden shoulders and décolletage...

"Julia, my dear, fetch my other slippers. My bunion's flared up, so these will never do."

At least she was spared the humiliation of wearing an apron and cap tonight in front of Richard. Miss Sallie told her to play the pianoforte from the parlor during supper, a thing Miz Jemima called "vainglorious." Julia thought if anybody could get Richard to pay attention to her it was Mozart.

When she returned with the slippers, John T and Joel stood near their mother's chair. Miz Jemima beamed at them, although

Julia could tell they were still unhappy about being called away from college just to see Richard. They moved out of the way, allowing her barely enough room to kneel and replace the slippers.

She thanked the Lord she already had the demi-handkerchief in place. Things had changed too much between her and the boys. John T had nothing but contempt for her since she'd rebuffed his clumsy attempts to corner her last summer. Now Joel had a way of staring...

"What do you call a congressman before he takes his oath, Ma?" Joel grinned. Jemima disliked jokes now; she had lost her sense of humor the day Dr. Theobald told her about the sugar sickness. The bourbon on Joel's breath had not yet caught his mother's attention, but it had John T's, who stopped him.

"I don't know about you, but I plan on calling him Your Highness," John T said with a bow of mock deference to Joel and his mother. When he swung upward, he gave Julia a cold, hard look.

"I see the Marshall boys have just arrived," Jemima turned to John, ignoring his sarcasm. "I'd keep yourselves well away from those two."

"On the contrary, Ma," Joel grinned. "Nobody's better company, and I plan to be a host to make you proud." He winked at Julia, "Maybe I'll come home more often."

"YOU PLAY AS FINE AS any young lady in Frankfort, Julia." Richard smiled down at her and spoke in the low voice that made her feel on fire. "But I am surprised that Mother allowed you to play something other than hymns."

His smile widened, emphasizing new lines around his eyes. She also noticed those eyes taking in her neck and arms. He had gotten older. Besides his new wrinkles, his hair was darker, like embers mixed with flame.

Her thoughts of him distracted her from playing well, however. She hit one wrong note, then another. The only thing that saved her from falling apart was the amusing thought of calling him "your highness". She wished he wouldn't talk to her as if she were Malvina. But at least Mozart worked; Richard stood by her, closer than she could have hoped, almost as close as the moment she raised his hand to her mouth an entire year ago.

"Fetch my heavy shawl, Julia, would you?" Jemima called from across the room.

Under Richard's spell, Julia had the irritable thought, why can't one of your dozens of grandchildren fetch it? But most of them had left the room, she grudgingly noticed. Richard straightened as he saw the necessity of saying goodbye to his brother James. She remembered her place and went quickly from the room, eager to return to Richard's presence.

Climbing the stairs, Julia relived each word, each smile he had shared with her by the piano. From the end of the hallway, a faint bit of candlelight escaped from John T's and Joel's room. The unmistakable sound of bottles thumped on the carpet then clinked together. Muffled laughter followed, high pitched like a girl.

She leaned over Miz Jemima's bed and gathered the long woolen wrap into her arms. A strong hand drenched in whisky pushed her down and shoved her face into the quilts. Her own hands were tangled in the shawl; she couldn't get free. She screamed, but the sound muffled deep into the mattress. Another hand yanked at her skirt and struggled with her shift and pantalets until the cold metal of breeches buttons pressed into her exposed flesh. She kicked with all her might, but a pair of strong horseman's legs straddled her thighs.

She gagged on the smell of sweat and liquor; her screams turned to sobs as he started to move down on her in a fast, jerking rhythm. "You know you're perfect, girl. Just perfect. You're the best of both worlds." The voice rasping in her hair was soft. It rose to an unnatural high pitch. "A white nigger. You have to do what I want, you know that don't you?"

Julia heard the door open, and her terror turned to mortification. Someone lifted her assailant off her body. She scrambled to breathe, to untangle her hands from the shawl, to cover her legs. She saw Richard ram the man into a wooden chair by the wall. His strength came down so hard, so fast on Lewis Marshall that he had no time to register shock or shame. Julia felt drenched in both.

Joel staggered toward her from the doorway, offering a shaky hand to pull her up. Recoiling, she sprang from the bed to the door, and covered her face with the shawl, pulling it tightly around her body to help her hide. She bit into her fist to keep from screaming, praying no one downstairs could hear.

"You're a pig when you drink, you filthy bastard, you know *that,* don't you?" Richard mocked him with the words he overheard. His hoarse whisper was brutal. "Julia's my family! You don't touch her!"

Lewis pinched his eyes tightly shut and laughed. "She's a nigger!"

Richard held him by the front of his shirt. "Shut up!"

"A white nigger!" Lewis laughed in a high-pitched giggle.

Richard slapped him with such force it knocked him out of the chair. "I've always wanted a good excuse to knock you to hell where you belong!"

When he turned, his face contorted in rage, he gave Joel a brutal shake. Lewis remained crumpled on the floor. "Oh, dear God, have you killed him? Is he dead, Rich?" Joel whimpered.

Richard kicked him onto his back. Lewis cursed, then made gurgling noises, proof he had not been seriously harmed. "More's the pity! Joel, I warned you about keeping company with this devil. Why didn't you listen to me? How could you let him near Julia?"

Joel jerked free and staggered to the chair, hanging his head over Lewis's tangled legs. Lewis moaned louder and made an effort to sit up before collapsing to the floor. "You're a pig, Lewis. Kissin' her's not the same as shamin' her! I'm a pig, too, for even talkin' to him about Julia. I'm so sorry."

"It's not me you shamed. Tell Julia!" Richard hissed.

"I'm sorry, honey. I'm so, so sorry," Joel slurred. He rose, took a few unsteady steps, and grabbed Julia's arm. She shivered and pulled away, pressing herself to the door frame. "You're just so pretty, he couldn't help himself. You're like my sister, you've been my friend forever. I should have protected you, not..." Saliva dripped from his mouth. He shuddered, and Richard grabbed a chamber pot just in time.

"Hold it yourself, Joel," Richard muttered between gritted teeth. He led Joel to the chair, Lewis still on the floor at their feet.

As Julia's sobs turned to gasps for air, Richard turned toward the door and gently folded the shawl away from her face. Her shame too fresh, Julia pulled away, but he wrapped her in his arms.

"I swear to you, I will kill any man who does you harm." His voice was husky, his breath hot in her ear. At the sound of heavy footsteps on the stairs, he released her, and their eyes held for a moment. He motioned her away.

Julia fled down the hallway, clutching the shawl around her, keeping her eyes on the floorboards. "Take that off!" John T ordered from the end of the hallway. Stunned by the anger in his voice, Julia looked up long enough to see Humphrey Marshall by his side. An involuntary whimper escaped her; she drew the shawl over her head and ran.

Jemima's seat in the drawing room gave her a good view of the entry hall. She frowned in annoyance when she saw Julia covered by the shawl. As the girl came closer into range, however, she took in the crumpled dress, the distorted features on her face. She motioned with her head for Julia to stay out of the room. Julia dropped the shawl on the foyer settee and ran to the cookhouse.

The sound of a fiddle and a dozen people's laughter coming from the open kitchen door failed to reach Julia's senses. She dashed past Miz Betsey's man, who silenced his music, past Lucy and Jacob, and a blur of faces. Henrietta quickly wiped a residue of crushed almonds from her fingers. "Finish up these tea cakes for me, Milly?"

She led Julia to the dark laundry shed behind a clump of bushes, safe from the kitchen's view. To Henrietta's relief, Samuel started a new tune; talk and laughter picked up again.

"It happened, Mama, just like you said." Julia's sobs shook her body. "It's all my fault. You warned me, but I just couldn't help wanting to look pretty for tonight."

Henrietta clung to her daughter, rocking her, listening to the story she knew all too well. Even though the young man had been too drunk to misuse her, enough damage had been done. She had to grit her teeth and tighten her legs to keep from spitting with rage and kicking a hole in the boards.

Once she had her anger tamped down enough to speak, she forced her voice into a soothing sound. "It's not your fault. Young boy or old man, not much difference when you have no say in the matter. And you don't."

She grabbed a cloth out of the soaking vat and pressed it on Julia's face then smoothed back her daughter's loose curls with a few drops of water. "Mas Richard saw? That's good. He's Miz Johnson's favorite."

"No, Mama, it's not good. He saw me—oh, dear God, he *saw* me!" Julia crumpled into her mother's lap, trying to block the image of what her bare legs and buttocks must have looked like. "And Joel saw me, too." Her tears came hard, soaking through to her mother's shift.

"It was dark, honey. They didn't see a thing." Henrietta clamped her eyes shut, strained to console her daughter, but the fight with her own rage, disgust at the image of her child's humiliation, made her words choked and unnatural.

Julia finally sat up, pressing the cloth against her eyes. She forced her mind away from her shame and picked up a thread of grief, instead. "Joel and I can't be the same after this. He was my best friend. But he let his friend—he didn't stop him, Mama. I heard them laughing before it happened. Joel must've known what he wanted to do."

"Can't ever have a best friend in our situation, Baby," Henrietta said.

Julia let the cloth drop back into the soaking tub. She'd said nothing to her mother about Richard's protective threat, the feel of his arms around her, could never try to explain the look in his eyes the moment before she fled. At last, she sat up straight and took her mother's rough hand. "I'll be alright now, Mama. I think I can be strong."

Henrietta felt a chill as her rage congealed into despair. There was never a time or place where a slave woman could be anything less than strong. Oh! She wanted to run, take Julia and Milly and get to the Ohio. But everybody in five counties knew her because of her cooking, and Milly had no fire for anything, much less freedom.

And Julia...she sighed and let that dream die for the ten thousandth time. "Stay close to Miz Johnson from now on. Don't get out of her sight. Because it won't take being liquored up for somebody else to try the same thing. There are plenty of men like the Marshalls just bidin' their time."

JEMIMA'S VOICE CARRIED outside to the breezeway. When Julia entered the house, she heard it all. "It's a crime what he did, and you let him, in my own house, in my very room. It'll take a week to get the stench of him out of there! I wish I could thrash you to an inch of your life! I never want to see the face of a Marshall on this property again."

Julia heard Joel and John T run down the foyer and out of the house with the sound of Robin's hard, fast steps right behind. She could not feel a shred of pity for her old friends. It was un-Christian, but she exulted in the abuse pouring down on them.

Straining to take in a breath, Julia entered the drawing room. Everyone had left; George and Henry had gone upstairs to their room. Jemima said nothing, allowing Julia to maintain her last scrap of dignity. She took up her post between her mistress and the door to show she was ready once again for service.

Richard quietly entered the room and asked her with his eyes if she was alright. With that look, her shame over what he might have seen suddenly fled. Although her mind and body ached from the incident, at that moment the more acute pain came from knowing he would soon be gone. And with a strange assurance that it was necessary to do so, she decided she must show him her heart.

When Richard bade his parents goodbye, Julia followed him to the door to light the way. After she helped him into his heavy cloak, he turned to her. "Thank God I had the good sense to go upstairs. When you didn't come back, I knew..."

The look of tenderness in his eyes was all she needed to propel her into forbidden territory. "You saw my shame, yet I don't disgust you," she whispered.

"Sshh," he consoled her, putting his fingertips over her mouth.

The gesture, rather than stopping her, drove her forward with even more conviction. "I love you, Richard." She said his name in a sigh of fear and relief.

His fingers moved across her face and stroked her cheek. He brushed away a fallen curl then looked steadily into her eyes. The creases of worry left his face, and he gazed at her as he had at her rescue. "I would never shame you. And you won't ever have to have another man touch you, unless he's your own."

She held his gaze. "God forgive me for being proud, but I can't ever be a true wife to...anyone, because of the law."

"I make the laws, now," he whispered.

It was the slightest brushing of his lips over hers, but sent a shock through her limbs that stayed long after he turned away and closed the door.

May 1807, New Orleans

Richard stood at the end of the ballroom balcony. He gripped his calfskin gloves and rocked back and forth nervously on his heels. His stiff posture gave him the air of a gentleman, but he could not feel the part as he looked down on a performance of human interchange that disgusted him. His old acquaintance, Alphonse Leclerc, stood next to him, grinning obscenely. Alphonse had dragged him to the plaçage ball, to see the improvements made now that it was in its fourth season.

"It dates back to the French court and the long-established rules of *le plaçage*," Alphonse boasted by way of introduction to the procedure. "It's the same tradition of royal generosity with this lovely twist—the men of New Orleans have this ball as a sort of parade ground for our girls of color."

Dozens of beautiful young girls wove through the room, towed along by their mothers. They all wore elaborately tied strips of silk or gauze wrapped over their heads. "I have a question, Alphonse."

His companion turned away from the view of the floor down below. "*A votre service, mon vieux,*" he grinned. "At your disposal, old friend," Alphonse translated himself.

"What is this hideous craze for turbans all about?"

"Ah! The *tignon*. It's a ridiculous law here that women of color cannot go bareheaded. The poorer girls wear a bandana, but our girls here fancy themselves little empresses of France. Josephine's dictates are even more tyrannical than her husband's, and much more willingly followed. You do know, don't you, that Josephine's of Creole origin?"

"No, I didn't, but then, have I ever had any interest in fashion?"

Richard struggled to control his anxiety regarding Suzanne. New Orleans had been her home for two years, although as earnestly as she despised slavery it seemed impossible to believe. Sallie told him she had married and set up a little shop. His throat tightened as he remembered the designs she called "empire-style," and this was the only style worn tonight.

To a girl, they dressed in white or palest pink, of fabric so sheer it left just enough to the imagination to make the men despair. Their mothers dressed in somber shades, reminding Richard of a jeweler's display. Were they attempting to make their daughters shine brighter? In contrast, the men, including Richard, suffocated in layers of formal attire. Only the skin of their faces showed.

Richard studied the girls, some so stunning they made even him stare like an imbecile. But each had the same broad smile frozen on her face. He searched their eyes. Some showed fear, others a fevered eagerness. The image of Henrietta and Julia flashed before him: this could have been their fate, for they were more beautiful than any of the women here.

Alphonse interrupted his thoughts with an elbow thumping his ribs.

"See there?" He nodded to a corner post, where a man about the age of Richard's father smiled up into the face of a statuesque girl, whose mama appeared to be pinching her into a more appealing position. Richard looked down in disgust, but Alphonse raised his glove to his mouth and laughed.

"Francois de Beaufort! He's practically bankrupted himself collecting courtesans. But this mama knows that he spreads himself so thin amongst them all that her daughter will have very few conjugal visits to dread. She'll have a house on the Avenue and a coterie of servants. But he will have to retire one of his older ladies."

"And what do the retired ones do?" Only one thing came to Richard's mind. Better to return to slavery.

"Many are so clever with their money that they've earned enough interest to live on the rest of their lives. Or they set up shops. They buy their own servants. Really, the *gens de couleur* here have the best of both worlds. Ah! There's one of the most famous courtesans in all New Orleans!" Alphonse gushed. "She's thirty now, so that would make her daughter there, Mathilde, fifteen. I know—my father negotiated with la Belle Louise sixteen years ago, when it was done properly in private, in the old style."

Richard stared at him. "Are you implying that her daughter is your half-sister?"

"No implication! Statement of fact. Can't you see the family resemblance?"

Alphonse grinned and held his head in profile for Richard to inspect. The forehead, chin and nose were practically identical, and Mathilde was as fair as her half-brother. She had a look of innocence mixed with expectation that broke Richard's heart.

"Louise is quintaroon. Mathilde hexadecaroon. If I were one of the more free-minded, I would gladly consider taking that little treasure under my wing."

"Such things are done here?" Richard's voice almost failed him.

Alphonse smirked. "Of course. There are ways of preventing..." He stopped short after seeing Richard flush.

"Dick, you're positively a fossil! A priest! No, I have it on solid authority that there are a few offspring of a priest or two here tonight. Your mighty clan with its dozens of pretty slave girls? Convince me you don't have any number of fire-haired dusky sisters!"

Richard swallowed the bitter taste in his mouth. "My dear Alphonse, my Baptist kin have a passion for only one thing, and that's for living in fear of hell-fire. Fornicating with servants is unthinkable to a gentleman."

If his friend weren't drunk, he would call him out on such an insult to his family honor. Look at him. Exchanging cards with passers-by and giggling. Instead, he wondered aloud: "Why did you bring me to this awful place?"

"In order to provide you with a most necessary understanding of the human condition, my dear boy," he replied, his dark eyes humorless. "You cannot go with your simple notions to the Federal City and sit down with the likes of Hamilton and Jefferson, as you are."

In an instant, his carefree tone returned as Alphonse lavished his attention on a young man who accompanied an elderly gentleman. They prattled in French. Richard froze when he heard "*ma petite Suzanne*". It was a common French name, but his heart told him the men spoke of her.

"Richard, allow me to present my uncle and namesake, Alphonse, and my dear friend, Etienne Delamar." With a flourish of his hand in mock grandiosity, Alphonse proclaimed, "Congressman Richard Mentor Johnson."

Keeping his gaze on the girls below, Uncle Alphonse bowed.

"*A votre service, monsieur,*" Delamar said, extending his hand in a brief courtesy.

"Johnson is a Kentuckian like your wife," Alphonse added.

"My dear wife is from New York, *mon vieux*. Her sojourn in Kentucky was, unfortunately, not a happy time for her. We do not speak of it."

"My error. I apologize, *mon ami*." Turning to Richard he bragged, "You see, I am the very Cupid responsible for my friend meeting his lovely wife. I met her on one of my tedious voyages to St. Louis."

Alphonse beamed in Etienne's direction then turned back to Richard. "She is truly extraordinary, Richard, so talented, just the tiniest slip of a woman, like a little wren. No, something more colorful, a..."

"Hummingbird?" Richard interjected.

"How charming! How apt a description! I lack your poetic gift, don't I?" Alphonse giggled.

Richard conceded that Delamar was not just handsome; he was beautiful. With those delicate features and small bones like Suzanne's, they must have made a perfectly matched pair. His heart sank, knowing it would be impossible for him to see her again.

Alphonse prattled; Richard forced himself to listen. "All of this is done strictly above-board, you see. I would think that, as a lawyer, you would find this fascinating! The legal papers will be drawn up over the next few weeks. The young ladies with several admirers—ah! The negotiations with their mamas will go on and on, but it will only add to the prestige of all parties concerned."

"It's rather like your famous Kentucky thoroughbred auctions?" Delamar interrupted. "*A la prochaine fois, mon vieux.*" Until next time, old friend, he said as he turned abruptly to Alphonse. He gave Richard a surly nod of the head that made it clear he could not tolerate being in his presence. He left with Uncle Alphonse in tow.

"I wonder what's gotten into Etienne. The least he should have done was invite us to his apartments. No, truly, Richard. We are more than friends—like brothers, really. It's not like him at all. How I would love for you to meet his little—what did you call her? Ah yes! Hummingbird!" He looked around. The observers like themselves were leaving. "Let's go back to the hotel for a drink, shall we?"

Alphonse walked with cat-like grace despite his tipsiness, and Richard followed him through a maze of carriages, footmen, and patrons. Richard tried to shake off the filthy feeling of the ball, the disaster of meeting Delamar. They found the hotel lobby where a throng of people were pairing up for an evening of gossip and flirting.

"There's a couple I want you to meet," Alphonse called over his shoulder as the crowd separated them. He pointed to an enormous Louis XIV style mirror so long out of fashion it was becoming fashionable again. Richard held his breath. The smell of horses and sweat had no effect on him, but he could not tolerate the mix of colognes—vetiver, cinnamon, and something nauseating, like incense in a papist church.

A man joined Alphonse's friends at the mirror. He stood over six feet and his hair and freckles gave everyone a start with his resemblance to President Jefferson. But it was the young woman standing by his side who made Richard stare in amazement. Except for a difference in height, she was Julia.

He heard Alphonse's voice: "Richard?" a question and a command to attention at the same time. "Allow me to present Francis Ball and his bride, and I believe their intention is to sail to the...Indies?"

"My father's sugar plantation in the Antilles. Curse of the junior son, I'm afraid," Ball cheerfully explained. "But Delia is not one to shrink from a challenge, are you, my dear?"

He spoke to her as if she were a comrade in arms, and when she smiled, her eyes keep their fullness, a peculiarity he had not seen in anyone but Julia. It took a conscious effort to break his gaze from her.

Although a bit quaint, Richard knew Virginians still considered it acceptable to compare pedigrees. "My mother's family are the Lees of Orange," he offered.

Ball smiled and took the bait. "From King Charles's secretary, Richard Lee? I assume you are named for him. So, we are cousins, then, though very distant."

"Are there any other kind in Virginia?" Alphonse laughed. "And you, Mrs. Ball? Are you your husband's cousin, too?"

"No doubt, though as yet undisclosed," she smiled. "My people are the Markhams of Rappahannock."

"Not possible! I mean—I beg your pardon," Richard hurriedly added. "It's just that you bear an astonishing resemblance to a young lady who is a member of the Chinn family," he stammered, looking back and forth between Francis Ball and his wife. "Prominent Virginians that settled Kentucky."

"That is astonishing, Mr. Johnson. You see, my wife was born Delia Chinn, but her parents died when she was quite young. She took the name of her aunt and uncle who raised her and her sister."

Richard held back from exclaiming, yes! We bought your household! The Balls turned to step away, but Mrs. Ball rested her hand on his arm for a moment. "Perhaps we will one day meet my twin, Mr. Johnson!"

Without thinking, Richard blurted, "I plan to have her by my side when I serve my term in Washington, Mrs. Ball."

Alphonse stared at him as if he had grown a second head. The Balls walked on, leaving Richard to explain.

"You've kept your hand very close to the vest, indeed!" Alphonse prodded.

"I had no idea myself, Alphonse, until now when I saw this lady. Then it became as clear to me what to do as my own reflection in that hideous mirror."

"Well? Tell me! Tell me all! Is she of a good age?"

"Seventeen. Nearly."

"Oh, dear boy, sublime! As lovely as that piece of porcelain, Mrs. Ball?"

"Lovelier."

"Handsome dowry?"

"Disinherited of sorts." Richard looked off, catching a glimpse of the Balls as they ascended the steps to the dining room.

"Hah! Well, you're rich enough, it shouldn't matter. Hint of a scandal, I daresay." Alphonse grinned and clapped his gloved hands, making a puff of lime-scented air.

Richard relaxed his shoulders and smiled sincerely for the first time that evening. "I feel like having some supper. Care to join me?"

Chapter 8

Return

July 1807, Great Crossing

James Theobald was curious. Only the most valued servants, with ailments beyond the ken of plantation mistresses ever received his ministrations.

"She's in here, Doctor," Jemima pointed to the little room adjoining the cookhouse.

Her voice had a quiver to it, and Doctor Theobald turned to look carefully at her, but the formidable Mrs. Johnson's eyes were dry. "You say she's had no complaints?" he asked.

"Hennie never complains about anything," Milly told him, panic raising her voice to an unnatural pitch. "But today wasn't the first time I'd seen her keeled over in pain. It's happened off and on all week. She just said it was a bad monthly. But I clean her room and I know for a fact she missed last month's."

"By her pallor, I'd say she's lost a great deal of blood." Theobald took hold of the woman's wrist and put his cheek near her mouth. The pulse came rapid, shallow; her breathing was the same. She made no sound but wore a look of peace, much as the dead. "You are suggesting that she may be pregnant. What is her age?"

"Thirty-nine," Milly whispered. Julia stepped nearer her aunt to hold on to her. They both looked away when the doctor lifted Henrietta's shift, not seeing the bright red trickle moving down her leg. But Jemima saw, and limped closer to her servant's cot to get a better look at the doctor's movements. When he pressed the right side of Henrietta's abdomen the trickle moved a little faster. He pressed the left side and within seconds blood saturated the little bed.

Theobald frowned. "Only recently I acquired a valuable book," he spoke rapidly as if to himself, "a compilation of studies and illustrations of women's ailments. In it is a detailed drawing by a Dutch physician of a tiny fetus growing inside a fallopian tube. It was sketched from the post-mortem of a woman who had successfully borne eleven children."

"As I have done," Jemima murmured. She shivered despite the oppressive heat in the little room. "It was the same as this, before she died?"

"The report was that she collapsed in pain, became unconscious and died a few hours later. The surgeon found her perineal cavity filled with fresh blood. I believe I would find the same here."

"You are telling me there is nothing to be done? That is, if your opinion is correct?" Theobald nodded, looking cautiously at Julia as she fell to her knees by her mother's side. Jemima gripped Milly's arm with her crippled fingers, making the sobbing girl stop her noise for a moment in shock at the pain.

"And you could not know for certain unless you were to cut her open? Like a slaughtered animal?" Jemima's shrill, staccato voice and her brutal words froze Theobald where he stood.

Never had Julia wanted to hate her mistress before. How could she give Mama a little ease in her dying hour and take care of this sick, cantankerous old woman at the same time? She choked down the bitter taste of her unshed tears, letting her young aunt's unrestrained sobs sound out grief for them both.

"Be strong, Julia," Jemima commanded. "Keep her skin cool with some compresses on her face and hands and neck. Milly, stop that noise. We're none of us helpless women here. Fetch a bucket of spring water so Julia can switch out these rags. And tell Lucy and Kate to start dinner."

Julia dared not look at her mistress; rage swelled through her chest and flooded her face. As she began to wipe her mother with a wet cloth, Jemima hissed, "Gently!" Julia looked up at the doctor for rescue. But his was a cool, and she feared, unfeeling nature. All she got was the sight of his swift, lean fingers slipping a thick wad of rags under Henrietta's legs. The movement made another heavy stream of blood gush onto the worn linen.

The sound of sloshing water made Julia turn toward Milly, who stopped crying at the sight of her niece's color-drained face. Milly set down the heavy bucket of spring water she'd been commanded to fetch, grabbed a fresh rag and wrung out a compress for Julia.

"I'm alright, Milly," Julia rasped, but sighed deeply as her aunt pressed the cool cloth to her forehead. And then, with a change sudden as a lightning strike, Theobald watched a grieving daughter become an obedient servant.

He felt compelled to stay to the end, he told himself, out of fondness for the household. But his professional curiosity made him wish he could convince Mrs. Johnson to allow a postmortem, to see for himself an ectopic pregnancy.

Although he was not a religious man, he had great reverence for the human body, the miraculous way torn or broken parts knit themselves whole again. He resented the religious constraints against dissection. It was nothing short of torture for him to see a body lowered into a grave to rot instead of serving some useful purpose in a surgery.

The doctor caught himself mid-thought. No, he could not muster any shame over his line of reasoning. He looked at the woman, still beautiful, without any disgust at his eagerness to cut her open. Neither was he concerned about the morality of slavery. He had no slaves, but it was the way of things, sure to die out eventually as it had in Greece and Rome.

He knew himself to be a good doctor with the potential to be a great surgeon, given the right circumstances. Field surgeons in Napoleon's battlefields all over Europe were documenting amazing discoveries now, because they had the sense to take advantage of what the dying and the dead had to reveal.

His fights were in tiny chambers such as this, but he knew this battle was already lost. At best, he could monitor and only estimate the amount of blood a woman might lose in this manner.

WITHIN FOUR HOURS, Henrietta was dead. Robin, Henry and George returned from their rounds, the noise from their horses and dogs alerting Theobald in time to meet them on the gravel drive. He gave them the news and a brief description of his suspicions, watching cautiously to see what the Johnson patriarch's reaction would be.

He followed the man as he walked slowly to the little room behind the cookhouse. Johnson stood gazing at the ashen body for a moment and rushed away without a word. Theobald wondered. It wouldn't be the first time, from the looks of Julia. He knew from ministering to Mrs. Johnson that it was her slave girl, not her husband, who slept in her room.

ROBIN WAS SHOCKED AT the news of his cook's sudden death. He had been a man of grief for a long time, longing for the one woman he had loved with all his might, as she deteriorated before his eyes. At first, her body shrank from rheumatism, curling her fingers and then her spine. In greater sorrow, he stood by while her mind lost hold. She had not confided in him for years. The only person she tolerated for more than half an hour was young Julia.

How was the girl taking the loss of her mother? Did she know of Henrietta's condition, or about any of such things yet? Jemima kept her backward; otherwise, she wouldn't have overreacted when Marshall lost his senses. Henrietta never had much of a chance to be a proper mother to her.

Henrietta, gone. From the first sight of her, it had been a long struggle to overcome his desire. Richard had compared her to Dulcinea, and that image had stuck through the years. Although he never gave into temptation, his wife thought he had. Betsey'd probably put that idea into her head.

He hoped Henrietta had been happy in their household; everyone treated her well, as her talents deserved. Protecting her from the advances of many men, both black and white, became his penance. But she never took an interest in any of them until Betsey's coachman played his fiddle. The only decent thing to do was let them be and protect them from Jem.

JEMIMA RETIRED AT DR. Theobald's insistence. Julia remained by her mother, still holding her hand, unable to weep. Did she not love her mother enough to grieve? Who had Mama lain with? That nice man, Samuel, from Miz Betsey's? Someone should tell him. And someone should send for the deacon.

Her mother lay there, so pale and beautiful. She reached out a finger and drew it along the rise and fall of that still face: the high cheek bones, the long, straight nose, the broad forehead and perfectly arched eyebrows. "What made her die, Dr. Theobald? I want to understand."

"It's rough. Are you up to it?"

"I've been with Miz Jemima on her rounds since I was ten. I've helped her midwife dead babies and set bones that were coming out of the skin. Before she got so crippled, we did work good enough to earn your praise, as I recall."

Theobald gave her a grim smile. "I'll show you what I believe happened to your mother." He took a scrap of linen rag from the pile of nearby stanching cloths. He went to the cookhouse and returned with some pieces of charcoal then drew a picture. It looked like a cow skull with bent horns coming down to its chin.

"A while ago the Dutch anatomists discovered that a developing infant—in its earliest and smallest stage, mind you—could get stuck in one of these..." he pointed to a bent horn... "fallopian tubes. The baby grows, the tube cannot. It bursts. And..."

"The mother bleeds to death, like Mama. I'd like to be a healer. Mama, Miz Jemima both, have taught me a lot." She picked up a cloth, wrung it over the basin of water, and carefully washed each finger of her mother's hands.

"Mama about herbs and poultices. Miz Jemima about splints and wrappings. She always tells me healing's about firmness with cuts and bones, gentleness with burns and fevers."

Her voice drifted far away as she draped the washed hands carefully over her mother's chest.

Milly, Lucy and little Kate appeared at the doorway. Lucy wiped away her tears with a dish rag before asking, "What can we do for you, Julie?" Milly turned away, sobbing.

"Could you rinse out Mama's good dress?" Julia stepped over to her mother's shelf and unfolded a white muslin dress yellowed with age. She hugged it to her before gently handing it over to Lucy, who hurried from the room.

"Kate, could you fetch an empty bucket and fill it with all the rags you can find?"

Little Kate returned quickly with a bucket and strips of rag, casting a terrified glance at Henrietta before running away. Julia turned back to Doctor Theobald. "Her soul's free, and you can't hurt her body. See what you can find out."

Theobald shook his head in disbelief. "You have the constitution and mind of a physician. If only you weren't..."

"A slave?"

"What? No. I was going to say, a woman."

Julia stood by the closed door and prayed for him to be quick. His back was to her, blocking the incision he made. She could see nothing but the strong contours of her mother's legs, her arms resting over her chest, her beautiful head. A distinct plop-plop sound came from the bucket. He was pulling one ball of blood-soaked rag after another from the opening he had made. She slid to the floor in shock at the amount of it.

What a terrible price women pay! Poor Mama! Maybe she had wanted a baby just to give her a little joy. Julia had seen girls younger than herself and older than her mother have babies. She knew childbirth was a wretched business; did the other hurt, too? Everyone seemed in a hurry to find out, but once they did, they never told her anything. She thought about Marshall's body squirming on her and she shuddered.

To distract her from those all too vivid, shameful memories, Julia watched Doctor Theobald. She admired his sleek form, his narrow face with the long nose, how his dark, straight hair gave way to tiny curls at the neck. He resembled a thoroughbred.

She conjured up Richard: muscled torso, full face, his thick red mane and gold-sparked eyes. A lion, with a power over her that made her willing to do anything. Her eyes closed, remembering the shock of his kiss.

She must have slept nearly half an hour, for the sound of Jemima's cane tapping its way toward the cookhouse made her jolt upright and onto her feet. "Dr. Theobald!" Julia whispered, terrified.

"Yes, I know. I am finished." He spoke breathlessly. "It is remarkable. No time to explain now, but I have seen it." With the final stitches of the autopsy tied off, Theobald tossed his blood-spattered makeshift apron on the floor. Julia put a large, clean cloth in his hand, and they were spreading an old sheet over Henrietta's body as Jemima entered.

Eager to see Jemima out of the room, Theobald offered his arm and a stern command to get off her swollen feet. Before he could steer her through the narrow door, however, she announced, "I've given instructions to Jamie to prepare Henrietta a proper coffin. She deserves more than a hemp shroud. Lucy will have her dress ready in the morning. We will all accompany you to the burial in the afternoon."

Julia's shoulders began to shake, letting out a sob that distorted the sound of her "thank you." Once alone, her tears came freely. She had shed tears of exhaustion, fear and anger, but these were her first bitter tears of regret. "Oh, Mama, I am so, so sorry I neglected you all these years."

Not your fault, honey. Not your fault.

RICHARD FOUND GREAT Crossing empty. Most hot July days like this kept his mother indoors behind thick draperies. He panicked for a moment, looking for signs of mourning, but saw no crepe or wreaths. The quiet sapped the joy from his homecoming. Walking out the back door, he saw a lanky servant boy leading a mare and her foal to pasture. He strode toward them anxious for company.

"Hallo, Mas Richard," the boy grinned, slowing his steps. "You sure been gone a long time."

"Simon, you rascal, I didn't recognize you from the porch. You've grown six inches! Looking more like your father every day, poor boy! Where's everybody?"

"Up at the cemetery, burying Henrietta. Your pa told me to hold the fort down."

Richard's chest tightened. "How's Julia taking the loss?"

"Alright, I'd say, but Mama says she's stuck." They reached the pasture gate and the horses stomped.

"Wonder what she meant by that?" Richard asked as he took the bridle and soothed the mare while Simon pulled open the gate.

With an expert eye the boy glanced over the pasture, checking for any breaks in the fence. "Well, she says Julie can't grieve too bad because she's got Miz Johnson to mama her. Always has. So, if she acts too sad, she'll only make Miz Johnson feel unappreciated."

Richard removed the tether to the colt then the tack from the mare. After a smack to her haunch, she bolted off toward a shady patch with the colt running eagerly behind her.

"Your ma's got more sense than anybody I know." He thought about how his own mother added so many complications to his plans for Julia.

Looking out across the wide meadows of the Crossing, he saw in the distance the group of mourners drudging toward the house.

"Simon, you run along now and curry that nag I brought back from the ferry."

His unwashed body smelled like horse and wore a layer of sun-baked dirt mixed with sweat. Any attempts to clean up would be hopeless; nevertheless, he lifted his hat and gave a rough swipe over his brow and neck with a handkerchief. He beat the road dust off his trousers and mopped his face again.

"Behold the bridegroom cometh," he joked to himself and headed toward them.

He marveled that his mother could endure the walk. As he neared them, he made out moving haloes of gnats over each head. Everyone's arms flailed in the air at odd beats, trying to keep off the insects. They reminded him of a boat with its oars out of rhythm. There was no doubt who was captain of the little ship crossing the huge meadow. A dozen of their people from the house and stables followed her. Jemima walked slowly, Robin steadying her on the left, Julia shading her head with a parasol on the right. Doctor Theobald followed close behind them, dressed like an undertaker.

What's he doing here? Richard wondered. Mother must be worse off than I thought.

But if that were true, why would Theobald allow her out in this heat?

Julia saw him first. Her back suddenly straightened, and her head lifted to meet his eyes. When he reached them, Julia did not smile or speak. Only the expansion of her nostrils and the slow closing of her eyes gave her away, and only he noticed.

Richard forced his gaze from her, took off his hat and greeted his parents and Theobald. He nodded to their people, but not a soul stopped in their slow march. It would have been impossible to recommence any movement in this swelter.

"Put your hat back on, son. Do you want a stroke?" Jemima commanded.

"Not on such a day," he answered with a wink aimed at Theobald, who returned it with a slight nod. Richard dutifully replaced his sweat-stained hat. Robin motioned to him and he got in step alongside his father. By bending a little, he could see Julia from the corner of his eye.

"I am sorry for your loss, Julia. We will all miss her terribly." His parents looked at the ground, giving him the chance to gaze at Julia for a long second. Any doubt he had about his desire for her vanished.

"We mind our manners, Julia, most especially in our grief," Jemima murmured.

"I appreciate your kindness," Julia answered softly.

"Properly address him," Jemima prompted in a cajoling tone.

"I appreciate your kindness, Master Richard." Julia looked at him boldly.

"Mama, this is not the time."

"The worst times are the best times for learning. We never forget what we learn in times of difficulty," Jemima intoned.

Theobald cleared his throat; everyone turned toward the sound. "I'd best get back to town. Unless I can help you further, Mrs. Johnson."

She would ask for nothing, he knew, having already proved her strength of will superior to his earlier advice to stay home. He wanted to bid farewell to Julia but felt unsure about the propriety of social niceties to a slave.

But for the life of him, he could not think of her as a slave. Since the postmortem on her mother, he felt a bond with the girl that bordered on possession of a different kind.

He settled on a wordless nod in Julia's direction, then bowed slightly to the Johnsons with the required lift of the hat. He and Richard exchanged another nod. As he walked toward the stable for his horse, Theobald found himself troubled by his friend's sudden appearance and strange restlessness. Travel fatigue, he concluded, although that did not satisfy.

Their group reached the shaded path near the spring. Lucy and the other servants quickened their pace and headed toward the house. Jamie, Sandy and Jacob headed to the stables. Only Milly lingered behind.

Lucy ached for Henrietta's sister, knowing Julia might as well be dead, too, for all the solace Milly could get from her. With a nod, she looked back toward Milly wordlessly telling her she'd manage without her in the cookhouse for a little bit. She hated to admit it, but she wanted to impress her masters. Milly was a serviceable cook but sorely lacking any of Henrietta's talent. Lucy hoped her flair would get her permanently out of the laundry shed and into the kitchen.

Jemima ignored her youngest sons, sulky from the heat and the forced attendance at Henrietta's burial. When their dogs came running to them from the barn, Robin mumbled, "Run along, boys."

"I'll be off to Betsey's," Joel told his father, throwing Richard a defiant look. John T added, "I, as well."

Jemima gave them a disdainful "hmph". Since the incident with Julia, Betsey had taken Joel under her protection, convincing the boy that Julia seduced Marshall and he was not at fault. John T did not even bother to hide his hostility toward her girl. Jemima had little use for any of them these days.

Julia, Richard, and his parents walked toward the stone bench by the spring. The ancient shade trees made this the most bearable spot on the property during summer. Julia propped the parasol against a tree, but the men had already gotten Jemima lowered onto the bench.

Richard's chest tightened as he noticed his mother's dress. Suzanne had made it for her, how many years ago? Only three, he realized. The dove gray dress Julia had once been so proud of had been dunked in blacking, leaving streaks of unevenness. His mother must be training her in the ways of proper mourning, he concluded. It unsettled him that nothing in life, no matter how banal, was anything more than a teaching opportunity to her.

Lucy sent Little Kate to them with a tray of cool tea and anise cakes, with a small bowl of sliced cucumber for Miz Johnson's ailment. The girl set it on the outdoor table, a slab of gray stone balanced between two tree stumps. She lifted the napkin off the cakes and took up her post, waving the cloth over the food to shoo away flies.

"Julia, pluck me some mint from the bank, that's a good girl."

Jemima watched attentively as Julia knelt near the spring head and gathered some young sprigs. When she placed them on the tray, Jemima grabbed and crushed them between her thumb and arthritic fingers, letting the smell revive her.

"Go on now, child, get a little rest. I'll call for you later this afternoon."

Richard leaned against a tree where he could get a good view of Julia as she approached Milly, who sat weeping on the back porch. Milly shook her head vehemently, wiped her face on her apron, but did not budge. Julia went inside without making the noisy porch door creak.

Jemima interpreted the look on her son's face as shock at her leniency. "What? She has nothing to fear. Joel and John T are gone, and if they drink again, they're gone for good. We can have no scandal, not now with you heading to Washington. We have no choice except to be the best house in five counties. And I want to tell you, Julia and I are training a whole crop of youngsters for house service. See? Look at Little Kate. She's coming along nicely."

Kate beamed at the attention and began to fan wildly over the tray in response to the compliment. "Gently, child. Smoothly. Always make your movements such that they do not draw attention."

Kate brought herself under control and swished the air with comic daintiness. How many times had Julia heard these kinds of corrections, Richard wondered? Not for the first time he marveled at her patience, but then she'd had no more choice than Kate.

His father had not spoken, only stared at the little trickle of water running from the spring house. The folks sat next to each other like strangers. They tamed a wilderness together, as if God himself appointed them to the task. What happened? His father finally looked his age; worse, he looked heartbroken.

Was he grieving the loss of his Dulcinea? He knew his father never touched Henrietta, but he must have suffered from longing as he watched her beauty waste away in the cookhouse.

"May I join you for lunch?" Richard asked suddenly. He had to find Julia, to comfort her, to tell her what they were going to do. Would she be on her cot in his mother's room? "I know I'm a sight, but maybe I could wash up a bit and make myself presentable."

"Only if your father lends you fresh clothing," Jemima answered as she munched on a slice of anise cake.

"I fear I'm practically threadbare," Robin sighed. "The heat. Then losing Lucy from the laundry to the cookhouse. But take whatever you need, son. Don't mind us."

When Richard walked up the porch, the soft scuffing of his boots on the boards stirred Julia, who had taken refuge in a dark corner of the drawing room. How was it that he should arrive when grief for her mother and this unbidden connection to Theobald had made her need for him so great?

She called his name softly when he stepped into the foyer. Relieved to see that the draperies would hide the sight of them together, Richard entered the dark room and carefully closed the door. They embraced until the dampness of their clothes forced them apart. He lifted her hand to his lips and as he kissed it, she kissed the back of his hand before moving it to her face.

"I am truly sorry you have lost your mother, Julia." He stroked her cheek tenderly with his thumb, alarmed by the redness and swelling of her eyes.

"She's free now. But God forgive me, I cannot grieve as I ought because you are home. Why are you here, in this room, with me?"

In answer, Richard kissed her slowly, softly, repeating her name and holding her gently until she felt her restraint give way. Her lips parted and she allowed herself to wonder at the taste of him: the dust of the road, the salt of his sweat, anise seed from the little funeral cake.

Mama, I am so, so sorry to have such joy in the shadow of your grave.

"You're mine, then?" he whispered, struggling to regain his breath.

"I am. I always have been." She pressed her forehead to his; he clasped her hands, and they swayed slightly until they found their balance.

For three years, Julia had dreamed of little else but this moment, never daring to share her hopes, even with her mother. Now, she felt trapped in the dream, afraid of waking before she could drain it completely of its sweetness.

"I will marry you, Julia. I will. It became so clear to me in New Orleans."

"Please make it clear to me, then," she pleaded. "How can we marry? Even being your woman will tear this family to pieces."

"You will not be anything less than my wife," he answered her with fierceness. "Wait and see how I will make you a life fit for a queen."

His intensity thrilled her, but he spoke like an overwrought child. "The life I have is better than most. I can bear my state knowing you want me," she said to calm him.

"It isn't enough! Nobody's going to order you around or trample your dignity when you're mine."

"No one orders or tramples me, now," she said gently.

"*Master Richard,*" he mimicked, "when you'd just left your mother's grave."

Julia lowered her head at the thought of her mother's scarred corpse, the secret she shared with the doctor standing close by her.

"No, Richard, please. Don't say such things. She really is so good to me."

"Not good enough. I'm going to free you from all of this." Taking her hand, he pulled her toward the door. "I told them I was going to get cleaned up. Help me, would you?"

Julia froze, uncertain of his meaning.

"You know me better than that," he replied to her look of alarm. "But if you'll find some of Father's linen and a pair of trousers, lay them out on his bed, and I can make up for some of the time I've stolen here with you."

"So much for no one ordering me about," she smiled weakly and stepped away.

"The difference is I'm talking to my helpmeet, not my slave."

When she saw the tenderness in his eyes, she knew he meant it. Reaching out, she took his hand for a moment, then quietly retreated from the room, leaving him alone.

After Julia left, what little light remained seemed dimmer. Wasn't it nearly three years ago she had risen from another dark corner and roused in him this desire for her? He swept the room with his eyes, chuckling softly to himself at his sudden fear of another girl skulking in a corner. Being ashamed of their love for one another was unworthy; admitting that theirs was a situation requiring secrecy was wise.

But for the love of heaven, why couldn't he take her with him now to Washington and marry her there? No one could tell she was a slave. Maybe he should act in haste. Within weeks of knowing Suzanne, he had wanted to marry her for love, but family decided she wasn't good enough. American, but not the right kind. White, but not the best kind. She hadn't known her *place!*

This time he swore no one would know about Julia until it was too late.

The heat slammed into him as he mounted the stairs and reached the landing. Julia had already slipped out of his father's room in her ghost-like way, leaving clean garments on the bed for him. Richard stripped, sloshed a wet towel over himself, and inspected his skin in the wash basin mirror: face burnt crimson; hands and neck tanned deep walnut; freckled white belly.

Alphonse's voice echoed in his head, "Mathilde's hexadecaroon." Where could the law draw a line between who was black or white? His own body bore at least three shades! He knew families of English stock with eyes as dark and skin as tan as Spaniards. And Julia, Henrietta? Slaves fairer than their masters.

He also knew dozens of men in dead marriages who found themselves in love with women like Julia. Look at the respectability that abomination of the plaçage had gained in New Orleans! And he'd never let Julia be mocked as Jefferson's girl had been in obscene cartoons and songs.

Anyone on the other side of the Ohio would marry them, and if no one accepted their marriage here, what would it matter? Julia would have her honor. So would their children. Blue Spring was his, but he'd use it to buy her off Pa if he had to.

He hurriedly pulled on his father's breeches and threw a linen shirt over his head, yanking it away from his sticky skin. At least he smelled better. The moment he gently knocked on his mother's door, Julia opened it just enough to reveal Little Kate gathering items to take downstairs. Her small apron sagged under the weight of fresh stockings, talcum shaker and hair comb. He quickly withdrew deeper into his father's room.

After the girl's footsteps retreated down the hall, he found Julia and pulled her into the little passageway between his parents' rooms. They kissed in the dark, hungrily, desperately. Suzanne's tiny form had made him protective and gentle. Julia equaled him in height and made him bolder, rougher. They collided as he pressed her against him; she worked her hands beneath his shirt, pulling him closer. Her grief made her reckless; his memory of Marshall's drunken attempt made him stop. He pulled away from her.

"I have to go."

"I know. They're bound to be wondering what's taking you so long."

"We'll have to continue our pretense a little longer, but believe me, darling girl, there's no one else. Are you sure you want me?"

"I've loved you since I was a child. There can't ever be anyone else."

Please Theobald, go away!

"You were—what, sixteen last year? Telling me you loved me. What courage that took, now that I think about it. And you seemed like just a girl. But the ten years between us doesn't amount to anything, now. Why is that?"

"Probably because I've come to think like a woman." She reached for him, pulling him back into her arms. "I've waited three years. Another three or four won't matter."

"My dear girl, it won't be three years," he laughed and chucked her chin. "Next summer, heaven willing, is about as long as I'll be able to stand." He lifted her hand to his lips and stepped away, reaching out with his other hand to wipe away the tears that started down her cheeks. She reached for him again, and he kissed her face, her lips and hair, rapidly, tenderly. Then he left.

Julia lay down on her narrow cot, unable to breathe. The heat of the room and in her body became unbearable. She removed her clothes and took liberty with her mistress's wash cloth and water, not caring if Miz Jemima chastised her. Richard possessed her now. She bunched up the linen towel in her hands and muffled her sobs with it.

Chapter 9
Arrival
October 26, 1807. Washington, DC

R ichard looked at his seat in the hall of Congress with the pride of a newly anointed king approaching his throne.

It was a slick leather chair on the smallish side with a low back and thin arms. He lowered himself into it slowly, reverently. *We did it, Ma. Pa.*

He smiled and offered his hand to those squeezing by on the way to their seats. He felt a few pats on his back from men who were still strangers to him, but word was most were Freemasons like himself, so they were already a brotherhood.

Pushing the chair closer to his small desk, he tried to relax his hands on its polished wood surface. They shook with excitement, not fear, but he pulled them back in embarrassment, anyway.

He breathed in the smell of fresh plaster and paint. Over a hundred and forty of them had to pack into this small chamber, for although the Capitol building was enormous, it remained unfinished. Richard was told to count himself lucky. The Supreme Court had to meet in the basement, and it was not only unfinished but dank as a dungeon, as well.

Three other newly elected congressmen sat next to him. On his right was John Rowan, age thirty-four. He had killed a man in a drunken duel over a card game, but his hometown judge dismissed the case. Next to Rowan sat Joseph Desha who was of Huguenot stock. He thought of Suzanne with an old, now dulled longing. Even though the man was forty with near-grown children, he was as smooth-skinned and beautiful as an angel. On the left sat Benjamin Howard who also had unearthly good looks. Howard seemed preoccupied as if he wanted to be anyplace else but the United States House of Representatives.

In front of them, the two senior members of the Kentucky delegation, John Boyle and Matthew Lyon, had their heads together talking. Out of their whole group, Richard felt more of a kinship to Boyle. They were both lawyers in their twenties who had outgrown Frankfort after one term.

The real character in the bunch—in all of Congress—was Matthew "Spitting" Lyon. Richard already knew the story. Roger Griswold from Connecticut called Lyon a foul name on the Floor of the House, and Lyon spat in the man's face. Two weeks later they beat each other's heads with a cane and a fire iron.

Almost as interesting was the tidbit Boyle mentioned on their way inside: Lyon was the only congressman ever elected in jail. But it had been for sedition under Adams's no-count Alien and Sedition Act, so the people made him a hero. What could he say or do over the coming months to make himself as memorable? He chuckled softly. Maybe the best thing was to keep a low profile and avoid earning a nickname.

Their entire Kentucky delegation voted Democratic-Republican, the party of President Jefferson. Unlike the president, however, they stood ready to declare war on England again. The question on everyone's minds was this: how fast can we go to war? Three months had already passed since HMS *Leopard* captured the USS *Chesapeake*.

No American could live with the shame of it. All the men back home told Richard to let the president know Kentucky stood ready to burn every fort between there and Canada, and to shoot Tecumseh and all the rest of England's Indian allies.

When Speaker Varnum pounded the gavel, the men's voices finally died down. Within minutes, Richard heard his name called by the clerk; he rose and spoke his first official word as a duly elected member of Congress. "Present."

Lyon looked back at them with a grin and drawled, "Hold on to your hats, boys, the windbags are about to blow!"

Howard whispered back, "Aye, and no spittin' in the wind if you please, Matthew."

November 1807

"The nation has arrived at a crisis!"

Not every eye in Congress turned to Richard, but the room grew silent quickly. The pages even stopped their message and tobacco deliveries for a moment when they felt, as much as heard, this strangely resonant voice. It rose and fell for several minutes, then crescendoed like an operatic ending with the shout: "We must receive satisfaction for the injuries that have been inflicted upon us!"

In response to the House applause, Richard simply bowed his head and returned to his seat. But what a struggle he had to restrain his impulse to grin like a triumphant schoolboy. Having been invited to an inner sanctum, the only committee privy to Jefferson's secret negotiations with England, it was his duty to be dignified.

He had also earned the appointment as secretary to the party's caucus and come quickly to the attention of their war-ready candidates, James Madison and George Clinton. And with all this, in the head-spinning speed of one month, he counted it a miracle that he could muster any restraint at all. How little he had known himself! The ease with which he took to being the center of attention astonished him.

Unlike the seasoned politicians who were taking a liking to him, Richard wanted no negotiating with England. Back home, the men who had elected him expected him to rise as a war hawk, and a hawk with the sharpest of talons. But all he really wanted was the attention of his life-long idol, Thomas Jefferson, the man who declared that independence was sworn on "our lives, our fortunes, and our sacred honor". He wanted it clear he was the president's man.

March 1808

Richard leaned into the hard wind tormenting the flower stalks and tree limbs bare of early blooms. The walk allowed him to work off the bout of nerves riling his stomach, nerves that made him clutch and unclutch the letter inside his pocket. He had gone weak at the knees, like a love-sick damsel, at the sight of the heavy paper with the president's seal upon it:

'I thank you for the good opinion you are pleased to express of my conduct in the administration of our government. It has been a source of great pain to me to have met with so many of our opponents who transferred to the person the hatred they bore to his political opinions.'

The words were meant to comfort Richard after the vicious attacks he endured for supporting the president's embargo. He imagined the hey-day his attackers would have if they ever got wind of Julia. Jefferson had suffered two elections filled with obscene references to his personal life.

God forgive him, but Richard hoped he could somehow find a tactful opening to this subject so like his own situation. Just how the devil to do it, that was the question. Should he lead into it with talk of Tripoli? No; that was three years ago. Or thank him for cutting the whisky tax? He might laugh to hear how Sallie said that had gotten a vote out of every man in Kentucky. No, he'll want to talk about the embargo, no doubt, or the war.

Better I keep my mouth shut!

As he mounted the steps to the entrance of the presidential mansion, he admired the smoothness of the unpainted gray sandstone. It fit the neoclassical style much better than the jagged dark stuff that built Great Crossing and Blue Spring. Suddenly, he felt like a rube, the ignorant country boy Alphonse Leclerc considered him. The wind had blown the torches out on the deep porch, and no lights shone from within; the president kept only a skeleton staff when his daughters and their army of servants were not here.

Richard dropped the brass knob against the plate. To his astonishment, the door opened at once and a dark-skinned servant of middling years greeted him. When Richard stepped into the foyer, the man picked up a flickering candelabra and walked away. Over his shoulder, in a hushed voice, he said, "Mr. Johnson, welcome. Mr. Jefferson will receive you upstairs if you will follow me."

The president lived without pomp or frills. They passed rooms shut off to save heat, and only a few pieces of furniture broke the monotony of the long hallway. Richard knew enough about the president to assume the Spartan appearance was a deliberate reminder to visiting Congressmen to trim the fat.

Keeping his eye on the large candelabra in front of him, Richard grew more and more impressed with the grace of this servant, who kept the lights wondrously even up two wide flights of stairs. When the melting wax sputtered, the memory of Julia's mouth on his scalded hand distracted his attention.

The servant knocked twice, then entered without waiting for permission. Jefferson welcomed Richard into the place where he held most of his informal evening interviews: his bedroom. He greeted Richard in a brocade jacket so worn the pattern no longer showed. His bony hand grabbed the younger man's, and Richard could not control the ghastly broadness of his own smile.

How alike we are, except in height. Same coloring, same deep-set eyes. But then we are distant cousins. Should I mention it? Shut up!

"Mr. Johnson! So! Please, step into my office," the president smiled, mocking his surroundings with a gesture of his hand. "All my guests must learn not to mind my projects—whims, really—that I feel compelled to work on as I visit."

"Mr. Jefferson," Richard cleared his throat, his voice betraying his nerves, "I am at your service under any conditions you may wish to prescribe."

As they walked toward the middle of the poorly lit room, the president began their conversation by asking, "You're a Kentucky man, so you must know that speechifier Henry Clay?"

"Indeed, I do. When he left here, he went back to Frankfort, and they made him Speaker. Nobody can string words together like he does."

Jefferson nodded. "He'll be back here in no time. Watch out for him, though, Johnson. He may be a family man, but he's a bit of a hot head, hmm? Beg pardon, while I finish my supper. I fear I am ruled by my unfortunate kidneys, and I must endure this broth several times a day if I am to remain on my feet."

He gestured to a pair of small, armless chairs near a table, bent under a staggering load of books and papers. Near the edge sat a bowl of bright yellow-green broth. A nauseating smell emanated from a pot of glue. Richard's mouth dropped open at the sight of a Holy Bible with strips and squares cut out of its pages.

"The Philosophy of Jesus, my current project," the president explained as he sipped the broth.

Richard forgot his hero worship for the moment. "But, sir, is this not a sacrilege of the Good Book?"

The president smiled benignly. "Would you not agree that it is the power of the words, not the bookbinder's skill, that is most important, Mr. Johnson?" Richard nodded half-heartedly. "You are of a purer religious bent than many here in Washington. Your family established a Baptist settlement before Kentucky statehood, didn't they?"

"Yes," Richard answered, surprised and pleased that the president would know about any of his family's history.

"So, the book itself is valued as an entity. The Baptists, however, speak too much of hellfire and damnation, but they are a younger sect and not corrupted as the Anglicans and Papists. Are you familiar with the Unitarian sect, by chance?"

"I am, but with the name only." Richard could hear the voice of Reverend Retting back home invoking God's protection against the anti-Christ Unitarians and Universalists.

"It is my belief that every American will someday be Unitarian." The president threw out this prophecy with the ease of a fisherman casting for trout.

Richard rose hastily to the bait. "Begging your pardon, sir, but I cannot believe that any Christian would follow a church that did not accept Christ as the son of God."

Seemingly satisfied, the president glanced up from his paper strips and squinted. "Well, it won't be the first time one of my wild notions gets proven wrong."

Richard wondered if this was an eccentric display of the president's charm. For his own part, he was disarmed, and felt as comfortable as he did at his boarding house dinner table, despite this little controversy over the Bible. He felt at home enough to continue in the spirit of debate. "If I might say, though, it's a far more plausible notion than the other one."

Jefferson smiled as he put the soup bowl on the floor. A terrier puppy scurried from under the bed and licked the bowl clean. "Which one, dare I ask?" he laughed softly.

"Of settlers reaching the western ocean by the end of our century," Richard answered.

Jefferson turned back to the table and re-arranged a few of the Bible cut-outs onto a piece of foolscap. "Ah! Well, there can be no doubt of that. My secretary, Lieutenant Clark, and Captain Lewis have proven it. Not all the Natives are hostile. You and I won't live to see it, but your grandchildren—they'll have the story to tell."

"Well, sir, I was just last year on the Mississippi, and I can tell you that the expanse of wilderness I saw weeks on end makes me marvel at it happening in a thousand years."

"It took only one generation to settle Kentucky. If we have people like you Johnsons, it will happen. That story of your mother hauling water past the hostile Indians is a legend."

Richard chuckled. "True, sir. My mother could've conquered the whole continent."

"Women are indeed the civilizing power, by all accounts." He wiped the glue from his hands with an old linen napkin. "Married yet, Mr. Johnson?"

Richard, although stunned by the suddenness of the question, recognized he had his opening. "I wish to be, sir. It is a most delicate situation, I'm afraid."

"Intriguing. How so?" he asked, corking the glue jar. After picking up a large document and unrolling it, he added, "Mind handing me that lot of weights behind you?"

As the president tamed the scroll with the paperweights, Richard forced his mind to concentrate. Jefferson was world-renowned for juggling ten occupations at once. All Richard had to do was remain coherent."

"You see, sir, the young lady in question is—despite her gifts and the good breeding of her father's family..."

"You seem to be struggling with some terrible proposition." Jefferson stopped his paperwork and looked into Richard's eyes. "What can I do to make you more comfortable?"

"Thank you, sir." The sense of ease he had felt only a minute ago abandoned him entirely. Now, he felt like a wicked boy about to confess stealing everything from the collection plate.

"As I said, it is delicate, yet I am determined to do the honorable thing and raise her out of her lowly estate and make her my bride."

"Excuse me, for I do not wish to be rude, but are you on intimate terms with the lady?"

"Good heavens, no, sir. I've thrashed a man for...but...she is like...was raised in some ways like a sister to us."

"So, your parents fear their ward may deprive you of making a more socially acceptable match."

"They do, sir. They do. They have notions of old Virginia aristocracy that I find truly galling, and not in keeping with their religious sentiments."

"I must offer, in their defense, that as a parent every ideal we hold dear often changes when it comes to our children."

"The case here, sir, you understand so very well. My mother, in particular, is so deeply attached to the young lady as to have made her a source of jealousy with my sisters and nieces." He gulped. "But there are legal, as well as moral, issues straining against one another that tear at me."

The president pulled off his spectacles and sat back in his chair. He looked kindly at Richard and waited for the telling.

"She is the beautiful daughter of a gentleman by the name of John Chinn. She favors his side of the family who are tall—and fair—and musically gifted."

"But since she is orphaned, no dowry, social conventions being what they are?" Jefferson tried to ease the strain.

"Her mother was our cook, sir."

The president steepled his fingers and tapped them against his lips. He closed his eyes and sighed. Richard, fearing he had pressed the president too far, considered how little time he had to explain the inexplicable. "My mother acquired the child when she was four years old and raised her as her own. She has been educated to do all of my mother's correspondence, and has even taken over her nursing and bookkeeping..."

"But she has the misfortune of being enslaved, am I correct?"

Richard nodded. "My heart is set on liberating her." He swallowed, barely able to speak the next words, which now seemed absurd. "And making her my wife."

They sat in silence for a long minute.

"My dear boy, you cannot pursue this. You have the makings of a great statesman. Do not throw it all away for a youthful affair of the heart." There was no mistaking the pleading in his voice.

There was no mistaking the despair in Richard's eyes.

Jefferson brought his steepled fingers to his lips. "You are no doubt aware of the Federalists' smear campaign against me on account of a fair-skinned servant woman attached to my estate. Do you remember what I wrote to you a few weeks ago regarding opposition?"

Richard quoted, "That hatred of a position is transferred to the person himself?"

"Yes, that's the idea. I can predict nothing for you except being reviled over this matter and being held in the utmost contempt. Should you somehow be able to keep your head above the fray, your family may not be as fortunate."

"But you were elected..."

"Barely! After many contentious ballots. My personal life played no small part in that fight. Factionalism was as nothing compared to the scorn heaped on me over personal matters. But my conscience is clear, and I have kept my promise to my wife, let God be my judge."

"Of course. What else can a man of honor do?" Richard offered awkwardly.

"And this is a matter of honor with you, isn't it?" The president paused and looked closely at Richard. "I'll assume you are going to ignore my council. If that is your decision, a little more advice. Keep her protected from the outside as much as you can. You are a man of property, of course?"

Richard nodded.

"Can you make it a world apart? And can you remain silent on the subject, as silent as Christ before Pilate? I tell you, that image was my strength through it all. The misery some men have caused you in Congress concerning my embargo will be as nothing compared to this, once it gets into the hands of your enemies. I hope you will be spared. But men, being what they are, I fear for you."

A world apart. Could he create a gulf wide enough between Great Crossing and Blue Spring? Blue Spring and Washington?

"It's been an interesting turn, this, to our conversation. To counsel you on matters so deeply personal was not my intent. So, let me lay out the real matter frankly, as I feel it is not altogether unrelated."

He patted his thigh, and the little terrier yapped as it jumped into his master's lap.

"I wanted to speak to you privately to caution you, and even more now you've made me your confidant. The reports I have had of you this session are impressive. But they have also left me anxious on your account."

"Sir?" Richard looked at him in surprise.

"See my puppy, here? He's a smart little thing. If you will be as wise as this little fellow, you'll wait till you get your teeth before going after the big rats. They're ferocious, and they'll stop at nothing if they think they can destroy you. Meanwhile, listen. Observe the mistakes of others. Do not take offense quickly, as there has been such a rash of lately. We cannot afford hotheads such as Burr and that upstart Jackson any longer. War is on the horizon, and my job is to keep it at bay for long as possible. From all your reports from the Caucus, my friend Madison will be sitting in this very spot a year from now."

"Yes, sir."

Jefferson stood and ran one hand over the page filled with the sayings of Jesus, cradling his puppy in the other hand.

"Remember the apostles. They did great things and spoke powerful words, only *after* Christ left them, not before." He gave Richard a warm smile. "Not that I am to be compared to Christ in any way! But do hold out. You have plenty of time after I am gone."

"Yes, sir. And thank you, sir. I will be forever indebted to you." They clasped hands, then the attendant motioned Richard to step into the hallway.

He walked back to his room at the Franklin Inn, oblivious of the ice in the stinging wind. He felt free from Great Crossing for the first time in his life.

"I WORRY FOR THE BOY, Anthony," Jefferson muttered.

"Yes sir, I can see why." Anthony nodded his head as he picked up the soup bowl from the floor, shooing away the terrier with his free hand.

"When I read his words in the Congressional reports, he gave me the impression of a man from times long past. So much talk of honor; too much faith in impossible causes. He intrigues me."

"I've heard tell he's been an effective advocate for your embargo."

"Precisely the kind of cause I am referring to! But I like him. All that earnestness of youth. Can't help but remind us old men how we once felt about all of this."

He sat back and took another handful of Bible cuttings.

"What were Madison and the rest thinking, giving pups like that license to run for Congress?" he mumbled. "Has to leave that personal business alone if he ever wants to be president."

Chapter 10
Escape
July 1809

Julia had little time to think about anything but Jemima and her world of need. When she had the luxury of thinking about Richard, her thoughts were usually as hopeless as the one that occurred to her now. *Two years since Mama died. Since he told me we would marry in a matter of months.*

One good thing about it: she had learned much, much more. Her piano and singing skills brought unabashed praise from Miz Jemima's guests. She knew every trick to getting done whatever the farm and everybody on it required.

Mas Robin and the boys were almost as scarce around the place as Richard, so it was no wonder the woman was crumbling. Everyone expected her to refill herself all by herself, just like that spring outside. Of course she needed Julia, as devoted as a daughter, loved like one. But, as she studied the small, clean line of her stitches on the pillow sham in her lap, Julia recalled how abruptly Miz Jemima changed when the little seamstress stole Richard's heart.

Suddenly, as if struck by prophecy, she knew her mistress would turn on her, would seek revenge. *If I leave her, they will sell Milly off.*

The Johnsons encouraged slave unions, and Julia suspected it was a means of not just getting more laborers or even more Baptist converts, but more power over them. Mas Robin's people stayed together as families unless someone tried to run. She had only seen it happen a few times over the years, but the howls and screams of those poor souls being carted off in different directions made her eyes water even now. And all their people being forced to stand and watch.

Maybe he'll bring Milly with us.

She closed her eyes and sighed. *How can you be fool enough to believe Richard still loves you? A future president if you take Miz Jemima's word into account. Marrying him is a fantasy. I'm a slave! A slave! Stop denying it!*

"Julia, are you having one of your headaches again? Stop clenching your jaw, and you'll get some relief," Jemima urged.

Little Kate entered the room in her smart uniform. On a napkin-covered tray lay a creamy packet. "A letter from Mas Richard, ma'am," she said with a curtsy. Her movements were delicate and her voice clear enough for Jemima's failed hearing to understand.

"Give it to Julia, Kate. And come back when you have finished your work. Julia needs to give you another lesson in proper hemming."

Jemima pulled off her spectacles and handed the letter to Julia. "I can't bear to wait till the boys get back. Read it to me now. But be careful—make it look unread." She smiled at Julia like a co-conspirator. "And sit beside me so I can hear you."

Julia tried to control the trembling in her hands. She shouted at herself, 'Be still! Still and strong!' First, she read too softly, making Jemima look up. Then she strained to speak more carefully, but in doing so made his jokes fall flat.

"Julia, why ever are you putting on airs? Just read, child!"

She nearly choked, however, when she read: '*I will close by saying, expect me within a week of receiving this, which you hold in your hands. I have some business to attend to in Ohio that may cause me a delay of a day or two, but have my pack of nieces and nephews ready for a grand welcoming for me, so I will be in a good mind to give them the new batch of trinkets in store for them.'*

"Whatever does he mean to do in Ohio?" Jemima mumbled. "Must be something to do with a horse, I expect."

"THAT'S HIM," JEMIMA announced. Despite her bad hearing, she made out Simon's welcoming call to a horse and rider coming up the drive. "We will have to do for his welcome. It's all he deserves coming days early like this!" Julia could feel the ruffle of excitement in Jemima's pulse as she helped her out of the chair. Her own heart had grown three sizes and pounded in her throat as well as her chest.

They stepped outside where the brilliant sunshine made them squint until their eyes ached. Julia looked in the direction of the sound of hooves crunching on pebble. The image of a dark blue shape with a halo of copper gold filled the tiny slits of her eyes. It was Richard, her destroying angel. He was off his horse and moving towards her. She felt lost, swallowed up in the sure knowledge that he had finally succeeded in annihilating her.

"You look rested and scrubbed, son. Got a good night's sleep at your place, I hope?" She embraced him as tightly as her stiff arms allowed and held him for a long minute. Richard let his gaze bore into Julia, who stood behind her mistress. She returned it with equal intensity. Two years? It seemed he had never left.

"Come in, come in out of this heat. Keep me company. Julia's restless, I can tell, and we can give her a chance to make our rounds without me nagging her about how she handles the wagon!" Jemima laughed, roughly patting Richard with her crooked fingers.

He hid his disappointment behind a broad smile. "I suppose she'd better go before the sun gets any higher." He exchanged a glance with Julia, then she was gone. His mother leaned heavily against him. How did Julia have the strength to do this all day long, he wondered?

When they reached the drawing room, he glanced at Julia from the window as she tied her bonnet. She looked cautiously over her shoulder, hoping to catch his eye. He watched her graceful figure take the reins from Simon, who seemed equally satisfied with the view of her. "That little so-and-so," he muttered. Well, he would hardly be a man if he didn't notice such a woman. "Mama, she can't make rounds alone. Where's Little Kate?"

"In the wagon."

"Nobody's in there. Just piles and piles of..."

"Look again, son. Why do you think we still call her Little Kate?" She laughed heartily at his confusion. "We finally got our shipment of work cloth. Despite the fact that it's southern grown cotton spun in northern mills, your embargo has delayed the shipment by half a year! Now, our women are going to have double the work. But I think Julia and the Singin' Sisters will find a way to get it done."

"I think she needs some more help," he said as offhandedly as he could muster.

"Send Simon after her."

"No! He ogled her like a barge hand. I'll go down myself in a few minutes. I haven't said hello to the old'ns in a long time."

"Suit yourself. Just don't delay her once you get started yapping. I need her back here." Jemima sat back in her chair. "Why this sudden interest in our girl's safety?"

He wanted to tell her just how interested he was. But there had been nearly two years of silence between them over Suzanne, and he dared not disturb their peace. Not yet.

"Well, go see the old folks, and get on back to Blue Spring. No telling what sort of mess McPherson's made of it."

He took advantage of her permission to leave. Another minute and she would have begun her favorite topic: marriageable young ladies who would be overjoyed to take on the role of whipping Blue Spring into shape. He ambled along on Pegasus, keeping to the Elkhorn's shade trees for a few hundred feet.

Seemed Mother had loosened the reins on Julia. From the letters Sallie sent him, Julia managed most things now, so their mother could hold court for visitors and grandchildren. Truth be told, their mother had fallen very low. The sugar sickness had crippled her feet and ruined her eyes.

He stopped several yards away from the cluster of twenty or so log cabins the field hands inhabited. As mistress of Blue Spring, Julia would need to be respected and obeyed, not loved. All the able-bodied were in the fields, at the rope walk or the mills, except for these: too old, sickly or injured to be of much use.

They treated her friendly-like, but with a bit of respectful distance. She fussed over their milky eyes, crippled joints and scabs with lineaments from her medicine bag. Little Kate stood in the wagon bed and tossed sacks down to Jamie, whose service as coachman ended when a carriage fall shattered his knee. How different their lives would have been, Richard thought, if Jamie had fathered Julia back in Louisville instead of old Chinn.

He rode closer and saw the faces of those who had fed and washed him, taught him to fish and skin a squirrel and a hundred other things.

After a few minutes of strained exchanges, he took his leave and motioned for Julia to walk with him to his horse. "It's just not the same, anymore," he sighed.

"They are afraid of you now. You're a very powerful man."

"Look more like you're helping me," he said, glancing around then handing her his hat. "I don't want Kate telling tales." Julia nodded and picked tiny bits of grass off the hat brim. "We won't have a moment alone, will we?" he muttered.

"No. Your big welcome home party is five very long days from now. Complete with several fatted calves." She smiled, overflowing with joy to be near him.

"Don't smile," he ordered.

Her heart sank. Pegasus lifted his forelock and shook his mane at the unpleasant sound in Richard's voice. The stallion took a step toward Julia, flicked his tongue at the hat in her hands and snorted as Richard put his foot in the stirrups. Seemed they both had the jitters around their master today.

In an urgent voice, barely above a whisper, he said, "I'm taking you away Sunday night. Across the river to Cincinnati. I have clothes—Julia! Look at me! We'll not be able to be alone again until we're on our way. If I ignore you or talk to other women at this shindig of Mother's, think nothing of it." His words hit her like a kick from Pegasus, their stern tone making her feel like a child getting whipped, not a lover being wooed. She nodded her head stiffly. Richard deliberately dropped one of the reins. When she handed it up to him, he squeezed her fingers tightly.

She passed her hand quickly over his hat, loosening bits of pebble and grass stuck to the damp headband. "Tell me how I'm to get away from...Jemima." Leaving off the obligatory 'Miz' felt like freedom already.

He looked back at Great Crossing. "I'll stay late after Sunday supper. Instead of going home, I'll have a horse with me down at the far end of the path by the spring. Get her settled in for the night and meet me there. Walk out of the house, speak to no one. Take nothing with you!"

Panic seized her by the throat. "She's such a light sleeper, she has me up three, four times a night..."

His whisper grated with irritation. "You're mine! Not hers!"

"I love you, Richard!" The harsh whisper tore at her throat. She stood only a moment in the dust, unable to stare after this stranger, wondering if it were still true.

LUCY PEEKED AROUND the corner of her cookhouse only to see another carriage of Johnsons pulling up. Lord, this family's like an ocean of people, she almost said out loud. They came in waves, each one younger and noisier than the one before. The neighbors from twenty miles around kept pouring in, too.

Miz Johnson hadn't been this worked up about a party since Miss Sallie's wedding fifteen years before. Henrietta had been baptized with fire by that mess right after she'd arrived at the Crossing. Been gone two years this month, and with her all the calm and quiet that made things turn out alright at times like this. She still couldn't get Milly to do more than go through the motions, for grieving over her sister.

And whatever the word was for Henrietta's opposite was what she needed for Betsey's stuck-up cook. The woman was driving Lucy to the brink of crazy, taking over the cookhouse and lording her fancy Virginia ways over them all.

Little Kate sat in a corner crying, stuck with baby tasks like stemming the watercress and mint. Everybody was on edge. Twenty of them worked like field hands, but they couldn't do justice to what looked to be two hundred mouths to feed, when Miz Johnson had told them to cook for sixty. She was too tired to think of that, now. No time to mix more dough and pluck more chickens and run to the buttery. The place was chaos.

Samuel pulled up in a wagon loaded with smoked meat, fresh melons and china. The light had gone out of him, too, since Henrietta died. "Miz Betsey's sent me with extra vittles and plates. But I don't see any help around here. What's going on, Lucy?" He jumped down from the wagon seat and hung his fiddle bag on the big oak's lowest branch.

"Everybody's helping at the stables. I got Miss Boss in there running me out of my own cookhouse, so I guess I can help you unload."

This was just about the only time Lucy had felt grateful that the Paynes lived within hollering distance. They usually did nothing but live up to their name, by being pains. She chuckled to herself, even though it had to be the oldest joke at the Crossing.

From the corner of her eye, she caught a glimpse of Julia near the spring house. A hand reached toward the girl to put some little white roses in her hair. Who could it be? She wanted to mind her own business but couldn't help looking back once Julia reached the porch. Mas Richard stepped out of the shadow.

Lucy hurried to rinse herself off and change into her fresh gray uniform. Transformed into a dignified house servant, she threaded her way between the guests in the parlor and the spillover on the porch, stopping only to pull back the drapes and open the windows. Miz Johnson had called out for Julia to play a piece by Moze Ott and then sing the low part of a song while Betsey's daughter sang the high part.

She hoped Miss Nancy wouldn't set the dogs howling when she hit those screechy notes. She could tell Julia was working hard to pull back and not steal Miss Nancy's thunder. She felt real proud of her.

Someone else looked real proud, too. Mas Richard clapped loud and looked at Julia like she was a blue-ribbon mare. Lucy knew a man didn't look at a girl like that unless he had trouble on his mind.

She had too much work on her hands to worry about it right that minute, but she figured Julia needed to be pulled aside real soon and given a talking to. All that trouble with Joel's friend a couple years ago might have made Mas Richard overprotective. Nothing like being rescued to make a girl get attached. But Julia was not a girl, anymore.

She walked around refilling glasses and felt better after seeing how Mas Richard gave the look to a lot of the rich white girls in the house. What were their mamas thinking, letting good Baptist girls dress like that?

Hours later, Lucy looked around the porch and the lawn surrounding the house. Scraps of food and dishes lay across five acres of Great Crossing. She saw the hands cleaning up way out yonder and wished them good picking on the scraps of all that turkey, venison and elk. Long as they didn't break Miz Betsey's dishes.

She watched Julia carry Malvina to the carriage. Glad that child's parents made up. But here now, something's not right—Julia looks like her heart's about to break. Lucy spotted Mas Richard down at the end of the drive where Jacob was bringing horses to the single gentlemen. Julia kept looking down that direction, too. Lucy dawdled, hoping to pick up more than just empty plates.

Richard and half the pack of his younger brothers—Robert, Ben and John T, for sure—walked back toward the porch. They sprawled along the railing. "Best coming-home party a man could have, Mama. I thank you. With all my heart." Lucy heard a catch in his voice. Why's he sad, too, she wondered?

"I turned a blind eye to the bourbon drinking going on behind the stables. But if you go and turn maudlin on me, I'll know you're drunk." It had been a good party, because Miz Johnson was teasing like she hadn't done in years.

Lucy noticed Julia jump when their mistress called to her, like she was a hundred miles away. Mas Richard was jittery, too. That settled it. Something was going on between those two. But how was she going to pull Julia away to have a good long talk with her? Even Henrietta couldn't get more than two or three minutes at a snatch with her. She hauled the basket, now heavy with collected plates and cups, down the back steps of the porch. Have to be tomorrow, before breakfast. I'll talk some sense into her.

AS SHE AND JEMIMA SLOWLY climbed the stairs one rise at a time, Julia listened to the men's voices reverberating through the stairwell. George and Henry's voices were deeper, except when they laughed or whined. Richard's voice was a larger version of Mas Robin's. It was easy to imagine him standing up in Congress, speaking with the power of a preacher. She felt his words more than she heard them and they thrilled her, like the notes of a song.

I will tell him this and so much else when we're able to say such things to each other.

Jemima leaned heavily on her as they reached the last few steps before the landing. "You are such a comfort to me, Julia. The boys are so cross with me."

Her breath came sharply, crackling near Julia's ear. "You've never treated me as though you were merely performing your duty. I cannot say that about any of my children. Not even my husband." Her voice trailed off. "Only you."

For the past few months Jemima had shown an increase of praise and affection, often holding Julia's hand or wrapping an arm around her when they walked. But why lavish so much on her this night?

"I love you, Miz Jemima," Julia managed to whisper. She meant it. She felt the truth of it more than the last time she had said the same words to Richard.

"Dear child," Jemima embraced her, seeing tears in her eyes. "Oh, I suppose it's all the excitement. Let's get my finery off and put away. Then we can settle down for a well-deserved rest."

For the last time, Julia slept at the foot of her owner's bed.

THE GREAT CROSSING Baptist Church stood as a testament to the Johnsons and Suggetts who had come to Kentucky with the mission of building such an edifice to God. After much negotiation, Julia had been allowed to attend the white services, sitting on a little stool next to Jemima's pew.

Never mind that her husband, sons and grandchildren were able-bodied and capable of taking her to church. It was Julia she wanted by her side, whose alto voice resonated soothingly in her ear when they sang the hymns. Julia knew the signs of her sickness and when to pass her a lemon drop or smelling salts.

Reverend Retting's sermon today was diabolical. "Entreat me not to leave thee," he quoted from the Book of Ruth. Both her lips and Jemima's moved silently as the reverend finished the text. "Thy people shall be my people..."

But we will be a family, Julia reminded herself as another wave of confusion swept over her. She will be my mother-in-law! The words dissolved like ash.

"The Lord do so to me and more also, if ought but death part thee and me." She wanted to run out the back door and scream into her hands.

I can't leave her. Richard will have to understand. He loves her, too. He wouldn't want her to be unhappy. She needs me so much more than he needs me. Where is our loyalty, our sense of duty?

She looked for the back of Richard's head. Give me strength, she prayed. To Richard, not God.

After the service, Richard came to them. He seemed more solicitous than usual of his mother's needs, making it even more difficult for Julia to meet his eyes. But he did not understand what her eyes were telling him. She hated him; she hated herself. She opened the parasol as they stepped into the daylight and hovered over Jemima to protect her from the morning sun.

At suppertime, Richard arrived at Great Crossing, radiating energy and good will. Julia felt like a wrung-out dish rag. All through dinner, she sat behind Jemima without eating, while Richard fomented debate. Politics were as much a part of every meal as cornbread, but tonight raged on for well over two hours. Why we should fight England. Why Madison was man enough to lead us in war; why war would be the best way to end the drop in hemp prices. She said a prayer of thanks that nobody mentioned today's sermon.

Richard ignored her. On the one hand, she dreaded that he wouldn't show up tonight. On the other, she panicked that he would, and she'd have no way to go back to the only life she'd ever known.

He stood to bid them farewell. "I have some business to attend to and won't be home for a few days." He did not look at her, or anyone for that matter, as he spoke. She had no doubt about her future, now.

"God speed, son," Robin offered from the porch, as Richard headed toward the stable.

JEMIMA APPEARED TO be sleeping. Julia nervously straightened a few toiletry items and clothes so whoever helped her mistress could find them easily in the morning.

When I won't be here to help her.

It was time. There was no use waiting for a better. She picked up her sturdiest shoes, the only things she would take away with her. Silently, she bid Jemima adieu, gave a parting glance to the worn, familiar objects in the room and crept to the door.

"Where are you going, child?" Jemima mumbled.

Julia began to shake, unable to control any part of her body. She managed to utter, "To help Lucy and Milly finish clean-up. There's still a lot from last night, and it being the Sabbath, I was feeling a little guilty on their account." She said a quick prayer of forgiveness for using the Lord's day in a lie.

"Come rub my feet. They've gone numb, and you know that frightens me so."

Julia turned back into the room, steadying her nerves as she hid the shoes behind her back and laid them on the floor near Jemima's feet. She hoped the quaking of her hands would not arouse suspicion.

Rubbing in vigorous, rapid strokes the way Doctor Theobald had taught her, Julia found the work exhausting but a good outlet for the shakes. Besides, Richard was fully aware of the demands made on her every hour of the day and night. He would just have to wait.

She looked down at the swollen, blue-tinged feet and rubbed until her hands ached. She feared to leave; she longed to leave. She worried for Little Kate and the others who would soon be forced to take on her enormous load of work. She longed for Richard and to have even a little taste of the life he had promised her.

Julia looked toward the window and caught a darkened glimpse of the face of some stranger.

I have no idea who that girl in the reflection is, much less who Julia Johnson's supposed to be tomorrow. I don't see how it will matter being free because slave or not, I don't know who I am.

Lucy knew who Lucy was. She was her own person down deep in her soul every bit as much as Jemima. So why, Julia longed to know, couldn't she feel that? At least Milly and Lucy complained about their lot, because they believed they should only belong to themselves.

But she acted like a woman who wanted to belong to someone. Jemima's slave or Richard's wife, wasn't that just the same dress worn two different ways?

Jemima's snoring turned deep, rhythmic. Julia rose and looked down on the sleeping woman who had been her life. Before she could lose her will, she bent and almost kissed Jemima's cheek, grabbed her shoes, turned and did not look back.

The breeze in the hallway gave some relief from the stuffy room that smelled of her fear. Mas Robin's door was open to get some benefit from the air. She held her shoes close to her chest and kept next to the wall. Creeping down the servants' stairs and into the linen press, her one longing was to say goodbye to Milly and Lucy. But Richard had warned her to tell no one, so she obeyed, opened the back door, and kept walking until she reached the spring.

When the night air hit her, she gained her senses and the awareness that her freedom, whatever strange texture it would be made of, lay just beyond the other side of the creek. She slipped on her shoes. Her steps became steadier, quicker, until she was running, hoping no tree root on the ground or branch overhead would catch her. Despite the threat of her heart pushing out of her chest, her equilibrium returned when she saw him.

He was there, standing by Pegasus, calming him, quieting him. Julia's feet kept moving forward. Turning away from his horse, he smiled and pulled her to him, held her face between his hands and looked into her eyes until she finally yielded up a smile. He swung himself up into the saddle, pulled her in front of him and they galloped over the Crossing, not slowing until they reached Blue Spring.

Julia remembered the place from visits with Jemima to comfort Sallie and her children during the year Sallie stayed here to punish her husband. Even in the darkness, she could tell Richard had transformed it. She heard the spring! Not blue like the sky, but indigo because no one had ever found the bottom of it. It had terrified her as a child; it terrified her now, but for a different reason.

As if taunting her fear, he murmured into her hair, "You're home."

There was no time to enter it, to accustom herself to the fact of it. A horse, already in the buggy harness, shook its head impatiently. Richard slid off Pegasus and pulled Julia down to him. He gestured for her to get in the buggy.

"Change quickly into those new things."

Julia wanted to make a show of trust to Richard, although the buggy could not possibly protect her modesty. Crouching and bending, her worn old dress glued to her, she gave a rage-filled tug and was free of it.

What she found on the buggy seat proved to be layers of gauze that fell over her head like a veil. She let out a sigh of surprise as it floated down her torso and draped over her legs in one slow, fluid motion.

Several yards away, Richard and the stable boy spoke together, giving her time to dress. Her hands shook uncontrollably, but she managed to fasten a few of the tiny buttons in back. Richard stepped into the buggy, making it spring up and down wildly. Despite the urgency of their situation, he seemed playful.

This is an adventure for him, like one of his boyhood stories, Julia thought, but to him, she whispered something she hoped would please him. "It doesn't seem real. More like a fairy tale."

"That's our life from now on, honey." He smiled and kissed the back of her neck as he fastened the last buttons on her dress. "Always a challenge when they're new!"

"And when did you become an expert on such a matter?" She tried to imitate Sallie, hoping to impress him with new-found confidence.

"Not what you may be implying, dear girl. But I shall look forward to a great deal of this from now on!" He grabbed the reins with one hand and tossed down her old dress. "Jerry boy, burn this!" The buggy jerked forward and the horse pulled ahead at a fast trot.

Jerry looked at the dress in his hands. "Granny Ann'd skin me alive burnin' something this fine."

Julia caught a backward glimpse of Great Crossing as the buggy rumbled over the Elkhorn bridge. In the late-night stillness, the noise sounded like cannon fire. Jemima never slept through the night. How soon would her absence be discovered?

I will not be forgiven.

Soon they reached the common road where the crops along the side muffled their passing, crops cultivated by hundreds of slaves owned by a handful of wealthy planters like the Johnsons, she brooded. There were no lights burning anywhere and clouds covered the moon. "I have to trust in your experience, Richard," she began in hopes of not starting an argument, "but I'm afraid they'll find me gone and follow us."

"They haven't got the slightest notion of anything other than sleeping off Sunday dinner. What, have they even noticed we've been in love for years?" He laughed softly.

She did not feel reassured.

"No one will follow us, and not tomorrow, either. I've taken care of that."

"A letter? You couldn't have left it when you were there at supper. It would've been found by Henry or...someone." She still could not say Joel's name.

"Jerry's going to ride over at sun-up and give something to Father." When Julia gasped, he turned quickly to her. "It tells him I've got you, and that's all. I've learned the hard way in Washington that it's better to hold back as much as you can from the opposition until you've gotten what you want."

"I hate to think of your family as our enemy."

"Not enemy, Julia. Opposition. There's a big difference."

"Oh, I hope so, I do hope so."

He gathered the reins in his left hand and put his arm around her. Without thinking, Julia pressed into his side and kissed his cheek then stroked his wiry sideburns. A clump of long, thick hair fell into his face and she removed his hat to set the strand right again. He pressed his head against hers and tossed his hat on the boards.

I can touch him now.

The thought made her body change and pull slightly away from him. "What if they believe I've seduced you?"

He exploded with laughter. The horse shook its head to rid its ears of the noise. Pulling her close again, he said, "Father will understand I have good intentions. Once the shock wears off, we'll settle the uh, paperwork."

Her muscles clinched. "Are you so sure he'll release me so easily?"

"Honey, he won't even talk about it. For Father it would be too...indelicate."

"So, you will let them assume I'm your concubine?" She made her voice light, joking, but her pride was shaken. "Everyone would prefer that over wife," she mumbled.

"You have a point. We have to go to them, instead. But we're going to have proof of our marriage on free soil to show them." His voice was serious again.

"You know, you still have time to change your mind. Only yesterday I saw no end of very wealthy women who wanted you."

"Perhaps. But I've known those girls all their lives, and their parents all of my life. None of them really wants me, they just want to get their hands on Blue Spring and prettify it!" The serious tone crept back. "Their families want to influence Congress through me."

He tightened his hold on her waist. "You're the only one who knows me inside and out and still loves me. That's something all those pretty little white girls are incapable of doing."

When he looked over at her, she saw a mix of anger and confusion flit across his face, then a question dart from his eyes. He needed her to reassure him!

"It's more than love, I'm afraid." She struggled to think of what to say, but nothing was equal to this task. "I have no way of expressing it. Not with 'white girl's' words, anyway."

He unwound his arm from her and took her hand, lifting it to his lips and keeping it there until a rut in the road forced him to grab the reins.

"Something hit me last week. Like that hole back there." She laughed a little. "I live two lives. One back home, one in Washington. What hit me was this: you've had the same problem. At home I can be free, but in Washington, I'm as bound down as you were taking care of Mother. And it made me angry with myself that I didn't run away with you a lot earlier than this. But you're never going to have to live two lives. You'll be mistress of Blue Spring, and that's that."

"And Washington? Can't we have a home there?"

Richard cleared his throat, hesitating before breaking the bad news to her so soon. "Before I actually lived in that swamp, I thought Washington would be a fine place to bring a wife. I was quite mistaken."

"I'm going to have to get used to being without you." She stopped herself from adding, without anybody. She leaned on his shoulder, pulled down by exhaustion.

"Believe me, after I've driven you crazy during the months I'm home on recess, you'll be glad to see me heading east!"

"So, you want to keep going back?" Hesitantly she added, "You want to be president?" She sat up. Maybe it was not Jemima's dream alone, but his as well.

"I don't know, yet. I've got many peculiarities, but I don't want you to be thought of as one of them. I want everybody to see you as my strength, and the way you take care of Blue Spring is how you're going to prove it. I know you can. Look at what you've done at the Crossing!"

When Julia gave no reply to his praise, he added, "I've been whipping Blue Spring into shape for a while, now. All you have to do is keep it going. I've made it a world apart, where we can both escape. I promise you it'll be the only world that matters."

"It sounds beautiful." Her voice faded. "A world apart."

But your other world is hundreds of miles away, and mine is only three, and that's not enough distance for me to make any kind of escape.

She turned to him and scooted forward on the seat so he could see her better. "Richard, I have gotten you into such a hornet's nest. If you must choose between me and your family, or me and your work, you must not choose me! I cannot bear the thought of you suffering rejection or ridicule on my account!"

Richard abruptly reined the horse to a stop, grabbed her shoulders and shook her. "Now you listen! I made my choice. I made it two years ago. I've thought of little else, and nothing—not my family, not my country—will keep me from having you. Stop your fear on my account unless it's just an excuse for your own. Or get out and head north if you don't want me, and let me turn around and go back to my worthless life without you!"

Stunned by his fury, Julia burst into tears, unleashing all the confusion and frustration she had held at bay for months.

"Julia, I'm sorry!" He took her in his arms and held her gently, shushing and rocking her like a child. "You're as worn out as I am with all this. Probably more." Pulling her face away from his chest, he kissed her tear-strained eyes and lips with a gentleness that begged her to forgive.

Drained of her strength and pride, a deeper, less familiar longing took hold. "I do want you! I'm the one who's worthless without you."

"Oh, no, honey. You'd fetch a high price." It was a reckless joke, and it made him even more reckless. "I love a slave woman!" He yelled into the woods surrounding them. "Slave" hung in the air, before it passed behind them like a phantom.

"Slave!" Julia whispered, her small sound lingering then following the one vanished before it.

Richard picked up the reins and the buggy jerked forward. They listened to the clomping of the horse and the churning of the buggy wheels for a few minutes before he broke the silence.

"Tell you what." The tenderness in his voice drew Julia toward him. "I'll be your slave from now on."

His eyes were wet! She was touched beyond joy. "'Intreat me not to leave thee, nor to return from following after thee.'"

"Hard to believe Joseph's sermon was only this morning. Seems like a lifetime ago. You know those words were spoken to her mother-in-law?"

"Yes, I know. They made me feel like a traitor to her all day. But I had no choice. I love you."

"When we get home to Blue Spring, you'll see how much I love you."

A few more anxious hours passed before Richard pulled into the shelter of a lonely way station to change horses. His arrangements of the previous week, along with generous payment, would ensure their secrecy, he told her. He was right; no one had pursued them or stopped them. No one would recognize them when they reached the Ohio River for their next change of horse either, he reassured her.

"You'll learn to trust me, Julia. I know how to take care of you."

Finally able to relinquish her anxiety, Julia gave in to exhaustion, sleeping on Richard's shoulder, arms cinched around his waist to steady them against the movement of the buggy. With the first rays of sunlight, she lifted her head, awed by the view of the hills in the bright pink light.

"It's so very, very beautiful," she whispered. The colors of the sunrise burst over her shoulder and lit up clusters of strange looking trees and a narrow river.

"The Crossing's much prettier than this, I think," he answered, his voice thick from lack of sleep.

"This is the first time I can remember seeing a sunrise anyplace else."

Richard said nothing in reply but watched her from the corner of his eye, trying to keep a steady hand on the horse. Her head turned away for a moment to take in more of the sky, but when she turned toward him again, he saw the face of Eve when she entered the Garden. He looked at the sky himself with bleary eyes and tried to see this patch of ordinary landscape with her eyes. He could not do it this time but promised himself to never stop trying for all the sunrises to come.

"SHE'S GONE, SHE'S GONE, Robin!" Jemima whimpered. She collapsed onto the stone bench by the spring but quickly turned away when she saw her reflection in the water.

"Richard's got her, I'm afraid. Jerry left this a little while ago." He handed Jemima a small, folded paper and left her alone with it while he scooped a handful of gravel out of the spring's water pipe.

The words made no sense to her. "He's taken her where? To Blue Spring? For heaven's sake, Robin, get the buggy and bring her back to me! I need Julia! I need my girl!"

"I don't think that's where they are. Remember? He said he'd be gone a few days." His mind raced. "But anything else makes no sense."

"What are you saying, Robin? Be plain!" she commanded.

"He's never shown any interest in her that way. But why be so secret? All he had to do was ask. Unless..."

"Impossible!" she whispered.

"He knows he can't elope. Not with a slave." The gravel in his hands fell to the ground.

"Robin, he's the only one of our children who believes he can do whatever he wants. All he has to do is dream it up. He's had his head in the clouds most of his life, thanks to you."

"I know. You do well to reproach me."

"No doubt he's taken her to Ohio. Not a soul there would suspect."

"Why the devil didn't he just take her to Blue Spring and keep her?" Robin kept his voice low, but he wanted to shout. Servants milled about everywhere. They kept a wide berth from him and his wife, but he was aware of their eyes and ears taking in everything.

She gave him a stricken look. He still had his strength. He was still handsome. He could easily have kept a woman if he wanted, and she knew he had wanted. She felt old and worn beside him. And now, without Julia, utterly alone.

After a long silence, Jemima looked at him. "I can see his reasoning. A concubine would be repulsive to his sense of honor. He would want to protect her honor, too. Marriage is the only way. To be *honorable*..." her voice trailed off.

But Robin's voice came to her like a blow. "He's not a boy playing make-believe. This is our Julia! We've raised her like a sister to the boys. It's...it's...repulsive!"

What little control Jemima had managed abandoned her. "What do you think I'm agonizing over? Do you think it's Richard I'm upset about? Richard be damned!"

"Jem, don't forget yourself! To curse your own flesh and blood is nearly unpardonable."

"Oh, shut up, Robin! I will curse the child I brought into this world if I want to. No! It's Julia. It's my girl." Her shoulders crumpled and she gave over to uncontrollable weeping. Robin stepped close to block the view of his wife falling apart, but she threw him off balance by wrapping her arms tightly around his knees.

"How could she leave me? How could my girl leave an old woman so devoted to her?" She sobbed, heedless of the stunned servants who stopped in their tracks at sounds they had never known to come from their mistress.

"How could she be so selfish? So heartless?" Jemima pulled her husband's large handkerchief from his pocket and choked into it.

"She had no right, none at all, Jem," he said, trying to calm her. "But you know good an' well she hasn't a willful bone in her body. She loves you."

"I know," she cried. He tightened his grip around her shoulders. She butted her head against his knees and began to wail again. "I know, I know," she repeated.

Her behavior unnerved him, putting him on unfamiliar ground as it did. He gave way to his own rage. "This is all Richard's doing. He deliberately set out to hurt us because of the fallout over that French girl. I know how his mind works, because I am guilty of putting ideas into his head. Werther and Quixote—rubbish! How could we expect someone as inexperienced as Julia to resist?"

She loosened her grip on him and looked up at his face. Her eyes had become a vicious red, making her look ancient. The thought pierced him with guilt, and he knelt down beside her. He took the handkerchief from her and patted her face, hoping her tears would stop. She squeezed her eyes tightly shut, and her face stayed dry.

"So thoughtless," she hissed, sounding like her old self again. "How could he shame our family like this and jeopardize his future? He's lost his mind."

Relief filled Robin now that she had herself under control. "We have to avoid a scandal, Jem. It will only take a day or two, and the county will be filled with gossip. The only way to deal with it is to dismiss it out of hand, to say he's made her his housekeeper, and let people assume what they will."

"No one who knows us would ever believe that Julia could leave me. And if we take that approach, the church will brand her a concubine and he a..."

"Pure hypocrisy. It's no secret certain deacons have their favorites among the wenches. People tend to make allowances. They're still considered good Baptists."

"*Considered* good Baptists? We *are* good Baptists! You, my father and my brother started this church here, remember? Our family is not only held to a higher standard, we *are* the standard!"

Robin watched as Jemima's back straightened and her will banished the broken woman that had clung to him only a few minutes before. He sat on the bench and strained to think clearly. Nothing came. After a painful silence, she spoke, her voice cold.

"We will say nothing. Not to anyone, not even the family. If anyone brings it up, we will stare them into silence. Promise me, Robin. Not a word, do you hear me?"

"Not a word," he muttered in agreement, relieved to let her take control.

"As far as...they...are concerned, they will not set foot in our home again. We will not speak directly to them again. We will have to be cordial to him in public for the sake of his political standing. I can't imagine he'd be so foolish as to bring her out with him. But I never want to hear her name again. Not as long as I live."

Chapter 11
Crossing
August 1, 1809. The Ohio River

They reached Gaines Tavern by the time the mid-afternoon heat made travel unbearable. The new inn sat like the figurehead of a ship in front of two hundred lush acres of bottomland. Julia admired the beauty of its design, so different than anything she had seen around Great Crossing. Richard left her in the buggy under a shade tree, disappearing under the eaves of the tavern entrance just as three well-dressed men walked out.

Julia sat stiffly, pressing her back against the seat. When the men passed by, the youngest of the three looked at her boldly. "Afternoon, Miss." She caught the glint in his smile as he lifted his hat to her.

The older man in the middle nudged him with an elbow. "Mind your manners. That's a lady," he growled.

Julia forgot the stifling heat. Addressed as 'Miss', called a lady. "Mama, I'm going to be free," she whispered into her gloved hands. She had to hear the words.

Richard stepped out of the inn and returned to her quickly. "It's alright. Not a soul here today that knows me. We've got just enough time to clean up, eat a bite and catch the last ferry." Hoisting their small bags over his shoulder, he took her by the hand and led her through the Gaines Tavern door.

As they stepped into the inn together, Julia tried to behave like a woman who belonged among the clientele, not the servants. But the place was busy, and no one took notice of her. She relaxed and allowed herself the luxury of breathing in the aroma of strong coffee and crackling sausage. After paying for hot water and fresh towels, they were led to a small room without a bed to clean up.

Julia excused herself to find a latrine and was thankful to find it clean enough to meet even her old home's standards. Returning to the little washroom as slowly as she could, Julia wondered if Richard might need more time to shave and change his linen. Should she knock or wait patiently in the hallway?

Just as she was getting up the courage to knock, he emerged fresh-faced, showing no trace of the long, sleepless night he had endured. Instead, he grinned like his old self and rubbed his stubble-free cheek against hers. "Get on in there, and make yourself even prettier. I'll find us a place to sit."

Although she had to spend a good two minutes of anxious searching, she spotted him in a corner near a window, smiling up at one of Mr. Gaines's ample daughters as she set plates in front of him. The room was hot, smoky, and crowded.

Julia felt she had stepped into a foreign country. Nothing in the orderly life at Great Crossing had prepared her for this. She relished it more than the food.

"Well, we'd best get on with it," Richard said, gulping the last of his coffee and wiping his chin with the tip of the tablecloth. Julia reprimanded him with a look straight from the face of his mother. He grinned like a boy in silent apology once the shock of the similarity wore off. Stepping outside, they brushed their clothes and bags free of crumbs and nearly stumbled when a dozen sparrows dashed at their feet.

Richard paid for stabling the horse and harnessing a fresh one—a liver chestnut large enough to pull a hay wagon. Julia waited in the same shady place as before, letting her eyes wander over the grounds until she spotted a row of cabins, worn to a dark gray.

At this hour, all the hands would be in the fields. She saw a curl of smoke rising from the cookhouse chimney. Even the noise of a dozen horses and wagons did not drown out the song of women working there, women who would still be cooking well past sunset.

Why do I get to cross the river and not them? Why can't we all just go down to the river? What makes us stay, like those cattle out there in that field?

She had no answers for questions born from so much new experience in so short a time. Richard took off his hat and waved to her with it from the stable. The sun made his hair spark like polished copper. Ragged-edge pieces of memory came back: her small hand reaching for him, his hair tickling her.

The fire-headed boy was taking her to freedom, to marry him. It was a tale as strange as the baby Moses going to the court of Pharaoh, then leading God's people across the Red Sea. She smiled at the irony. Jemima's girl from Great Crossing was about to make it over the river. The only great crossing she'd ever make.

They had been on the bustling road going down to the Ohio for less than a mile when a gust from the northeast made Julia struggle for air. Her lungs fought to escape the stink of dead fish and rotted wood. Something else—acrid, familiar yet overwhelming—left a metallic taste in her mouth. "What's that smell?" she gasped. Richard didn't seem affected.

"Salt. From Great Lickings. Leeched into the water. Been doing it for eons."

"Great Lickings?" Julia managed to choke. The missing half of her old home, she grimaced.

"Used to be huge herds of deer and buffalo that'd make their way over just to lick the salt rock. They've been killed off."

"What killed them? This smell?"

Richard barked out a loud laugh, taken by complete surprise at his serious Julia making a joke. "Indians in the old days, mostly. Between the herds and the hunters, they made the Bullskin Trace. It's a pretty decent road, now, goes all the way to Lake Michigan."

Julia knew from family stories that Robin had killed Indians on both sides of the river during the days before statehood. Never a braggart, her old master would not talk about those fights, but his youngest sons had, plenty of times. A dozen years ago, John T had grabbed hold of her hair pretending to scalp her before Benjamin had come to her rescue. Benj. She would miss him.

To escape her thoughts, she asked, "Have you ever killed an Indian?"

He gave her a puzzled look. "Never had to. Before my time. But if their new confederacy keeps getting guns from the British, I would." He added under his breath, "With pleasure." Julia kept still, although her instinct was to shake her head in denial.

The sounds of people preceded the sight of the river, providing a welcome distraction. How many of her friends at the Crossing would have given their lives to get to this place! Then she heard the sound of the river itself, like a windstorm made out of water.

Recent rains had swollen the Ohio, and the current looked ten times as powerful as the Elkhorn, which had always frightened her. Julia had no love for water. A river, large or small, made her think of only one thing: being swallowed up. She'd have to steel herself for this crossing and make a good show of being brave.

Richard jumped down. "Might as well stretch your legs. It'll be a while." Julia looked over the long line of travelers. Single men with their horses; buggies and wagons; families with knapsacks filled with all their possessions. Here and there children held rope-leads to goats. A few women carried wicker boxes full of hens.

"I don't see any business trade, just people like us, Richard."

"Did my homework. This is the ferry for ordinary folk, run by the Kottmyers. Germans know about rivers."

"It looks like very hard work," Julia added, watching the young men strain against the current with their pulls and poles.

"Dangerous, too, and unreliable," Richard said, a crease growing deeper in his brow. "During dry months of a bad year folk can ride horses over. Some winters, you can walk on ice."

Dangerous. Unreliable. The words swirled in Julia's head, making their own storm current.

Over this river, I'm free. I don't have to marry Richard. No matter how much he thinks he loves me, I will ruin his life. No! This is the jitters, that's all. The ferry will get you across, and Richard's not going to hurt you.

She felt her face flush as she imagined tonight and turned her head away from Richard. But she made herself turn back; she studied his face as he talked. Her eyes lingered on his mouth—wide, curling into a smile so easily. How many times had he kissed her? The memory of his body pressed against her made her change and ache.

She studied his eyes. Deep-set, their green, blue and yellow specks a perfect contrast to his dark copper hair. She glanced over his body. The huge chest and shoulders, the thick-muscled thighs. She understood why her body pulsed, why running away from him was impossible. Whether she would be free to do anything else, at least she would be free to love him without restraint.

Their turn to board the ferry came, and theirs was the only buggy. They stood alongside it, soothing the unfamiliar horse. A few other passengers joined them, clutching their baskets and lead ropes with one arm and the ferry's thick rope with the other arm. The Kottmyer boys, their muscles straining against the current, started their pull to the other side.

Julia prayed with her head pressed against the horse's neck. When she opened her eyes, she saw the river. She relaxed her grip as she began to marvel at the striations of color in the water. Green then blue swirls suddenly streaked with red from great chunks of soil dissolving in the current. The colors in Richard's eyes and hair. By the time the ferry reached the calm shallows, her fears of the river and of Richard had disappeared.

"Thank you," she whispered in prayer.

Richard answered, "We've crossed our Rubicon, my girl." He looked back at Kentucky. "You know we're not going back the same." They stepped off the ferry together onto the free soil of Ohio.

"WHAT KIND OF NAME IS Cincinnati—Indian?" she yelled over the noise of wagons and tradesmen.

"Latin. Order of the Cincinnatians." Richard answered distantly, his mind on finding the little chapel. "Men who fought the Revolution. They called this place Columbia for a little while, but before that, it was named Losantiville." Julia giggled. "No, don't laugh! Our own Dan'l Boone thought that one up. Remember that game my folks used to play with us? Where you take apart words then make new ones out of the parts?"

"Yes! It was one of our favorites." A pang tightened her heart as she thought back.

"I can't remember what words he took apart, but thank heaven Losantiville didn't stick," Richard chuckled.

Cincinnati had no pretentions. Everywhere Julia looked, she saw people doing almost anything they pleased. They headed farther down Front Street, the only road of any substance in the town, past a mishmash of wharves, warehouses, and taverns. Richard spotted a cabin-like structure set back several feet from the dirty street.

"That's it!" he grinned at Julia. "Can you see the cross over the alcove?"

Richard brought the horse to a halt, jumped down and tethered it, then caught Julia in his arms as she nearly fell. Her dress snagged on a splint of wood, tearing the thin fabric several inches. It was a bad omen, even for a faithful Baptist girl.

"Never you mind," Richard reassured her when he saw the dismay on her face. "You're going to have more beautiful dresses than you'll be able to wear in a lifetime!"

He raised her hand to his lips then tucked it around his arm. "And parasols. Like the one I forgot. Can't have my girl getting as freckled as I am."

Julia thought of her fourteenth birthday, the last time he had mentioned her and freckles. They walked the few steps to the church but had no chance to knock. The narrow door opened, and a cloud of dust and gravel flew around them. They swatted the particles away from their eyes as fast as they could. A girl with a broom in her hand and a coarse kerchief on her head yelled, "Watch out!" far too late to do them any good.

The accidental barrage of little pellets had done nothing to dampen their spirits, but a sharp voice from the back of the church did. "Emma! What have you done?" It sounded like thunder from heaven and made Julia's heart stop. Emma cringed and managed to shrink to an even scrawnier size.

A man rushed towards her, but the sun flooded the doorway, making him squint. He saw the outline of two figures, but their presence had no restraining power over him. He yanked the broom from the girl and pushed her outside past them. More like a rag doll than a child, she struggled to gain her balance but fell to her knees, scraping them on the rocks that formed the little path to the church entry.

"Here, here!" Richard admonished, bending down to help the child to her feet. He took out his handkerchief, daubed it with his tongue, and wiped it over her scraped knees until the debris fell away.

Julia picked up the kerchief that had fallen off the girl's head and bent down beside her.

"Thank you," she mumbled, but there were no tears in her gray eyes. Julia knew that a child used to that kind of harsh treatment could only have had a life of nothing else. Emma ran to the back of the church out of their sight.

"I beg your pardon. She's the little brat of a neighbor's indentured man. More ignorant than I can endure, but out of pity I give her a penny to sweep. The road makes everything dirty again in minutes."

"We were hoping to find Reverend Dennison. Are you he?" Richard asked, barely able to control the urge to throttle the man. How he hoped this was not the minister.

"He's out yonder at one of the docks, preaching. I'm...guess you could call me Esau." He laughed coarsely. "His brother. Not pious enough to be even a deacon in this..." he swung his arm around to indicate the whole of the little chapel..."religious edifice."

Richard realized the man was well into his cups and pulled Julia back into the little yard. "Would you happen to know if he is east or west of here?"

"Probably in the bottom of the river by now since you're asking. Thrown in by some heathen riffraff." He punished their ears with another laugh.

The more Julia heard, the more she feared for Emma, and hoped the girl had run away. Julia had been spared encounters with drunks most of her life because of the sobriety of the Johnson home, Joel and John T the exceptions. The memory of her assault made her pray that poor Emma did not know that awful fate, but the empty look in the girl's eyes made her fear the worst.

Except for witnessing a few willow branches across the backsides of the youngest Johnson boys, violent treatment was foreign to her.

What kind of grim unhappiness could make someone as cruel as this man had been to a child, on the threshold of a church?

"Esau" suddenly underwent a change of countenance. Julia turned and found the source of this: a small man with the face of a bulldog. "Sorry. I failed to introduce myself, proper-like. I am August Dennison, and this..." he held his arm out to the man behind them, "is the Reverend Alexander."

"And you are?" the Reverend asked Julia and Richard, avoiding his brother. His voice was hoarse from preaching at the docks but had a mild and sweet tone to it.

Richard extended his hand. "Dick Johnson, sir. My friend, Miss Chinn." Julia wondered if Richard were thinking the same thing: the tall, deep-voiced drunk of a brother fit the part of a hellfire preacher more than the small one who actually wore the mantle.

"You're strangers here, I take it. Is there some way I can help you?" he asked, his manner direct but without rudeness. Richard and Julia relaxed a bit, and some of their earlier hopefulness returned.

"You can indeed! We are hoping you can marry us," Richard said.

"I should be able to oblige you, Mr. Johnson. What is your religious persuasion, may I ask?"

"Raised in the Baptist faith," he answered, hoping the man would not ask him if they'd been baptized. Julia had been as a child. He and John T had held off, waiting for the Lord to show a better way. He hadn't quite, yet.

"Follow me, then, please." He stepped between them, stopping in front of his brother. "Could you fetch Brother Stevenson and his wife, Auggie?" The brother ran his hand through his hair, tucked in his shirt and moped off. "Forgive him. It's a bitter pill taking orders from his younger brother. He lost his wife and son last winter shortly after we arrived here."

"How awful," Julia offered. Still no reason to mistreat a child, she wanted to say, but kept her place.

"A bitter pill indeed, poor fellow," Richard agreed. "But perhaps he could show more kindness to the little girl." He exchanged a look with Julia, who squeezed his arm in approval.

"Emma? What happened?"

Richard described their welcome. "Perhaps your wife could intervene."

"I lost my wife before we set out from Virginia. November last. It's not been easy. Only nine others of us, besides my brother and myself."

They followed him through the chapel into an antechamber that served as office, study and kitchen. When he shut the door, Julia noticed a beautiful Geneva robe hanging from it. An educated man, like Reverend Retting. She pitied him almost as much as she did little Emma. He motioned Richard to a stool by the small fire grate, then squeezed himself between the wall and a shelf laden with shabby books and tightly folded clothing.

Reverend Dennison opened the church ledger and began questioning them in an authoritative tone. Julia winced as Richard stated her father's name. As Dennison wrote, he gave no indication of recognizing any names, but Richard decided to bend the next answers to protect Julia. "Place of birth?"

"Virginia, and Ohio," Richard answered. He squeezed her hand; she kept her eyes forward, willing her face not to move.

"Age?"

"Twenty-eight and nineteen."

"Consanguinity?"

"Very distant cousins." Julia suppressed a smile.

"Any colored?"

"No." He squeezed her hand. She fought to keep her head up. How she hated to lie! No, I am not lying, she told herself. But Richard is, and you are about to become one, so it's the same thing.

"One dollar for the marriage performance. One dollar if you'd like a certificate. A small fee I share with the witnesses, or you pay them yourself if you don't want the paper." He turned in his chair and took a tin box out from under a well-worn pair of deerskin breeches. "And sign your names. You can make your mark, Miss, here."

Richard handed him some coins, dipped the quill and signed the thick sheet of paper, pressing his hand heavily on the opposite side of the ledger to make the page lay flat. He continued to hold the book while Julia signed her name in her small, light cursive. She felt a surge of pride at seeing their names side by side on the paper.

"We have so few in these parts who can write," Reverend Dennison told her by way of apology. "Rarely a woman. If you'll excuse me..." he made a gesture with his hand toward the chapel, as he rose from his chair. "It would be more fitting if I made myself presentable." He smiled amiably, giving them the impression there was nothing he found more exhilarating than performing a marriage.

They stepped back into the chapel, then sat side by side on the split log bench in the near darkness. Julia wanted to ask Richard, was it true they were cousins? She knew why he lied about her race. Odd that he would lie about the other, but perhaps it was just his old teasing self come out to break the tension. And what was wrong with telling the man they were Kentucky-born? But she trusted his judgment, and decided it was high time she bowed her head to pray and ask forgiveness from the Lord.

Richard seemed content to sit next to her without talking, unusual for him. How he loved talk! But their peace was short-lived. August entered the little room with an attractive couple about Richard's age. Julia made a shy attempt at conversation with her, but the reverend entered the chapel just as the woman began to reply.

The transformation was remarkable. Although he did not wear the Geneva, his black suit lent him stature. With his hair combed and face scrubbed, Alexander Dennison looked as if he could minister in the court of God. He radiated power.

They got to their feet, and he began immediately, as if some urgent business pressed upon him.

"Let us pray," he invited them. Bowing their heads, they heard him say, "O God, our mighty Heavenly Father, lend thy Spirit here in this, the least of thy houses, to the joining in thy presence of Brother Johnson and Sister Chinn. In the Lord's sacred name, amen."

"Take each other by the right hand," he commanded.

Julia and Richard obeyed.

What words they repeated, neither of them could tell. The exchange of vows did not pass between them with their words. It went through their fingers and the air they shared as they breathed; it merged with the shaft of light pressing under the door that seemed like a sign of divine presence.

Without breaking his gaze upon her, Richard removed the ring on his little finger and coaxed it onto the ring finger of her left hand. He held both her hands between his own, pressing them tightly. The band, new to her finger, refused to yield and caused a burst of pain, but she delighted in it. Dennison pronounced them man and wife. He proclaimed a new prayer over their bowed heads, invoking heaven's blessing as they went forth to multiply and replenish the earth; for Richard to succeed in working by the sweat of his brow; for Julia to be spared in childbearing.

With that final amen, Julia felt her being expand beyond the confines of the little church into the presence of her mother, her unborn children, and others she could not see but knew were there and loved her. Love stretched backwards and forwards through time all around her, flooding over Richard and the preacher, covering his drunken brother and the strangers called to be their witnesses. She heard the clinking of the coins Richard put in their hands, the brush of a paper passing into his pocket. She saw the tormented eyes of August remembering his wedding day; the dirty head of little Emma peeking from around the corner, the smiles of the Stevensons and Reverend Dennison as they walked with them outside into the sunlight.

"God speed, Mr. and Mrs. Johnson," the booming voice of August Dennison called after them as their buggy joined the noisy traffic on Front Street.

They drove down the main road of Cincinnati and headed north. Within a mile, the stores and warehouses gave way to farms. "Are we on the Bullskin yet?" Julia asked.

"We were, back there before we turned. So, tell me, what else is on your mind?" He smiled at her long enough to make her heart struggle against her ribs.

"Nothing. I can't think of a thing, except how much I love you." She added softly, "And want you."

Had he heard her? By the way he pulled her next to him and kissed the side of her head, she knew he had. "You aren't afraid, are you?" He laughed a little. She squeezed his leg and kissed his shoulder. "Because I'm scared to death. I've never..."

Julia wasn't sure about that, had doubted he would ever tell her the truth about such a thing. That he had set aside his male pride, truth or lie, made her feel like a wife. She tried to sound womanly, as confident as she could despite her nerves.

"We've kept this in for so long, Richard, we won't have to think about it, and I trust you so completely, I don't care what happens." He kissed the side of her head again and said nothing more.

They drove down a narrow trail overhung with tree branches. On both sides grazed the fattest sheep Julia had ever seen. Richard stopped in front of a plain, white-washed house. The narrow front door wore a heavy coat of dark green paint that matched the shutters folded back from the windows.

When he knocked, a smiling woman in a cap and apron opened the door. "Ah, Mr. Johnson! Mrs. Johnson." She stepped outside and indicated by a nod of the head that they should follow her down the gravel walk.

"Julia, may I present Mrs. Turner?" The woman looked back at Julia and half-way smiled but did not stop walking.

"Jonah's a godsend, Mr. Johnson. Between my son and him, I do believe they will be able to do most of the work my husband did."

"Who's Jonah?" Julia whispered.

"A boy I got out of debtors' prison. Brought him with me coming home this trip." He didn't explain how Suzanne's terror of those places had spurred him to crusade against them.

Making no secret of having overheard, Mrs. Turner added, "My husband had business with your husband's family for many years. Sometimes it helps to have friends in high places." She gave Richard a knowing look that hinted of a smile.

Their walk led them to a frontier cabin that had the advantage of mortar and paint. Mrs. Turner entered and quickly pushed aside the shutters at the windows. The breeze and late afternoon sunlight spilled into the single room.

"As I told your husband the other day, we have three cabins on the property, but the other two are rented out to tenant farmers. This one was built by my late husband's parents and has survived many a Shawnee raid. He never had the heart to raze it. Since he died last year, I've become an innkeeper of sorts."

"It's charming, Mrs. Turner!" Julia smiled shyly. She was pleased with the clean, simple room. But a lingering confusion over how little she knew about Richard's friends and activities—like rescuing boys—had weakened her confidence.

She caught Richard's surreptitious glance at the trencher of smoked meat and bread on the table. The longing in his eye for her only minutes before had now transferred to the food. It made her want to laugh. He was just a man like any other, with the same appetites. And passions. Her body began to tremble, her mind to darken.

"The privy is behind the big house. We've left an extra bucket of water in the cabin, and if you want it hot, there's a kettle and some firewood in the grate. Just come in the back to supper—it's at sundown. Breakfast's any time after sunrise." She straightened the linen on the washstand, gave them a nod and shut the door behind her.

"What shall we do till sundown, Mrs. Johnson?"

To Julia's surprise, Richard turned to her and ignored the table. He untied the ribbons on her bonnet, then gently uncovered her head. He took her hands and removed her gloves. When her hands were bare, she pushed his jacket away from his shoulders. She ran her hands across his back and arms as she pushed the sleeves away from his body. With his arms free, he wrapped them around her, unfastening the back of her dress, kissing her again and again. When her dress fell to the floor, he knelt to pick it up, draped it over the little wooden chair by the table, and stayed on his knees. He coaxed off her slippers then reached up to pull down her stockings. She caught her breath, unfamiliar with the aches in parts of her body she'd never known were there.

Under a quilt in a dizzying pattern like nothing they had ever seen, they loved each other for the first time, and wept when it was over, and lay there astonished at how easy it was, being man and wife. When the setting sun turned the cabin purple, it was impossible not to take each other again.

Toward the end of supper time, Mrs. Turner told the boys to go ahead and help themselves to the extra food. "They've been traveling a long time. I expect they fell asleep before sunset." When the boys went off to bed, she took a moment to go outside and look up at the stars, wondering why God has taken her Joseph and left her so alone on a night like this.

RICHARD LED JULIA DOWN the gravel path to the back door of Mrs. Turner's home. It opened into a pretty little dining room. They found an enormous breakfast waiting for them, set in a puddle of sunshine on a polished maple table. Julia blushed when they met their hostess.

"The boys and I ate a while ago, so it's all for you—hope you enjoy it." Mrs. Turner excused herself to see to her morning chores, trying to keep her smile discreet and her envy at bay.

"Oh, Richard, look how she set out her best china and linen. Isn't it lovely? Whatever must she think of us for missing her supper?"

Richard avoided answering her question. He watched his bride and made small talk about the food. How he loved her! The way she bent her head to say grace, poured his coffee, bit her biscuit. She sat opposite the window, the bright morning light creating a halo out of her hair. The sun bleached the color from her skin and eyes. She sparkled and nearly blinded him. "You're like a jewel, darlin'," he told her softly, unable to take his eyes from her. "My jewel of great price," he grinned.

"I think it's 'pearl,' Richard," she squeezed his hand for the compliment.

"Nun-unh. Pearls may glow a little, and they look mighty pretty in candlelight. But you're as bright and sparkly this morning as a diamond. I've never seen a woman as beautiful as you in broad daylight."

She stared at him, unable to absorb his adoration. "I only hope you won't regret the price!" she laughed, but the words came from the depth of her soul.

Chapter 12
Exchange
August 1809. Great Crossing

Julia had begun to shake the moment they crossed the Elkhorn. She felt pure shame when she saw the look on Simon's face as he took the reins from Richard. When Richard helped her down from the buggy, she pulled her hand away from his arm; he clamped it back tightly with his other hand, to make sure it stayed.

Little Kate opened the door but would not look them in the eye. Richard loudly hallooed the house and made pleasantries with his youngest brothers who were coming in for supper. George indicated with a nod of the head that the folks were in the study, and Henry let out a soft whistle as he raised his eyebrows at them. Julia felt Richard tugging her along against her will. Her feet had turned to lead. She felt like a harlot in her fine dress and bonnet.

When they stepped into the study, his parents did not greet them. Jemima sat by the grate, a tiny fire of slow-burning cedar providing a dry heat and sweet aroma. Julia knew this was a sign that Jemima's rheumatism had grown unbearable. Jemima was breathing hard, handkerchief near her mouth. It fluttered from the shaking of her hand.

"We're married. In the eyes of God." Richard's voice shattered the air. Julia fought off the room as it crushed in around her.

"No, it is not in His eyes. It's against the law everywhere. Or did you create your own law? Never mind. You can't take what isn't yours," Jemima said rapidly, so softly they were forced to move closer and strain to make out her words.

She leaned away from them but could go no farther in the chair. Julia shook violently but stayed bound to Richard's side. He held out the marriage certificate to his father, who nodded his head and turned away.

Like a small boy with his finest schoolmaster's report, Richard bent to show it to his mother. Glancing at it for only the briefest moment, Jemima snatched it out of his hand. She threw it on the little flame at the edge of the grate. The frail paper turned to ash in a heartbeat.

Richard let out a groan of anguish. He dashed toward the fire. Jemima yelped, fearing he would strike her, but he only knelt in front of the ashes, grabbing his hair with his hands. He turned to his mother with a look of rage, but she kept her eyes on the flame, refusing to acknowledge them.

Richard took Julia by the arm. They left the house, unable to speak, unable to think. But he turned back as she climbed into the buggy; his father had motioned to him from the porch. In Robin's hand was a sturdy white paper, the ink smeared from being blotted too quickly.

Richard knew his wife was now being turned over to him in the only way recognized by Kentucky law: property law. A filthy exchange. One paper so precious, now gone, a second so vile, in his hand. He would never let Julia see it. The illusion of freedom was all he had left to give her.

"You've killed your mother," Robin told him, but his eyes looked straight at Julia. The sting of the words were meant to thrash her, but she bore up, looking stalwart on the outside. Her heart, Richard knew, was crumbling.

His heart, however, was hardening. Richard had stood up to the greatest as well as the meanest men in America. Only two years in Congress had taught him well how to wait for the final word. He met his father's glare with an even gaze. "Take care of her then, Father."

Jacob came out when his master went back in the house, and stood next to Simon, who still held on to the buggy. Richard took up the reins, and Jacob offered him a puzzled smile, a nod to Julia. "I wish you both well, Mas Richard," his tone as solemn as a grave dedication.

"Looks like we've been expelled from the Garden, Jake!" Richard answered him with a peculiar lift in his voice. "Maybe someday you and Lucy can join us at our place."

"I'd like that. What a stable we could breed at the Blue Spring."

The wind picked up and made the horse jitter just as Lucy ran from the back of the house.

"Julie!" she whispered, hoping to stay out of sight and hearing of her mistress. She held out a little packet that rested on the palm of her hand. "Kate told me you were here. Take this. It's your mama's good apron and handkerchief. She had a notion for me to keep for when you jumped the broom."

"Lucy!" Julia's eyes were wet, and she fought to get her voice steady. "Keep the apron and give it to Milly. Just give me the handkerchief."

Lucy tore off the straggly piece of twine. Julia bent down to hug her friend, holding the frail handkerchief to her mouth. She whispered, "I am free now, Lucy. Married and free."

Lucy looked with sorrow into Julia's gray-green eyes and squeezed the gloved hands with her calloused ones. The buggy pulled away with a jolt. Jacob steadied Lucy at the waist, and Simon ran a few yards after the buggy. They knew their master and mistress would be difficult to deal with at a time like this; they couldn't be caught lolling about in front of the house.

The wind gusted and filled their nostrils with the green, fishy scent of the Elkhorn. Lucy folded Henrietta's apron back into a small square as she watched the buggy leave. "Jake, you know that girl isn't ever going to be free."

"Whole lot freer than you and me, honey."

"You know what I mean, now."

"How she's goin' to be stuck in a lonesome spot?" Lucy heard a note of devilry in his voice, probably brought on by a fit of envy at Julia's freedom.

"Well, what's she going to do?" she asked crossly. Jacob sighed, disappointed that she had to get all this talk about Julia out of her system.

"You mean about how not a solitary servant's gonna mind a thing she says? And not a single whitey gonna acknowledge her as one of their own, either?"

Lucy always wondered how he read her mind, words falling out of his mouth like they were on a string pulled from her own. She looked back at the drive.

"She's going to wither and die at Blue Spring. Ol' mean Curtis McPherson has Mas Richard fooled, but he won't fool Julia. She's Miz Johnson all over again, but with all the sweetness still in her. She's going to have the knowledge of what to do, but not the respect from anybody to get anything done!"

"Luce, she's not our child. She's a grown woman, and she's married—married one of the most powerful men in this country. Lord tellin' what the girl can do with all that education Miz Johnson gave her."

"No, Lord tellin' me that she hasn't got a friend in this world when Mas Richard goes to Washington, and he gone over half the year at a time."

Jacob stayed quiet a minute then sighed deep. What dreams of escape he'd been forced to kill to keep Lucy from dying of fear! Why couldn't he feel happy for Julia instead of this bitterness? To spare Lucy more uneasiness, however, he avoided talk of their freedom, tried to find something to say about their friend, instead.

"Well, Blue Spring's got near twenty field hands. And runnin' the house he got ol' Granny Ann, when Miz Betsey sold her off for little of nothing. And he's got three of her grandchildren, too, though Mary's a puddin' head. Julie gonna be fine handlin' that small a crowd."

"She'll wind up doing most of the work, you wait and see," Lucy shook her head.

"He's hoping we can get over to Blue Spring. Things goin' from bad to worse over here for us, and he knows that would make Julia happy, got to say that for him."

"You know Miz Johnson's not letting go of Katy, not now. After all this," Lucy sighed. Their daughter had been running her little legs off trying to replace Julia, but nothing was going to make that old woman happy ever again. Well, it had only been a week since those two grown fools turned everybody's lives upside down. Maybe in a few months, Miz Johnson would settle down. Or die.

As they reached the cookhouse, the muffled sound of crying came from under the heavy oak table. Katy huddled there, tears streaking her face, glimmering over a purple welt. The child had been struck hard. Jacob reached under the table and beckoned her out. He wrapped his arms around her, while Lucy squeezed out a wet rag in the basin. Jacob held the cool cloth to her cheek, exchanging a look with Lucy.

"Not your fault, Katy-did," Jacob said as he rocked her in his arms.

"She's been wanting to hit somebody else," Lucy whispered, forcing her rage away so Katy could calm down and not attract any further unwanted attention. "Daddy's gonna take you back to our cabin, Sugar, and Mama's gonna hurry and clean up around here before the mice get to feeling like I left them an invitation." She forced a smile, and her daughter smiled back.

Katy clung to her father. He carried her like a baby to their cabin. In seventeen years at the Crossing, Jacob had been struck by an overseer and a mill boss, but never by Mas or Miz. He knew Lucy had been spared, too. Why couldn't one of them have taken this blow? He clamped down tight on his rage as he looked at his daughter's bruised face.

He'd witnessed all the boys, even Mas Richard—Henry especially—get a leather strap or a willow branch across their backsides, because a Johnson boy was a good Baptist boy, a thing never to be spoiled by the sparing of the rod. But Miz Johnson had always had the patience of Job with her house people. All that kindness went out the door with Julia when she ran away.

As Lucy swept the cookhouse, she pushed her anger at the old woman out with the dirt as best she could. She tried not to get her hopes up about going to Blue Spring. If slapping Little Kate was any indication of what the future had in store, nothing was going to go right for her and Jacob from now on.

BOOK TWO
Blue Spring

Chapter 1
A Tour
August 1809

J ulia forced her eyes open, defying the bright sunlight that drenched the bed. Richard, turned on his right side, held her captive in a sleep embrace. His arm pinned her chest, his left leg both of her legs. Light bounced off a froth of gold and copper hairs covering his body.

Freckles of every size covered all his limbs, his back and chest. Only his feet were unspotted. The dots mesmerized her, and after staring at them for some minutes, dozens of patterns and designs began to stand out like constellations of stars.

She used a strand of her hair to brush his arm, and watched his skin turn to goose flesh but he continued to breathe heavily, his broad chest pushing against her side like a bellows.

Had she ever slept when the sun was up? She didn't think so, not until she'd married Richard. Since her mother and Jemima had risen well before dawn, so had she. Mama had no choice, yet even when rheumatism and the sugar sickness had confined her movements, Jemima still found something to occupy every daylit minute.

That meant Julia had always found herself equally occupied. Now she had to fight the urge to get up, just as she had fought the need to weep last night when they left Great Crossing. She stayed idle in bed for the same reason she had held back her tears—to avoid troubling Richard.

No matter how she fought it, her mind relived the scene again and again until she smelled the little paper burning, heard the animal sound of pain from Richard's throat, felt the clamp of his fingers on her arm as they stumbled out.

Blotting tears on a corner of the bed sheet, she forced her mind to consider other things, anything. They had arrived after dark, lit only one candle, and dropped their clothes haphazardly before falling into bed. Both heartsick, there had been no talk of what had happened, no interest in food or even each other. Only after several hours' hard sleep had they wakened in the middle of the night, made love, and drifted off again.

The room appeared dwarfed by his bed—their bed—a massive four-poster made of oak, each finial carved into the shape of a giant acorn. But look how he had barely enough room to walk between the bed and wall! She would offer to sleep on that side. A little table seemed comical in proportion to the bed: it was only large enough for their candle holder and a small book. She was curious to see the title page but dared not move; when would he have the chance to sleep uninterrupted again?

An ugly dresser leaned against the wall, and on it rested a pivoting mirror; but there was no brush or comb, only a small painting of a horse. Empty washstand, no linen on the rack. What were the house people thinking? She would have to impose some standards, the first one being that the master of the house always had his room ready.

From her uncomfortable position, she had a window view of a tree-covered hill. For most of her nineteen years, the only treetops, clouds or stars she had seen upon waking had been those from Jemima's bedroom window. She fought back new tears, but there was only one way to escape them—to get up. She had to get up!

What will the servants think of us being so lazy?

She blushed, realizing what they would think. Would they believe she was his wife? Oh, what did it matter? Had she ever had time to stand about listening at doors and peeking through key holes? Their people wouldn't either.

With a slow, careful movement, she lifted Richard's arm and freed her upper body. He opened his eyes. The light proved too much for him, however, and he turned with a moan from it, freeing her completely. She sprang from the bed, only to be grabbed and pulled back down.

"THERE'S NO WATER IN the basin," Julia pointed out. Richard pulled on his breeches and threw his shirt over his head. When he dashed out the door, he nearly tripped on a pail, towels and soap. The water had turned lukewarm, but it was pleasant enough for a summer morning.

"Here you are, honey!" he offered her the linen towel draped over his arm. "Mary must've brought it up ages ago, but it's still got a bit of warmth to it. Tidy up and I'll be back after I check on...somethin.'" He grinned, kissed her astonished face, and left her.

Never had she felt more grateful for the gentleman in him. She'd been overcome with embarrassment at the thought of using a chamber pot in his presence but feared she would have to before she exploded.

When she emerged from their little room into the upstairs hallway, she had to fight the urge to turn back and collapse on the bed. Working all hours of the day and night had been her only life, but being a wife was already taking its toll, making her head blurry and body sore. She needed her kit—but no, it was not hers, had never been hers. The salve she needed for pain was at Great Crossing. But surely Granny Ann would have something? At least now she knew what her first task had to be: putting together her own medicine bag.

Richard slammed the heavy front door and bounded up the stairs. He grabbed her by the waist and swung her until she shrieked with laughter, a sound so unfamiliar to her own ears she stopped.

"Don't stop. I love hearing that laugh! It's all I want to hear out of you from now on," he said, giving her a hard kiss. "Let me show you our house, Jewel." He pulled her hand like an eager little boy, his face ready to burst from grinning. "You've seen one of our little guest rooms, where we were last night."

"Guest room? You mean that's not our room?"

"No, you nit! What kind of a groom would keep his bride pent up in a little space like that? Come on!" He pulled her from one door to the next, saying "this is for guests" or "this will be good for our boys." At each portal, she smiled or blushed, squeezed his hand. Until they reached the end of the hallway.

When he pushed open the double doors with a flourish, she gasped. "Oh, Richard!"

"Well, go on in!"

"I can't. Not yet. I want to take it all in," she said in an awed voice. He stood behind her with his arms around her waist, then planted a lingering kiss in her hair. To her right, against the wall shared by the door, loomed a clothespress that nearly reached the ceiling. To the left was a large fireplace built of cream-colored limestone.

Impossible to keep clean, Jemima's voice echoed in her mind. She banished the thought. The mantel was freshly painted in glossy black, and before the fireplace lay a plush carpet in a swirling pattern of black, red and cream. Two wide chairs covered in black damask flanked a low oval table loaded with sweet rolls, boiled eggs and berry compote. The small silver coffee pot was a work of art, with little paws for feet and a spout shaped like a kitten's tongue.

Julia felt like a visitor.

The four-poster bed was hung with gauze and its linen glowed from starch. Over the windows hung valances of red damask that matched the color in the carpet. But what wrung her heart was the vanity table. Richard had carefully arranged an exquisite toiletry set on it. She walked over and gently passed her fingers over the jars, trays, combs and brushes.

As her shoulders began to shake, Richard came toward her, pulled open one of the little drawers in the vanity, and took out a delicate cambric handkerchief. He sat her on the cushioned stool and blotted her face, picked up the largest of the brushes, and passed it over her hair.

She watched him in the mirror as he looked down at his work, pulling the brush through her curls, flattening the hair with the palm of his free hand then stretching downward with the force of each stroke. With each release, her hair bounced into curls again. It made him smile in a childlike way she hadn't seen in a long time.

No one had brushed her hair for many years. Her mother, always harried with preparing meals, had nudged her to complete self-sufficiency by a very early age. She remembered one of her first days at the Crossing, finding a scrap of Sallie's ribbon in the grate and weaving it into her braid. Beaming with pleasure, she had gone back to Miz Jemima's side.

"What's that in your hair, child?" And with a sleight of hand the ribbon was out and tossed into the stream. "It's pleasing to the Lord for His servants to be plain," Jemima had told her, though she couldn't have been older than four.

"Penny for your thoughts." Richard put the brush down and kissed the fresh part down the middle of her scalp. She hesitated. "I'm your husband, Jewel. I love you. Tell me what's in your heart."

"It's so silly. I hesitate because I don't want you to remember me as a child."

He laughed. "I barely noticed you, remember? But ten years doesn't make any difference between us, now." He stooped beside her and ran his hands along her ribs, nuzzling deep into her neck and sending chills down her arms. He looked at their reflection in the mirror. She looked at it, as well, and in this way they gazed into each other's eyes until she could no longer tell on which side of the mirror their real selves existed.

"A vain little memory, of a scrap of ribbon I found, and it was pulled from my hair and thrown in the spring."

He turned her face and looked into her eyes, putting a stray hair behind her ear. "If it takes my entire life, I will make up to you everything you had to endure as a slave."

"Richard, I wasn't out breaking hemp stalks. You have nothing to..."

"Yes, I do. And what you put up with! Field hands have to put their backs into it, but you never got a rest from that woman, not for a minute. She sucked the life out of you! I couldn't stand it."

He stood and pulled her up from the stool. "I will never stop making it up to you, Jewel." He led her to the enormous clothespress. "It's an armoire! Now look in there. Armor for a lady," he grinned. "Give the knobs a yank!"

She tugged the handles and the doors opened onto a dozen frocks, one a beautiful gown of ivory silk and lace that she knew was too fine to ever wear. The contents reminded her of a giant vase of flowers, colors swirling around each other.

"They're all too beautiful! Where will I be able to wear such things?"

"Here! In our home!" He took a peach-tinted dress from its hook and held it up to her. "It's not a sin to please your husband, is it?" He chucked her chin gently and kissed her. "And when I take you to church, or out for a ride, when I give my speeches..."

She looked at him, hoping the pain in her eyes stayed well
hidden.

Why is it that I see things so much more clearly than he does?

She heard herself say, "Thank you, with all my heart." She gulped
down tears of gratitude and frustration. "I hope they fit!" she forced
herself to smile.

"Of course, they'll fit! They're designed to adjust." He grabbed a
ribbon beneath the bodice; it gathered in the fabric. "And this!" He
showed her the back placard of three rows of tiny hooks and eyes.
"When you're expecting. And at the rate we're going, that could be
any day now."

She blushed. How she longed for the ability to be outrageous
like Sallie and tease him back. Instead, she answered him with the
only power she had. Putting down the dress, she pressed herself
against him. "You *have* thought of everything. Where do they come
from?" *Please not Suzanne in New Orleans.*

Holding her close, he ran his hands through her hair, down her
back. "I started looking in Georgetown—the one in Washington,
not here." She could feel his breathing change. "Those tradesmen do
a fine business with us poor saps in Congress. We get so homesick,
buying things is a way to remind us we still have a home to get back
to."

Between kisses, he refused to stop talking. "The best are from
Alexandria. I found a woman in a shop there, pointed out a tall girl
about your size then she asked about your hair and eyes, and showed
me some fabrics."

He broke away from her and pulled out the drawers below the
armoire doors. "I wish you were in these right now," he grinned.
"Look how fine they are." With a careless gesture, he destroyed the
arrangement of petticoats and demis, nightgowns and thin summer
wraps.

"These were more difficult," he said, pulling out the bottom drawer. "Last year, I snuck into Ma's room, found your Sunday shoes and traced them on an old piece of linen."

Richard looked so triumphant, she did not have the heart to tell him those shoes were his niece Nancy's castoffs, and fit poorly. She picked up one of the silk slippers, and held it in her hand, rubbing the smooth fabric with her thumb. If they gave her blisters for a month, she wouldn't care, she could wrap her toes in lamb's wool. He had done nothing but think of her. Of her, his mother's slave girl! He had ridden all the way to Alexandria, wherever that was, and hauled these things home over hundreds of miles.

"Richard, I am overcome. All I wanted was you."

Tenderly, he wrapped his arms around her as she gave way to more tears. There were too many of them for the flimsy cambric, so he mopped her face with his own ample handkerchief.

"You're just hungry, Jewel," tilting his head in the direction of breakfast. They sat in the new chairs at the oval table, said a little grace and inhaled the food, laughing at themselves for their bad manners.

"Now stay put. One more thing I've got to take care of." He left her with a kiss and a warning not to leave the room until he came back.

Get on with your duties, her mind nagged her, but what were they? Everything in the room looked spotless. How could Granny Ann's weak-minded Mary and the other child do all of this?

She busied herself picking up the beautiful breakfast dishes. But there was nothing left to do but put on a new dress. For Richard. She let the peach tinted creation fall over her body then slipped on her very first pair of new shoes. Shoes no one else had ever worn. Painted linen mules.

Next came something she had never done for herself, had only stood by as she attended to other women: her toilette. Despite her best efforts to find joy in the process, however, she felt overcome by shame. Jemima's voice nagged her about the sin of vanity and the downfall of the proud. She had to turn away from her reflection in the mirror to find any relief from that voice.

Julia unhitched the latch of the nearest window, letting in the sweet scent of grass. A mockingbird swooped down at the dogs in the yard; they jumped and snapped at its tail feathers. She gazed at the dense woodlands in the distance. Her old home was in the opposite direction. A part of her needed to run to a window on the other side of the house, to see Great Crossing and ease her mind. But Richard had told her to stay put.

Soon, she heard him running up the stairs and greeted him with a guilty smile as he burst through the door. By the way he shook his head and sighed like a boy over cake, she knew he was pleased. He grabbed her hand, nearly pulling her out of her slippery new mules. "Time for you to see the rest of your house, Jewel. I've got everything ready now."

Nothing in her small life had prepared her for a change this complete. "You make me feel like Queen Esther."

"Good! You deserve nothing less." When they reached the bottom of the stairs, he guided her to the left and threw open the doors.

This was their dining room, painted the color of robins' eggs, with green damask in the valances to match the covers on two dozen chairs. Four tall, narrow windows, two at the front, and one on each side of the fireplace, welcomed in the morning light.

"Oh, Richard! It's as beautiful as our room. The fireplace...it's the same! And the furniture, it's...I don't know the word. Graceful? I thought you'd prefer the style your sisters have."

"Nun-unh. French Empire's undemocratic! This is good ol' American, made in New York by a fella name of Phyfe. I had enough of everything French in New Orleans."

The table's mirrored finish reflected a disturbing painting that hung above the fireplace. In somber colors, the artist had placed a castle ruin too close to a cliff, looking down on violent, crashing waves. It made her queasy, the way all wild water did.

"I have to confess, I won't miss all the usual antlers hanging over our dinners."

"But you don't care for this painting, do you? Jewel, you have to speak plainly with me. I'm not my mother."

"Be patient with me—this is an entirely new life for me, Richard, and I'm overwhelmed!"

When she put her arms around him and closed her eyes to receive a kiss, he obliged without hesitation. Feeling a little more confident, she ventured to say, "I know a little about music, but nothing about art. This makes me think the artist must be a very unhappy man."

With a laugh, he told her, "Not this artist. He's far from that. He's doing my portrait in Washington...mine and Clay's, so you know he has a sense of humor if he thinks we're staying around long enough to hang on a wall in the Capitol."

She sighed and looked into his face. "You really are an important man, aren't you?"

"Don't let it go to your head. I surely don't let it go to mine. In Washington, we keep each other cut down to size."

"Still, the fact that you're a member of the most powerful group of men in the country is incomprehensible to me. Can you tell me why you chose this painting?"

"I suppose I didn't think about it at the time. More of an impulse." He paused to study it for a minute. "It evokes Burns for me, or Goethe, perhaps. See how that castle is defying those waves? It makes me think that even a ruin can still stand when something powerful's trying to destroy it."

She smiled, but his sober answer troubled her. "I'll try to look at it through your eyes."

Noticing how uneasy she'd become, he began clowning. "Exactly what I did when I had this room redone. I said to myself, my girl isn't the kind to want carcasses hanging from the wall where she eats her berries and cream!"

He flattened himself against the wall and stuck out his neck, making moose antlers with his arms.

This was the Richard she'd watched growing up, tormenting his brothers. He grabbed her, and she let out a little scream. She pulled away as best she could. "It's the most beautiful room I've ever seen. Everything is so...I don't know how to describe it. Harmonious? Would that do?"

"It does, perfectly. In fact, I have one last room to introduce to my beautiful wife. And I'm positive you're going to find it even more harmonious than this one. It's your wedding present."

They nearly ran as he pulled her to the other side of the hallway. He opened the doors into the drawing room, a mirror image of the dining room. This was a room for a woman, with only one nod to the masculine: the portrait of General Washington hanging over the fireplace. The walls were painted a deep rose; the settee and side chairs were covered in cherry red damask. A clock of white porcelain touched with sugar candy roses in pink and yellow ticked quietly underneath the portrait.

"Richard, this is even more beautiful!" she exclaimed. "I couldn't cherish anything more. Thank you!" She touched it carefully, marveling at the workmanship.

"Hold on," he laughed. "That's not it! That's just an ol' Dresden. Come over here."

She turned to see him standing in the corner of the room by a new pianoforte, its top held at an angle by a decorated pole, revealing its strings, hammers and interior, a pastoral scene in dark greens and golds. It took a full minute to overcome her shock.

When she regained her composure, she whispered, "Thank you, oh, thank you, Richard. You are too good."

"Play," he said, kissing her fingertips. He sat down in a side chair by the instrument and waited.

"What shall I play? What should be the first notes? A hymn perhaps?"

"That little ditty you sang to me at Mrs. Turner's cabin would suit me fine," he grinned.

And so, she sang to him Mozart's most popular song, this time fully clothed. "La ci darem la mano," she began.

Through the open windows came a sound that had never been heard at Blue Spring. It cast a momentary spell over the slaves at work. They stopped to take it in—a woman's deep voice singing words they couldn't understand, with little bell-like clanking noises underneath.

It was pleasant enough, but not worth getting on McPherson's bad side. A few minutes after the music stopped, the workers nearest the house looked over and saw their master with a tall young woman, walking toward the center of the yard.

"Jewel, this is where you belong. You're finally home." Gently taking her by the shoulders, he turned her to face the house. It took her breath away. Blue Spring stood solid, a mixture of iron gray and silver stone mortared in milky white. Sunlight glared off the slate roof forcing her to shield her eyes. The chimneys on each end looked like giants holding it all in place.

Off to her left were paths to the cooper, blacksmith, and carpenter sheds. Beyond stood the barn and horse corrals. To the right she made out a new laundry, cookhouse, and storerooms. Everything was built of stone and oak and looked capable of standing through the Lord's millennium.

She leaned against him. "It's magnificent."

"Take good care of it for me, honey," Richard murmured into her hair. "You're the heart and soul of it, now. I'm more or less a visitor, you know."

Chapter 2
First Sabbath

"**I**'m starved. What have you got planned for my breakfast?"

"Chicken sausage. Biscuits and gravy. Anything else you have a notion for."

"I've had my 'anything else' for the moment."

She pretended to smack him with her slipper for that and quickly tied her bed jacket around her.

"And you know I can eat my weight in biscuits any day of the week." He smacked her backside with his hand, no pretend to it. With a bounce out of bed, he pulled on old work pants and a hemp shirt. "But I don't smell anything going on in the kitchen, yet. You can't be too soft on Granny Ann, or she'll be ruling the roost instead of you." He wagged a finger at her, then pulled on his socks.

"I should have asked you, I know, but it's the Sabbath, and our first one, and I want to get it right from the first, Richard. So, I talked to Granny, and she's more than willing to make an extra batch of victuals Saturday so she can go to church. I hope you won't mind."

"Honey, that's all well and good, but..."

"Do you know how many Sundays my mama got off from that cookhouse?"

"I imagine none, what with that army of boys Ma had to feed."

"And Granny's a good bit older than Mama was when she died, so I reckon we'll have a far happier cook with a little kindness.

Besides, I'm a good cook. What little time I got to spend with Mama she made count."

Richard said nothing for a moment, taking in her fragile self-confidence, this first evidence of it as she bragged about her cooking. His heart swelled with pride and just a touch of pity, like the time his niece had given her first wretched embroidery sampler to him. Instead of berating her, he decided to let her try her hand at the reins. "I'll be down at the spring. Call me when you're ready to feed me!"

Julia hadn't bragged. She could cook. He enjoyed his breakfast more than any he'd had since Henrietta's early days at the Crossing.

They nervously washed and dressed for church. Richard had a few misgivings about presenting Julia as his wife to the rest of his family in public, but it had to be done some time, and doing so at the church would prevent even Betsey from making a scene. As lovely as Julia looked in her new frock of lilac muslin, even his parents would have to forgive them. Besides, they'd had time to accept the fact he'd married her, and no one wanted to repeat the pain of separation they'd suffered over Suzanne.

After lifting Julia into the buggy for the short ride to Great Crossing Baptist, Richard gave her another surprise. "While you were making breakfast, I sought out McPherson and told him that all the servants were to go to church. Him, too. You should have seen his face! Then I told Jerry to get cleaned up to go, and his grin was as big as McPherson's scowl. Must be sweet on one of the girls from Betsey's place. No boy that age wants to go to church except to see a pretty girl."

He looked over at her, taking in her beauty. A yellow demi-kerchief covered her décolletage, much to his disappointment, although he couldn't have expected Julia to do otherwise. Now she fiddled with her new gloves. "I'd forgotten how long your fingers are. I'm going to need to get you a new pair next time I'm in Alexandria."

"Should I even bother to tell you not to?" she said with an anxious laugh. And at sight of the parishioners mulling about in the church yard, her heart began to pound so loudly it drowned out even the noise of horses and crying infants. Simon stood nearby, holding her former master's carriage, but looked at the ground as they rode past. Shaken by the boy's snub, she fumbled her parasol clumsily when Richard handed her down from the buggy.

Richard tipped his hat and grinned pleasantly as they walked toward the familiar faces waiting to enter the church. His appearance with Julia, however, had the effect of hurrying the congregation indoors, and Reverend Joseph Retting, not accustomed to such a breach in his protocol of greeting the flock, turned to see if perhaps a bear were coming up behind them. To his relief it was only Dick Johnson.

And what was this? An entrancing young woman, as tall as Johnson, clung to his arm with a sweet, shy look on her face, the kind of expression he had seen on many a new bride. It was obvious to his experienced eyes this was a couple deeply in love.

Reverend Retting smiled as they walked toward him, although he had to squash his pique at not having been asked to perform their marriage. Strange, Sister Johnson made no mention of it; stranger still, when he remarked upon the absence of her Julia he received only a stony glare.

When the bride stretched out her hand, and said, "Good morning, Reverend Retting," it struck him like a thunderbolt. Flustered by the shock of revelation, he stammered, "Good morning, Julia." So complete was the girl's transformation, he had not recognized her.

Richard pointedly corrected him, "Mrs. Johnson, please, Joseph—I mean, Reverend Retting."

The Reverend accepted the teasing rebuke, but he'd meant no offense. The church congregation became uncharacteristically quiet, however. Their ears must be burning, he concluded, unhappy with their ill-reasoned reverence. He stared at the couple for a moment, then quickly peeked at his silent flock.

As Richard and Julia moved to step over the threshold, he gently rested a hand on Richard's arm. "And so, Brother Johnson! You are married," he stumbled, voice dipping and rising unnaturally. "Please, tell me who performed the nuptials?"

Richard, who assumed his status would overshadow any question of their attending church, now understood that he was being denied entry. His face colored deeply as he stared at their old family friend. He glanced quickly at the people sitting quietly within, no one daring to turn and stare, but straining all the same to follow the situation on the porch. His mother, seated on the front pew as she once had been in the old days, held her head exceptionally high.

Turning to address Retting, Richard let his voice, in contrast to the low, intimate tone of the reverend's, ring clear, knowing how much more the good Baptists of Great Crossing were enjoying this than any sermon.

"Why, my dear friend, we were married Monday afternoon, in the eyes of God, by the Reverend Dennison, in Cincinnati." A long pause followed; Richard drew Julia close to his side. He wrapped her arm in his, allowing her weight to lean against his body. They both steadied themselves. The reverend held more sway over the hearts of Scott County's people than ever Richard did as their congressman.

"Brother Johnson, such a marriage is forbidden in the eyes of God, as well as in the law of the land." The minister's voice always had a practiced tone of regret and sorrow, but Richard noticed true concern. He saw heads lightly bobbing up and down in agreement with the preacher, silently cursed them, and prayed for Julia to survive this.

Just as Richard felt he was losing the battle to control his anger, inspiration came. "No more forbidden than that of Ruth and Boaz, although they were considered of different race in days of old. And yet they are the progenitors of our Lord Himself."

Jemima put a restraining arm on Robin, who had tightened every muscle to keep his place beside her. Never had they felt so betrayed, and this public humiliation of the entire family was by their favored son. Henry squirmed; George chuckled in discomfort.

Betsey focused on her younger children, wiping noses that were clean, pulling up stockings still straight. She reflected bitterly that Sallie, the one who could have put a stop to this nonsense, had given up on church ages ago. She tried not to listen, but Richard was being such a showoff as usual, that everyone heard every syllable.

The only advantage of being on the front pew was that only the choir and deacon could see their faces. That group could barely contain themselves when her seven-year-old William whined, "I'm tired, Mama. Why doesn't Uncle Dickie stop talking so Reverend Retting can yell at us?"

The reverend honestly considered the resounding truth of Richard's argument, and admitted that he was willing to accept the Bible story in this remarkable new light. As he stepped aside with a conciliatory nod, motioning them to step through the doorway, James reached them, panting with the effort to restrain his rage.

"Dick, Julia, why don't we visit a moment, and let the good reverend get started on his service?"

"God bless you, Reverend," Julia said quietly, acknowledging his willingness to accept her changed circumstances. Retting took her hand for a moment, then quickly made his way down the aisle to the front, signaling the choir to begin the opening hymn. 'O God, Our Help in Ages Past,' Julia heard as they stepped away.

Richard wrapped her hand securely around his arm as they retreated down the church steps. Turning to his elder brother, he whispered, "No need, Jimmy, no need to say anything."

"Just tell me, is it true?"

Richard looked at James for a moment, wondering what exactly he already knew. But his brother was never one to prevaricate, so he replied openly. "Yes, we are married, by a Baptist minister, on free soil. It's legal."

James let out a low whistle. "I'll be damned, man. The folks refuse to tell us anything. They won't even speak your name." Making no effort to hide his contempt, he looked at Julia and added, "Or yours."

"So, we're to be shunned, like rebel Quakers?" Richard asked.

"You're a damned fool," James sighed.

"He who calleth his brother a fool is in danger of hellfire," Richard retorted with a grim smile.

"Well, I *am* my brother's keeper, and though I don't give a damn for your personal life, your political career is a completely different matter. I don't want to be the one living in Washington to mollify our parents! I have a family!"

"So, do I!"

Even James could not miss the pain in his brother's voice. It did not soften his heart, however, and as he ascended the church steps he hissed, "We'll see about that."

Without looking back, Richard and Julia walked toward their buggy, the entire day dying with each step. "Richard, James frightens me. He can't take me away from you, can he?"

The terror in her voice made Richard want to drag his brother out of church and lash him. Through clenched teeth he spat, "Not he, not anyone, can take you away from me. If he wants to fill his role as oldest brother, so be it. But nobody intimidates me, least of all that self-righteous hyprocrite."

She strained to think of something, anything, to say to him, to distract him from his rage and her from the tears of frustration choking her. The parasol. "'We don't want our birthday girl getting freckles.' I remember you telling me that five years ago, right here at this tree."

Richard looked at her, bewildered, before realizing what she was trying to do. "Yes? When was that?"

"Your Fourth of July speech. You stood there with Miss...with Suzanne. You and your mother seemed to have some sort of game going on between you."

Richard's heart tightened at the sound of Suzanne's name from his bride's lips. He grimly smiled at the memory of his plans to make Julia their housekeeper. As he helped her into the buggy, he muttered, "Believe me, honey, my mother and I never had any sort of game going between us."

"Game isn't the proper word, then." To explain herself, she added, "It always seemed that she was aiming to move you in a certain direction."

"Ah! You mean maneuvering. I suppose game is as good a description as anything. What did I do?" He loosened the reins, and the horse trotted toward home.

"Tried to wiggle out with a joke or a compliment. But you were always kind. I never heard you say the things George or Henry or even John T did. But then she was always making them do things they hated." *Like attend my mother's funeral.*

"Yes. Well, the Knights of the Round Table rubbed off on me more than it did my little brothers. Except Benjamin, possibly. I always respected Ma. She had a lot of courage. If I had half of it, I'd be a formidable force in Congress."

"What was that about the Quakers you said to Mas...to James?"

"You mean shunned? A custom amongst the strictest Quakers, of literally turning their backs to anyone who breaks with their ways. Parents have shunned their own children, children their parents."

"Standing there on the porch, we had a hundred backs to us, your family included. That was shunned, indeed."

"But not for long, not forever, Jewel." As they headed back to Blue Spring, Richard's rage hardened into bitterness, something he did not want to inflict on her.

"Look at me?" The new bonnet cupped her face making it narrow at the chin like a cat's. She dazzled him as she had at Mrs. Turner's table. Beauty spilled from her and onto the spring-fed creeks and summer flowers all around them.

"'This is the day the Lord hath made; rejoice and be glad in it.'" Julia sighed. "I'll miss church. It was always the highlight of my week. The hymns especially. You need to go without me."

"You're the one baptized, not me. This just gives me more reason not to be."

When they reached the narrow road leading to Blue Spring, Richard pulled the buggy to a halt. They could hear the creek water, the buzz of insects, the breeze blowing through the trees. Off in the distance stood their home.

"Look at all this, Jewel." He pulled her close to him. "It's been mine for nearly five years. But in only two days, you've made it seem like we've always been here together. Get it through your head, girl! I'm your husband, and I love you." He took off her glove and kissed her hand. "What they do to you they do to me."

"Thank you," she said softly and shook her head. "I don't deserve you."

He laughed. "Nobody does, least of all an angel like you! Tell you what. We'll start our own church in the good ol' Baptist tradition, 'where two or more are gathered,' just you and me. We can sing and pray and read the Bible, can't we?" She nodded her head, refusing to let the hour's bitter mix of shame and frustration sour the gratitude she felt for his love.

He flicked the horse into action again. "Did I ever tell you about the visit I had with Mr. Jefferson in the Presidential Mansion?"

"Not directly, but I recall reading one of your letters to your mother over and over. I do believe that was her favorite. She couldn't reconcile herself to his Philosophy of Jesus, but she had memorized the parts about your future in politics. And she loved saying, 'we're distant relatives, you know.'"

"What a perfect girl to marry. You have my pedigree down by heart, no doubt!"

"All except the part where we're cousins."

"Oh, it's there alright, the Chinns and Johnsons go way back to old Virginia days, but I have no intention of charting it out. That's for thoroughbreds, not people."

"What did you talk about that wasn't in your letter?"

"You." Richard slowed the horse to a walk as they neared the house. "He told me that if I went ahead with my plans to marry you, I'd need to create a world apart." As she looked over the trees, his fields and home then up to the sky, he followed her gaze.

"Always remember this, Jewel, I created this little world right here for you."

Jerry took the reins when Richard brought the buggy to a halt. He looked almost polished in some of Richard's old clothes and genuinely pleased with his church-ready self.

"Mas Richard, Granny Ann's a mighty proud woman, and she'd never dream of asking you, but I'm asking you. Can I hitch up a wagon to carry her and the little ones to church?"

Seeing the anxiety on Julia's face at Jerry's boldness, Richard felt a much-needed surge of goodwill. "Alright. That ol' cart mule will think it's a load of feathers compared to what he's used to pulling."

Richard walked around to the other side of the buggy to hand Julia down. Over his shoulder, she saw Patsy hurrying down the path to the servants' quarters, in a dress vaguely familiar. It hadn't been burned but cut down to fit the little girl.

With a shudder, Julia saw the burden of her servitude draped over those small shoulders. Now, as a free woman, Julia vowed to herself to do everything in her power to alleviate as many of those burdens as she could.

Curtis McPherson galloped up as Julia entered the house, the glare he gave Jerry easy enough for Richard to read. "Am I to take it you told the boy he was not to have use of the wagon?"

"That's right." McPherson dismounted.

Richard knew that his overseer was, like many in the profession, a brute. He kept the man bridled by a combination of rewards, praise when it was due, and threats. Blue Spring, like Great Crossing, was not a farm where crippling or severe beatings were used to keep people in line.

The whip was Curtis's preference, but Richard followed the Johnson way: keep servants in families, and they'd do almost anything to avoid having a child or mate sold off. And in a good year, when the harvest quotas were exceeded, everyone got rewarded in some way or another: workers with food, clothing, and blankets; McPherson with coin.

He could not let things get off to a bad start between the man and Julia just because she wanted to make a charitable gesture to their people.

"Jerry, come here!" The tone of Richard's voice brought Julia to the drawing room window. This was a voice she did not know, and her immediate fear was that he would take out the morning's frustration on the boy.

"Did you ask McPherson for the wagon?"

"Yessir. I did. And he told me no. We'd all have to walk."

"And you explained about Granny having an understanding with Miz Julia, did you?"

"Best I could, sir."

"Then listen here. McPherson is my overseer, and what he says goes. If you come to me or Miz Julia with any kind of request, you better tell us that you asked McPherson first. More than likely, we're going to back him up on what he told you. Any double cross, you'll be out in those fields, you hear me?"

Jerry hung his head and muttered, "yessir." Richard told him to get back to hitching up the cart. His overseer spat and stared at the ground.

"Now McPherson, I expect Miz Julia's going to change your orders from time to time. You're going to have to expect it to happen. Blue Spring is a big place, and we can't hand deliver you messages." Richard narrowed his eyes. "You're overseer, it's true, but whether I'm here or in the Federal City, I expect you to follow my wife's wishes. She's had a lot of experience at the Crossing and knows how to manage a farm. She knows my plans for this place as well as I do, and when I'm gone, she'll read to you my instructions if there are any changes to be made." "Yessir," McPherson growled, looking toward the house. He caught the shape of Julia at the window.

"And if you're in disagreement with the way my wife and I handle the place, you're welcome to give notice. I hope it won't come to that."

"Beg pardon, sir, but you can have runaways on Sundays just like any other day of the week, that's all I'm thinkin', and a wagon is a might faster than leavin' on foot."

Richard studied the man; was this pride or something else? Soothe the pride, he decided. "I appreciate you looking out for my interests, but you understand my family has trusted our servants with horses and wagons in these parts for thirty years, with never a runaway. It's a mule cart, for heaven's sake, man, not a thoroughbred."

Richard watched McPherson ride off in the direction of his quarters. He would have to warn Julia about him, but not today. When he stepped into the house, he called her name.

She peeked out of the drawing room. "What have I done?"

"Nothing!"

She's nineteen. How can I leave her at the mercy of McPherson, or even Granny Ann? He forced a note of cheerfulness into his voice. "Now, how about our little church service?"

Once she pulled him into the drawing room, she led him to the settee and stood over him with the large Bible in her hand. "It's here, where you talked about in the Book of Ruth. That was brilliant, what you told Reverend Retting. He didn't even mention Boaz in last week's sermon!"

"Inspired, Jewel. I swear the thought had never occurred to me, and then, there it was, as if I'd pondered the idea for a month." He pulled her onto his lap, but her long legs dangled at a ridiculous angle.

"The problem with you is, I'm either going to have to grow half a foot or get a much broader lap!"

"That's why I plan to have plenty of daughters for you. They'll be just the right size, for a few years at least."

He kissed her before reminding her, "My family's not much for girls, in case you haven't noticed. Boys outnumber them five to one."

"Mmhmm, I've noticed. But maybe we'll be the lucky ones."

"Nothing would please me more than to have a dozen little girls, as long as they take after you." He kissed her again then swung her in one motion off his lap and onto the settee. She handed the Bible to him.

"I can't imagine anything more despicable than a bunch of little devils like me running around."

Chapter 3
Callers
September 1809

J ulia rubbed her finger over the embossing of two smooth ivory
calling cards. 'The Honorable Richard Mentor Johnson, Esquire.'
'Mrs. Richard Mentor Johnson.' Both cards were beautiful, hers
utterly useless.

She smiled sadly at the irony of knowing all the prominent
women in the region. They had shown her great kindness over the
years...when she'd been a slave. As the wife of the most in-demand
gentleman in the area, she would be shunned.

Once, she had asked Jemima why their calls were always so brief.
Jemima told her it was a sign of good manners. "It shows that we
are sensitive to the fact that those with new spouses, or infants, or
problems are bound to be distracted at any moment." Julia missed
her. Richard did not. They never spoke of her.

Men called on Richard every day. There were constituents
seeking political favors, even neighbors just venting grievances. They
talked for hours of horses and keelboats and war, arriving before
breakfast. She had to greet them, feed them, endure their stares.
Richard introduced her to each of them, although most had known
her all her life. He even invited them to come back with their wives
for their 'at home' Wednesday afternoons.

"Once people see how good you are, they'll flock to you, Jewel," he assured her after his visitors cleared out.

But don't you see, Richard, I know the rules. It's not that they won't, they cannot.

The words formed in her mouth, but she could not say them. Instead, she gave him an encouraging smile.

Richard decided they needed a temporary butler. For most of his five years there, Blue Spring had been as informal as a log cabin. As a bachelor, he personally opened the door to all his visitors because they were either family or male. Since Jerry was the only manservant anywhere near the house, he would have to be taken in hand.

"But a butler's a rarified position, Richard! It takes years. Remember Jasper?"

"Impossible to forget!" Richard grimaced at the memory of Sallie's prim man who had ruled Blue Spring during Sallie's year in residence. He had been sorry to see his sister go back to her husband, but glad to be rid of the high and mighty Jasper.

"But you've trained a dozen servants at Great Crossing in deportment, honey. What's so difficult about answering a door and taking people into another room, anyway?"

She knew he understood all too well the difficulties. But for the sake of avoiding a debate about butlers, which he could do for hours, she gave in.

"Alright, you win. But we've got to do something about his horse smell."

Granny Ann got Jerry into a washtub handing him a boar bristle scrub brush and lye soap, but the real insult was the toilet water Julia lavished on him after he was dressed.

"You smell like magnolia! Too bad!" Richard teased him. "I prefer horse lather."

"Horses have a perfume all their own, and that's a fact," Jerry added soberly.

EVEN POLITICAL CALLERS who had never heard of Julia
stayed away from Blue Spring for their first 'at home'. Richard put on
a good front for her and sat in the drawing room, dressed in his best,
poring over Tacitus while she played the piano. When they heard a
buggy rattle up the drive, Julia stepped quickly over to Richard. He
closed his book and they stared at each other like surprised children
caught in a prank.

They heard Sallie through the window telling her driver not to
dismount. She tapped at the door with the knob of her parasol. Jerry
opened the door, and she laughed out loud.

"Why Jerry, I've changed my mind about you. You've definitely
got the makings of a silk purse. But I won't tell Jasper. Where's my
brother?"

She pushed past Jerry, but stopped in the hallway where she
watched, holding her breath, as her brother tenderly straightened
the pearls around Julia's neck. He looked giddy with tenderness. The
sight of them changed everything.

Sallie realized she had never really bothered to look at Julia
before. Her hair, no longer hidden by a cap, fell from an upsweep
of light brown curls down her neck. Instead of a dull little uniform,
she wore an exquisite ivory-colored gown of silk. Julia responded
to Richard with something she had not seen since poor Suzanne:
adoration.

Her fury towards them vanished. She forgave their folly on the
spot; worse, she envied them with all her heart. She tiptoed back to
Jerry who was laughing with her driver about his butler get-up.

"Jerry, announce me properly to my brother. You need the
practice. Tom, take the carriage into the shade. I'm staying for a little
while."

With the wind out of her sails, Sallie entered the room with the
quiet restraint she reserved for funerals.

Richard beamed when he saw her, took her hand and led her to Julia, who looked at them with uncertainty. "Mrs. Ward, might I have the honor of introducing you to my lovely bride?"

Julia performed her courtesy, just as she had once taught Sallie's children to do. "How do you do, Mrs. Ward?" Her deep voice thrilled Sallie with its beauty.

"How do you do, Mrs. Johnson?" she replied with a solemn courtesy in return. "Congratulations, Richard." Sallie kissed him softly on his cheek. He wanted to hold onto her, to sob on her neck in relief, but he patted her hand and smiled gratefully, instead.

"Won't you be seated?" Julia indicated an armchair for Sallie as she and Richard shared the divan. Julia, with a nearly imperceptible lift of her finger, signaled to a small figure at a side door.

Patsy carried in cool water with mint sprigs, and a plate of impossibly thin tea biscuits. Sallie snatched up a glass, her mouth nearly too dry to speak. "Blue Spring has the best water, don't you think?" She smiled, trying to break the melancholy that had overcome her. She watched Richard and Julia, who looked as doomed as Romeo and Juliet.

"I agree. It seems sweeter," Julia replied shyly, looking over at Richard, who gave her a smile of encouragement.

Sallie's glance traveled to the gleaming pianoforte. "What a gorgeous instrument! Wherever did you get it?"

"My husband says it was made in Philadelphia!" Julia beamed.

Sallie's throat tightened when she caught Richard patting Julia's hand. She tried to nibble a wafer, but it was no use; she could restrain herself no longer. "We have to do something about you two."

Richard put his arm around his wife. "And what do you propose, Sallie?"

Allying herself with her favorite brother was nothing new, but she had no power to circumvent the whole of Kentucky society. "You do understand this is the only social call you'll receive?"

Julia nodded in agreement, but Richard frowned. "Sallie, it isn't necessary to..."

"Look, Richard," she put down her glass with a little thud of annoyance. "Julia may be young, but she's intelligent. She's been our mother's protégée all her life, and that means if she thinks like anyone, she thinks like Mama. So, Julia," Sallie turned and looked directly at her. "What do you think Mama's doing? What do you think about...well, about everything? My brother didn't force you into this, did he?"

Richard squirmed and dropped his arm from Julia's shoulders. "Sallie, this isn't necessary. I never forced Julia to do anything, and I will deal with Ma. I don't like Julia being upset..."

"Oh, shush, Dickie! Look at her! Does she look upset? Julia knows precisely what I am saying, and I want to hear what she thinks. You always have things to say, so let somebody else have a chance."

Julia forced back a smile. Getting a fair share in a discussion with her husband challenged them all, but Sallie shared that trait. Richard started to protest again, but Julia straightened and tried to speak to Sallie as an equal.

Sallie remained spellbound by Julia's transformation. She wanted to do nothing but sit and stare. This was like a grand experiment, something no one would believe: a mousy slave girl turned alluring woman.

"First, thank you for coming. You're the first hope we've had of...any understanding." Julia dipped her head and swallowed. Her courage returned when she saw how carefully they were listening. "Richard gave me a choice, the night we left, if freedom were all I wanted, I could run away once we reached Ohio. Perhaps I could've provided for myself...a woman who can read and write is a rarity, it seems."

Richard froze. It never occurred to him that Julia would have thought about another life.

"But Miz—your mother—had been my whole world. I really didn't mind. She was so kind to me." Julia's voice faded and she quickly took a sip of water.

Sallie looked down at her hands. Oh, the times she had resented her mother being so easy on the girl!

"But Richard's my world, now. I want to make Blue Spring something he can be proud of. My life won't be so different from most women living on a farm. And from what I noticed, making calls with your mother, most ladies turn into busybodies. I don't want that."

Sallie nodded. She knew from sad experience how powerful the allure of gossip was.

"I don't expect you to champion me socially. I understand your position. As for your parents...they'll leave us alone, don't you think, Richard?"

He nodded and, to her surprise, remained silent. "But your brother James troubles me. You know he threatened us at the church. He's always been jealous of my husband, so I worry about what he'll do. I don't think we should trust him."

Julia continued, "You recall how your mother always ignored children at the beginning of trouble? She'd say that a child will turn himself inside out for a little attention, and if you didn't give it, they'd soon learn that being inside out wasn't too comfortable."

Richard and Sallie both laughed at the painful reminder.

"I believe she thinks Richard's going to come around...that I'm...what did you say about the painting, Richard?"

"An impulse," he murmured.

Julia turned back to Sallie. "But you know the most important thing to her is Richard's success in Washington."

"Oh, yes! We've all known that well enough for a while." Sallie rolled her eyes at Richard in an exaggerated display of peevishness.

Julia laughed softly. "So why would she stir up a hornet's nest over our marriage? It would draw away attention from the good he's doing in Washington. I believe she'll say nothing and continue to say nothing. She'll simply pretend the situation doesn't exist. To her way of thinking, eventually we'll turn ourselves right side out again."

"She's right, Dickie. Julia, you're a gem. But what are you going to do with yourself? Richard's gone half the year."

Julia hesitated. Richard waited, eager to find out. He was ashamed for thinking so little about her life, her feelings. He had always prided himself on being a gentleman, but here, he hadn't used even a little imagination in considering what life would be like for her. He glanced at an engraving from *The Iliad* hung on the wall near him. Had Paris ever given a thought to how Helen would feel once she got to Troy?

"There is so much I want to learn. Richard can send me books, and I want to write."

Richard looked at her, astonished at this revelation.

"I have so many concoctions and poultices from Mama, and from your mother. And so many words of wisdom and comfort they taught me that seem to work better on healing people than medicine. It's bound to be useful to someone."

"It's a worthy task, Jewel. I'll ask Theo for some books to help you." Richard squeezed her hand gently. He felt like he was discovering her for the first time.

"And Sallie, we will have a big family."

"Is there any other kind for us Johnsons?" Sallie quipped before turning serious. "What about your children? If people can't accept you, as perfectly lovely as you are, what will happen to them?"

"Perhaps things will get better in time, Sallie." Richard interjected. "In New Orleans, the *gens de couleur* have prestige..."

"But look at her! She hardly even qualifies as a person of color. So why all this fuss?" She answered herself. "But there's going to be fuss and more fuss, just like that Sunday. I feel like going back to the church just so I can leave it again for the way they treated you."

"That was an appalling situation, but strangely, Sal, I have no animosity...none! Perhaps it's because I had hoped people wouldn't treat us like that but knew in my heart of hearts they would. I know Julia feared as much, more for my sake than hers, poor lamb."

"Well, if you want my advice, which you probably don't..."

"No, you're so wrong. Whatever you can offer would mean so much!" Julia interrupted. Sallie glanced at her brother. "Alright, then. You heard her! It's just this, Julia. Go right on holding your head high. None of us chooses our birth. But for that, you could have easily been a member of society. Keep yourself lovely, dress well, enjoy all the good things Richard's so eager to give you. However, please don't subject yourself to any further humiliation by going back to that church, or by going a-calling."

Julia looked down, and nodded her head, while Sallie caught Richard's eye. He looked like he wanted to cry for his wife's sake. Sallie hurriedly added, "But you shouldn't sequester yourself at Blue Spring, either. Go out in your carriage! Try some of the merchants. They'd be fools not to welcome your trade. They're not of our class, but make friends of Mammon, as the Good Book says."

She rose and straightened her dress. "And now, my pets, I really must leave you." She pecked Richard on the cheek and embraced Julia. "Forgive me if I am not able to call on you very often in the future. But I promise that I'll never speak about either of you unless it is to praise you. I'll stare down any who dare to bring up the subject of you two," she said with mock severity. "That, I must confess, is going to be great fun."

Richard walked his sister to her carriage and helped her up the step. "Thank you, with all my heart, for being so kind to my wife." He leaned in through the window. Sallie tousled his hair.

"Your wife. Little Julia, *your* wife!" She sighed. "Well, believe me, it was not my intention when I started over here this afternoon. I had planned on wringing your neck and throttling her. But seeing you both...you're happier than I have ever seen you. And Julia! She's like...oh, I don't know." She struggled to find the right words. "Like a princess. She is so unbelievably lovely." She patted his back. "When did all this happen, by the way? The little ones used to adore her, but honestly, I never dreamed you'd taken any notice of her. Now, I can see why, but..."

"New Orleans."

"What? But how...did you see Suzanne? You know, you never told me what happened on that trip."

"And you've wanted to know all this time if I saw her? Why didn't you ever ask me?"

"You know very well why. I felt so responsible in a way for all that disaster."

"You weren't. You only tried to help," he sighed. "But no, I didn't see her. I did meet her husband, though."

"What was he like?"

"Not like me, I can assure you," he chuckled sadly. "But he had one thing in his favor. He absolutely believed in her, accepted her completely. She's become quite a success, which is something I could never have tolerated."

"More's the pity. But what does New Orleans have to do with Julia?"

"This horrid ball..."

"The plaçage ball? Yes, my husband's been."

"I assume Alphonse made him go?"

"Oh, yes! But there was no bending his arm, I assure you." She looked away for a moment. "I have to confess, it sounds intriguing."

"If you like the grotesque. It was nothing more than a dressed-up slave auction. Young, fair-skinned girls, pure girls, mind you, because these lechers demanded their virtue as part of the price. And they were dressed up in finery, paraded around by their own mothers in front of those scoundrels. It made me disgusted with my sex." He looked back at the house, wondering if Julia stood at the window, questioning his absence.

"So, you decided you would rescue our fair little Julia?"

"It wasn't so much the ball as it was an encounter that astonished me beyond belief. Alphonse introduced me to a friend and his wife. Turned out to be Delia Chinn. I saw her when she was a child. When Father bought out their household." Including Julia, he thought with shame. "The girl was the spitting image of Julia. We talked about our lines, you know how that goes. She's Julia's great-niece, if such things were openly admitted."

"I always wondered who her father was. The old man, then. You know, this entire matter has made me see things so differently, but I am a terrible coward. I know I'll go on accepting things the way they are and saying 'what a pity'. Can't you fellows change all of...this?" She waved her hand, taking in the house, the land, the slaves.

Richard sighed. "Washington, Jefferson, now Madison. No one seems to know that answer any better than you do. Gentlemen regret it but accept it. I've adopted Jefferson's view. If you're good to your people, they're certainly better off under your care than out in this heartless world on their own."

"Well, I'm not so sure about that. Jasper could rule the whole world on *his* own. I'd free him, except I can't survive without him. Then there's the likes of you, a gentleman, even though you like making a high drama out of life. Still, I admire your misguided gallantry. At least you're never dull, like most men."

Sallie gently pushed him away from the door and told Tom to head over to her mother's place. She had no plans to make a case for her brother or for Julia. But the love she had just experienced had been like a religious conversion. Sallie wanted to share a little of it with her mother, to connect the two houses.

She found her mother in the linen press with little Kate, who was stretched on tiptoe and straining to bring down a stack of dinner napkins. "Get down from there, Katy, and I'll hand them to you," Sallie said as she reached up and easily removed them. "Where do you want these, Mama?" she asked sweetly.

"Take them to the dining table, Kate, and mind you check there's not a speck of food on it before you put them down."

Gone was Jemima's gentle, mannerly tone that Sallie once found so irksome. Whenever her mother spoke these days, servants or family, it was with weariness underscored by vexation. Jemima pretended to inventory the table linen, counting audibly. She hadn't greeted her daughter or even looked at her.

"I've seen them, just now." Sallie never wasted time on prelude. Her mother stepped away from her and hobbled towards the dining room.

"I have guests this evening, Sallie. Don't trouble me," she barked.

"You don't fool me a bit. You're dying to know everything."

"The only thing dying here is my memory of those two. I told you all never to speak of them. Now, let me be."

"No Mama, let *them* be."

"Enough!" Jemima hissed, and circled the table, pretending to flatten the linen.

"They are deeply in love. Divinely happy." Sallie said softly, with all the pain of a remorseful marriage in the words. "They understand why you...we...feel the way we do. They expect nothing from any of us. But you should see them! And the house! It's already sparkling.

Jerry's become a butler, and Richard bought her an ivory frock that makes her look like a princess."

Jemima stared at her daughter, and shouted, "He's the one who thinks of her as a slave! I never did!" Her face crumpled into a hundred lines. Between sobs, she choked, "She was everything to me. I never thought I had to free her. We don't free family!"

Sallie embraced her and held on for a long time.

Chapter 4
Expectations
October 1809. Blue Spring

"Ever heard the expression, 'If the mountain won't come to Mohammed? We're going to open this house up to everybody for the next two weeks before I go back to Washington!" His powerful voice echoed through their dining room, empty except for the two of them. They dined on veal cutlets swimming in gravy, surrounded by autumn vegetables. Their plates were hand painted china newly uncrated, gifts from Alphonse Leclerc. Everything Richard did smacked of excess to Julia, desperate to make everyone see her through his eyes.

Julia did not delude herself that the parade of people who came to their home were there for any other reason than to satiate their curiosity about her. After the first few evenings of elaborate dinners followed by expensive cigars, the women stopped coming, but the men continued to make themselves at home.

She presided as hostess at table and held her own with what questions anyone tossed her way. Richard settled upon their own solution to the awkwardness of the absence of the ladies: at the end of dinner, he raised his glass to her, then she excused herself with the most dazzling smile she could manage and retired to their room. There she practiced the art of self-control. Seeing her with swollen eyes and a red nose would only hurt him. If she looked and acted happy, he'd be satisfied that he was succeeding at making her happy.

She took a little comfort in knowing Richard had pride in her. On several occasions, she had caught him enticing people into a room just to boast, 'Julia did this.' But clearly people would not accept that she was anything more than his housekeeper by day and his mistress by night.

There was no work to complain about, either. Granny Ann ruled the cookhouse, laundry shed and kitchen garden like a hen, ready to peck anybody that got in her territory. She protected her oldest granddaughter, Mary, with fierceness. Mary could follow Granny's orders to peel potatoes or pluck feathers, and she did it without a word...just a long stare in the direction of her grandmother's voice then at wherever Granny pointed.

Julia tried to take Mary under her wing, showing her how to polish the furniture, but she ate the beeswax instead. When she put a broom in the girl's hand, she just stood and swept the same spot over and over. Julia gave up.

Seven-year-old Patsy turned out to be a different matter. She was as sharp as her older sister was dull; she even glowed with a copper sheen to her skin and hair, sending out sparks of energy with every task. Overjoyed at the prospect of getting out of the kitchen and laundry, she took pains to show off the speed and thoroughness of her work.

"Patsy seems to be growing a little fond of you," Richard remarked one night. "But don't turn her into a pet the way Ma did you!"

Then what am I going to do with myself when you go? Julia wanted to scream.

As the day for his departure neared, Julia forced herself to live up to his expectations. He could have no fears for his beloved Blue Spring on her account in his absence. When the day came for him to leave, she held him close and kept her tears to herself. As she stood in the doorway on that crisp morning in late October and watched him go, she wondered why she had kept the news of the baby to herself, as well.

JULIA STARED OUT THE tall, narrow window at the front of the dining room, longing for a walk but staying indoors, afraid of slipping on the pavers that landscaped the grounds. With so little to do, her mind turned to cataloguing the minutiae of her surroundings: seven streaks in this glass pane, only three in that. The twenty green bubbles in the center pane reminded her of creek ice about to thaw.

She watched Jerry at work. With Richard gone, the house had no need of a butler, and the boy far preferred his horses. Leaning against the frame of the stable door, sheltered from the stinging sleet, he kept his hands busy with the task of braiding thin strips of leather into a collar. Though not as tall as Julia, he had a way of squaring back his shoulders and moving his head and limbs with ease. She could imagine him springing from the ground and landing on the back of a horse without any effort at all. He even braided his leather scraps with a confidence and surety that gave her a pang of envy.

Jerry looked African in the way she imagined her ancestor had. Mama had spoken of their forefather with reverence and an admonition to pass his memory on when Julia had her own children. Tradition held that he had been skilled in medicines, from a land of strange animals and plants that grew tall as trees. He had been brought to Virginia on a slave ship in the time of the first King Charles and acquired by the Chinns who had owned him, then his descendants, for six generations.

A horse and rider trotted toward the house, prompting Jerry to put down his craft work and pull his hat down over his ears to meet the man. The two exchanged pleasantries; Jerry waved before hurrying up to the porch. She met him at the door.

"Somethin' from Mas Richard," he said. None of the servants said, "your husband." None of them called her Miz Julia or even ma'am. They didn't call her anything. What was the point of correcting them? She had just as little idea of her place as they did. Jerry handed her a hide-wrapped packet then stomped back outside to the stable. It was the first communication of any kind from Richard, and she clung to it like a drowning woman desperate for a lifeline.

He had left her two months ago, in charge of Blue Spring and to the mercy of the family and neighbors. In that short time, the entire county had turned against her. Richard's enormous family, which she could not escape in any direction, blamed her for making—how was it Betsey's daughter Nancy put it?—"brazen attempts to claim legitimacy to her lie of a marriage".

As if she had carried out single-handedly their elopement into Ohio and coerced Reverend Dennison into pronouncing them man and wife. Nancy had been her childhood playmate and friend, rare girls in households of boys. She had been in the throes of preparing for her wedding to that shy boy, Sabret Offutt, when she humiliated Julia on a public street in front of everyone.

After settling into Richard's chair in his study, Julia clawed at the seals until they broke away and revealed his writing. With a quick glance at the whole of it, she saw with joy that it covered a dozen pages of foolscap, front and back. She spread everything out on the desk.

Illustrations of farm plots. Instructions for building a new barn. Plans for diverting the spring to bring water to the house; nothing but directions for that horrible man McPherson. What she craved were words for her, to embrace her and crack through the chill of this place and her sense of isolation.

Through her tears of frustration and disappointment, she managed to find them. A smaller page, covered front and back, lay hidden between the drawings. Her relief stopped her tears, and once she got control of her shaking hands, she devoured his letter. The date was November twenty-fifth. She thanked the Lord it had arrived so quickly.

"My dearest girl, how fares my crowning Jewel?" He talked to her from the paper, describing his room at the Franklin Inn and old Matt Lyon's snores, the smell of muddy boots and damp wool in their cramped room. He made her laugh, a sound so unfamiliar it brought Granny Ann from the pantry to peek in on her.

"I'm fine, Granny. Just a letter."

"'Bout time. Dinner in a hour."

"I am leading out, along with Clay, and they refer to us as the loudest of the war hawks, which I take as a compliment, not only for myself and Clay, but for all Kentuckians." Then *"Knit me up more socks, for the darning needle grows rusty in my hand, and the washer women are so brisk I fear they'll break the darned threads!"*

She laughed at his pun and the cartoon he drew of himself. *"Pegasus adores O'Neale's new stable and pasture, even in the rain and muck, which is all we are getting this season."*

Julia missed the stallion. She closed her eyes and remembered the night they escaped Great Crossing.

"Dinner at the Inn is even more rambunctious than it was at home when I was a boy. We try out new rails on each other to use the next day against the Federalists. Then we adjourn to a library the O'Neales set up for us, and their little Peg plays Methodist hymns, though they run to melancholy unlike our homey Baptist songs. What I would most love to hear is my own girl playing and singing Herr Mozart. When I long for you, I think it's good to be a bachelor in Congress. Nothing but my obsession with our country keeps me away from you, and as the dreary months roll on, I have the consolation that they move me closer to the

time when we shall be together once more. Send me good news, for I am pining for my girl. Your adoring" and his initials scrawled large at the bottom.

Julia rocked back and forth in the chair, crying, kissing the paper, grateful no one was there to watch her going mad. Every day since he left two months ago, she had written. By now, he should have received dozens of letters, but made no mention of even one. They'd arrive like an avalanche, probably. It was costly. Would he reproach her? She wondered how long it would take before he read the one with the only good news that mattered.

Chapter 5
A Friend
December 1810

Exactly one year ago, Julia had written Richard that, God willing, he would have a son by the first of June. But God hadn't been willing. It had been lost New Year's Day. Women at the Crossing had always gotten on the subject of childbirth and miscarriages, and she was grateful for the preparation it had given when that nightmare came upon her. She had been without him then and would be without him this time. She tried not to take comfort in thoughts of Theobald.

Richard had been home mere weeks when the letter came from Washington, calling for the third session of the Eleventh Congress. Aren't there supposed to be just two?" she'd asked. "Yes, but the President can call a special session anytime he wants, and with the war coming..." then he'd cut off the conversation, rubbed the tiny bulge on her stomach and told her to sit down. "Worrying's my job, and I deal with worrisome things quite well."

He had left early to avoid the norther' blowing in from Canada. The other congressmen who rode with him did not want to take any chances on arriving late.

They'd had five months together. She knew she was with child by her birthday, but she didn't tell him until the end of August, wanting to make sure it didn't end like the last one. Nor did she want him to protect her, gentleman that he was. She wanted as much of him as he was willing to give, and their hunger for each other seemed insatiable. That made his leaving all the worse—a tearing-away after feeling his body next to her each night and staying near his side much of each day.

When she sat alone in a room now, the memory of his presence became like a comforting ghost to her. She could feel the weight of his breath, the little whoosh of air caressing her as he passed by, the touch of his fingers on the little curls that fell down her neck. The strain of the joy in his presence followed so quickly by the grief of his absence left her reeling. Even after five weeks, she could not accept that he was gone again.

Over the fifteen months since their elopement, loneliness had become as bottomless as the Blue Spring, as impassable as the Crossing. The women trapped her in the most painful isolation of all. Even Granny Ann reflected Betsey's resentment. Jerry, Patsy and Mary gave her trouble, as well, although Jerry and Patsy had warmed up a little. Richard often talked of bringing over Jacob and Lucy, perhaps Milly. But after a year of wishful thinking, she was giving up on that ever happening.

She refused to complain to Richard about her loneliness or anything else. Complainers riled her, a bequest from Jemima, as well as her mother. Neither of them would have had sympathy for any of her complaints. "Complaining shows a lack of faith in God's will," Jemima's voice rattled in her head. Most of the time, she couldn't hear the difference between that voice and her own.

After the first day Jemima put her to real work, she'd cried in bed about the pain in her legs. Was she even five years old? Mama'd told her to "keep your mind on what you see and hear, not on what you fetch and carry. Pay attention. Everything you learn is another tool in your kit in case you find yourself free one day. And if you can't be free, at least you won't be burning up at the rope walk or slaving in the fields."

I listened, Mama. I'm free. I've learned how to do everything Jemima taught me and then some. But I'm so, so alone.

As constant as her childish chores had been, as pointless as her tasks were now, they had no comparison with minding hemp and tobacco. She watched their people trudge in from the fields, and she looked over at the stones barricading the land they worked. Slaves, like stones, had no choice but to bear their burdens and couldn't complain. And she had not been able to lighten their loads or bear their burdens, not even little Patsy's.

McPherson rode up the main drive to the house, then headed toward his place. His bent head made clumps of sleet fall off the point of his hat rim. She sighed with relief, not feeling up to the task of dealing with him. Perhaps he'd missed lunch and only wanted an early supper. Why did he make her uneasy? He avoided being alone with her and never came in the house unless Richard was there. She wondered what her husband had threatened to do to him if any harm ever came to her. But what had her husband said to their overseer about the other girls at Blue Spring? McPherson or any man from the village could easily come down the hill onto their property, corner a girl and find a place to damage her.

Stop! She told herself. Every plain, ordinary thought these days turned dark. Jemima used to fret over Betsey for the same reason. "Melancholia overtakes many an expectant mother because Death breathes so heavy down their necks. But it's just the good Lord's way of reminding a woman to set her house in order."

Julia had already turned her rounds over to Daphne and Phoebe. They'd probably been born about the same time as Richard, a period of madness for all names Greek and Roman, like Richard's Mentor and John T's Telemachus. The sisters had six children between them, midwifed babies and served as healers before she came to Blue

Spring. They'd been a bit put off by her arrival, she found out much later when Granny Ann dropped one of her hateful insinuations.

Perhaps it was a trick of her mind, like Betsey's melancholia, but she felt an urgent need to pick up a quill and begin a letter of farewell to Richard in the event she died during childbirth. He wouldn't be home until April. She got herself comfortable at his little desk in the study, but her resolve to remain level-headed crumbled after she wrote the first words, "My darling husband." She persevered for over an hour until she had something to leave him in case the worst happened.

Patsy came to the study, carrying a tray of broth and toast with a dish of fig preserves balanced precariously on the edge. Butter and fried foods made Julia's stomach burn, and Granny Ann had been insulted by her food staying untouched. This combination allowed Julia a little relief and kept Granny from resenting her too much.

The child built the fire a bit higher, then ran when her grandmother hollered. Julia finished the broth and started on the toast she had spread thick with figs. A jolt hit underneath her navel. She put down the food.

The next jolt made her cry out. She tried to stand, but collapsed to her knees, and saw the crimson stain on the chair cushion. Julia watched in horror as the blood followed the pattern thread by thread. "Patsy!"

Julia screamed when the next pain ripped through her, starting in her chest and ending in her thighs. She dropped to the floor but had to drag herself across the room to the door. She pried it open a few inches. "Patsy! I need you!"

It was Mary, carrying an apron of kindling up the stairs, who heard her. The girl dropped the sticks, and Julia heard them tumbling down the stairs. "Mary, get Granny Ann," she grunted between pains.

"Blood!" Mary told her grandmother as she tugged her toward the study.

"Fetch Jerry," the old woman said through gritted teeth. After grabbing a stack of clean rags and a pitcher of water, she headed to Julia.

"Granny," Julia panted as dizzying nausea welled up. The pressure in her abdomen exploded and she screamed in a long wail. Blood seeped through her dress onto the floor. Mary and Jerry found their grandmother making a hopeless attempt to stanch the blood pouring from Julia. "Mary, get me some thick blankets and some sheets and spread them on the sofa. Run now, hurry," Granny Ann coaxed.

"Jerry, yell for Patsy. The three of us can get her on the sofa. Then you fly to Doc Theobald."

"Take the wagon? The buggy?" he panted, weakening at the sight of Julia's ghostly face and the pool of blood beneath her.

"No! Too slow. Just jump on a fast horse, soon as you get Patsy for me." But Patsy was already there, kneeling beside Julia, taking a rag and wetting it, swabbing off the beads of cold sweat on Julia's face.

Mary spread a sheet on the sofa. "No, child, put blanket first, then sheets," Granny Ann instructed her quietly. "More sheets. That's my good girl."

Julia's eyes opened. Her face contorted in pain before she let out a shriek. When the pain subsided, they lifted her onto the sofa. Jerry tore off for the doctor. Granny removed the gown and undergarments, hiked Julia's shift above her knees and covered her with a sheet and blanket.

"Mary, fetch a bucket and come back for these things, then get 'em soaking right quick. We may be able to rescue that gown."

Granny wedged the rest of the pile of rags under Julia's hips, hoping to stop the flow of blood. Julia's eyes fluttered open, and she looked with despair into the soft brown eyes of her cook.

"I'm losing the baby, Granny, aren't I? I've attended other women, doing this..." She moaned, but it rose out of control into a scream.

Granny Ann looked at Julia's bunched, hard abdomen. "Do you feel like you have to push, child?"

"No, not yet. I want to throw up, though. I feel so sick, Granny," she whimpered.

"It happens that way, sometime. Listen child, I've sent for Doctor Theobald. We've got the blood stanched for now, and if you don't feel like pushin' you may be keepin' this baby." She motioned to Patsy to light the candles. "I've seen it happen when lots of blood comes out, but if the mama stays put till it's full time to have it, well, those babies seem to turn out just as good as any other, so don't you be worryin'."

Granny Ann's throat tightened as she looked down on Julia's blanched face.

She's just a scared child. Lord forgive an old woman.

It was under an hour, but by the time Theobald rushed into the room, Julia's urge to push had become too great to control. Within minutes, the doctor held in his hands a perfectly formed little boy the size of a large yam. He folded the lost baby in a piece of cloth from the pile of stanching rags.

"I want to see him," Julia commanded.

"Let me clean him up a bit for you, child," Granny offered, exchanging glances with the doctor.

"No!" Julia gasped. "I want to see...everything."

Granny dabbed at the little body with a damp cloth. She loosened the tiny fists, then hesitantly placed him in his mother's hand. He covered her palm, his legs dangling onto her wrists. She stroked him as she would a drowned kitten, tears silently streaming down her face, sobs ratcheting her chest.

"We were going to name him George, Doctor Theobald. I found he was coming just a few weeks after George's accident."

The doctor shook his head. The baby was a grim reminder of standing helpless over that handsome Johnson boy whose neck had broken from a horse jump gone wrong.

"I know this baby helped me forget losing the other one a little bit. I had hoped our baby might help Richard get over losing his brother."

Theobald had little to say at times like these, but he made an effort for Julia's sake. "Life always has a way of helping us get over death, it's true."

"Granny Ann, I have a rosewood box on my dressing table. Send Patsy up to get it. We'll bury him in that."

She raised the baby to her lips and kissed him. Granny Ann carefully lifted him away.

Once again, Julia's face contorted in pain, and her body shuddered. She expelled the afterbirth with another gasp of pain. "The blood," she said, lifting her head toward Theobald. "It's like Mama. There's so much of it. What happened?"

"My guess is that he tore away from the uterine wall," he answered absently as he inspected the afterbirth. "Had you been riding, or running up and down these stairs, as you ought not?"

"No riding. I promised Richard from the beginning. But the stairs..." Her weak voice trailed off to a whisper and tears fell from the corners of her eyes. "I've been preparing all month. Jemima always said that staying strong, that stairs and such, made you stronger for your lying-in."

Theobald exhaled, his mouth a tight line trying to contain his frustration. "The Suggetts and the Johnsons are like Adam and Eve, Julia. They're practically made of iron. But you...come from more delicate stock."

"But I am strong, you know that!"

"Strong in mind and will doesn't necessarily mean strong in childbearing. There's much more to be considered, like the shape of the pelvis and..." He stopped his lecture, softening his tone. "The point is, my dear, you need to dissuade yourself of following her old ways. You need to take more heed of me. I am very fond of you and Richard, and I would take it as a personal affront if you miscarried again, or worse—far worse—for want of following my advice. I shall write your husband directly and emphasize to him the importance of you not overexerting yourself."

"He'll be so very disappointed in me." She closed her eyes and let the tears fall.

"Nonsense. I will tell him he should be wild with joy that you didn't hemorrhage to death."

"But he lost his son because I was so foolish."

"If you are very careful, and do exactly as you're told, there will be more children, probably." In truth, her pallor and feebleness troubled him. He needed to find the proper words to rally her mental strength. "When does your husband return?"

"April," she whispered, her throat swollen from weeping.

"Good. That will give you ample time to regain your strength and be ready to give him a proper welcome when he does return. Meanwhile, you are to lie here as still as possible, for at least three days, perhaps longer. Do you understand?"

Her beautiful eyes, emerald from tears, looked at him in alarm. He felt her pulse, weak but steady now, then took her hand gently. "You need rest, dear girl, for your mind as well as your body. You are not to reproach yourself under any circumstances. These things happen to most women at least once or twice, and it is nobody's fault. You're strong enough, and young. And you can bring more help into your house so that you need not come to such a state again."

"Yes, alright," she mumbled. Her eyelids fluttered. "Thank you for your care. I have come to believe you are my only friend. Besides

Richard." She smiled wearily at him then closed her eyes and fell into a deep sleep.

PATSY AWOKE, FORGETTING for a moment where she was. When her eyes adjusted, she remembered her grandmother had fixed a pallet of blankets for her in front of the fireplace. The doctor sat by her mistress, holding her hand then raising it to his lips. He kissed it as gently as Julia had kissed that little dead baby. Patsy lowered her eyes. Her heart jumped at the sight of the doctor giving way to soft feelings.

As soon as he noticed her, the mean look came back to his face. He put his fingers on Miz Julia's wrist, but that didn't fool Patsy.

"Go back to sleep."

Used to getting orders, this was one she was happy to obey.

Theobald poked the embers in the fire; the room was cooler now, which he preferred for his patient. It would be the ruin of him if word of his sentimental gesture got out. He had a wife now and didn't need any bad feelings between them. He looked over at the child, asleep already. Perhaps she hadn't seen anything. He, on the other hand, could not sleep.

He scanned Richard's bookshelves: an enviable collection of nearly one hundred volumes, most on the subject of law, but some on philosophy, and a surprising number of titles from literature. How he wished he had the money to indulge in his own passion for books.

Deciding to practice his rusty German, he settled on a volume of Schiller plays and began *Die Jungfrau von Orleans*. But after reading a dozen pages, he found himself berating Richard. Young women like Joan of Arc lived on in those like Julia, willing to sacrifice everything, and for what? Richard seemed unaware of what Julia's life was like. What difference did it make if they burned at a stake or bled to death in miscarriage? Both were a waste of women with valuable spirit.

Julia stirred and made an effort to raise her head, moving as if to arise from the couch. With his arm outstretched, he managed to just stop her from getting up, but the precious book fell from his lap. "Stay down," he ordered.

Her eyes opened and surprise gave way to relief. "You're here with me!"

Resisting the urge to return her smile, he answered awkwardly, "You need to take a little nourishment." He poured a cup of broth from the kettle left on the fire. Julia lifted her hands to the cup but they slid to her chest.

"I must try!" she insisted.

"You must do nothing but stay still," he replied too sternly. "I'm quite capable of feeding you a little broth," he added in a kinder tone, putting the spoon between her lips. She sputtered, and it dribbled down the sides of her mouth.

"Let's raise your head a bit, shall we?" After helping her, he picked the book from the floor and saw that the soft leather corner had bent in the fall. "Damnation!"

"I'm sorry," she whispered.

"Why? I dropped one of Richard's books, and was giving myself a well-deserved curse." When he sat down by her again, she offered him a shy smile.

"Can you manage a little more broth?"

Julia nodded. She answered his questions about her discomforts between sips. "It's all to be expected, under the circumstances," he said, trying for a note of assurance in his voice. "I will tell you honestly, a few hours ago I wouldn't have thought you'd be here having Granny's broth."

"So, that's why you stayed."

"Richard would never have forgiven me if I'd left you at the mercy of an old woman and two children with death knocking at the door."

She managed to drink more of the rich broth, which heartened Theobald. He changed her stanching cloths and found the blood flow down to a trickle. He stirred the coals in the grate again, rousing Patsy. "Go back to sleep, child. You as well, Julia. Sleep, if you can."

"Would you read to me, from the book you dropped?" she asked.

"It's in German...will you understand?"

"No, but I love the sound."

Within a stanza, Patsy fell back to sleep. Within a few pages, Julia slipped off. It's just as well she cannot understand the words, he thought; they'd break her heart, as did everything Schiller wrote.

Unable to sleep, he wandered about the downstairs of the house like an envious ghost. The beautiful red parlor, now black and gray in the dark, had a pleasant scent of clove and orange pomanders. When he reached the pianoforte and passed his fingers gently over the keys, he thought of Julia's skill and how she had improved over the years.

He couldn't shake the old nagging wish to take Julia in hand and give her real medical training. Her little book about herbal treatments had been such a good idea. Too bad she'd given up on it.

Julia's case was unlike anything in his experience. Not this miscarriage mess—that was ordinary enough in the scheme of things—but the breach with society, the flaunting of propriety. When he called on patients, he had to listen constantly to all the nonsense about these two.

Richard came off unscathed more often than not, and Julia, who had no freedom or status, who had to make do without a husband most of the time, bore most of the rancor. She had no friends, as she so pathetically told him. And why had Richard insisted on those damned soirées and dinners? Couldn't the man see the torment his wife experienced under the scrutiny of these people?

At least she possessed Richard, mind and body. The man was mad about her—any fool could see that, and any fool could understand why. He thought the Johnsons utter, stupid fools, too proud to take back their son, as well as the girl they had raised almost as their own.

He pulled back the drapery; the rain had stopped, and a faint hint of dawn tinted the horizon a grayish pink. He was exhausted; he needed to be home in his own bed, embracing his own wife, not letting his thoughts and emotions run away from him.

But he knew himself well enough to realize that Julia's spell over him would break with the coming sunrise. At least this night he'd gotten a sense of the desperate solitude she experienced day after day. If she survived the week, he hoped she'd be able to keep her sanity.

He walked back to the study and checked on his patient. She had slept soundly for several hours and was probably out of danger. He, however, was not. He put Schiller back on the shelf, being careful to avoid stepping on Patsy. Granny Ann and Mary made scraping noises in the pantry, and he smelled good food—sausages and coffee. He knew it was intended for him, and he had enough of an appetite to do it justice.

Granny pushed open the pantry and nodded to him. He followed her to the dining room where Mary had a fire going, and soon found himself in Richard's armchair devouring everything before him. As he finished, Granny asked if he would step out to the pantry. Two slave women wrapped in blankets waited to talk to him.

"Yes, what is it?" he asked.

"Doctor, this here's Daphne and Phoebe. They do the healing down at the quarters since Julia's been confined. They were telling me she sent Jerry down to 'em yesterday sayin' to come to the house this mornin.'"

"You told them about the miscarriage?"

Granny nodded. Turning to the women, he asked, "Which of you is the stronger?"

"That'd have to be me, sir," the taller of the two spoke up. "Phoebe."

"Can you lift Miz Julia's weight?"

"Sure, I can. She's tall but not much bigger round than a tobacco stalk."

"You'll have to keep her still, feed her, put the chamber pot under her, for five or six days. And promise me, you'll not give her any of your medicines. I can't risk her having a reaction to some herb—she's barely survived this. Do I have your word?"

Phoebe nodded. "I can do all that. Long as Granny here don't mind. And Miz Julia don't mind me being in her house. And Daphne don't mind looking after my kids."

"Alright. If anything happens, have Jerry come for me." The women nodded to him with several 'yessirs' and went in separate directions. He gathered his coat, hat and bag and walked quickly away from the house, forcing himself to leave his thoughts of Julia where they belonged.

RICHARD'S EYES FLASHED open. It was an old nightmare followed by a new one. Old Senator Marshall was firing at him with a pistol from the far end of the rope walk. The noise of the gun shots, so real in his dream, had startled him wide awake. But it was only Matthew's sharp, popping snores.

Too bad. He regretted that Clay had only wounded that bitter, angry fool last year in a real duel. Humphrey Marshall and his poison newspaper were making life hell for him, Clay and just about anybody else who held office in Kentucky.

The new session would start in a few hours. He had an opening-day speech that was sure to fire up this stale group to finally grant Louisiana statehood. He needed it to temper his reputation as a war hawk. He'd been warned to leave off his bellicose style because his party didn't like him being derided as a windbag. Ha! Too bad. His calls to war last session had rallied quite a number to their side. He saw his role as Madison's spur to action. But he'd spurred and goaded for three years, so he had to admit it was time to do something different.

He thought about Suzanne reading today's speech. Truth was, he'd written it for her, and she'd know it, too, if she ever saw it. If it wasn't buried between auction notices on the last page of the New Orleans *Moniteur*. He felt a slight ache near his heart, like the press of her head upon his chest.

Julia made him happy, but she had none of Suzanne's flash in a good argument, no flare for matching wits. His girl had no experience with the world; how could she? Her only exposure had come while sitting quietly in a corner with her sewing, catching the gist of debates. At least she had more education than most women, free or slave. Thanks Ma, for that if nothing else. He wondered how Suzanne had acquired hers. Funny, they never had talked about such things.

A new idea made his mind race: why not a bill in favor of public education for women, maybe for slaves, or even Indians. The thought of a new crusade suddenly energized him, until reality hit. It would be easier to annul slavery than to get those fellows to support anything that had to do with education. People had to take care of such things on their own.

Should he make a plan to further educate Julia? Let her alone, fool, he chided himself. He'd heard earfuls about stubborn, opinionated wives on the trips back and forth to Washington. No man could have a more perfect wife. Didn't he get enough of debate and ideas while he was here? What man wanted to discuss work with his wife, anyway? He had better ways to spend his time with her.

The thought of killing Marshall in that dream flashed into his head. He could not stop his mind from repeating over and over, entirely against his will, the man's words. The newspaper had held out against him for over a year, but now Marshall's writing had turned vicious and personal. Richard knew his district was secure and he didn't fear being voted out. What he did fear was his family being torn even farther apart. The entire Marshall family seemed bent on destroying the reputation of all the Johnsons.

He lay there playing a forced memory game, trying to recall every dealing between the Johnsons and the Marshalls over the years. Their families were both wealthy and influential, but not so different from hundreds of others. Most of Marshall's latest attacks had centered on Pa, not himself. Marshall and Pa were the same age. Maybe all this came from an old grudge.

Maybe Marshall wanted to get to Henry Clay through him. Did he have enough to sue for libel? That was the kind of duel he could fight and win. It would show his father that he cared about him.

Richard missed his father and hated the void that separated them. The distance between Great Crossing and Blue Spring had become as wide as that which lay between home and here. He lay there listening to his roommate's brisk snores and had to laugh. Ma always snored when she was expecting. Did Julia snore yet?

A slosh and a scraping noise of pottery on the floorboards outside his door alerted him to the arrival of the hot water. He rolled out of bed, glad to have the chance of beating Matthew to it. As he crossed the chilly bedroom, he had a pang for the warmth of his room at Blue Spring. He'd have a son, maybe a daughter, a month old by the time he got back. He'd have to write Theobald tonight.

Chapter 6
Preparations
March 1811, on the Cumberland Road

Richard suffered from wretched irritability. He and the rest of the Kentucky delegation were forced to a snail's crawl by the wind and freezing rain. For two weeks in the saddle, he'd been unable to shake this melancholy, despite the good-natured talk of his fellow travelers. The attacks from Marshall had intensified. As foolish as it sounded, he had decided to take Henry Clay's remedy and challenge him to a duel. No reasoning, legal or otherwise, had gotten through to him. Maybe a bullet would.

He brooded on images of the son he'd fathered. Julia wrote that he had been a perfect child but so tiny he'd fit in her hand. One thing he'd learned and repeated to himself over and over: common sorrows become extraordinary when they become your own.

He wondered what Julia would really be like. Her letters were cheerful enough, too cheerful in fact. Theobald wrote how she had told him she preferred death to disappointing her husband. How was he ever to make her understand what she meant to him, to exorcise the slave from her mind? He gave her everything a woman could want. He'd left his family behind for her. *God, give me strength to help her think like a free woman.*

Clay and the others had lost children and learned to accept it, not that they were heartless. He'd been the recipient of their

223

generosity and loyalty for four years. But discussing his loss, his Julia, seemed too sacred a pearl to cast before anyone. He had an innate wariness when it came to talking about her.

What would he say to her? Nothing would suffice, he feared. Perhaps pretend it never happened. No, that was what his mother did. Julia wrote about placing little George in her beautiful rosewood box, giving him a proper burial under one of the maple trees, and marking the place with a white stone. The image of the two of them standing over the little marker suddenly gave him some much-needed peace. "Peace I give unto you, not as the world giveth..."

His heart felt lighter with that, and as he rode along getting stung by the sleet, he had no doubt that God had put that in his heart. He'd let her know that he loved her more than sons. This recess would be different; he would spend his time by her side, and perhaps she wouldn't object to trying again for a child. And perhaps he wouldn't kill Marshall.

Late summer 1811

J ulia wandered through the herb bed in her kitchen garden,
putting sprigs into her basket. She needed to concoct an infusion
to fight off nausea and constipation. Richard and Theobald
sauntered in the shade near the house while Jerry got the doctor's rig
ready. The sight of them together left her a bit giddy and more than
a little confused. The doctor hadn't known she was expecting again
until Richard told him this morning. This visit must have had
something to do with the mess they had gotten into with the
Marshalls.

Last week, Lewis Marshall stabbed Richard's oldest brother
James on the courthouse steps. William, as the next oldest Johnson
male, chased the assailant all the way to Lexington to challenge him.
Then Humphrey Marshall and Richard got involved with their own
drama. But somehow, the final two players in the duel had come
down to Lewis and Richard. She couldn't help blaming herself for
that awful night five years ago when Richard had nearly killed Lewis
for her sake.

"I'm warning you, Richard, if you go through with this duel,
you'll be the death of this new baby, and maybe Julia, as well. We
came too close to losing her last time." Theobald managed to keep his
emotions under control, but he wanted to throttle the man.

"I've explained everything to Julia. She agrees that our family
honor cannot be defended any other way."

"What else was she supposed to say?" Theobald muttered
irritably. Richard would have said Julia agreed with him even if she

225

had begged him on her knees not to fight. Which was probably closer to the truth.

"Lewis Marshall is a notorious drunk. Your brother's stab wound is superficial, and his life is in no peril. There's simply no reason for you and your brothers to pursue this."

"Impossible. You know the Marshalls have given our family no peace for years. What I'd rather do is burn their newspaper." He gave Theobald a wicked grin. "Writing endless rebuttals to their libel's one thing, Theo, but letting them get away with attempted murder?" Richard had the gleeful attitude of a schoolboy setting up a prank. How could he be so cavalier? It smacked of arrogance, Theobald fumed, returning the impish smile with his own version of a schoolmaster's warning scowl.

"What is this all about, Richard? I've known both your families for quite a few years, and this feud seems to have come out of nowhere."

"Petty politics. Jealousy. Our family's more influential, that's all." Richard glanced toward Julia. No; she would never have confided Lewis's attack on her to Theo.

The doctor continued to glower. "Then use your influence in a rational way. Didn't you people learn anything in Washington after Hamilton's death? What if, God forbid, something should happen to you? Julia and this child would have no one. Who's going to defend them?"

Julia looked up as the doctor's voice escalated. Their eyes met for a moment; she turned quickly away. Richard turned to look again at his wife, and a thought shamed him: *Theo sounds as if he loves her more than I do.*

He watched Jerry drive the doctor's rig onto the pebble drive. As he and Theobald walked the few steps toward it, he felt a pang of jealousy, but dismissed it. Impossible for his devoted Julia to find anything attractive in such a cold fish. The thought made him want to laugh.

"Tell you what. I believe we have an honorable way out. Marshall has choice of weapons, and I know he'll choose rapier. I'll say—and it's the truth—I cannot use a sword. He knows I'm a crack shot, but he's terrible with a pistol. Why do you think he stabbed James? I'm betting that will be the end of it."

The dogs and horses made too much racket as the buggy left for Julia to say a word. She stood and waited for the din to die down, holding the crushed mint under her nose until the churning in her stomach died down, as well.

"The duel?" she asked, not wanting to waste any time finagling an explanation out of Richard.

"You wouldn't be too disappointed in me if I found a way around it?" He took the little basket of clippings from her hand and held it to his nose. It made him sneeze, and they both laughed at the thunderous sound he made.

Julia was glad for the chance to quash her anxiety with a good laugh instead of a cry. "Honor can be saved in all sorts of ways, Richard. But what changed your mind?"

"He is the oddest man, Theo."

Richard put his hand on the small of her back and headed them toward the bench he had built near little George's grave. When they sat, he took her hand and kissed it. "He reminded me that I have to protect you and this baby first. He called me up short."

She closed her eyes for a moment and saw those long, elegant hands holding little George's tiny form.

"I understand why you want to protect the entire family. Their newspaper has ridiculed everybody, even your sisters. But I've never been able to get worked up by them because they've left us alone. And I don't understand, Richard. I'm such an easy target. Why pick on Betsey and Sallie instead of me?"

"I hope it's because I scared enough of the devil out of Lewis on your account already."

He sat quietly for a minute, watching the wind ruffle the thin fabric of her summer frock. When one of the hounds sniffed them out, he picked up a stick and played a game of fetch for a few minutes. Julia knew something weighed on him that he wanted to talk about, but all she could do was wait.

Finally, he stood and put his foot up on the bench, letting the stick fly out of sight so the dog would give them some peace for a minute. "It's hard to talk about dying, Jewel. This duel won't happen, but war's coming, and the diplomats can't keep it at bay much longer. Besides, you know me, and you know I've been the loudest voice shouting for it. I'm going to have to fight, and there'll be no way out of it for me."

"You wouldn't want a way out of it, you mean." She squinted as she looked up into his face. He moved to block the sun from her eyes, and she thanked him before venturing a guess at the reason for their conversation. "You must have a will, but I don't know what's in it. Are you worried about what's going to happen if the war takes you?"

"I love how you read my mind," he said with a little smile. Just like my folks used to, he thought. "My fear is this, darlin' girl, five of my brothers have gone into law. I've left Blue Spring to you and our children, but if this baby doesn't make it, and I go to war in a few months and get killed, you may not have a chance against them. I've got to find a way to arm you to fight your own war."

"I'm not afraid, Richard. I have learning. Even if they take away everything you've given me, I'll have my freedom."

He looked toward the house and the reflection of the sun off its windows. "Yes. Well."

Chapter 7
Prophecy
December 1811. Washington, DC

"War is necessary," Richard began softly, like a preacher. Only a few in the House chamber refused to nod their heads in agreement. "Great Britain has failed to fulfill her promises or to offer redress for the wrongs she has committed. Regardless of our moderation and justice, she has brought home to the threshold of our territory measures of actual war. Upon the Wabash and within our territorial sea the war has already commenced! We must now oppose the farther encroachment of Great Britain by war, or formally annul the Declaration of our Independence, and acknowledge ourselves her devoted Colonies!"

As the hall filled with shouts of encouragement, he let his voice soar. "I pledge myself to this House, and my constituency to this nation, that they will not be wanting in valor, nor in their proportion of men and money to prosecute the war with effect. I shall never die contented until I see England's expulsion from North America and her territories incorporated with the United States!"

The Speaker of the House, his comrade Henry Clay, grinned and pounded his gavel.

"Couldn't have said it better yourself, Henry!" Richard goaded his friend as they walked back to the Franklin Inn hours later.

"Of course, I could've! Damn irony, being Speaker of the House. I don't get to speak nearly as much as I used to. Have to leave it to the likes of you."

At dinner that night, Richard sat down to a tribute of knives clanging on water glasses. "You spoke bravely for all of us Kentuckians, Johnson. I think we all, to a man, would march out with you and have Canada annexed this time next year!" Sam McKee gushed.

"I don't think it'll be long," Richard replied with a huge grin. "General Harrison's victory at Prophet's Town has surely stirred up a hornet's nest." Word of the November seventh attack on the Shawnee village near Tippecanoe Creek had only recently reached them.

"If anyone deserves the nickname of prophet, it's you, Johnson!" Desha laughed. When Lyons decided not to run again, Desha had been installed as Richard's new roommate. "Now, if you could just foresee a way to afford raising an army!"

"There's no mystery in that. We're a country of militiamen," Richard said. Between bites of pork chop, he pointed out that Napoleon had trained thousands of men to attack on horseback first, then let the foot soldiers clean up. "I've no doubt that I could muster a thousand men in Scott County alone willing to train with me to make up a mounted militia."

The men passed his idea around and chewed on it like part of the meal. McKee argued, "You've got too much faith in our men back home, Johnson. It's thirty years since the Revolution. They may talk like a passel of hot heads, but just you try to round 'em up and organize 'em!" McKee switched to a high-pitched twangy voice. "I ain't gonna let my prize stallion ride in front of British regs! You lost yer cotton-pickin' mind?"

They all hollered. McKee was a born mimic.

Desha stopped laughing long enough to add, "He's right. I can't think of a single Kentuckian who'd let one of his prize horses onto a battlefield. And let's face it, back home *all* our horses is prize horses!"

McKee took over again. "This war that's coming isn't the same as the old one. The war for independence was about honor, and all sorts of ideals. Men no longer cling to sentiment. Men today are all about themselves, making farming a business, and that's what this is really about—business! Should we go to war over trade rights and access to waterways?"

"Easterners may take that line of argument, but I've heard too many men back home say they'd rather fight than negotiate one more trade deal with the British," Richard answered. "After all, McKee, our livelihood is our honor."

"You're forgetting the Tecumseh alliance, aren't you?" Anthony New, their freshman congressman, asked.

"Not a bit," Richard answered. "Your district as well as mine has been affected by the way his confederation has messed up trade along the northern territories. And we have us a war started now, between Harrison's troops and Tecumseh's. It's no secret the British are supplying his people. I still think a militia on horseback, trained to shoot at men instead of game, would be as unstoppable as Napoleon's corsairs."

McKee cackled and added, "Any one of my horses is smarter than any man here! They wouldn't be fool enough to gallop headlong into a blaze of rifle fire or cannon. Not like all you war mongers seem willing enough to do."

"Clay, you're a horseman. We got plenty of breeds back home that would probably do as fine in a battle as they do on the hunt, don't you think?"

"I'll put my mind to it, Dick," he said. "Meantime, Little Peg, ask your mama if she's got any more of that sweet potato pie." The girl ran back to the kitchen.

"Wouldn't you agree you can't get much more stable a breed than our quarter horses? There's something almost unearthly about their intelligence. And they're plentiful back home," Richard put in.

Little Peg came back to the dining room. "Mama said there's pie coming out of the oven, but it needs to set, unless you men want it running off your plates!"

Clay smiled at her and patted her hand. "Well, you tell her we'll enjoy her pie with our spoons instead of our forks and love it all the same!"

Peg rewarded him with a hug and trotted back to give her mother the message.

Desha spoke up. "Well, I wouldn't be too concerned about any of this. If we go to war, it'll be over in a matter of weeks. What with the trouble Napoleon's giving everyone on the other side, King George'd be hard pressed to spare his regs for a full-scale war over here."

"He may have enough here already," Richard corrected. "The Great Lakes are plagued with their schooners. And with Tecumseh's confederacy, they only need as many Brits as necessary to train the Indians."

"The Shawnee need to train the British, to my way of thinking. You can't get a finer warrior," McKee said.

"You can count on war not going according to plans. There's going to be plenty of battles to go around on land, but the entire mess we've been in with England since independence has been at sea. Madison has my vote to get the naval works over yonder at Anacostia fired up," Desha said.

"The goal of warfare is to weaken your enemy, then destroy it, no matter where you engage them," Richard raised his voice to talk over the clamor: Mrs. O'Neale had just stepped out with her pie.

"And the redcoats patrolling the western forts and supplying the Indians—don't you know they would relish any excuse for incursions into Indiana and Michigan? Our trade stations and settlements just look like ripe fruit waiting to be picked. I foresee this threat in the west, and for my money, Kentucky has the only men who can stop them."

Desha, refusing the pie, handed Little Peg his napkin. She laid it in the basket on the sideboard, ready for tomorrow's breakfast. "Like I said earlier, Dick's our new prophet. Better listen up, everybody!"

Chapter 8
Imogene
February 17, 1812

It was cold. Theobald would be happy for that, because birthing was a bloody business, and this time Julia wanted to keep as much of her own blood as possible. For three months after losing little George, she felt like a rag doll without any stuffing in her hands and knees.

Since this wasn't exactly her first lying-in, she had an easier time relaxing. Knowing the pain hurt like a torture did not help too much, but it gave her the good sense to know she would most likely survive. She had a few relaxing herbs from Daphne and Phoebe that she didn't plan on mentioning to Theobald. She'd set pretty ornaments and figurines about the room to distract her a little.

Julia knew she was ready and thought how like preparing for battle it really was. Most women came through alright, though too many died, and medicines for childbirth now dominated her book since she had gone back to compiling it. A new farewell letter to Richard lay safely tucked inside his top desk drawer. Since she had begun writing in earnest this year, she found the letter she wrote to him last time so poorly crafted it shamed her.

She wrote one to the child, too, expressing her love, and that she would be watching from above, and to have faith in God. Granny Ann said it was bad luck to do such a thing, but Richard said in these enlightened times there was no place for luck, only the will of Providence and good medical skill.

Theobald's suspicious attitude toward Daphne and Phoebe disappointed her. Over the past year, those two had provided her with fascinating anecdotes about midwifery and helped her refine and adjust countless concoctions for her kit. During her pregnancy, she had to stop making her rounds to keep Richard and Dr. Theobald satisfied. But an inspiration had come to her—she set some funds aside to "hire out" Daphne and Phoebe to do it. She hoped they would earn enough to buy their freedom. Their men earned extra from smithy jobs, but to free the whole family would still take years' more baby deliveries and iron work.

The number of people at Blue Spring had already doubled since their marriage. Julia's ledger now listed fifty-five names. Putting each name in her book as McPherson or Phoebe brought her the news of a new acquisition or birth filled her with a mixture of loathing and helplessness. Although Julia and McPherson remained wary of each other, they accepted the fact theirs had become a conspiracy to make Richard think he deserved all the credit for making Blue Spring a success.

Theobald now used a midwife to cover the hours of early labor. Charlotte Lindsay was a Scotswoman who came with her husband and two teenage children to run one of the mills at the Great Crossing village. Her name evoked images of a delicate and feminine person with curled hair and lace trims.

The woman preparing the bedstead with knotted ropes and a stack of stanching cloths a yard high had her hair in a severe coil and wore the plainest dress imaginable. Her arms showed muscle through the fabric, and although the woman was not as tall as Julia, the power of her frame made her look taller by three inches. She smiled easily enough and her voice, though she had so far only spoken about ten words, was soothing.

"I'm to send word to the doctor when your water's broke. If all goes well, you'll be done by sunset."

Julia took a deep breath.

"You've had breakfast?" Julia nodded yes. "Then no more food except for some of that tea I've brewed up."

Charlotte shooed away Patsy and her tray, saying, "Best you and the others stay downstairs, child." She then closed the door to the bedroom.

The restlessness and unease started yesterday. Julia felt like one of the mother cats she'd seen mewing and circling about in the hours before kittens came. But she had prepared everything well in advance. Last night, dull pains started, and by sunrise had become regular. When she lost little George, there had been no warning of any kind. The pains had been violent and immediate, the tragic results within three hours.

Charlotte made her walk the long upstairs hallway, breathing long and deep, blowing air out when the pains subsided. Her water broke before noon. She heard Jerry gallop off, making her heart pound at the thought of Theobald's arrival. It made her ashamed to be so eager for his presence, too much like the way she felt when Richard was due home. This attraction alarmed her now, because it was not her husband's face she envisioned smiling over their baby, but Theobald's.

She could barely walk for the pains. They were close, regular and relentless, like jabs from a knife in her flesh, and blows from a hammer on her bones. Nausea overwhelmed her, and she panicked for a moment. She leaned against the wall and pictured little George again. When she looked down, there were no signs of blood, despite the intense pain.

At last, the midwife had her go to bed and lie on her side. She held on to one of the ropes while Charlotte massaged her back with a salve that turned warm on her skin.

There was no talk between them. Words added to her distress, taking on labor-like edges of their own. The silence soothed her. It allowed her to hear the surging of blood in her head and made her wonder if the baby's heart was synchronized with her own, or if it had a separate rhythm now that they were about to be parted.

She fell asleep between pains, naps no longer than two minutes, but she dreamed—of her mother, Jemima, and the Johnson boys when they were little. She heard the gurgle of the old spring water pipe and felt the stiffness of her cot at the foot of Jemima's bed. Then the strangling, tightening pull in her abdomen woke her, revealing the contours of a little head or foot. Or perhaps she dreamed that, as well.

"The doctor's here." Charlotte said but stayed by her side. As Theobald climbed the stairs, Julia fell asleep again, then opened her eyes wide when he placed his hands, so soothing in their icy coldness, on her abdomen. He pressed firmly. "Good positioning, everything's progressing rapidly, Mrs. Lindsay. It will be soon."

"Thank you for being here. Charlotte has done well..." Julia's face crumpled. She gasped, trying to breathe properly, but to no avail. "This is different now. It's so very...severe..."

Her voice slid out of control. She writhed, reaching out for Charlotte's hand, which she squeezed with ferocity. Between her clenched teeth, she let out a scream, pushing down urgently, despite her intention to be strong.

When the contraction subsided, Charlotte let go of Julia's hand and hurried toward the fireplace, where a kettle boiled on an iron plate. She poured steaming water into the basin, mixed it with cool water from the pitcher nearby, and had a shallow bath ready for the newborn. Julia felt a surge of hope as she watched Charlotte make this preparation.

"The head is showing now," Theobald told her. "Push. Harder than ever." Charlotte came to her side, and Julia gripped the woman's strong arms as she experienced a ripping, slamming force on her right pelvic bone that made her scream like an animal. Hot liquid seeped over her hips and up her back. A tiny wail grew louder and louder until it was drowned out by Charlotte's announcement, "A lass!"

Doctor Theobald smiled. Julia could not remember ever seeing him smile. He beamed at her, his narrow face suddenly beautiful as he met her eyes.

"Well done, Julia. Well done," he said quietly.

He finished the delivery of the afterbirth while Charlotte cleaned and oiled the screaming baby. Once she was swaddled in flannel, her cries subsided. With what little strength she could muster, Julia held out her arms for her daughter.

"Imogene," she whispered.

"What's that?" Theobald asked, smiling again. Relief at the success of this birth made him euphoric.

"From Shakespeare. Imogene. Faithful despite all the falsehoods told about her."

He nodded and stepped away to wash up in Richard's basin.

"She's rooting. That's a good sign." Charlotte turned her attention to the stanching cloths, cleaned Julia and removed another bloodied layer of linen, plopping it into the wash tub at the side of the bed.

The sound brought back the memory of her mother's tiny room, the hour when she and Theobald became bound to each other in some inexplicable way.

"Not a hitch to this birth, Doctor. As perfect as ever I've attended, am happy to say." Charlotte pulled a sheet and blanket over Julia's legs. "Mind if I stoke that fire now? There's no sign of unusual bleeding at all."

"Yes, the baby could use the warmth." As Theobald unrolled his sleeves, he walked back to Julia's side. "You know, a woman of your station should have a wet nurse."

Julia kept her eyes on the baby this time. "I've thought of it, but I want to do it myself. No one calls here, and I call on no one. My station, as you so kindly put it, is not acknowledged by anyone but you. And I thank you for that."

She looked like a dissheveled Madonna, and his heart began to beat fast. He needed to leave. "As you wish," he muttered, turning to Charlotte. "Can you be spared a while longer from the mill, Mrs. Lindsay?"

"Oh, aye. My children are old hands at turning and bagging. Ralph'd prefer me out of his way, truth be known."

"Then I'll have Jerry deliver word to the mill that you'll be here overnight." He reached the door, anxious to leave. His attraction to his patient, even after seeing her in the worst circumstances, unnerved him. He had to get his head clear. A good dose of cold night air would do it.

"I'll stay till sunrise, and come back after Ralph's had his breakfast," Mrs. Lindsay assured him.

"Good!" Looking again at Julia, he asked, "Are you comfortable with that arrangement, or would you prefer I stay?"

She fought the urge to ask him to stay, instead giving him a sleepy laugh. "Go home. A much happier outcome than our last adventure." By the time he turned to reply, she was asleep.

As Theobald waited for Jerry to bring him the buggy, he shook off his unwanted feelings for Julia by thinking about his own wife. He hoped his Nancy would prove as strong when her time came. But Imogene was an impossible name.

Good thing she hadn't chosen something worse from the Bard, like Cymbeline. Or Ophelia.

"I HAVE A DAUGHTER," Richard closed his eyes to hold back tears. He put down the letters from Julia and Theobald. No spring recess. Just as well—fathers didn't signify to a baby.

"Congratulations!" Clay replied, looking back down at his newspaper to protect Richard's pride. "Love my daughters. Great deal easier on the eyes and ears than the boys."

"I'm relieved they both came through it. And I am glad it's a girl. The last was a boy. I was afraid that she'd never be able to think of this child in the same way if it had been a boy, as well," Richard confided.

"Women take those kinds of things hard, alright," Clay muttered behind the paper, growing a bit uncomfortable. He'd heard the tales of Julia from gossips in his parlor back home. He had his own doubts about the validity of such a marriage, but Johnson had been honorable enough to stand in front of a minister to make it right in God's eyes. Clay had reservations about that part, too, but he could see both sides of the argument. At least Johnson had enough sense to keep his life to himself.

Getting on neutral ground, Clay asked, "Anybody from your neck of the woods mention that big earthquake out Missouri way? Paper says here nothing's left of New Madrid."

Richard chuckled. "They felt it back home, alright. China and pewter falling everywhere—scared my sister Sallie to death. She even went back to church. Once."

May 1812, Payne Farm near Great Crossing

"Listen to this, Bets," John said from the bedroom study. It was half past ten, and they finally had some time alone. He had before him the latest edition of the *American Republic*. "'*If they have war, they are told by their oracles, Richard Johnson and Henry Clay, that they are to have taxes*'—of course, we'll have more taxes. We can't fight a war without money, the idiots!—oh, here it is: '*Congressmen and their families, like the Johnsons, may get contracts and become rich.*' He didn't say 'like the Clays,' did he? They aggravate the hell out of me, and he goes on to call Dick a wind mill..."

"A *great* wind mill," Betsey corrected, "but it's just another one of those blasted Marshalls."

John looked up at her. "Since when have you taken an interest in the papers?"

"Since Lewis Marshall attacked my brother, and since the governor re-commissioned you a general. Since war is all anybody has talked about for..."

"Alright, I get your point!" he offered her a conciliatory smile. "I have to agree with his critics, even those evil Marshalls. Except I'd say he's more of a hurricane than a windmill. It takes him a hundred words when five will do."

"Well, maybe it takes that much to speak up for all of us back home. Be proud of him, honey."

"Yes. Well. You, of all people, know why I find that a bit difficult, being the oldest in a family he's torn apart."

John buried his head back in the paper rather than lose his chance to read it. He never should have given Betsey a chance to start on her brother again. He agreed with Richard's long-time evaluation of the situation: "Betsey thinks she owns me just because she saved my baby scalp from the Indians."

"That girl was more like one of our own children, John. How many did we have when Papa bought her?" Without waiting for an answer, she continued, "Three! She knew her place so I let her play with our daughters. But Mother spoiled her rotten."

"Well, she must've picked up something, because Blue Spring's doing better than everyone else's place," he muttered.

She ignored his attempt to be rational. "Now that she's finally had a baby, she'll think she actually owns Blue Spring!"

John stayed quiet. Part of Betsey's problem these days was the fact that she was carrying their thirteenth child.

"Why him, John? Why can't you, or James or William run for Congress? All three of you are more imposing. Surely you can't be satisfied with just being in the state legislature?"

"Simple, Bets. It's a day's ride to Frankfort, and nearly a month to Washington if it's bad weather. I can't speak for your brothers, but I prefer having a wife in my bed most nights."

"Well, he's in good company with the likes of Clay," she said, calming down.

"Might as well start painting their banners for president and vice president," he joked. "But if I were you, I'd be upset with Henry Clay for stealing Dick's thunder. He's not even a real Kentuckian, you know."

"Oh, we're all Virginians when you get to it. But what troubles me is this, Johnny. My brother and Clay are going to be blamed for this war if it doesn't go well. Remember what Dick said in his last letter, about Congress being determined to declare war before they adjourn?"

"Honor calls for decision, and all that. Honor's surely his most overused word."

"I remember a memory game Papa used to play with us. He'd pick a word, and then we'd each have to give him back a quote. It amazed me how Dickie fixed on that word, honor. We older ones were always envious of how he could best our father."

"It was the only way a child with four clever older brothers and sisters could make an impression. Looks like it worked if it left such a lasting one on you."

"No, it's just this—he was the first in the family to fall under the spell of the power of words. I just wish he'd chosen to be a minister instead. Maybe then, he wouldn't have thought it so honorable to pretend to marry a colored girl and give her children."

Chapter 9
Hephzibah
July 1812

Richard hadn't laid eyes on Blue Spring for nine months. McPherson had followed his drawings to the letter and proof was in the new stable. It looked finer than any in Lexington. And he saw how Julia filled her time. There was a freshness all around the place, with rose beds, trimmed hedges and pebble walkways from here to there. He felt the jitters coming on as he thought about meeting his little girl, and it seemed like years since he'd last held Julia.

Jerry sauntered toward him. The muscles across his shoulders bulged from his work shirt.

"Jerry, you devil, nobody'd mistake you for a butler these days! You look like you've been picking up horses and throwing 'em over the barn!"

"Good to see you back, Mas Richard." Pegasus nuzzled Jerry in greeting, and he smiled. He loved that horse, and Pegasus knew it.

"Take care of him for me. I'll be back, and you can show me the new foals."

Richard's eyes took a minute to adjust to the dark interior of his home. He heard Granny singing, and a rhythmic brushing—Mary, probably scrubbing the back rooms for his arrival. When he stopped in front of the dining room, he noticed it was decked out in flowers.

He caught a blurry reflection of himself in the punch bowl on the sideboard. He looked like a mess, but he grinned all the same. Would the Lord feel this gleeful sneaking up on everybody "in a day you know not"?

After walking quietly through the front rooms, he peeked into the half-open door to his study. Julia slept, her head wedged into the comfortable side wing of his reading chair. Her thinness alarmed him.

Then his eyes fell on a tiny hand covering Julia's breast. He stood frozen, listening to them breathe, feeling like an intruder or a guardian angel, not sure which. He pulled up a footstool and sat next to them. His daughter's fingers dangled within reach and when he put his finger out, she held on.

"Dear God in heaven, I am so happy," he whispered.

The three of them stayed motionless, Richard adjusting to his new life, Julia and Imogene unaware of his presence. And then they stirred, as all sleepers do, not knowing what has changed in the air around them.

Julia opened her eyes. "Richard!" she whispered. "You've met your daughter, haven't you?"

He shook his head and let the tears fall as he kissed her. When he kissed his daughter, she moved at the interruption of her dream and opened her eyes in irritation. She stared at her father, frowned and went back to sleep. Julia surrendered their baby into his arms.

"Thank you, dear girl," he whispered to Julia. "I am happy, truly happy."

RICHARD'S FIRST NIGHT home did not go as he expected. Julia did her best to please him, but exhaustion drained her strength; she was spent in a matter of minutes. After sleeping a couple of hours, he awoke to the sound of Imogene's fretful cries.

As tender as his feelings were for his infant daughter, the first thing he did upon entering their bedroom was to move the cradle to the unused nursery. But Patsy should have been sleeping in the nursery, as well.

Julia awoke in confusion, milk quickly saturating the front of her nightgown and part of Richard's nightshirt. She stumbled down the hall and Patsy met her halfway, Imogene in her arms. They returned to the nursery where Julia rocked and fed the baby back to sleep. Of course, her husband needed rest. But why did he have to ruin her blissful arrangement?

Before dawn, the baby fretted again for Julia, who was on her feet before the milk let down, before the noise roused Patsy. Heavy snoring at the Franklin Inn had meant nothing to Richard, but he hadn't dealt with the screeches of a baby since he was fifteen. One night was enough.

He let Julia sleep after the sun rose and ate the breakfast Granny Ann took obvious pains to make him. As he ate, the thought occurred to him that declaring war against England last month had proved easier than getting a good night's sleep. Their daughter was more of a tyrant than King George.

He carried his plate to the pantry and hollered down the walkway toward the cookhouse. "Granny Ann, are there any women in the quarters with a baby?"

When she heard his voice close by, she ran out to answer him. "What's that, Mas Richard?" He repeated his question. "Hephzibah just had a little girl Miss Julia put down in the book as Rose."

"Send Mary down soon as you can and bring them up to the house."

He returned to the dining room sideboard and piled a platter with biscuits and ham for Julia. Patsy was dressing the baby as he passed by the nursery, but even he knew a high-necked gown and bonnet were no good for a baby on the first day of August.

"She'll have prickly heat in five minutes in that thing," he said.

"Miz Julia just wanted her to wear somethin' special for her pa, but now that you've seen her, I can put her into something easy."

"Patsy, you're a smart one. Get her changed and take her on downstairs for some fresh air."

Julia stood in front of the washstand mirror, her chemise down to her waist, attempting to wash away the smell of curdled milk. She caught his eye as he walked in and covered herself with a linen cloth until she knew they were alone. He grinned at her with a biscuit stuffed in his mouth. She shook her head.

"Thin as a stray calf, Jewel. Except for these things." he stood behind her and cupped her breasts in his hands.

"I'm warning you, you'll have milk all over yourself if you don't stop." She leaned back on him and closed her eyes. He kept his senses, however, and allowed her to get back to cleaning up.

After she changed her chemise, she wrapped a lightweight corset around her waist. "Pull the ties, would you?" He obliged, and watched her place flannel rags, folded into thick squares, between the chemise and each breast.

"You look mighty fine in corset and pantalets, Miss Julia. Here, eat some breakfast." He pulled her toward the table.

"What I'm dying for is just a big glass of water. I don't think I can choke down a biscuit."

"Uh-hunh," he grunted, pouring water into a delicate teacup. He sat down and stretched his feet out, resting a foot on the fireplace grate, playing with her hair while she chugged down the water.

"I'm bringing Hephzibah up from the quarters to nurse the baby," he announced.

"But Richard! I don't want anyone else to..."

"Don't you see what's happened to you? I hardly recognize you. You're not going to spend another night like last night. There'll be no more giving in to the demands of our daughter."

Julia tried to chew on a biscuit, but her mouth got drier. Tears rolled down her cheeks, making her feel like a child herself. "But I don't give in to her, I enjoy every moment with her."

"Watching you stagger around last night was not a picture of enjoyment. And I'm not going to have my wife looking like a scarecrow. You look every bit like one of those poor Irish women on the Ohio. I am baffled that Theobald would let you get to such a state."

"What does he have to do with anything?"

Richard tilted his head, surprised by such a petulant tone at the mention of his friend.

"I haven't had need of him since the delivery. And as you may recall, I grew up taking care of all the babies in your family. Besides, weaning an infant takes time, and I'm not ready."

Richard fought back the impulse to raise his voice, reminding himself that he wanted to help her.

"I don't wish to argue, darlin'," he lowered his voice. "My concern here is for you. Imogene seems healthy enough. She's a baby without a thought in her head. She won't know who is feeding her, nor will she care, so why are you upset?"

"It's nonsense, I know," she replied, trying to find her dignity. Exhaustion and the strain of getting to know Richard all over again were taking their toll. Each time he returned from Washington, the real strain came from having to turn control of her life and their home over to him. Now he wanted to take over their daughter after being back less than a day.

Fatigue made her resentment all too transparent. "It's very hard to explain to a man what a mother feels like having her child at someone else's breast. You must understand, Richard, she's all I have."

He swallowed back his frustration. She never argued, so why now? "You have me, Jewel," he said, hoping she caught the hurt in his voice he intentionally put there. He knelt by her chair and embraced her.

"I need you, too. There's a war on, you realize!" He chucked her lightly under the chin but despite herself, she refused to give him the smile he always expected with his pet gesture.

"I don't know when—soon—I'll be leading a regiment going to Fort Wayne. Does it seem too much to ask to get my wife back before I have to go?"

She wiped her wet face with a napkin. "No, of course not. But you said nothing in your letters about Fort Wayne or anyplace else."

They sat in silence for a minute while she tried to eat. "It's so quiet. Where's the baby?" she asked, a hint of panic in the rise of her voice.

"Getting some fresh air with Patsy."

"Oh," she sighed. After she finished another cup of water, she forced herself to smile but managed to avoid looking directly at him.

"Let me dress and make arrangements for Hephzibah. But I can tell you right now Sandy Miller isn't going to like having her out of his sight."

Richard laughed. "If I had a woman like that, I'd be relieved to have some peace and quiet for a change. Which means you won't have much yourself while she's here, but between her and Granny Ann, I'll wager they'll get some meat on your bones."

He kissed the top of her head before leaving. "I'm going to find our daughter and get acquainted. See you downstairs."

Alone, Julia confronted herself in the mirror. She was thin, her face chalky, her cheeks hollow. Why had she not noticed before? She looked like a stranger to him and felt like one to herself.

Yet, last night, at his touch. He could have been anyone—my mind was too tired to want him, but my body was so eager. Could it be what people say, because of my African blood?

The thought angered her. Richard came home after weeks of hard travel, yet had no difficulty finding strength to do as he pleased with her, and there was no African blood in him. How many times had she heard conversations between Jemima and other women about the necessity of pleasing their husbands despite their own needs!

He has no understanding for the complications of weaning a baby, she brooded while she dressed. She knew that binding was painful, and yet he would have no sympathy for her. Women's difficulties were part of Eve's curse; she knew her lot was to bear up and suffer without comment, but it rankled, all the same.

Theobald might have some modern suggestion instead of her homey ointments. But it was impossible to see the man until she was sure none of her unwanted feelings toward him would show. If he came today, she'd be unnaturally aloof, and Richard would think that strange.

"Damn the man!" She cursed as she slammed her comb onto the dressing table. How could he march in without a word of appreciation for all her improvements to Blue Spring, demand her to break her bond with her baby, and treat her as if she had no brain in her head? Did he still love her?

Did she still love him? Three years ago, to the day, they had been married. Now she felt like a stranger not only to him but to herself as well.

She put her elbows on the vanity table and folded her hands together to pray. "Father in heaven, forgive me for cursing my husband. Forgive the rancor in my heart. Help me to bite my tongue and swallow my anger, and submit my will to my husband, for you have made him head over me, and I must know my place. In the Lord's blessed name, amen."

She waited, hoping to have the pounding in her heart and the anger vanish in a miraculous manifestation of blessed grace. She waited longer.

Nothing happened.

As she put on a ridiculously impractical but beautiful dress Richard liked, her resentment grew. She had proven her ability to run Blue Spring despite three pregnancies and caring for a baby. Even McPherson gave her grudging respect. Many carefully made alliances with tradespeople at the village and in Georgetown had brought the farm's expenses down considerably. Meticulous records of every penny earned and spent, every birth, injury and illness, proved one thing: she knew this place better than Richard did.

The answer came as she walked downstairs: *I'll do what Richard wants when he's home. I'll do what I want when he leaves.*

It would be an easy way of keeping peace with him and maintain a little dignity for her. But when she saw Richard with Imogene in the crook of his arm, she smiled despite her resentment, and Richard smiled back, although it might have been for Jerry and the splendid roan yearling trotting past.

There in the shade of the stable overhang sat a very miserable Hephzibah and her sleeping month-old baby. Imogene began to fret, but Julia made herself walk past her daughter and felt milk let down, quickly drenching the flannel rags.

"Don't get up," Julia said quickly. Hephzibah's stature made Julia feel like a child; she felt stronger standing over the woman at her feet and knew she'd need every ounce of strength to hold her own with Richard's most valued worker.

"My husband has decided that Imogene needs a nurse."

Hephzibah looked up at Julia then down at her own infant. It was a strain to talk to her or look at her pale face. Without her fair skin, the woman standing over her would still be a slave. But here Julia was, giving orders and messing up the good situation she,

Hephzibah, had only yesterday thanked the Lord for—a man who looked out for her, and their second beautiful baby.

"I know it will be hard on your family to have you at the house. But it will be comfortable for you. And little Rose." Awkwardly, Julia added, "And Sandy and Tommy can keep your rations for themselves."

Hephzibah nodded but refused to raise her eyes.

"When Imogene starts walking, you can wean her and go back to Sandy."

Hearing her own voice, Julia knew she sounded girlish, as well as apologetic, and Richard surely would have criticized her for that. She cleared her throat to sound more authoritative. "We'll need to get you some house clothes, and I'll have Mary make you up a bath in the cookhouse."

As the woman rose to her feet, Julia realized the tub might not be wide enough. Hephzibah made two of Julia. Her arms, shoulders and back bulged from muscles built by twisting hemp into rope. Even her facial features seemed strong, masculine in their sharpness and definition. The powerful way Hephzibah moved as they walked to the cookhouse exuded a confidence that Julia envied with all her heart.

By the time they got to Granny Ann, Julia had thought of something to sweeten the job. "You'll be free from your other work, and you can walk down to the quarters to see your family at sunrise and supper. But you'll need to stay in the house at night, for Imogene. You'll have extra food, all you want."

Since it was clear Hephzibah was not going to talk to her, she muttered, "I don't like it any more than you," and walked away.

Feeling like a lamb to the slaughter, Hephzibah submitted to the preparations for her new station. The bath water was so hot it made her head pound. Was it her rage keeping it at near scalding temperature? The smell of floral soap turned her stomach, a smell she forever would link with the bitterness of being taken from her family. Would anything ever be hers? Nothing belonged to her, not her days toiling for a high and mighty Johnson and his pasty "wife", not even the milk meant for *her* child, not *theirs*!

Without a word or a smile, Granny Ann wrapped Hephzibah in a sheet and sat her next to the cookhouse door to dry. Rose lay asleep in an extra dough trough Granny had lined with a piece of old quilt.

Patsy relieved her master of his daughter, now screaming at having her hunger ignored. She brought her to the back of the house where Imogene's new nurse sat, still wrapped in a sheet.

When Hephzibah sighed and put the baby reluctantly to her breast, Imogene curled her nose and turned away, howling. "They know their mama's smell, you see," Hephzibah mumbled to Patsy.

"What are you going to do?" Patsy asked, more curious than concerned.

"Just wait till she's hungry enough to try something different." When the first drops of milk fell, Hephzibah put them on her finger and rubbed the baby's mouth. The crying turned to a whimper and, within moments, Imogene rooted at the generous breast.

"You're gonna be just fine, little girl," Hephzibah chided the greedy infant in her arms. Alarmed at the strange voice, Imogene broke away and looked up at her nurse's sullen face, with a pair of startled eyes too much like her grandmother Henrietta's. Hephzibah and Patsy steeled themselves for a tantrum.

Instead, the baby smiled and lifted her fat, pink hand to Hephzibah's chin and patted it. Without thinking, Hephzibah growled and pretended to gnaw on the little fingers, earning squeals of laughter from Imogene. Overjoyed to know the baby had charmed the terrifying Hephzibah, Patsy backed away quietly and ran to report to Granny Ann everything she'd witnessed.

Looking down at Imogene, Hephzibah said in a warning tone, "Alright, I will feed you for the sake of your grandma. No tellin' how many times she broke rations to give Sandy and me something good." Letting her eyes rest on little Rose, she whispered, "I won't let myself forget."

Julia found some soft cloth in the press, shook out the dried lavender caught between its folds, and set to work cutting out a dress, kerchiefs, and apron. Patsy put to good use the sewing skills Julia had taught her and began stitching the seams: a simple shift with cap sleeves and a drawstring top to make nursing easy. She had it ready to wear before sundown and presented it to Hephzibah as carefully as if it were a wedding gown.

Passing her reflection in the window, Hephzibah hardly recognized the image. Her curly, shoulder-length hair was tied back with a calico kerchief instead of a sweat rag around her forehead. After a moment's study, she thought it balanced her square jaw and large chin and made her look womanly. The new dress softened the lines of her muscled shoulders. Sandy always told her he loved her strong face and body, but she knew all too well her appearance was different from other women.

After she fed both infants and washed herself, Hephzibah put some food into her new apron pocket and convinced Patsy to keep the babies. She ran to her cabin. Tommy huddled on his little cot, crying that his ma was gone forever. Sandy stood at the doorway, sulking. He was a big man, large enough to block Hephzibah when he had a mind to.

"You look mighty fine, Miss Hephzibah. But who's going to be feeding us with you at the house? And when am I going to see our baby girl?"

Hephzibah glared at him and stepped gently over to Tommy. "Just look what Mama's got for you, sugar!" she cooed at him.

"Mama! I thought they'd taken you away."

"No, honey, I'm just a little ways up the path from you now at the big house! I'm nursing Mas Richard's baby girl just like I do your baby sister!" She choked back her tears.

Sandy undid the cloth around the bread, corn and chicken. "Looks mighty good, Heph, but I need to know what's happening to us."

She began rummaging among their small store of rations, quickly mixing some mush. Feeling guilty and flustered made her work like a madwoman.

"Make us a little cook fire right quick, Sandy, and Tommy, go see if you can round us up a carrot or two out back." Her son stared at her, fearing she would trick him and disappear again.

"Go on now," Sandy reassured him.

After getting the fire started, Sandy came back inside. He wrapped his arms around her from behind and stood there a minute kissing her shoulders.

"You smell sweet, like flowers. A new dress, pretty new apron." He rubbed his calloused hands across the fabric of her dress then down her ample sides.

Sandy's size and strength made him indispensable to McPherson, and Hephzibah could outwork any man in the fields or the rope walk. For years they had been given grudging respect from their overseers, first at Great Crossing and now at Blue Spring. This was the first time as a couple their master had disrupted their lives on a whim. It brought them both up short, slapping them once again with the hard reality of their enslavement.

Hephzibah began to fear the house job would change everything, especially how they thought about themselves. But she was not about to say any of this out loud to Sandy. Better not plant a seed that had no business growing.

"Mas wants his baby wet nursed. Julia looks like a scarecrow, an' it probably made him sick to look at her sack a bones las' night." She went weak with relief when he laughed.

"Good thing no baby can suck the meat off your fine haunches, Heph," he laughed some more and nuzzled deep into the side of her neck.

She hesitated, knowing the worst had to be said. "But I have to go back. I have to stay nights till the baby sleeps through. And I get extra vittles, and no heavy work till she's weaned. But honey," she turned away from her mixing bowl to look into his face, "that could be wintertime. Even next spring."

The look on his face said he understood what she left unsaid. "Don't worry about anybody turning my head. I'll just thank the good Lord for a string of sleep-filled nights from now on." Sandy gently lifted the bowl from her hands and kissed her.

"So, we're going to be alright," she wanted to make it a question, but wanted even more to show her faith in his love for her.

Sandy gave her a reassuring "mm-hmm", but he felt sick at heart. She was being taken from them, and he needed no reminding that so few choices were their own.

"I can come before sunrise and make your breakfast. I'll be here at night to make supper. And maybe Tommy could make himself useful at the house, so he won't get underfoot at the rope walk?"

"He's handy fetching for me and the others, and it's about time he let go of your apron strings. Besides, I don't want him learning prissy house ways."

She should have known better. His contempt for house hands went way back. It didn't help that he still thought of their master as that stub-nosed white child on the back porch of the Chinn place fifteen years ago.

As Sandy and their son ate, Hephzibah felt the pinch in her nipples as the milk let down. "It's time to go back now," she said sadly.

Sandy half-heartedly tugged Tommy's hands off her pretty new dress. She dared not turn to look back, but she heard Sandy tell their boy, "Son, we'll see her and Baby at breakfast. And Mama's going to have somethin' real good for you to eat."

Hephzibah waved her hand to signal Sandy she heard and would follow through. The cookhouse lantern glowed ahead of her, and she ran the rest of the way to the house.

THE MISERIES OF THE past few days brought Julia close to hating Richard. Binding her breasts had come with the painful awareness that her body would never be her own. Excruciating throbs pulsated through her back and down her arms. The soreness, along with the smell of rancid milk, forced her to finally cut the tight strips away and release the pressure.

Julia stood in front of her dressing table, unable to look at her hollow eyes and gray mouth. As the bindings fell away, she sucked in a gasp. Angry purple streaks ran from her nipples under her arms, and when she touched a vicious red circle on the side of her right breast, she buckled with nausea from the pain.

Richard heard her gasp, climbed out of bed and stood behind her, dumbstruck. He clamped his hand against her forehead. "You're burning up, Jewel!" He carried her back to bed and carefully placed her on her back. After he dressed, he sent Jerry to fetch Theobald, despite Julia's protests.

Patsy kept Imogene away from her mother while Hephzibah looked at the infected breasts. Within minutes, she had hot cloths pressed around them. "They're plugged. Just like moss in the spring pipe!" Julia managed a feeble laugh, grateful for this letting-up of tension between them, even though it was a joke at her expense.

"Thank you, Hephzibah." Julia gnawed her lips. "I know you don't like me much. But I remember how you and Mama always got along."

"Sandy and Hen went way back, long before you were born." Against her better judgment, Hephzibah looked at Julia with a bit more compassion. "Anyway, what difference does it make if I like you or don't?"

"You must think I'm being high and mighty. But I'm not. It's what I have to do," she muttered.

"You do what you got to do, but in the meantime, we got to do something about this fever making you talk out of your head." Had Julia felt it? The strange and slippery way she turned her power over to Hephzibah? "Mary, fetch more hot water, and bring me plenty more rags."

Hephzibah further took control of the situation when her master crept back into the room. "She'd be more comfortable with Miz Charlotte from the mill than with the doctor. Lotta times these things get better with poultices and such like instead of cutting and bleeding."

Richard looked from his servant to his wife. After tugging at his hair a moment, he headed back down stairs, relieved.

Hephzibah had been wet nurse for only four days, but she hadn't needed even that long to take new measure of the man she'd had to call "master" since she was fifteen years old and he barely any older. She gave him begrudging credit for his kindness to her Rose. But he was used to getting what he wanted when he wanted it, and now was never soon enough.

Mary sloshed a bucket of hot water at her feet. Hephzibah quickly squeezed out the rags floating on top. "Get ready for some heat," she warned. Julia winced as the scalding rags seared her skin but, within seconds, she felt relief from the throbbing and let out a deep sigh. Hephzibah kept the heat steady across Julia's chest, and started pressing cold cloths on Julia's forehead. The cries of the babies forced her to leave.

Richard bounded up the stairs at the sound of the infants and took Hephzibah's spot. "Mrs. Lindsay's in the pantry making some nasty concoction she swears will put you to rights." He wrung out a fresh cloth in the basin of cool water. "I never knew this could happen, Jewel. Me and my know-it-all ways." Confronted by a glimpse of the ugly striations, he felt overcome by a wave of shame. He kissed her cheek and pushed several strands of hair behind her ears.

When Theobald arrived, Richard changed a final cloth and covered Julia with a sheet. The doctor squelched a laugh at his friend's pointless gesture to protect Julia's modesty.

"It's been a long time. But from a patient's point of view, that is a good thing." He offered them a restrained smile. He had missed her.

"Charlotte's here," Julia muttered, averting her eyes from Theobald.

"Yes, we spoke downstairs." He uncovered her breasts one at a time and pressed at the inflamed spots. Julia sucked in air and bit her lips with each prodding. Worse than labor in its own way, she grimaced with the thought.

"Mastitis. Blocked milk ducts," he said curtly to Richard. "Much like a milch cow gets from time to time. Whatever gave you the notion to bind yourself?" he chided as he glanced back at Julia. "I believe I've warned you off old-fashioned ideas."

"It's my doing," Richard confessed. "But only because she was at the mercy of Imogene's every whim."

"If you were feeding her as often as your husband implies, Julia, it was inevitable that this would be the outcome if you suddenly stopped. The infection is mild at this sta..."

"You call red circles and purple streaks mild?" Richard interrupted.

"Almost black, with pus extruding—forgive me, Julia..." he turned to her then back to Richard, "that would be considered severe. For the present, I can lance two of the nodules I've palpated, but it will be most unpleasant, and may not be very helpful at this stage."

Richard ran his hands over the top of his head in a gesture of frustration. "Is there any way she can be spared more suffering? What else can be done?"

"Mrs. Lindsay's old remedy is basic enough—nothing more than a poultice of pokeroot. Such things sometimes work wonders. But I advise you, Julia, to take a few precautions which will be difficult with your fever. Drink only when you can bear your thirst no longer. Then sip something rich, like strong broth instead of water. We need your body to have very little with which to produce further milk. And have your wet nurse keep the baby away from you for the next three days. No contact, do you understand?"

Julia nodded and brushed away a few tears. She looked like a pitiful rag doll instead of a grown woman of twenty-two, Theobald thought. When their eyes met, they both looked away quickly.

The men left when Charlotte brought in a bowl of dirt-smelling paste.

"Richard, take the baby off Julia's hands as often as you can. Just the sound of a baby's cry can stimulate milk in its mother." His voice faded. He chastised himself for wanting what he could never have.

"It's strange. I grew up watching my mother with all my younger brothers, then my sisters with all their children. I never knew—well, just never cared—what they went through."

"No soldier suffers more than women do. From my point of view, Eve's curse seems terribly unfair. Sweat of the brow is nothing in comparison."

Richard grunted in agreement. As they stepped outside into the sunlight, Theobald looked off in the distance at the haze over the river. "There's rumor of Governor Scott putting together battalions across the state. If you need a surgeon, I'm your man."

"Then you're in. When the time comes," Richard replied.

"And when do you believe that will be?"

"Any day now. General Harrison has his hands full between Fort Detroit and Turtles Town. He's written me to stand ready."

Jerry brought the creaking buggy around and held the dapple-gray steady while the doctor settled on the seat. "She'll be fine," Theobald reassured his friend. "She's much stronger than you realize." He turned to add, "Send your boy as soon as you have news from the governor."

"THAT FOOL HULL SURRENDERED Detroit to the British!" Richard's shout made the walls vibrate and the babies cry. Julia followed him, desperate to think of some way to calm him so the ceiling wouldn't fall on top of them. He stomped toward his study, reading the rest, and when he reached his desk, spat out, "His officers think there's treason, for they could have held it easily." After adding his own comments, he signed the circular then handed the paper back to the courier.

Another messenger arrived two days later. The threat on Fort Wayne long ago predicted by Richard had finally materialized. Harrison wanted a battalion of mounted men to come to their rescue. Richard was transforming before Julia's horrified eyes into a warrior, eager for the fight. Like the knights the boys used to imitate at Great Crossing, he drew maps, cleaned weapons and snapped orders, only this time for real battle.

For years, he had urged Congress to action. But what made her fear for his sanity along with his life, was his talk of Kentucky as the savior of the nation. She had to restrain herself from being Jemima's mouthpiece, but in her head was the voice of his mother: "Pride cometh before a fall, son. God created Kentucky, not the other way around."

She spent a lot more time on her knees praying not only for his safety but a good dose of humility.

By the time the week was out, however, Julia began to believe her husband was right. Nearly a thousand men with their horses and equipment gathered and set up camp between Blue Spring and the Crossing. They looked like bullies and talked like killers, but a lot of them had a Bible open across their knees around the campfires every night.

RICHARD WAS LEAVING in the morning with his militia. Julia took Imogene from Hephzibah's arms and carried her out to the stables, where Richard and a dozen men selected the last of the horses. She had done nothing for days but direct workers in preparing dried foods for the men to eat in the saddle, sturdy clothing that would take them into winter, and bandages for Theobald's surgery wagon.

The feeling that something more had to be done tugged her back to the house, but she forced herself to stand still and simply watch Richard from a distance. Would God give her a presentiment of his death?

She stared at him for several minutes before he noticed her. Their eyes met and he smiled imperceptibly, but it was the only acknowledgement she needed. She took the baby back to Hephzibah and headed toward the drawing room to do something she had neglected for days.

The room needed air. After she propped the doors open, she unlatched all four windows, and the early evening cross-breeze revived her. A few insects headed toward the candelabra on the little side table, but the flies had plenty of attractions outside and mercifully left her alone.

She began a simple Haydn piece that had become a popular hymn, and before long, the sweetness of the notes managed to rise above the clatter. Some of the men picked up the song and their voices melded into a strange concert with the shouts and curses of soldiers, and the noises of restless animals and workers.

The music served her well. Before she finished, all the resentment that burdened her fled. Then Richard appeared and sat beside her. He gave off the smell of iron, leather and horses, and the heat from his body made her break into a sweat. But the power of his presence filled the room so often empty of him, and she played out her love in notes that she hoped would linger with him on his journey north.

As she played, she asked the question that had weighed on her mind for weeks. "Do you feel any presentiment of danger?"

"Meaning death?" He looked several seconds into her eyes. She nodded and played louder, faster, until he lifted her hands off the keys.

"No, none." After he stared at the portrait of Washington above the mantel, he added, "I think there's more for me to do."

He stood up and put his hands on her shoulders, then bent and kissed her hair. "Go on, finish your songs. I'll be back, much sooner than you'd expect."

Chapter 10

Tecumseh

October 5, 1813. Thames River, Ontario

Last year Richard told Julia he would make it back in one piece, and he had.

But this time he had his doubts. Only hours ago, a few volunteers joined in his plan, the kind of plan always called "the forlorn hope". They did not expect to live out the day. It had taken some doing, but General Harrison himself had given the go-ahead for Richard's wild and probably suicidal idea.

One branch of the Kentucky boys charged in plain view of the British and Indians. The forlorn hope, however, hid under cover of the brush near the Thames River swamp. They figured Tecumseh and his equally suicidal warriors would be there. They were.

Had anyone else gotten out of that cold muck alive? He regained consciousness just long enough to realize he was in no shape to have the kind of conversation that would get him any answers.

Somehow—he'd forgotten the details—he'd been shot and knifed by the Shawnee in the swamp woods. His men dragged him out from under his horse and propped him up against a tree so he could watch the rest of the fight. He looked down at his blackened left hand, laying across his lap like a piece of raw liver.

Had he fainted? Must have, but the tree held him up. He came to in time to fire off four shots from the pistol in his good hand. He aimed directly into the face of a handsome Shawnee who had a bludgeon in his left hand and an exquisite English pistol in his right. The warrior fell backwards.

Look at the strange way we're tangled together. Feet and hands pointing outward. We're like a human compass, he thought before he passed out. When he came to, the Indian was gone, drag marks going off into the bushes. Some of Richard's own boys hollered that he'd killed Tecumseh.

They picked him up and planted him on top of his saddle. He heard Theo give orders to his new aide-de-camp, Labadie, to "hold the colonel on that horse". He knew the horse—Jerry's pure-white little mare he had taken into battle at the last minute after his stallion took a fall.

His nephew, Willie, walked beside him to keep him from sliding off. He wanted to joke with the boy, to say something like "you can call yourself a man now that you've seen a battle at the ripe old age of fourteen." But all he could manage were a few ungodly groans.

The battle raged, cutting them off from the little clearing made for triage. Theo led them to General Shelby's camp. "Mitchell!" he heard Theo shout. "Richard, if A.J. Mitchell's here, we can get you out of trouble, you hear? He's the best we've got."

All he heard was the panic in his friend's voice. When the men pulled him off the little mare, he saw a blur of red, not white. Her pelt was saturated with his blood and her own. She collapsed onto her knees and died right in front of him. He began to howl like a baby. How she must have suffered carrying him behind the lines!

Willie and the others hoisted him onto a bare, narrow table in the governor's surgery. "Colonel, calm yourself," Theo repeated in a voice that was anything but calm.

Suddenly, he felt the shock of freezing air on his bare skin and open wounds. His blood-soaked clothes fell to the ground in wet thuds—new clothes his mother had sent him as a peace offering, with a note. *I pray for angels to guard you home and not the heavenly home, either.*

A second wave of shock came with the bucket of river water Labadie dumped over him, chunks of ice, algae, and all. As the wounds came into clear view, Theobald, Mitchell, and Labadie all swore in unison. Richard heard Mitchell curse and mumble to Theobald, "Don't know how in hell we're supposed to fix that. This hip and thigh have gaped so wide we'll need two men to hold him in place while we stitch him up."

Richard threw up and passed out.

When he came to, he could no longer see his hand, but he felt each beat of his pulse bang against a splint. His chest, groin and thigh were wound tight with bandages, and he had to force himself to breathe. Mitchell cursed some more and told Theo, "Stay right with him. Maybe somebody can help you at Fort Detroit if he can survive the loss of blood. At least his vitals have escaped."

Labadie, Willie, and a couple of other boys lifted him onto a blanket stretcher and carried him outside the General's tent. Richard's adjutant, Major Barry, rode over. By the look on his face, he was expecting to see a corpse.

Richard opened his swollen eyes, grateful for the warmth coming from the nostrils of the major's horse. "I will not die, my friend," he said with a forced smile. "I'm mighty cut to pieces, but my vitals have escaped." He hoped Mitchell told the truth about that. He needed Barry to spread the good word. It was bad for morale to have leaders succumb to their wounds. Better to die in the thick of things, like a hero.

There was nothing heroic about the state he was in now.

Some of the men behind the lines secured a cart. They found odd pieces to cushion his litter against the skull-splitting jolts of the wagon. It made him sick at heart to leave his men, as well as so many members of his family—a dozen of them—brothers, nephews, cousins. He could hear the battle winding down and wondered if any of them besides Willie survived.

They neared the rotting dock on the Thames. What a sense of humor the Canadians have, he thought, looking through the gaping wagon slats at the pathetic excuse for a river. Captain Champlin hallooed from the deck of a scorched and battered schooner, the name *Scorpion* painted clear enough for Richard to read. The captain looked pleased with himself. Word around camp last night was he'd taken the British vessel in a skirmish upriver. The boat stank of blood and worse, but then, so did Richard.

Other men were carried aboard, too wounded to talk about the outcome of the battle. The stretcher bearers reported that Redcoat General Proctor had fled, and Colonel Johnson had killed Tecumseh. This Richard did not know for certain, but since the men hadn't recognized him, they weren't just saying it for his benefit.

He felt a grim satisfaction and wondered if the dead warrior whose feet had entwined with his own on the battleground had indeed been the greatest Indian leader who'd ever lived. Or died, he smiled to himself. It's not so much the killing that a soldier minded, after all, but not getting the credit for a good one. If it was true, it might make him as famous as the Shawnee chief. He wondered which, if any, of the wounds in his body were Tecumseh's doing.

The craft hove into the river current. The wounded and their attendants fell silent, letting the sounds of the water soothe them into a stupor. The thought crossed his mind it was good he'd gotten Julia pregnant again, because it was probably for the last time. Over and over, the thumping pain that started in his groin crawled down his thigh then shot back up to flood his abdomen with fire.

Good thing the swelling in his face made it impossible to see anything—if there was anything left to see down there. Whether he was a whole man or not, she'd have to go through the birthing business alone. If the loss of blood didn't kill him, gangrene would probably do the job over the next few weeks before he could get home.

He had spoken to her of his fear that James and the others might find a way to disinherit her and their children. Dying was out of the question, then. He grimaced at that thought, because all his pains, so unique to each region of his body, so indescribable, probably had no remedy except in death. The words "just die" then "can't die" kept a rhythm in his mind with the hammering in his left hand and the ragged thud between his hips.

He was overcome by thirst. Where was Theo? Where was Labadie or Willie? Buried deep between the scarred boards of the boat, he had only one view: upward at the sky. He prayed, but his prayers sputtered out of his head like sparks from a dying campfire, scorching him with their fall.

Pain of slow dying. Pain of a woman in labor. Had to be about the same, he concluded, though he'd known plenty of men and women to come through a lot worse than a battle or a birth, only to be struck down by something as no-count as tripping over a tree root or eating a rotten potato. The thought made him laugh, but it hurt, and he stopped himself.

Finally, Theo came toward him. He held Imogene in his arms! She ran to him, but he cried out from the pain when she fell on him. "Oh, Genie, I scared you. Papa's sorry!"

"He's raving. Get me another blanket, anything, man!" Theobald ordered.

"I've done everything they wanted of me. Theo, you know it, you're my friend," Richard felt the doctor mop his head and neck.

"But she's my daughter!" Tears streamed down his cheeks into his ears. The warmth felt comforting.

Theobald whispered into Richard's ear. "Calm yourself, Colonel. You're raving, man. It's the fever, but the men here…"

Yes, the men. He was an officer and had to pull himself together. He knew he wasn't thinking right. He never would allow himself to think about their "situation", but now that he was dying, he had to. All it took was a drop, just one drop of African, and you'd be Negro forever. Even my own child, smarter and fairer than anybody else in the family, but she didn't count because she was tainted.

"Can't die, Theo."

RICHARD AWOKE WHEN *Scorpion* dipped into the waters of the St. Clair. The winds, not the river current, had taken charge of the boat's progress. Despite the ceaseless throbbing of his wounds, his mind felt steadier. An image came into his mind of a lone knight standing vigil at a long-abandoned round table. Was it Percival or his old friend Quixote?

All the Johnson boys had gone off to fight their dragons without looking back. They were all with him in this war, except George, who would have loved it. And Robert. The war took him on that trip to Fort Wayne last year.

Had James made it out alive? Or Henry? It would break Ma's heart to lose her oldest son. But her baby—that would kill her, and what prayers he had left he used on behalf of his youngest brother.

Cousin Jimmy probably made it out since he was a chaplain now and kept close to the wounded. He knew for sure Willie was alright, and General Payne wouldn't have been in the middle of it. Maybe it wouldn't be a waste if the Johnson boys got some glory out of it. And he had no doubt his Kentucky militia had done some real damage to the enemy. If it weren't for his fear of leaving Julia at the mercy of his brothers and Betsey, he'd say the battle was worth dying for.

October 17, 1813.

"Happy Birthday!" Richard opened his eyes and made out the forms of several men crowding around his bed. James and Henry grinned down at him. Behind them stood their brother-in-law John and his boy Willie, with cousin Jimmy Suggett standing off to the side. James held a steaming enamel bowl under Richard's chin. Detroit's bitter winds had easy work getting through the chinks in the wrecked fort's walls, and the steam warmed Richard's skin as it rose from his breakfast.

"Nun-unh, not so fast there!" James admonished when Richard strained to sit up.

He hadn't seen that much solid food in days. The smell of hominy and ham made him feel ten years old again. He reached out with his good hand for the wooden spoon.

"Mind your manners! You need to stay still. I'll do the feeding around here." James wrapped a piece of linen around the neck of his patient to serve as a bib, then pulled a camp table near him with his foot. Willie mixed the hominy with cream and a generous ladle of fresh maple syrup.

"Sounds like movement outside. What's happening?" Richard asked between gulps. It hurt to chew and it hurt to swallow, but it was the kind of pain that felt good for a change.

"I'd say in honor of your birthday that Shelby's marching the men home. The only way we could think of rousing you out of your stupor, my boy," his brother-in-law explained.

Richard had been seven years old when Betsey married Payne, and the man still patronized him. The rumble of wheels over gravel, sounds of horses and rattling equipment passed under the window, then slowly faded as the soldiers descended below the ramparts.

"When do we get out of here?" Richard asked in a feeble voice that sounded strange to his own ears. "It feels like the Arctic's moved to this place."

"Doc Mitchell has the final say, but he thinks you need another week. That'll give our Georgetown boys plenty of time to finish rigging up your carriage. We'll get out of here before the snow hits."

The ambivalence in James's voice told Richard they didn't think he'd be leaving soon. He shuddered. If he didn't die, he'd lie here on this cot in a fort nearly as cold as outdoors. He calculated the trip: three hundred miles overland to home would take a fortnight, in good weather.

Rain—more likely snow—was in the air. Couldn't they smell it? Bad weather would make it impossible to get over the roads, for the horses to graze. He told them as much.

"And what if you split yourself open, start bleeding all over again? In case you've forgotten, there are five holes patched up on your carcass." For a chaplain, Jimmy was short on politeness, but Richard appreciated him since everyone else continued to tiptoe around the truth.

"Right! And by the way, thanks, Uncle Dick!" Willie said. "We were saying to the boys how you took a bullet for each of us."

"You're telling me all of you got out of this without a scratch, except me?"

"We've all got scratches and plenty of them," Henry reassured him.

"But odds are none of us will bust open the first time we hit a tree stump on the road," John added with that irksome parental tone.

"I'm mending." Richard hoped it was the truth. "Just weak, is all. You in charge?"

"Like Jim said, Mitchell's got the say-so," John hedged and looked away from Richard's eyes.

"He's still here? Why didn't he pull out with Shelby?" Then it became clear. He was in a truly terrible state if Mitchell felt obliged to stay on.

He attempted a smile. "Well, we all outrank him, and I'd rather eat a little of Shelby's dust than get snowed in here for six months."

"Why don't I go check on that carriage?" Henry grinned. John and James followed him out and left Willie to finish feeding his uncle breakfast. Cousin Jimmy lingered to pray and read from the Bible. He let the book fall open where the Lord would lead. He began, "Blessed are the poor in spirit."

"He looks like hell. I don't believe he'll survive either way," John whispered to his brothers-in-law once they got outside. They headed toward the smell of food, but none of them had any appetite. They debated several minutes over their options to put the rest of their Kentucky militia in movement.

"Alright. I'll take my men and join up with Shelby," John decided. "James, do you think you could stay with some of the boys? Get together an escort for Dick and the rest of the wounded?"

"I'll go and tell him." James stepped back into his brother's room as Cousin Jimmy read, "Rise, take up thy bed, and walk."

James gave out a nervous laugh. "Not so fast! Dick might take that for a sign!"

He did.

It took two hours to clean Richard's wounds and re-bandage them. Cousin Jimmy had mercifully provided him with a bear skin to throw over his only article of clothing: a heavy night shirt. His brother William wrapped his feet and calves in flannel covered in strips of an old woolen blanket. He looked like a poor Indian. Under the disapproving glare of Doc Mitchell, the slayer of Tecumseh stood unsteadily on his own two feet for the first time in twelve days.

"Just one step, one is all. Matthew chapter nine verse seven, right, Jimmy?" He looked at his cousin.

But he couldn't pull it off, and he submitted to Theobald and William dragging him along. The fort's infantry stood in silence and saluted as they stumbled by. When he collapsed from the exertion, three young infantrymen bore him to the carriage.

A bed of rough boards straddled both seats, but it was cushioned by a pair of buffalo furs and someone's prize goose down pillows. As the men helped him onto the makeshift bed, Richard gave a little prayer of thanks for whoever sacrificed those luxuries on his behalf.

Theobald got in and sat at his feet, intending to keep a close eye on his patient's chest, hip and leg wounds. Mitchell sat near his head and did a quick review of the bandages to determine if anything had split open. He carefully cradled Richard's fractured left hand and arm.

"Some men are too noble for their own good," Mitchell muttered to himself as he looked out the carriage window.

The first snow fell before sunset.

THEY KEPT TO THE BULLSKIN Road, that ancient Shawnee trail stretching from Detroit to Cincinnati. If a fort was not visible from the road, an inn or hostel was conveniently in sight. Most of them had been spared destruction at the hands of the allied tribes because of the determined presence of militiamen.

The three men rode in silence. Richard struggled to keep his groans to a minimum so Mitchell and Theobald could get some much-needed sleep. Between him and the other wounded at Fort Detroit, the two hadn't had ten minutes' peace in days.

When the carriage came to a stop, Theobald readied the honey pot and, with great effort, Richard relieved himself. He fainted from the effort, but came to in time to hear that there was still a trace of blood. Mitchell insisted that he drink a great quantity of watered-down wine, and he did so with an eager pleasure that he feared his doctors would find revolting.

Sergeant Briggs climbed down from the coachman's seat and tapped at the carriage door. "Scouts rode ahead to Ft. Miegs to tell them we're comin.' Should be there around midnight."

The fort was small compared to Fort Detroit, almost as cold, but surprisingly clean. Briggs mentioned it was ready to be decommissioned, and Mitchell took it as a sign that the war was ending, and in their country's favor.

Two young privates brought a litter to the carriage, lifted Richard out and hauled him inside before the doctors had time to get their gear unloaded.

"The Roman surgeons noticed that wounds healed cleaner when they fought in Gaul," Mitchell said to soothe Richard, convulsing in the cold as his wounds were checked. "A gash as deep as the one in your thigh would cost a soldier his leg in a summer battle. We don't know why, but cold helps, thank God."

"Believe me, I do," Richard forced out between chattering teeth. "Do you think my wife will be able to handle this when you leave me?"

"How far advanced is she?" Mitchell asked, more of Theobald than Richard.

"She began her confinement last month. I've received only one letter since," Richard had only to look at Theobald to know how Mitchell knew such a personal detail about his life.

"Then in that case, no, I do not believe she should be subjected to the trauma of seeing wounds of this severity."

Richard smiled weakly. Mitchell spoke as stiffly as Theo! "Tell him, Theo. Hercules wouldn't be able to hold her back." He closed his eyes and kept a stoic smile on his face while he endured the surgeons' ministrations. When they took their leave, it was with a stern warning not to move a muscle.

"Sirs, the thought will not even enter my mind."

They gave instructions to his orderly, then hurried through their rounds, checking on the other wounded. It appeared that Richard's heroic survival had the benefit of making the other men feel their injuries an embarrassment by comparison. Their colonel was boosting morale by suffering more than anybody else.

"I do not understand how the man has managed to survive all this." Mitchell shook his head.

"He has a strength of will peculiar to his family, and I would dare to say that, of all the Johnsons, he is the most peculiar," Theobald replied.

One of the orderlies led them to the small, private quarters the fort surgeon had readied for them. It was nearly too small to share, but they had no strength to make a fuss. They collapsed onto their rickety cots and bid each other good night. The odds were against them getting much sleep for long. Theobald snuffed the candle between them.

"Just curious?" Mitchell's voice sounded uncharacteristically high.

"Yes?" Theobald frowned in the dark. He was so bone tired.

"Can it really be true? The story about his so-called wife, and all that."

"What's the version told in Frankfort?" Theobald asked cautiously.

Mitchell hesitated, embarrassed. "Something about revenge for his mother thwarting a romance and running off with his father's mulatto slave. Having a little daughter he keeps hidden away because she looks African. It sounds absurd, I know."

Theobald sighed too loudly for close quarters. "It's true to some extent. Gossip always has a hint of truth to give it wings, I suppose. His mother did indeed disapprove of a lovely girl he had chosen to marry. But it was several years later that he eloped with Julia into Ohio. Some Baptist minister married them."

Theobald closed his eyes. How could he describe his friends to anyone, their devotion to each other? He could say nothing of the suffering Julia endured being cut off by the woman she thought of as a mother, by the family she grew up loving as her own.

"But even in Ohio such marriages aren't allowed," Mitchell prodded.

"Julia, to all appearances, is white. Their daughter, as well."

"Ah! Well then, they could get away with fooling a religious idealist."

But not such a refined judge of slave flesh as you, Theobald thought bitterly.

"Of course, the silliest gossip is that she bewitched him, that she is a practitioner of jungle magic." Mitchell's voice halted.

Theobald sighed. He resented being kept awake by a man he thought far above such idle talk. He turned his face toward Mitchell.

"They say that because she has a gift. You know how it is in our profession, how one man has great technical skill, yet his patients fail while those of another with less skill thrive? The sick respond to her. You know he turns the care of Blue Spring completely over to her when he's in Washington, and they have over fifty slaves, for whom she is entirely responsible. And their little girl is the brightest button I've ever seen. He adores them both."

Why did he ramble? He sounded like a man besotted.

"You speak as if you know them," Mitchell said.

"I'm one of the few who does. I've attended his mother for years, and now Julia. A slave has more freedom to move about among the community than she does. It's cruel how she is ostracized."

"But why is he not? He continues to be voted into office. His men chose him to be their commander in this war. How does he get away with it all?"

Theobald turned his back, ashamed of himself for having said too much. "I suppose people always trust a man of honor, depending on how they define it."

Chapter 11
Adaline
November 17, 1813

Richard lay by a comfortable fire in his study, trying to grit out the pain in his hand and thigh. But it could not compare to the hammer in his head set off by Julia's pitiful wails.

He had missed all this when Imogene was born, getting the news in a letter he was able to leisurely pick up at the close of a day in Congress. He felt no agony then, only comfortable pride at the pretty picture in his head of Julia and their baby girl propped up on pillows and smiling into each other's faces.

Stupid fool, he thought. This had gone on a day and a half. Blue Spring was built of stone, cedar and oak, but he heard everything through the floorboards over his head. He could tell she was trying with all her might to keep quiet for his sake. But each time he heard her whimper, the sound drew on like an arrow being pulled out of his own belly.

He was glad now that his worst wound ran from his groin to his knee. It gave him a taste of woman's medicine. He prayed she could live through this, because so many women did not. But he couldn't dwell on that. If he'd survived, so could Julia.

He wished he had someone to talk to. The whole damned lot of Johnsons was keeping away from Blue Spring right now because their illustrious brother was getting another child off their slave girl. His nephew Willie came by last week, against Betsey's orders, with the happy news that James and his wife named their new baby Richard Mentor in his honor.

James probably thought I'd be dead the same day.

He hung on in hopes of seeing his own son. Maybe he would name this baby after his fallen brother, Robert, he thought nervously. Robert had been the closest thing to an angel the family ever had. Add George to it, even though he'd never been an angel. Or George Robert in the order of their deaths. They'd have to call him Robert, though, since Julia still clung morbidly to talk about their Little George.

Richard's rambling shattered when Julia let out a shriek. She must have been powerless to hold back and the thought made him involuntarily shudder. He sat up with great effort, mopped the perspiration from his face, and waited for someone to run into the room with news. The house fell eerily silent.

Jewel is dead. It's all my fault.

Then he heard the high, squealing sound of a puppy. Within seconds it grew to a wail that became a long, steady scream broken only by terrifying chokes. Then he heard laughter. Julia! He fell back onto his cushions, struggling to breathe. He ached to run up the stairs and share the bond of blood between them while she and the baby were still fresh from their battle. When the door finally opened a few minutes later, he was greeted by Theobald, wrapped in a spattered butcher's apron.

"Well, Colonel, you have another beautiful little girl."

"Is Julia—I heard nothing, then I heard her laugh..." the attempt to sit upright exhausted him, and he fell back against his pillows.

"She's fine. It was a rough delivery, but the forceps got her out." Richard blanched at the mention of the instrument. Theo, odd man that he was, had proudly shown him the polished steel thing before going upstairs, taking time to gleefully explain the technique and his first-rate training in Boston. He brooded over his observation that the war had brought his friend back to life, as if it had given him new purpose.

"I expect she went into labor early out of shock from seeing you, but the baby's a fair enough size and as you can hear, has inherited her father's knack for the stentorian." The din upstairs grew. From the way his new daughter screeched, she had a terrible temper.

Theo laughed again. "I'd say those lungs are a good sign she won't be one of those babies that up and dies in the middle of the night!"

Richard felt unusual warmth coming from his friend's voice but for some reason it gave him little comfort. "Can I see them? I feel certain, with a little help from Jerry..."

"Good heavens, no! Julia will be able to get out of bed in a few days. You, on the other hand, need another month of rest. You'll worsen if you rupture any one of your wounds, and even the most ordinary of movements could ruin everything we've done."

"It's so difficult to lie here and do nothing when they need me." He wanted to cry from frustration. Pain he could endure, but this helpless state was driving him to the brink.

"You still don't seem to understand," Theobald glared at him, the smile gone instantly. "I tell you bluntly, you're in death's shadow. For their sakes," he nodded toward the ceiling, "take no risks. None."

Mrs. Lindsay waited until Dr. Theobald signaled for her to come in. "Your wife was eager for you to see. What do you think of the name Adaline?" she asked, kneeling to show him the baby. Within a mass of swaddling, he saw a dark red face that all but disappeared when she yawned. Then she closed her eyes, and her plump mouth dropped open. She'd gone to sleep!

Richard's eyes watered, and his chest tightened with emotion. He had to hold back his sobs because of the pain.

"Please hold her closer, Mrs. Lindsay." With his good hand, he lifted the front edge of her little crocheted cap. Thick hair, straight and dark, poked out. For a moment he had the disturbing thought an Indian fathered her.

"She looks very much like her sister, doesn't she? Except for the hair?"

"Imogene's hair was the same," Charlotte reassured him, reading his thought. "This dark lot will fall out in a few weeks and then she'll be bald as an old man until her real hair grows in. I'm guessing from the sound of those lungs she'll have a lot of your copper color, sir."

Charlotte, who had always held herself a bit aloof from the high and mighty congressman, found herself talking to him in the easy way that came to her around the dying. From the smell of him, death stood at his shoulder, despite the doctor's protestations otherwise.

When Richard first laid eyes on Imogene, she had been nearly seven months old. Nobody could have told him that anything would get that much love out of him again. But this child, alive for less than an hour, grabbed his heart and took possession.

"I can't die now. Adaline." After he passed his fingers over her tiny form, he dropped his hand onto the cover, drained from the effort. Then he wept openly.

"Beg pardon, sir." Charlotte backed away and carried the baby back to the warmth upstairs, but she choked back her own sob as she went. Poor man, seeing this new little life so close to his own death. A few decent fellows shed a tear or two when they came to understand how perilous their wives' deliveries had been. All cut up himself, he had the greater sympathy, even though Charlotte doubted he knew how badly this breech had torn her. No, mutilated her, much as he'd been by the war.

Theobald fell asleep in the armchair next to Richard. When he awoke, he watched his patient for a minute, sizing up his capacity for suffering. "Colonel, can you bear up under more bad news?"

Richard jumped as if startled out of a deep sleep, although his eyes had been wide open. "Julia's not dead? The baby?"

"No, no, nothing so horrible!" This was never the kind of news a man wanted to hear at any age, much less in his prime, and he was off to a poor start.

After a moment of hesitation, he decided to continue. "You know Julia had a hard time of it. A footling breech, with the complication of..." How much should he explain? "I'll spare you the details. Now, Imogene was a surprisingly perfect delivery, but this one..."

"You're trying to tell me this is to be our last child, aren't you?" Richard felt duty-bound to relieve his old friend. Theobald nodded, grateful for the help. "After what I heard, how can I think otherwise?"

"It was admirable how hard she tried not to upset you." Theobald forced himself to concentrate on the task at hand instead of thinking of Julia. "Another might possibly be the end of her. She hemorrhages so easily. You probably guessed that we almost lost her along with that little boy. Thank God, this time we were able to get it under control."

Richard cleared his throat to stave off tears. Theobald avoided his eyes, stepped nearer, and fussed with the bandage on Richard's hand.

"Never mind me," Richard offered as an excuse. "The house is so deathly quiet."

"Everyone's getting some much-needed rest. You should, too."

"God knows I try, Theo, but waking or sleeping, my imagination runs to extremes. It's no good just sitting, doing nothing."

"When Julia's better, she'll want to read to you. I can too, you know, although I must confess, I'm enjoying the rest I get coming over here!" He met Richard's eyes and was grateful to see a hint of a smile. "In a week or two, you can receive visitors."

He swabbed at the wound between Richard's elbow and wrist. "This is coming along nicely. Pus minimal, scabs lifting off your new growth of skin."

Richard made an odd grunting noise, a cross between a laugh and a cry of pain.

"She has some fool's notion that she needs to have a dozen children to make you happy."

"Sounds like her," Richard sighed. "But with me gone over half the year, it would be indecent to leave her with a big family." He winced at the pressure in his arm as Theobald applied a new dressing. "I can't get her to understand she has nothing to prove."

"She's in your mother's shadow, and I, for one, am convinced there's not a woman on earth who could live up to that."

Richard chuckled despite his pain. "Ma's gaining mythical proportions, I'm afraid. I told you about Jefferson?" Theobald nodded. "They'd love Imogene, and this new one. I hate this alienation from them, Theo! All my greatest joys are only a source of contempt to them." Richard exhaled and gritted his teeth at the throbbing in his arm.

"Too tight?"

"Just a little." As his doctor adjusted the linen strips, Richard poured out his heart. "You know, Ma is the last person I want Julia to be like. It's good for a man to feel protective of his wife, instead of unnecessary."

Theobald agreed. His Nancy was showing more and more signs of that particular "talent" and often made him think of the formidable Johnson matriarch. But Richard's idea of protectiveness left much to be desired. Some day when his patient healed, he might find the tact to tell the man just how neglectful he was.

Richard shut his eyes, determined to ask the question haunting him since his trip on the *Scorpion*. "Theo, do you think I'll be able to function? As a man, I mean."

Theo was relieved Richard had his eyes closed. "You took some bad damage to muscle and skin in your groin and thigh, but the other...chances are you'll be fine. Once you get on your feet and start walking again, I'd venture to say you'll get your strength back quickly." With some reluctance, he added, "You both need a couple of months to mend."

"How old's that boy of yours now?" Richard changed the subject.

"Oh, maybe fifteen months? Haven't been home long enough to have Nancy remind me. One thing, he skipped walking—just runs everywhere."

When Richard opened his eyes, he saw another of Theobald's rare smiles. "Go home to your family, Theo. We'll make out alright."

Theobald patted Richard on his shoulder and bade him good night. Phoebe took up her post by the door with a basket of freshly ironed bandages to fold. Before he left, he ran upstairs to check on Julia. Her color was a little jaundiced, but her breathing was heavy and rhythmic in her sleep, a good sign.

Hephzibah still had the gift of generosity as a wet nurse, he was relieved to see. She held this new baby in her arms, rocking and humming softly. Mrs. Lindsay knelt on the floor, washing bloodstains from the bedroom carpet. Why the woman didn't leave that kind of cleaning to servants he could not understand. It made him even wearier watching her. She had more stamina and worked harder than anyone he knew. Perhaps Blue Spring didn't weigh her down as it did him. He quietly gave her instructions that he knew she did not need, but which she expected him to give. As soon as he stepped away, she went back to scrubbing.

He fought off the urge to glance back at Julia and counted it a small moral victory that he succeeded. The woman did indeed inspire a man to feel protective. While he would not deny himself the hidden satisfaction of knowing that he, not Richard, truly understood her, he got away from Blue Spring as quickly as his horse could carry him.

Chapter 12
Jemima
25 February 1814

J ulia watched the funeral procession from a little hill where ice and a layer of snow covered the branches of the trees and hid her from view. Looking down from her hiding place, however, gave her the nightmarish sensation that all the Johnsons were dead and she the sole survivor left to mourn them.

Richard had limped back to Washington only ten days earlier, despite her pleas and his brother William's worsening condition. When he returned after a brief farewell visit to his brother, Richard seemed unable to accept the situation. "How could God spare me and bring him so low from a common camp fever? He hadn't even seemed ill when we left Detroit."

Granny Ann then told her that Jemima had insisted on taking over William's care after his wife collapsed from exhaustion.

When John T and his bride stepped aside, the coffin came into view, its wooden lid giving off a shimmer from a fine veil of ice crystals. She watched the plumes of breath rising from the nostrils of Robin and his many children and grandchildren. Only William was missing. But the others were all there, including Robert and George, whose graves had worn level with the rest of the cemetery.

Off to the side stood the house servants. Julia's heart tightened into a knot so hard she thought it would choke her when she caught sight of Lucy and Jacob and their children. Little Kate was nearly as tall as her mother, and Simon towered over all of them. But there was no sign of Milly. She must be preparing the funeral feast.

Jemima left behind so many men. "Men are too careless of their womenfolk, Betsey." Julia could hear that crisp, staccato voice in her ear. "Like greedy children. So unaware of the demands they make on our bodies, so heedless of the power of their thoughtless words upon our souls. I have spent my entire life learning to stand tall instead of withering away at the snubs and insults to which my husband has subjected me. He is a better man than any I know, but I would have been used up five times over if I had been made of weaker stock."

Here below, she saw the words proven out. Over four years ago, when Julia left Great Crossing, Jemima was already ravaged by age. Julia pictured her as she had been that last time—the bent back, curled-in fingers, the missing teeth distorting her mouth line.

Robin was nearly seventy, a full eight years older than his wife, but he stood tall and straight, still broad across the shoulders. The cane he leaned on merely lent him an air of patriarchal respectability.

Jemima had been worn out, like a sturdy piece of broadcloth given no break from daily abrasions. The rag that remained was all that lay in her coffin. Julia wiped the tears from her face, and whispered, "Now you know what freedom is, Jemima. Go and make a run for it."

March 1814. Washington, D.C.

Richard looked up at the sound of Little Peg running toward him. "Little" no longer applied. She had just turned fourteen but had all the makings of a siren. Already the sons and nephews of the most powerful men in Washington—even the powerful men themselves—sent her invitations she was too young to accept and gifts no Christian parent could allow their daughter to take.

Rhoda O'Neale bent his ear the first few days after his arrival, under the pretense of making him more comfortable. What she wanted was a chance to reassure him they were a respectable, God-fearing family, and that he shouldn't be taken in by malicious gossip about their very moral (though very lively) daughter.

"Colonel, this came for you today. Do you think it's about your little girls?" Peg smiled, and a sharp pang of lust made him feel thoroughly ashamed of himself. Theo never mentioned this side effect to his injury.

An equally sharp pain in his thigh helped him regain his senses. Walking from the Franklin Inn to the Capitol was helping him regain his strength, but each step took a toll and the pain cost him hours of sleep. At least he got his speeches written and committee reports read while his wounds throbbed in the middle of the night.

He looked over the address on the letter, which was in his brother James's hand. He sensed something wrong and lost his balance. Little Peg wrapped her arm around his waist to steady him, which only made him more agitated. As they came through the door, she called for one of the servant boys to settle Richard into a well-cushioned chair by the fire.

"May I bring your supper to you here, sir?" she asked.

"Thank you, Peg. That would be a good idea." He cracked the seal on the thick paper and read James's old fashion handwriting.

"*Mother left this world last night. Theo said her kidneys failed and put such great pressure on her heart it could no longer function. I know what a shock this will be to you when you receive this news. Will seems to be taking it hard, and has had a setback in his condition, as he blames himself for the strain his illness put on her. I fear you need to brace yourself for more bad news on his account, but God knows the beginning and the end, and you are a wondrous example of His grace and good will in our family's behalf. God bless and strengthen you. Mind yourself so that you do not falter, either in your health or in your service to our nation's best cause of freedom. This more than anything else, would honor her memory.*"

Ma dead. All the speeches of explanation and reconciliation he had practiced in his head over the past four years were no longer of any use.

"Bad news, it appears?" Peg put the tray of soup and bread on the table in front of the fire, then stepped toward him and wrapped her arm around his shoulders.

The sobering news had done wonders to put his moral compass back to work. "You're a kind-hearted girl, Peg," he swallowed, checking his emotion.

"I hate for anyone to be sad, that's all. Nothing's gone wrong for your little girls, has it?"

"No, but I have learned that my mother is with God this past month now."

"You live very far away, don't you? In Kentucky."

"Why Peggy, we've been looking everywhere for you." Mr. O'Neale struggled to speak as he caught his breath. "Your mother needs you to start setting dinner out."

She lay the napkin open across Richard's knee and gave it a gentle pat before she left. Mr. O'Neale offered an apology for her impertinence.

"Why, she's been around all of us her entire life, O'Neale! We're her family, not anything special. She's a comfort when we miss our own children." He smiled as O'Neale bid him good night.

The next day, he sought out his friend, the Reverend Obadiah Brown, and asked if he could take him up on the offer of renting his spare room.

Chapter 13
Robin
October 1815. Great Crossing

The gravediggers covered Jemima's little mound with fresh dirt as they dug the final resting place for Robin. William's widow placed a fresh bouquet at her husband's headstone, and Sallie's daughter Malvina put some flowers on George's and Robert's graves. Sunlight warmed the soil just enough to give off the smell of decay. When Robin's coffin lowered into the grave, everyone wept except his stoic young widow.

In Betsey's overstuffed drawing room some hours later, the perfection of the autumn day outside mocked their loss. But it was the ungenerous nature of the talk between his sisters that made Richard want to turn his back on the whole lot of them and head outside.

"Papa was seventy years old, Dickie. Fanny, barely eighteen! How do you think I felt? Or any of us felt, for that matter? Our youngest brother is four years older than she is!" Sallie shrieked.

The image of Peggy O'Neale flashed into his head. His father's young widow, Fanny Bledsoe, had none of Peg's beauty or energy, but he and every man in the room could understand why a vigorous man like their father could envision a new family with a young wife. Pa had even set up a new town at an age when most men were willing to give up and die.

"At least she was decent enough to let us have Papa buried by Mother." Betsey drowned out her own words in a sudden burst of tears.

"All I am saying is that we can't throw her out on her ear. Father built Fredericksburg for her." Richard answered. "It's two days' ride from here, for her, at any rate. She won't want to have much to do with us."

"And why did he call the place Fredericksburg, anyway?" Betsey sniffled. "If he was going to start a new settlement, he could've named it after himself."

"It was probably her idea. And what is she going to do with it? The house is too big for her all alone," Sallie snarled.

"She's not alone. Her father has already moved in! That's what I'm saying. Is it her property? I don't think it is, and I think she should just move back to her father's old parsonage, and we can all pretend that this ridiculous marriage never happened," Betsey said.

Richard leaned on his cane and bent toward her. "Widows have a few rights to property in Kentucky. At least I hope so for your sake and Sallie's." And Julia's, but he left her name unspoken.

"But Papa stipulated in his will that they should be married at least five years and have at least one surviving child before she could lay claim to that property!" Sallie fumed.

"Why didn't he consult one of us?" John sipped casually from his glass of bourbon. If it hadn't been for his wife's hysterics, he would have been content to leave the Bledsoe girl everything. "What's the good of having half a dozen lawyers in the family if you don't make use of any of them?"

"I say we let her have the house, the land, the whole lot in Fredericksburg. But Ma and Pa's people here need to stay in our hands. I have to get Jacob and Lucy in exchange," Richard said abruptly.

Betsey's usual indignation against him rose to a fevered pitch. "In exchange?" She leaned on the last word. "And what about the rest of us? What would any of us be getting *in exchange*?"

"That's not what I meant." Richard waved his hand in front of his tired eyes in a motion of irritability. I'll buy them." With four days left before his departure for Washington, it was going to be impossible to negotiate with his remaining seven siblings.

"But that is the point, Richard. Who do you pay? That chit he married? Her father? I can't stand the man. It all seemed like a scheme of his from the beginning to lure our father."

"He's a minister, Betsey. I don't think there was anything underhanded going on." Richard strained to remain calm.

Benjamin finally spoke up, his calm voice barely audible over Betsey's noise. "Don't you think it odd that a father—a minister, no less—would be willing to marry his daughter off to a man almost twice his own age, old enough to be the girl's grandfather and then some?"

Sallie shivered. "That was sickening enough, but I still can't forgive Papa for marrying that girl when Mama had been gone barely a year."

"He and Mama started growing apart after Henry was born," Betsey said. "After Henrietta came." Everyone had the good sense to ignore that comment, but eyes wandered in Richard's direction.

"And where is Henry to go? What is he to do, since Papa promised young Willie the property after you all got back from the war?" Sallie added.

"The folks left Henry his own parcel. You know that," John answered, his words slurring a bit as the bourbon took effect. It was no secret to anyone that Willie was his favorite son. He looked at Richard for support, knowing how the war had brought his son and brother-in-law close.

But Sallie was too quick. "It's not right that Willie should lay claim to the old place. He'll be in West Point another two years and it'll be years after that before he'll marry." She scanned the room uneasily. "Where is Henry, anyway?"

Richard had to think only for a moment. "Where else would a heartbroken young man be but at his father's grave? We all have more than our fair share, for ourselves and every member of our family. All we have to do is agree as Father's joint heirs to turn the land up there at Fredericksburg over to Fanny."

"Let the Bledsoes keep the property, as long as they stay clear of Scott County, and make no claim to relation with us," James suggested evenly.

It was something that Betsey and Sallie could agree on, but minor quibbling continued for several minutes, until Henry entered the house. His red eyes and swollen nose testified to the depth of his mourning, and it brought his older brothers and sisters up short. The contention vanished.

James wrapped his arm around Henry and mumbled, "Great Crossing's yours as long as you want to stay. John and Betsey don't care, and Willie doesn't need it." They all nodded in agreement. Sallie gave her older brother a conciliatory peck on the cheek and took Henry by the hand. She made him sit on a divan in the corner, then busied herself getting him to take a sip of tea, smoothing his wiry hair behind his ears as he did.

Richard limped out, accompanied by John T. When the sound of their boots on the porch steps receded, James remarked, "Strange isn't it, that Dick should be the one to suggest our need to keep a distance between ourselves and our father's fool notion of a child bride."

Joel looked at him with a hint of scorn in his eyes. "No one understands that kind of foolishness better than he does. Haven't we all managed to keep our distance from his mistake?"

RICHARD AND JOHN T led their mounts down the path that ran along the Little Elkhorn. John T broke the silence. "Why did you decide to get baptized this trip home, Dick? I mean, all those years you held out against Ma and Grandpa Suggett. Why'd you wait until after she died?"

"You're asking whether I did it out of guilt?"

"Yes, I suppose so. "

"Partly. Hit us all hard losing Robert and Will and Ma so close together. I had no real love of the church, and then I've always gotten a certain spiritual fulfillment from being a Mason."

"I must admit that I find comfort in the Lodge, as well, at least, the brotherhood of it. I imagine the apostles felt something like that for each other. But I'm still waiting for...something. I know there's more out there, but I cannot find it here."

"What's changed me is living with Obadiah Brown. His prayers before Congress are stirring, you know. We talk constantly about the gospel. And he makes it so clear, so simple. Just repent and be baptized."

"You think it was Reverend Brown and his simple Baptist preaching, not the heavy hand of death on us Johnsons?"

"So much death, being so close to death myself, it makes you think of eternity in a way nothing else can do. But Reverend Brown is very persuasive."

"Rumor has it his daughter Mary is, as well."

Disappointed more than surprised at his brother's insinuation, Richard answered him carefully. "She is bright, and I enjoy discussing theology and philosophy with her, but I am twice her age."

"Age didn't stop our father, did it?" John T pressed him.

Alright. He wouldn't back down, either. "No, but having a wife and two little girls puts a check on me."

John T slumped a bit in his saddle and took a long look over the river. Finally, he said, "I don't think I'm going to find my purpose in life in a church. Might as well look for it in Congress."

"If you run, you'll win, I've no doubt in my mind." Richard felt it only fair to add, "But Washington's the last place to take your wife."

"Not your kind, anyway," John T muttered.

Richard turned Pegasus toward Blue Spring without another word.

Chapter 14
Survival
August 1816. Blue Spring

"Mama, may I go outside and play with Rose?" Imogene asked in a voice of such moderation and restraint that Richard looked twice to make sure another adult hadn't snuck into the hallway.

"I see no reason why you can't, as long as you wear your coat," Julia answered. "Patsy, give Adaline an extra layer. She's not over her cold yet."

Patsy was overjoyed to get outside. For a fourteen-year-old, she had an overdeveloped sense of problems brewing, and she wanted no part of them. Granny Ann's ally in gossip was that stuck-up Kate, who was her age but acted like she was her mama Lucy's age. And since Kate's face, unlike her body, still had the look of a little girl, she gave adults the impression of ignorance, when she was just culling tidbits of news for the cookhouse.

Patsy had other things on her mind, like politics in Washington. She put Julia's teaching her to good use by reading the journals to the Colonel whenever his eyes gave out. That happened more and more these days. He liked helping her with the hard words. The latest articles, however, had more to do with the weather than anything else.

Must be like Preacher said, at the End Times you won't know what season it is. But the Colonel said that was an old papist notion and not in the Bible anywhere. It sounded enough like the Bible to her, though, and it sure did fit what was going on.

First, winter got so mild they opened the windows and never lit a single fire, and the trees sprouted new leaves. By spring it got cold and a black haze blocked out the sun for nearly a month. Now summer was just plain freezing cold, putting frost on the corn and making it good for nothing. The hemp and tobacco stalks, what little had grown, got ruined last week from the weight of *ice*! If that wasn't a sign of the end of the world, she didn't know what was.

All she heard right before they were sent outside was, if they couldn't find more seed from last crop, they'd have nothing next year. They had next to nothing already. The kitchen garden put out just enough to make a little soup in the evenings, and everybody from the field hands to the Colonel looked mighty lean. Thank goodness, the chickens were still laying eggs.

She watched Imogene, Adaline and Rose play for a little while. Off in the distance she saw Tommy Miller grooming one of the ponies. He was a handsome boy, but younger than she was, even though he was the size of her brother Jerry. With parents like Hephzibah and Sandy, he was going to be as big as Goliath. Maybe she'd start calling him Goliath. No, he'd get his feelings hurt, and she didn't want to make him feel bad.

Anyway, she had her heart set on Simon, who had the most important job at Blue Spring, as far as the Colonel was concerned. He trained the thoroughbreds for all kinds of money to the farm. When he moved to Blue Spring last year along with his parents and his stuck-up sister Kate, she thought she'd die at first sight of him. He was a grown man and had no interest in her, but she'd heard Julia was ten years younger than the Colonel, and that was exactly the difference between her and Simon.

She led the girls around the yard, chased the chickens and the dogs, but she didn't want them to catch sight of that pony because there would be some hollering trying to keep them off it. Despite her devotion to Simon, she had no use for horses of any kind, and a pony could kick you in the head same as a giant stallion.

As hard as Julia worked trying to keep the little girls unspoiled, it all went out the door the minute their daddy came through it every year in the spring, and nothing made that man happier than the way those children took to his horses. He had them in a saddle before they could walk. She would be willing to bet that as soon as she had them back inside, he'd swoop one of them up to his shoulder and giddy-up around the room, out the door, and over to the stables before his bad leg gave out.

Horses ruled their lives. For the past two years, since the Colonel passed a law getting all the men repaid for the horses killed in the war, all anybody did was come to get their dead horse papers in order. Seemed like an awful lot more horses got killed than did any soldiers.

Patsy began to gallop in little circles so the girls would chase her, more to keep herself warm than anything else. Lately, every time she played with Adi and Genie, she couldn't help but think about the strange situation they were in.

Nobody around Blue Spring talked out loud about it, but even she knew Julia was one of their own, though for the life of her she couldn't see any African in the woman. Nobody'd guess these little girls were a slave's children. But they stayed apart from just about everybody for the months the Colonel ran off to Congress. They went nowhere except to see Miz Lindsay or a few nice trade folks in the village.

But that little Imogene was already learning her letters and smart enough to make a few all by herself on a slate! She'd seen it with her own two eyes, although she couldn't see what it signified for a five-year-old to be able to write anything. It sure made the grownups come close to crazy over it. She liked Imogene because she was eager to please. Just one look from Hephzibah or her mama with even a hint of crossness to it made her a lamb.

That Adi, though. Either laughing or crying her head off. It made Patsy feel bad for Imogene how everybody petted the little one so much more. White folks—she put Julia in with them—just didn't seem to have the knack to see the obvious.

They played until her nose ran as much as Adaline's. "Let's get on in now, before we turn into icicles!" Patsy said.

When they came into the foyer and got off their hats and coats, Lucy shooed them upstairs to the playroom. "Kate'll bring you up some warm milk and a bite to eat. We got ourselves some trouble brewing and the girls need to be out of shouting range," she confided to Patsy.

It was true; Patsy heard the Colonel getting worked up, and ol' mean McPherson's voice getting loud. It felt like the whole world was turning upside down. As she got the girls up the stairs, a terrifying thought took hold of her. What if the crops were ruined and they had to sell off Blue Spring? And her, their family and friends?

Another thought made her smile: if it really was the end of the world, Jesus would set them free.

JULIA LAY IN BED LISTENING to Richard pace from the dining room to the study. She never claimed the gift of second sight, but the eerie sense that the world was ending—her world, at least—drained her of feeling alive. Richard seldom smiled anymore unless one of the girls got a mild chuckle out of him.

He rarely touched her, and during nights like this, when she longed to have him near her, he limped back and forth downstairs, sometimes rustling stacks of papers, sometimes dragging his weary body outside to look at the horses. If his loneliness were anything like hers, they both might as well be dead.

What did it mean this ice in summer, the blackened sky last spring? Everyone's hearts failed them. Hers could barely beat unless it was in her throat or her stomach. What haunted her was the thought that her marriage was as unnatural as the weather, as false and unstable as the seasons they were enduring.

Perhaps the same thought had come to Richard, or perhaps it was plain ordinary human nature at work: he had fallen in love with Reverend Brown's daughter in Washington.

Julia huddled into a ball under the pile of blankets on their bed and cried.

THE SOUND WAS UNMISTAKABLE, and Hephzibah stood outside the bedroom door a full minute arguing with herself about going in uninvited. Julia still had a lot to learn about men, especially bossy men like the Colonel. Hephzibah's move from wet nurse to laundry matron last year made her more aware than Julia would have liked of what went on in that bed. Whole lot of nothing, mostly. She didn't think the problem came so much from their messed-up bodies as their confused minds. Julia was so betwixt and between everybody, she had no one to talk to.

"I didn't think you liked me," she remembered Julia saying that morning years ago. And that was the truth, then. Hephzibah had grown to love her like a sister once she realized Julia still saw herself as a slave. But she let no one in, too afraid of being seen as weak.

Hephzibah sighed. *Guess I'm just going to have to let her be strong all by herself.*

Fall 1816. Payne Farm at Great Crossing

"**I**t's a good plan, James," Richard forced himself to admit to his brother. They had discussed the possibility of creating their own steamboat line since Fulton's impressive success in 1811, but for the life of him, he could not understand why James chose now, when they all faced ruin. Most of all, Richard wondered why he himself had stopped dreaming great things.

"And Shreves just made it in his steamboat, going upstream from New Orleans to Louisville in less than a month!" This kind of schoolboy enthusiasm was so out of character for James, the rest of the brothers turned and looked at Richard for help. Only John Payne sat back in his chair, sipping his usual bourbon, above any petty bickering his pack of brothers-in-law might instigate.

"Well, financing this will be just about impossible without a grant. The banks have already got too tight a grip on you from your war supply contracts. We could apply for federal money, but getting it is tricky business, and for a congressman to be seen advocating for his family...it could be the end of my career in Congress."

"If you're worried that we would be perceived as opportunists after this year's crop disaster..." James stammered.

"No, that's not the problem. From the reports in the papers, ruination has been pretty general since the Tambora eruption. There'd be nothing special about our family in that respect."

"I think I know what you're getting at, Dick." John took another sip from his glass. "I remember an article in the *Republic* a few years back, accused us of getting rich off government contracts."

"Before or after that duel business?" Joel asked with a smirk.

"After, I think," John answered before he could stop himself. Betsey may have played favorites, but Joel rubbed him the wrong way. Twenty-seven, and still couldn't hold his liquor.

"Has anything come of your proposals for building that armory or military academy out here?" Benjamin asked, hoping to steer the conversation back.

"Calhoun simply wouldn't get behind either idea. Clay's star is rising, however, and he'll be able to get appropriations for the west, but it's going to take time. Don't forget, Clay and I both pushed for a congressional pay raise, and every man in Kentucky's ready to hang us. We're going to have to go back to Washington with our tails between our legs and rescind it before we can start pushing through anything for the good of the state. Much less for our family."

Richard got up and paced a few steps to stretch his sore leg.

He looked out the window, grimacing in pain. The youngest four of Betsey's enormous brood were playing chase with a couple of hounds. How he wished he could run again, throw children high in the air and catch them. Have more children. Not quite thirty-six and he felt sixty. He returned to his chair by the fire as John T spoke up for the first time.

"What about the home industry idea we talked about during that jaunt up to Fort Miegs in '12?"

"I've got a little support on that but haven't made a formal resolution on the matter. I got as far as telling them our military uniforms should be made here. We have a thousand times more waterpower in the west than they do in Massachusetts. We could build a cloth mill right here in the Crossing village. The machinery's the problem."

"I doubt if the Lowells and their ilk in New England would put up with that idea," James argued. He didn't like having his thunder stolen and wanted to get back to the steamboat plan.

"But that's the entire matter, isn't it?" Richard shot back. "We've got to get the west established in industry. We're the future out here, and it's against every principle to be beholden to New England on the one hand, and the South on the other. Why shouldn't we have factories turning out rifles and furniture and cloth, too?"

They laughed. John T raised his eyebrows. "Dick, you're with us! No speeches, please!"

"Just remember how hard it was for us to get our army supplied during the war," Richard continued, ignoring their attempt to calm him down. "We need to be able to take care of our own out here."

"But we still need more help from the government to get trade routes open," James interrupted. "The roads depend on whatever time and money locals can spare with their stretch of a road. The riverways are too irregular, but with a few dredges and dams we could keep stretches of water flowing all year round.

"And then our steamboat line could make runs from New Orleans all the way to the Erie. I'm telling you, boys, this is our future. Between our land speculations and making highways on the water, we could be the most powerful family in America. It's what Ma and Pa worked for. It's my duty as the oldest son to make sure it hap..."

"Now, who's giving speeches?" Benjamin cut James off by plopping a fresh cigar in his brother's mouth.

Betsey flung the door open, choked on the tobacco smoke and walked over to James. "Head home, baby brothers. I can't feed you and my sons tonight. I wish to high heaven God had never created volcanoes. Or cigars!" She yanked the cigar from her brother James's mouth and stuck it behind his ear.

Chapter 15
Lily
March 1819. Blue Spring

Hephzibah enjoyed the freedom of getting away from the big house on a cold day without having to wrap up. She and Lucy'd put a little meat on those scarecrow bones of Julia's, but she'd put a lot more of it on herself. The hard-muscle days at the rope walk were long since gone and she often found herself overheated and out of breath, as she was now, just from walking the couple hundred yards to the wheelwright shed.

The aroma of the chicken dumplings she was carrying out to Sandy and Tommy got the better of her. She stuck her finger under the pot cover and licked the cream sauce off with a sigh. Granny Ann had always been too stingy with the butter and lard. Not Lucy.

Tommy must have smelled the dumplings. He lay his heavy work apron aside and came grinning towards her. Handsome didn't even begin to describe her boy. Fourteen, but looked like a man. Tall as Sandy now. He hated when she mothered him. It was hard to hold back. "Don't you think it's about time the Colonel built you a proper workshop, honey?"

"Just glad to be out of the rope walk, Heph, and back in my trade." The wheelwright shed did need to be rebuilt. It let in too much cold air on days like this one. In summer, the only thing that spared him and Tom were the breezes coming off the spring every once in awhile.

"Fast as things are happening around here, the Colonel's gonna be the richest man in Kentucky, and all these old out-buildings will get replaced with stone ones," Tommy told her. She smacked his hand when he stuck his finger in the pot before she could even put it down on the work bench.

"You hold on, there. Papa's got to say grace," she scolded.

Sandy thought prayer as good a way as any to break the news to her. He put his tools down but kept his apron on. "Lord, thank you for good food and a fine mama. Keep us, her and young Rose safe while we go on this Yellow Stone expedition. May it be the means of our salvation, as well as our freedom if you could arrange it, amen."

The look on his mother's face made Tommy lose his appetite. "Son, you go on and eat. I'm gonna take a little walk down to the spring with your ma," Sandy said.

Hephzibah had gone blazing hot with shock when she heard the words of Sandy's prayer. Now, as they walked toward the cold water of the blue spring pond, she shivered uncontrollably. "Tommy going, too?" she asked through chattering teeth.

"Yes. You know he's got no choice."

"No, but you've got influence with the Colonel. You just have to say."

"Say, what? Tommy's a man now, and he's gonna have a chance to see something besides five square miles of Great Crossing and Blue Spring! We're going to Leestown with the Colonel next week, get on the *Calhoun's* first trip. What are you afraid of? He'll be with me. Jerry's going, too."

"What about Simon and Jacob?" she demanded.

"Staying for the horses, you know that," Sandy answered, looking over the water toward the tangle of woods on the other side.

"You know what I'm afraid of," she finally said.

"The Indians aren't near the problem everybody talks up. It's them dirty scoundrel traders ruining everything on the river, Colonel says."

"Indians don't bother me." She shivered, took a deep breath, and tried to hide the panic in her voice. "Have he and Jerry got a plan for running? Because if they do, you have got to stop them any way you can. Tommy's still a boy, a big innocent baby, Sandy! He couldn't be out Lord knows where at the mercy of bounty hunters! I'd shoot my own self and Rose and you, too, if he runs and ol' mean McPherson come cart us away from each other!" Hephzibah broke into sobs.

Sandy wrapped his arms around her, muffling her cries in his chest. "He hasn't told me about any such plans. And I imagine Jerry wouldn't run because of his sisters and Granny Ann. But Julia wouldn't let the Colonel sell off an old woman from her soft-headed granddaughter. Not any of us, either. He needs us too much."

"Julia can't do anything. And that man has a hard streak in him when it comes to doing what he says he'll do. How else can he keep all of us pinned down, and McPherson off our people's backs with his whip?"

"Look, Heph, this is what I'm thinking. Colonel, he's gonna be making so much money off this expedition from the government and trade, he'll be softened up to letting me buy us all outright. Another year and I'll have enough from my hire-outs."

"Is it all still there where you buried it?" she sniffed, wiping her face with the corner of her apron, relieved to think of something besides the destruction of her family. Times like this she felt to thank God she never did have any more children.

"It's safe. Safe as the grave it's next to."

May 1819

A bushel basket filled with spring peas sat between Lucy and Milly. Normally, the little girls would be put to shelling them, but the day was quiet. The Colonel had steamboat business down the river in Leestown, and with him out of the way, nobody bothered to visit and nobody except themselves required feeding.

"You remember Miss Suzanne?" Lucy asked, her question breaking the rhythmic snapping of the pea stems.

"Lord, now, wasn't that a long time ago? Before Henrietta died. Made that pretty little dress for Julia that started her getting big ideas." Milly always spoke low and mumbling. Lucy was one of the few who could understand her.

Lucy knew better than to allow Milly any room for grousing about Julia. This gossip was good, so she jumped to it. "Our new girl Lily's one of her husband's."

"One of his what?" Milly looked up with a sneer on her face. Sometimes Lucy thought her old friend was the unhappiest soul earth side of hell.

"Fancy girls. Seems Miss Suzanne found out about her husband setting up a house and all for Lily. Since she makes most of the money, she hollered about how she wasn't working her fingers to the bone and ruining her eyes just so he could go out on her."

"All that weasel Alphonse's fault, I bet," Milly added.

"That's what Katy said. When she went in with a tray for the Colonel and that awful man, she said the Colonel gave him a tongue thrashing like no man'd give unless he was still crazy about a woman.

He said, 'what am I supposed to do with a fancy girl?' and Alphonse said, 'I thought by now, your girl would've run out of her charms,' and Colonel smashed that glass of bourbon out of old Alphonse's hand and made Katy run out of the room."

"I'm guessin' she heard a lot more standing outside."

"She didn't even know what she was hearing. Alphonse saying nymph–somethin' and laughing like a fool, then talking about things she'd been doing since she was thirteen years old. Katy didn't want to hear anymore out of God-fearin' good sense, he was so nasty. Colonel said he wasn't gonna pay good money for trouble, 'specially when he didn't have money to spare."

Milly finished the last handful of peas and ran her hands through the basket, picking out tendrils of vine and flower buds and dropping them in her lap. Her apron looked like a work of embroidery when she finished. "But she's still here. Looks to me like Satan's come on in and set down for supper." She crossed her arms, stretched her legs out, and pursed her lips as if to add, nobody's got a lick of sense around here but me.

"It wasn't the Colonel. It was Julia. I know Jemima raised her to think sharp, but she's got that old woman's weakness for strays."

"Now just how do you know all this, Lucy? Katy couldn't have heard a thing if Julia'd gone into the room."

"Julia told me! She said, 'Lucy, the Colonel's old friend from New Orleans has brought us a real gem. She speaks French and embroiders like an artist and has the most beautiful penmanship I've ever seen. At last, I am going to have some help training my girls.' I felt so sorry for her, I kept my mouth shut. But somebody has to tell her she's got a serpent to her bosom."

"It's not going to be me, if that's what you're fishin' for," Milly replied. "Get fat ol' Heph to tell her. They're thicker than blood."

Lucy hated Milly's old ploy for sympathy. Julia showered her aunt with favors and never gave her any work Julia wasn't willing to do herself. But the fact that Milly remained a slave and Julia did not embittered Milly and poisoned her affection.

"Well, that's what I'm going to do, soon as I get these peas on the stove," Lucy sighed.

Milly sat for a while longer, letting her mind wander. She imagined different ways the presence of a slut like Lily on Julia's proper farm could play out. It was a welcome distraction from her own problem. By her best calculation, this baby would come around Christmas.

For three years, she and Curtis had been careful. When he came into the house to go over accounts with the Colonel or Julia, they avoided each other. Her freedom to move around Blue Spring on her own horse was just about the only good thing to come out of being Julia's aunt.

She'd been terrified of men mainly on account of Henrietta's horror stories, stories she never had a chance to tell Julia, who was always in Jemima's shadow. But "mean ol' McPherson" was the kindest, quietest soul she had ever known.

Would he keep her? She didn't know. She had to tell him soon before she started showing. Lot of women her age were long done having babies. But this was her first man, and her first child. She hoped her patience—even if it had come out of fear—would pay off and earn her the same kind of freedom Julia had.

July 1819

The day was barely underway and already Julia, Patsy and Hephzibah were drenched in sweat. Somehow Richard had gotten word to President Monroe, who was journeying on his western progress, and invited him to stay at Blue Spring. Word returned that the president would be delighted to stop over for the night following his appearance at Lexington's Independence Day celebrations. Richard acted like it was just an ordinary thing. Invite the president. Why not?

So much for her birthday. Julia didn't mind, but Genie and Adi might. Having a visit from the president was not nearly as important to them as making paper flowers and animal cookies for their mother. Richard always spoke at Great Crossing's July Fourth levee. He loved coming home to find his lunch plate trimmed with unidentifiable marzipan creatures.

What would President Monroe think of her? Was he the kind of man open to facts, or subject to rumors? By all accounts, he was a dour man, as was his wife and oldest daughter. But, since Richard showed no hesitation in proffering the invitation, he obviously had not considered her to be an embarrassment. He never hid the girls away when they had guests, and their existence had to be credited to some kind of mother. Perhaps he had talked to Monroe about her, as he had Jefferson? Perhaps he didn't think of her at all.

"This room just won't do, Julie." Hephzibah let out a sigh so hard it moved the ruffle on Patsy's cap. "He'll melt in his sleep, and the whole lot of us Johnsons will be strung up for assassination."

Julia was grateful for a reason to laugh. She couldn't explain why, but for the past month her friend's spirits had been so high every problem turned into just another reason to joke. "Let's move him across the hall to the northeast corner, then," Julia said when she stopped laughing.

"That little room with the acorn bed?" Patsy asked, but the note of scorn rubbed Hephzibah the wrong way.

"That little room's twice the size of my old cabin. Whole family could sleep in it."

Julia ran across the hall and checked over the room. It was small compared to Richard's and hers but by no means inadequate. The cool air that greeted her as she opened the door left no doubt it was the right place for the president to get a comfortable night's sleep. She rested her head against the door frame, indulging in the memory of her first night with Richard in this house, this very bed. It made her smile until that empty feeling set in.

"We'll need to bring in a cot for his valet," she said over her shoulder to Patsy.

"How many people are with him, do you know?" Patsy asked. Julia noticed the frown lines deepening on the girl's face and rubbed her shoulders for a moment to relax her.

"Twelve. Like the disciples," Hephzibah answered with a grin. "It does feel good in here, though," she said, walking over to the window. As she passed the small fireplace, even the updraft felt cooler. That entire side of the house benefited from the wind as it came off the blue spring in the summer. Winter was an entirely different matter, but that was not their concern today.

"We have to air out this mattress and retie the ropes. Run on downstairs, Patsy. Get Katy to help you. I'm gonna throw the feather bed from the window soon as I see you and then I want you to give it a real good shaking."

Patsy looked out the window and sighed. She headed out of the room with a bundle of sheets and pillows in her arms.

"What's the matter with our girl?" Julia asked.

"Love's what," Hephzibah chortled. "Simon. But I think somebody's got him hooked."

Julia gave an absent-minded "hmph" and squeezed between the wall and the bed. "I have to get this right, Hephzibah." She pulled up the tight covers, freeing the feather bed. "Lord knows what the men in his entourage will say if I dare to get one of them out of the right pecking order."

As she came back around the bed, the room looked dark and shabby. "Let's get some of the boys up here to move out this old dresser and bring in the chest of drawers from the blue room. This chair's too ratty as well. Maybe get one from my sitting area."

"Alright, but I think it's a whole lot of trouble for nothing. For one thing, he's old. And it'll be dark. Nobody notices spots on a horse once it's in the barn."

Kate fetched her brother and Simon from the stables so they could move the furniture. She left Patsy to beat the feather bed on the wash line all by herself. From the way she was hitting the thing, she must be remembering the sight of Simon and the new girl Lily going to it in the barn. Think people old as them would have found a less obvious place.

"Wash up those filthy hands and put your shoes on the back porch before you go into Julia's house," Kate told her brother crossly.

She headed back to the laundry shed to finish her work: rinsing a dozen sets of sheets. Her back hurt. How could something as no-account as a sheet weigh as much as a horse once it got wet? Lily was practically worthless. If that woman wasn't three or four months gone already, before her brother even got to her, then Kate was queen of England.

She hadn't told her mama about the goings-on, but Simon was so green he might not even know what Lily was up to. He'd figure it out in about six months when Lily started calling him daddy.

BLUE SPRING BUSTLED, just the way Richard liked it. The place had not felt so alive since 1812. But, just like the time during the war, Julia couldn't sleep for worry. No matter what he said to reassure her, she countered with an argument that always ended with "but he's the *president*, Richard!"

It was a waste of good labor pulling men and women from the rope walk and the mill to help her with the house and side yards. He would have preferred her to take it easy, too. The president might be past his prime, but the sight of a beautiful woman usually did more for parlor politicking than the sight of a speck-free floorboard.

He let his mind wander, replacing Julia's image with Lily's. He wanted to hate her for hurting Suzanne, but it wasn't really the girl's fault. God should never allow a seventeen-year-old to look like that. Julia had talked him into taking her, but now didn't want her in the house! Katy gossiped, no doubt in his mind. He'd see to it that she got a pretty dress and cap and serve the president his after-supper tray. Julia always retreated from their guests before that and wouldn't have a say in the matter, or he'd put his foot down.

He needed a pretty face to help him seal the plan he and Monroe had worked out for Indian education. He'd softened Congress up regarding the funding. The president would request it if he liked what he saw at James's little Indian school. But Richard envisioned a full-size academy, describing it to the president as a West Point for Indians. It would fit well at Blue Spring where he had room to build in any direction.

He had alerted his choice for headmaster, young Reverend Henderson, to be ready at a moment's notice to drop by for an introduction. Theo would be a good addition. He was about the only person he knew as serious as the president. He jotted a quick note to his friend and whistled for Jerry to deliver it.

"REMEMBER, HE PREFERS to be called "Colonel Monroe", not "Your Excellency."

Richard spoke so calmly Julia wanted to shake him. It sounded like a hundred, not a dozen, horses coming up the drive. She straightened her cap and brooch, remembering how he'd frowned when she came downstairs and criticized her for being too buttoned up for a warm summer evening. "Your lovely hair. Your charming shoulders," he opined. But she wanted the president's respect more than his admiration. Hephzibah stood with the girls in front of her, their ringlets perfect, their dresses flawless.

Milly and Lucy refused to leave the cookhouse for this assembly on the portico, but Granny Ann hobbled out, leaning on Mary's arm, just in time. Julia noticed the young people preening themselves at the last second—all but Lily, who stood completely still, staring straight ahead at the group of riders, a hint of a smile on her lips.

Richard walked forward, his limp controlled by the tightening of his stomach, and grinned at the gray-haired man who dismounted first. As Jerry whisked away the president's horse, Richard extended his hand. "Colonel Monroe," he grinned.

"Colonel Johnson," the president returned the grin with his own version of a smile: a thin-lipped grimace. As they started up the steps, Adaline broke free and ran to her father.

"My daughter, Adaline." She curtsied but could not take her eyes off the president's chin.

"How old are you, Miss Adaline?" Monroe said, giving her a courtier's bow in response to her curtsy.

"I will turn six in November. My father almost died right when I was born. The Indians shot him lots of times. Have you seen his great big scars?"

Julia moved toward her, but Richard squinted to tell her to stay put.

"I have not had the pleasure, no," Monroe said, and knelt to look at her closely.

"Have you been in a war? I think you have to be in a war to be a colonel."

"Yes, I have been in a war or two."

Julia and Hephzibah both gasped as Adaline stuck her finger in the deep dimple on Monroe's chin. "Is that where the Indians shot you?"

The president's staff froze in place. Julia felt her knees grow weak, and even Imogene shook her head in disbelief. Monroe stood up and threw back his head in laughter. He gathered Adaline in his arms. "I have a granddaughter who likes that hole in my chin, too," he said.

Richard presented Imogene. "My eldest. Already a talented little musician."

"I have two daughters also, Miss Imogene," he said kindly.

"*Je voudrais bien chanter pour vous.*" I would like very much to sing for you, Genie said solemnly, keeping her eyes on the president's boots.

Monroe's face lit up. Despite his rough years in France as ambassador, he still loved the language. "*Alors, tu vas chanter pour moi, ce soir?*" Then you're going to sing for me tonight? He asked kindly. He looked over at Richard. "A pleasant surprise."

"Julia's doing. She has a gift I am happy to say Imogene has inherited." Richard turned and reached out his hand, but not for her to take. "Julia?" he said, bringing his arm down. "Please, come forward and meet our guest."

Hephzibah stepped forward also and took Adaline from the president. Julia curtsied and smiled shyly. "Would you prefer to take refreshment or see your room, Colonel Monroe?" She addressed him quietly, receding into the background.

Throughout the week as she prepared for the president's visit, she wondered how her husband would handle the delicate matter of introducing her. How she longed to hear him say "my wife" or "Mrs. Johnson" as he had ten years ago.

But they rarely shared each other as husband and wife anymore. At least he showed no shame in admitting she was the mother of his children. The surprising kindness Monroe showed the girls and her lessened the sting of Richard's ambivalence.

Like well-drilled troops, Julia's small army of servants led the president's entourage to sleeping quarters scattered throughout the house and grounds, then back to dinner. Milly and Lucy prepared a spread that would have made Henrietta proud.

Julia was a little surprised to see Theobald and the new neighbor, Reverend Henderson, follow Patsy into the drawing room for Imogene's little performance after dinner. As she accompanied Genie's song, the sight of Theobald made her hands fumble over the keys, earning a wide-eyed stare from her daughter. She looked up, hoping to dispel his influence on her, and saw him immediately look away from her and toward the portrait of Washington.

Except for Adaline stealing a little of her sister's thunder, Genie's performance went off better than Julia had dared to hope. She stood by the doorway as the girls made their goodnight curtsies. Her eyes met Theobald's for a moment and his brooding face lightened with the hint of a smile for her. But he glanced at something behind her that changed his look to a frown. She turned and saw Richard pulling Lily aside for a few private words.

The girls ran to their father just as Lily headed off to the pantry. Richard lifted Adi into the air for a good night kiss, then bent over

Imogene to compliment her performance. Hephzibah took them upstairs with a worried look over her shoulder at Julia.

"What did you want with Lily?" Julia asked with a forced smile. She swallowed back her jealousy, however, when she remembered Theobald.

"I told her to get a clean apron on, then bring in the smokes tray."

"Patsy's already doing it."

"Then she can bring in the bourbon."

The stillness of his expression, the lack of small talk about the girls, put her on edge. Warily, she asked, "Do you think it wise to bring out whisky with the new reverend here?"

"It's Kentucky, Julia. The president expects it. And Henderson's a man of the world when it comes to politics. He's not some fanatic Campbellite." Richard stepped away from the stairs and headed toward the drawing room. "Good night," he mumbled.

She could have been a stranger.

When Richard entered the crowded drawing room, Theobald made a quick exit, hoping to find Julia. She stood, motionless, at the bottom of the stairs. For a moment he hesitated, thinking of his wife. Her demands for a beautiful home, her disgust at his embraces, her refusal to have any more children. He felt, as he knew Julia did, trapped in a life of hidden misery.

"Tired?" He asked. The word must have startled her.

The tears in her eyes destroyed all his defenses. "Julia," he whispered, and led her down the hall toward the study, the room that held the most memories for him in this house. He had kept vigil in this room for her. He had helped Richard hang on to life here.

In the past ten years, he had watched Richard grow in strength and influence while Julia had shriveled before his eyes. Now he felt nothing but contempt for Richard. If Julia were truly his wife, which he doubted more and more, then treat her like a wife, not a wretched housekeeper.

The hallway was abandoned, thanks to the president. They reached the room unseen. He shut the door. Only a little light bled through a break in the draperies. He untied her cap and put his hands firmly on each side of her head. The darkness made their faces featureless, but he found her mouth and kissed her with the passion he had denied himself an entire lifetime.

Julia had been given no time to think about what was happening to her. The indifference of her husband, the pain in Theobald's eyes, the yearning to be loved, all combined to make her yield to his impulse. She kissed him in return, hungrily and greedily, until he broke away from her with a sob.

"Julia, God forgive me, but I have loved you for so long." He wiped the tears from his cheeks and grabbed her again, holding her close.

"May God forgive me, too, James." Julia buried her face in his chest, not daring to meet his eyes.

"Our lives should have been together." His voice faltered. He struggled to control the emotion that choked the words he had so little time to say. "We could have done so much good. I know I am in the wrong to do this, and I promise not to trouble you. But you deserve to be loved. Treasured."

He lifted her face to his and covered her eyes, her hair and neck with his touch and with his lips. He felt her skin quiver and heard her quick, shallow breathing. Her warmth and eager response to his touch drove his desire to the brink.

He could not let her go. He held her close, swaying her, covering her body in long strokes of his hands to imprint the feel of her upon his mind. She pressed her head against his heart, letting her tears soak into his waistcoat.

The sounds of loud laughter near the window dragged her miserably back to reality. She pulled away from him just far enough to find her cap. He meekly placed it on her head, then tucked in a few stray curls before tightening the string in back. His gentleness broke her heart.

"I have to go." She dropped her head against his chest again.

"And I have to let you go, don't I?"

She nodded.

"I'm so sorry to have destroyed your trust in me..."

"No! Nothing could ever destroy it. I have never trusted anyone as I have you."

"This is our only time. Julia." He whispered her name. "My Julia." He pulled just far enough away to wipe her tears. "I feel free of the most enormous burden I have ever borne." His long fingers moved down her neck and shoulders to her arms until he found her hands. He lifted them to his lips. "Know, whenever you need to know it, that I adore you."

"And I you." Slowly, she pulled her hands away, feeling as if her soul were being rent from his.

When she left, he dropped onto the sofa, put his head in his hands and wept.

OVER SIXTY MEN CROWDED together in the drawing room. Richard had an innkeeper's eye for his guests' comfort, and his idea to have cheerful serving girls instead of sour faced butlers succeeded in making everybody happier. At least a third of the men here tonight were kin, and all of them, from his nephew Willie to his brother-in-law John, ogled Lily like barge hands. Even the president seemed to bid for her attention.

Richard watched her appraisingly. He had been impressed by her ability to choose a cigar, trim and light it for a guest. She was making a pretty show of waiting on Monroe, Theo and a few others standing in a tight circle. Her banter got a chuckle out of everyone except Theo. Richard had never seen the president so relaxed. Despite his abhorrence for all New Orleans's decadent ways, he had to grudgingly admit their girls had the corner on feminine wiles.

Patsy walked away from the group, leaving Lily to enjoy the attention unhampered. Her path led her in the direction of her master. The bottle of water on the tray was still full, the decanter of whisky nearly empty.

"Slow down on the bourbon. The president has to be up early for the Georgetown parade, and then he has a long ride to Frankfort."

"It's not the president, sir," Patsy whispered. "It's the doctor."

"Theobald? He only uses liquor on his patients," Richard quipped.

Patsy hurried away to get the tray restocked. Curious, he headed Theo's direction, stopping to make a joke or add a comment about the size of the crowd as he passed among the men. Some of the younger fellows took the hint and stepped onto to the porch to get some air. Others took off toward the lawns. Within a few minutes, the temperature and the noise became bearable.

Aware of Richard's intent to seek him out, Theobald made his courtesies to the president and stepped away, approaching his host. "Her French is native. If you like the New Orleans accent, that is. My skill in the tongue may be a bit weak, but I think our president plans on them having a *tête-a-tête* later on."

"Think that's the bourbon talking?"

Theobald reached unsteadily for the little chair by the pianoforte. "Medicinal. I have a cold." Richard looked him over. His eyes were red. His thick black hair needed a good combing. He had some nondescript stains on his waistcoat.

"You know, Dick, you have lived a charmed life since the volcano set the rest of the world back. You are a lucky man. Luckiest I know. Stores, leases. The mills. Now the steamboats. Going to make you the richest man in Kentucky."

Richard noticed an edge in his old friend's voice and shifted away a few inches.

"Oh, by the way," Theobald continued, grabbing Richard's arm, and pulling him back, "I put in a good word for the school to our president. He's worried about diseases coming off the Indian boys. Told him most of our best cures come from the Indians."

He took a long draw from his glass. "Or our slaves." His voice had grown louder. A few of the adjutants nearby stared at him for a moment before returning to their conversation.

Richard smiled and nodded toward the drawing room doors. Theobald sat instead, put his glass on a stack of Julia's music, and stared at the piano forte. Without engaging the keys, his fingers moved over them, palpating them softly as he would an injured man's bones.

"He wanted to talk about his sick little wife. Bad case of melancholia, my opinion, but of course I didn't tell him that. Living with a politician's enough to break any woman."

Theobald's dark eyes looked deep into Richard's. Then his aristocratic face contorted with a huge, unnatural grin.

Monroe stood at the farthest end of the room, but Richard could not stop the reflex of turning to make sure Theobald had not been heard by a nearby aide. He leaned over the piano. With all the compassion he could muster, he said in a low voice, "Go home and take care of yourself, Theo. I'll get one of my boys to drive you."

Theobald rose abruptly. He seemed to tower over Richard. As if the bourbon had never touched him, he spoke in his old, distinct voice. "No need. My head will clear in a moment."

He stepped toward the foyer. "Give Julia and the girls my regards. I did not get to pay my respects this evening."

December 1819

Freezing rain clattered against the roof of the carriage, reminding Theobald of grapeshot on the battlefield. Among soldiers, his courage never failed him. Why did it fail him now? Fool, he derided himself. Utterly stupid man, he added for good measure as the memory of Julia stirred him. Where was his regret, remorse?

For nearly six months he had avoided Blue Spring. Richard had been back in Washington for weeks. By most accounts, the man's health seemed greatly improved by the distractions of his steamboat line and the prospect of the Indian boys' academy. His newest diversions were a hankering to become senator and ridding the land of debtors' prisons. So noble. So self-serving. Julia's devotion was entirely wasted on the man.

And my feelings for her are a waste as well, for we are not adulterers.

Nancy had looked up from her mending with a sigh and clicked her tongue when Simon appeared on their doorstep. He stammered uncomfortably about two babies coming at once. "Julia's handling Lil's and my baby without a problem," Simon told him with a mix of pride and fear. "But Phoebe can't handle Milly, and Milly don't want Julia at her and McPherson's place. She's old, Daphne says, and having a terrible time."

His wife had not even helped him on with his coat.

When Julia heard the carriage spitting up gravel along the drive, she hurried down the servant's stairs, leaving Daphne with Lily and her newborn daughter in Lily's dormer room. The girl was built for having babies with the least amount of effort, she thought bitterly.

Everyone had suspected Simon was not the father, although Julia halfheartedly hoped he was. He certainly wanted to be. Lily had been heard boasting within Julia's hearing that the father was "the most important man in the country". But the baby's good size and strength lay the blame on Suzanne's husband, or that scoundrel Alphonse. Someone a good two months before Lily ever saw the president.

She tossed off her bloodstained apron, grabbed the heavy shawl she kept by the back door and headed to the carriage, blaming the sleet, not Theobald, for making her shiver uncontrollably. "Simon, fetch Jerry to take the doctor out to McPherson's house. Then go see Lily. There's somebody you'll want to meet."

Theobald moved to open the carriage door, but Julia stopped him, watching Simon run toward the quarters next to the stables. Finally, she climbed into the carriage and sat across from him, his long legs forcing hers to press against them. Her head bowed, she stared at his hands as he removed his gloves, as his fingers sought for, then surrounded her own. He held them solemnly, as if they were exchanging vows. Neither of them had the will to break the silence.

When the crunch of boots on gravel alerted them to Jerry's approach, Theobald closed his eyes and willed his hands to release her.

"You have saved me many times. Save Milly?" Julia pleaded. He nodded glumly, then opened his eyes just in time to see her tears.

He grabbed her hands again. "God help me, but I cannot bear parting with you. Stay with me. It's the only way we can be together."

"Milly doesn't want me..."

"*I* want you. In the only way I can have you—working by my side. Please, Julia."

She nodded, opened the door, and told Jerry to drive them the mile to McPherson's place. Theobald's demeanor swiftly changed from frustrated lover to controlled physician. She moved to sit next to him for the few minutes' journey while he swiftly explained some of the procedures he expected her to perform.

She thought of Mrs. Lindsay's strong arms and gentle sturdiness and the struggle of bringing Adaline into the world. Suddenly, she felt overcome by exhaustion and rested her head against Theobald's shoulder. He stopped talking mid-sentence, cradled her head against the bumps in the road and held her close to him for the brief minute they had left together.

"How could I be so selfish? You've already delivered a baby. That's enough for one day."

She laughed softly. "Practically the only thing I had to do was make sure she didn't get out of bed after giving birth. I didn't know it could be so easy for some women."

"That's because nothing has ever been easy for you. And I'm afraid I'm only making things harder," he sighed. Jerry pulled the carriage close to McPherson's porch. "Let's see what we can do for poor Milly."

He pushed open the door, and Julia scrambled out, tightening her shawl against the freezing rain.

"I fear it's going to take a miracle," Julia replied. She knocked gently at the door.

"I can do miracles with you by my side," he whispered. When the door opened, the despair in McPherson's eyes told them it might take much more.

May 1821

The breezeway to the cookhouse looked like a ship in full sail. Winter had all but devoured spring, and Hephzibah had decreed that every scrap of bed linen needed the benefit of a good airing. This was the first mild day of sunshine and soft breezes in months. Hephzibah and Katy had carefully spread the sheets over a network of hemp twine, and all the women of the household passed along the cloth inspecting for holes. Julia had already begun darning the sheet nearest her, desperate to set her mind on something else besides their latest money crisis.

Richard stood on the brink of losing everything they had. When she passed by the dining room and glanced at the painting of the castle by the sea, her eyes would play the mean trick of putting the figure of her husband on the edge of the cliff.

The gloriously named "Yellow Stone Expedition" he and James organized had ended in disaster. Sand bars and Indians had torn up two of their beautiful steamboats. The government had confiscated and scrapped the others after the entire country's banking system collapsed.

He no longer pressed his plans for the Indian boys' school out of idealism, but for grant money. That would not be forthcoming until Congress could get the economy out of a hole as deep as the blue spring.

Imogene, Rose and Adaline had the eighteen-month-old "Christmas twins" on the porch, trying to teach them pat-a-cake. Leticia caught on to the rhythm in seconds. Patience, however, clapped on odd beats and laughed the entire time. Her only words were "mama" and anything that rhymed with it.

After months of coaxing, Julia convinced Milly that Patience would talk if she played around other children. Theobald had confided in Julia after the baby's delivery that she might have a hard time in life. The umbilical cord had tightened around her neck before he could deliver her. He had seen it before, mentioning that Mary had probably suffered the same fate.

Milly had named her Patience as a tribute to her own long wait for love and motherhood. It certainly seemed inspired, for Julia's aunt had been transformed into a most loving and patient mother.

Bored with the game, Patience scampered under the billowing sheets and came out near the cradle where Lily's new baby was sleeping fitfully.

"Patience, get on over here by your mama. You don't want to wake up little La-la," Milly gently coaxed.

Within seconds, Lily jumped from behind a sheet, yanked Patience away and roughly picked up the baby. "Keep that little puddin' head of yours away from my baby. And her name is *Lydia*. I do not want Leticia or Lydia to have any kind of pet names. Ever."

They all turned when they heard the porch boards groan. Hephzibah dropped her armload of down pillows.

"And just what do you have to be so high and mighty about? At least poor little Patience got a mother who wants her! If the rest of us weren't around to look after your girls, they'd been run over by a wagon or drowned in the blue spring. A dog's a better mother than you!"

Julia signaled to Imogene to take the younger girls inside to play.

"You are just angry because Lydia is not your son's child," Lily shot back.

Hephzibah moved forward, chest heaving. "My boy's got more sense than to lay down with a little tramp like you."

Lily stood her ground, looking Hephzibah up and down with a sneer. Speaking softly so only Hephzibah could hear, she said, "Look under the bench at Little George's grave and you will understand how much he loves me."

Sandy's freedom money. That Tommy could betray them was unthinkable. But how could Lily know where it was buried? Hephzibah took a step back, shaking her head in disbelief. "You worthless slut," she choked, rage distorting her features. She grabbed a sheet and began twisting it. "I'll break you like a stalk of hemp!" She ran after Lily, struggling to get her huge body near the girl.

"No! Heph, that's my grandbaby!" Lucy yelled, yanking at the sheet in Hephzibah's hands. Kate ran to help her mother. Granny took Mary to the far end of the porch while Patsy leaned against the side rail enjoying the ruckus.

Julia cried out, "Stop it, all of you!" Everyone ignored her.

Lily clutched her baby like a protective shield. Lydia wailed from the pressure of her mother's grip, but Lily shouted over the noise.

"I can't help it if he loves me! All men want me, whether I want them or not!" Her voice rose to a screech. "I have been loved by the greatest man in America! By the richest in New Orleans. If your master's old whore Suzanne had not ruined my life, I would be a free woman, with my own houseful of slaves! Like her!" She kicked a clod of dirt toward Julia.

Contention rarely disturbed Julia's home. For the past several years, the women of Blue Spring looked to one another as indispensable members of a complex family, bonds forged between them as they dealt with and survived crisis upon disaster. Until now. Julia stepped toward Hephzibah, who had buried her face in the sheet meant to wring Lily's neck. She mumbled a few words of consolation and sent Hephzibah back to the porch.

The delicate balance between hope and despair in their lives often hinged on the smallest slights or privileges. Julia was skilled at maintaining balance in these subtle matters. But nothing was small or subtle with Lily. Julia's lifelong confusion about her place made confrontation a torment, and Lily preyed upon that weakness. The girl was eager for a fight. Not with Hephzibah or Lucy. Only Julia.

Mustering all her self-control, Julia kept her voice low and steady. She carefully approached Lily, who stood near the billowing sheets with a wild, careless look in her eyes.

"We don't think about being slave or master here."

Lily let out a sharp laugh. "*Menteuse.*" Liar.

Julia steadied herself. She had watched Jerry many times control a skittish colt with a few calm and gentle words.

"We are just women, working to help each other get through another day. If you'd only try, you'd discover that every one of us has had more than their fair share of heartache. Even more than you think you've suffered."

The softness of Julia's deep, soothing voice irritated Lily to distraction. Only in her native tongue did she have the skill to destroy her so-called mistress. In French, she hissed, "I don't *think* I've suffered! I know I have. I know a lot of things about this place, about you and your so-called husband. I know who you really love. And I have seen our master's eyes take in the young girls, and why he has no use for you in his bed. I know of his despair over losing the steamboats and all of his money, and I know what a man who has lost everything needs."

Lily stopped, anticipating the effects of her words on Julia. A strange quiet fell over them. No one broke the silence. The only sound came from the sheets snapping in the wind. Without understanding the words, everyone had clearly understood Lily's menace.

Milly walked toward them, then stood next to Julia, taking her by the hand. Lucy stepped out from the maze of sheets and took her other hand. Hephzibah struggled down the porch steps and stood behind her like a belligerent guardian angel. Kate and Patsy, Granny Ann and Mary joined them.

Julia had never felt so much love in her life.

Chapter 16
Independence Day
July 4, 1825

Simon perched five-year-old Lettie on his shoulder and leaned against the fence rail. Her hands were full of long, sweet grass to feed Old Hickory, the Colonel's favorite mount. Tommy guarded Lala's hands closely as she patted the buckskin's withers, careful not to let her near the horse's mane for fear she might give it a good yank. Not a soul dared call her Lydia; Lettie hated to hear her baby sister called anything but Lala.

The two men had finally come to an uneasy truce over the girls. Although Lucy had convinced her son he had not fathered Lettie, she'd been powerless to help him bond with Lala, his actual daughter. Lily had tormented Simon for months with images of Tommy as her lover, and in his mind Lala belonged to his friend.

Though Tommy knew that Lala was not his own, Lily's insistence that he was the father made him take responsibility for her. All that mattered to Julia, Lucy and Hephzibah was seeing these children receive the love and protection their mother had no interest in giving.

The Colonel sorrowed only a little to see Alphonse take Lily away from Blue Spring. He reserved his grief for Alphonse's news that Suzanne had died from one of the fevers all too common in New Orleans, buried without the devotion she merited.

To her credit, Lily shed tears over leaving her daughters, but no one wept to see her go—not the men she had used for amusement, nor the women she had tried to divide, nor the children she had brought into the world.

Lucy hollered at them to come for breakfast. "Let's go see what Mammaw has for us this mornin'," Tommy said. The men put the little girls down and watched them run toward the cookhouse. They followed slowly, surveying the grounds and the work laying ahead for them. "We get one more rain, the grass might come back from all the stompin' down it got from that Frenchy's visit," Simon mumbled.

"Lord, I don't know. Five thousand folks, that's ten thousand feet, trampin' all over this lawn and their horses tearin' up our pasture." Tommy shook his head. "What was the Colonel thinkin' having ol' Lafayette come here?"

"Heard talk about the Indian school, probably. Wanted to see if such a thing could really exist. You know those Frenchies always got along with Indians. Lots of Frenchy half-breeds." Simon regretted mentioning that and wondered if his talk of French people made Tommy think of Lily as it did him.

"What I want to know is," Tommy took a long pause. "How come Washington needed some prissy Frenchy to help him fight? Littlest man I think I ever saw."

Simon laughed. "Liked our horses, though. Knows his horse flesh."

Tommy headed to the school grounds. He was the new slave driver on the construction site of a bigger dormitory for the Indian boys. The place was busting at the seams. All their workshops and sheds had been converted to something for the school and he resented it.

He had no love for these boys. They threw dirt clods and rocks at the workers when Reverend Henderson wasn't looking. Colonel had given him permission to take matters into his own hands next time it happened.

"Tommy, you're bigger than your pa," he'd said. You know how scared a little scrawny Choctaw boy's gonna feel right up next to you? Go over there when you're carryin' one of those big slabs of stone. Give 'em a contest. Bet it'd take ten of 'em to even budge it off the ground. Teach 'em some respect."

"Why don't Reverend Henderson just whoop 'em?" Tommy had asked.

"He does. But they've been trained from babies to endure pain. Hunger, cold, just about any hardship. Ever hear of the Spartans?"

Tommy said no, and the Colonel told him about the old Greek tribe. He felt sorry for them. He felt sorry for the Indian boys a little, being so far from their homes and families. But not sorry enough to put up with their insults. What held him back was knowing he and his pa would soon have enough to buy the family free.

As he passed his father's wheelwright shop, Tommy saw a few buggies and people on horseback draw up and look over the place. Since the Indian boys' arrival, and the Frenchy Lafayette's departure, Blue Spring had become famous. People stopped on the main road and stared at the property, talking with the Colonel if he happened to be out with some of his people or the horses. Julia'd made him proud by turning out a bigger party than any white lady ever had in the whole country.

Lately, when Patsy lay next to him at night, she'd giggle about how the Colonel had gone back to lovin' on Julia. He didn't believe it; she only said it to get him going.

THE BEDROOM DOOR OPENED, and Richard strode toward Julia, carrying an armful of flowers. She watched his movements in the mirror, looking hopefully for any sign of genuine affection, any indication to drop her defenses.

"Happy Birthday, darlin'," he smiled. "I'm going to take the girls with me to the flag raising. Think it's about time they heard their old pa in action!"

She pivoted on her stool in front of the dressing table to get a better look at him. This was a direct approach meant to disarm her; instead, her protective instincts took over. Once, his insistence on ignoring the cruel reality of her situation had made her love him even more. But to ignore it where their daughters were concerned ranked as blind stupidity. Before she could control her tongue, the words escaped. "Oh, Richard, no!"

Richard dropped the flowers, dew spreading over the damask settee where they fell. "What?" He tilted his head and leaned toward her, the gold and turquoise of his eyes shining with hurt and latent fury.

"They aren't prepared for this kind of rejection, not public humiliation in front of you." When he remained silent, she hurriedly explained, "I thought we had long ago accepted the rules of society where the girls and I are concerned. You've never before wished to expose us to public shame." Her hands began to tremble; she turned away from him, put down her hairbrush and rested her hands on the edge of the vanity.

"I don't believe you need fear that," Richard said in a slow, even voice. "You saw how Lafayette and everyone else raved over their performance at our levee. I think my experience in these matters deserves more of your faith. This is the beginning of the world opening up for them."

He paced around the table and chairs then shoved the flowers aside, annoyed at the dampness on the divan. "And I think your negative tone is the only thing that causes them pain. Don't you understand that your predisposition to look at the dark side of everything hurts them?"

This insult, rather than shaming Julia, emboldened her. She stopped shaking and said in an even voice, "It's not being negative. It is being realistic. You don't know what it's like to be scorned." Moving toward the armoire, she glanced back at him before pulling out the lower drawer containing her undergarments.

Richard stood up and followed her, watching as she changed her pantalets and demi. When she put her day frock over her head, it stuck. He gave it an impatient tug and sighed as the thin fabric drifted over her curves. They were victims of familiar routine now, actions that never interfered with their thoughts, which had become quite separate over the past difficult years.

"What do you think I go through every day that I am in Washington? It's nothing but constant rejection."

Always it turned to him! Away from her and the girls and back to his life, his needs, his everything. She had little sympathy for the kind of rejection he dealt with in Washington. And why, in her distress, did the image of Miss Mary Brown come to mock her? Even she knew that the Browns still had hopes for their daughter becoming Richard's "real" wife.

Julia failed to hear the tension in his voice or acknowledge the determination in his eyes. She noticed nothing. A new image crowded out Miss Brown: that of Scott County's puffed-up white women shoving aside her daughters. She had to keep herself together because Richard respected self-control and not much else, anymore.

"But isn't that a rejection of your ideas, not you as a man? Richard, you built us a world apart, and over the years, people have been kind, but only when they come through that gate out front. Just a few yards off our property, on the main road, they change. Those who smile at us here do it for your sake. Out there, they ignore our existence. If our town rejects them out in public just once, they will be duty bound to continue to reject them the rest of their lives. Please, I beg you, allow the girls to stay home where they're safe!"

Richard took a conciliatory step toward her, reached for her hand and kissed it. "I am sorry for all you have endured because of me, Jewel."

He had not called her that in a long time, but she knew all his little ploys to disarm her. Aware of what he expected her to say, she matched his polite comment with her own forced words. Kissing her hand? Speaking gently? Done only out of his sense of gallantry. Such things were no longer his personal truth. The duality of his nature in Washington had become so much a part of him, it infected the man she once adored in everything he said and did once he was home.

"I've endured nothing that I didn't expect to encounter all along. But the girls? They shouldn't be fed on false hopes. Our little bit of pride is all that keeps us feeling human."

Richard began to circle the chairs and divan. "That's all changed. It changed because of Lafayette, when he treated them like they were his own granddaughters, in front of every one of those old dragons that have made your life so unhappy. Even my mule-headed sister praised them to the rafters, and James? James, of all people, kissed them!"

"Only to impress Lafayette! Richard, you have to see things as they really are! You have to try and under..."

"How can you twist their kindness like that? They will be there to support me and the girls today. And for all the other old biddies, this is the perfect opportunity to build on what Lafayette did. We have to act now while it's fresh in all these people's minds."

She kept still, swallowing back the nausea that rose when she had to contradict him on any matter. Worked up as they both were, Julia knew she must handle him more carefully. Over the past ten years, Richard had become unpredictable in his treatment toward her. She blamed it on the physical pain he endured from his war injuries, the financial disasters after the volcano's ruination and the Yellow Stone expedition's failure.

He had come under even greater pressure since the Marshalls had begun their new attacks and accusations of fraud and graft. They ridiculed his campaign to end debtors' prisons, and wanted the Indian school shut down. He had to succeed, to keep favor with the locals and Congress.

Not even throwing her body over the girls would stop him from going through with this, but in one final attempt, she tried a compromise.

"Then please, just take Imogene. She's thirteen going on thirty."

At least, he chuckled at their old joke.

"If she's not treated with the respect due your daughter, she will know how to behave. Adi, on the other hand, will make a scene. She falls apart at the least slight, and nothing prevails upon her to be sensible."

"But how can I show favoritism to one over the other? I could no more deprive Adi of this than I could Genie."

She should have known better. Richard loved their firstborn, but Adi had him completely under her thumb. At the thought of their youngest, Julia's face convulsed. "This is going to crush their spirits. Why can't you see that?"

Rising terror made her reckless; she grabbed his arm with both hands. "I refuse to let you do this to them!"

He tore away, forcing her nails to drag across his arm, leaving a jagged trail of broken threads in his shirt.

"You 'refuse'?" He mocked. His voice froze her, stopping her feet and her heart. "What kind of talk is this? Are you jealous of your own children?"

"How can you say that to me?" Julia stepped past him and headed toward the door to find the girls.

He caught her wrist and held her fast. "I do not like you this unreasonable and stubborn," he said in a mild voice, barely above a whisper, the vein in his forehead now a dark blue ridge. "Mind yourself, Julia. I will sell you off before I let you interfere with me and my daughters."

She broke her wrist free from his grip and shrank from him. "*Sell me off?* What could you possibly mean with such a threat?"

Richard's voice fell on her like a hammer. "Father did not free you. He transferred ownership of you. To me."

As she stared at him in disbelief, his features blurred into an unrecognizable mask. It couldn't be true. She never saw what Robin wrote that agonizing day, but no record at Blue Spring bore her name. So why would he say it?

"Is there any love left in your heart for me if you can be so cruel?"

"I would never have told you if you hadn't pushed me, but you act like it is you who own Blue Spring, like you are the girls' only parent. I take insult and debate from everyone, my family, all my colleagues in Washington. You were my only source of peace. Now, I see I will have to find it in the girls."

She dropped onto the edge of the bed to stop her fall, to still the crashing waves that pounded in her head as she drifted away from him.

Tell me, Lord, how can my heart even beat any longer?

Richard seemed to want something more from her as his hand gripped the door, but she sat beaten and emptied of every good thing he had ever done for her or given her. Far worse, he was bent on leaving and taking the girls, forcing them to take a shaming as unthinkable as being stripped naked before the town.

"It is more important to have peace in our home than anything," she choked out the memorized phrase, her oft-used olive branch.

Nothing before had ever stolen their peace so thoroughly. When she refused to look at him, he closed the door and walked down the hall. She heard him talking to the girls, encouraging them to look their best, getting giggles out of them that she herself never elicited.

Julia sat on her hands and bit her lips to keep from grabbing the bric-a-brac, from throwing it at the door and screaming at the top of her lungs. As her family walked downstairs, Richard made excuses for her: "She's not feeling well and wants more rest."

Despite her resolve, the tears began to flow. A sardonic little laugh escaped her at the thought that, when they had faced near-bankruptcy, he could have sold her off to pay down his debts! She had felt trapped for many years but had taught herself to find joy in life by devoting every thought to her daughters. Repenting of every longing for James. Clinging to any scrap of genuine affection her husband tossed her way.

But for Richard to threaten her. Not since that night on the road to Cincinnati when he told her to get out had he been cruel. That time had been to prove how much he wanted her, needed her to stay. This time proved he did not want or need her.

Slave. But he had married her! On free soil! Didn't that make her free? And if it did not, why hadn't he freed her legally after all these years? Dear God, how was she going to endure being a slave for the rest of her life?

The sweet faces of Rose and Mary came to her, swiftly followed by ugly images of Granny Ann's bent back, of Hephzibah's swollen feet.

"No!" Julia cried into her hands. "I'm not going to fight myself again. I am a mother. More than a wife, more than a slave."

She had to concentrate on the girls. Sooner or later, they would walk through the door of their home, and she had to be ready for them, whatever the outcome. What could she do to ameliorate their pain?

"Sufficient unto the day is the evil thereof," Mama used to say to her. Get them through the day; get them to forget, just for today.

Julia bitterly wished she never had to lay eyes on Richard again, although she would be overjoyed for the girls' sakes to have him lord over her that he was right. She had felt the town's backside of the hand and had learned to live with it, but her daughters were too young to grapple with this kind of hypocrisy.

Hoping the girls would not think her truly ill, she changed into a cheerful pink frock she had not worn in years, one that Genie had loved as a little girl, though Richard said it was too youthful for her to wear any longer. Thirty-five today. That wasn't so old.

Why couldn't he have complimented her on keeping her figure, instead? Too youthful? How unfair! He was the one getting thick. And gray. She pinned her hair up in a style that Adi liked, and found the little pearl earbobs the girls had given her three years ago.

Wishing to avoid Mary and Kate, she carefully descended the stairs. But it was her birthday, and they would be busy helping Lucy and Granny Ann prepare the little celebration Richard always held for her. Would he throw it over? No, he would do it for the girls' sakes, at least.

She grabbed a straw bonnet, headed toward the potting shed for her flower shears and tried to find some solace in the garden. Sandy waved to her from his wheelwright works, and she looked over the meadow where Jacob had the new crop of foals scampering around him. Lucy sweating in the cookhouse; Simon and Tommy hefting stones for the new dormitory; field hands loading wagons. Burden upon burden never lifted from their shoulders.

It seems I am the one seeing things as they really are for the first time.

BEFORE JULIA FILLED the basket, the carriage came up the drive. It was a good two hours before the Fourth of July event should have finished. She reminded herself that her only task was to console her daughters. That, unfortunately, required controlling her rage at their father.

Jerry held the reins loosely, letting the horses walk at their leisure until he halted them in the breezeway. Julia put her shears on a fence post and moved toward the carriage, clutching the handle of the basket so tightly it hurt. Richard did not wait for Jerry to help the girls out of the carriage.

He gave Julia a quick glance; she kept her face frozen in a smile as he handed the girls out. Imogene returned her smile with a weak one. Adaline's face looked blotchy from tears, but she beamed unnaturally with a forced grin and kissed Julia on the cheek.

"For the vases in the dining room." Julia held out an equal share of cuttings to each of them. She tossed the basket into the carriage and walked toward the house, an arm around each of them. Richard removed her hand from its place at Genie's waist and gave her a tug. She fought off the instinct to shake away his touch.

"I'll be in soon, girls," she said.

"Oh, no, Mama," Adi replied. The strained cheerfulness in her voice cut Julia's heart so deeply she had to choke back tears. "We have a few presents to get ready for you."

Genie's eyes met Julia's, and they wordlessly agreed it would be best if she left them alone for a while, presents being the least of reasons.

Jerry drove the carriage toward the stable, leaving them alone together. Richard refused to let Julia pull away her hand. He slowed down and waited for the girls to enter the house before he turned to her.

In a broken voice, he apologized. "I'm going to need to spend the rest of my life undoing the damage of my attack on you this morning. I am so ashamed, Jewel. Of myself, of my kin, of this town—it was like reliving that time we went to church after we were married, you remember?"

How could she ever forget that day, or this? But at least, he was man enough to admit he was wrong. She forced herself to nod.

"Aurelia Scott and my own niece, Nancy, approached us. They took the girls by the arm, like they were best of friends, and then they started talking in that sickening sweet way: 'There simply isn't even the tiniest bit of room—and your barouche is so comfortable. Don't you think you'd be better off watching your father from there?'"

If the situation had not been so horrible, Julia would have laughed at Richard's mimicry. But he had mimicked her well enough this morning, and with that memory she tugged away. He pulled her back.

"No, Julia, you've got to bear with me. After that, the girls did the most wonderful thing—they kissed my cheek and walked back to the carriage as cheerfully as if they'd only forgotten their parasols. I was so proud of them..." His voice cut off and he looked away.

"They smiled so sweetly, and even Adi..." he swallowed, rubbing his sleeve over his face, "Adi held Genie's hand, and nodded to the people as they walked back to the road. I was honor-bound to give my speech, but all I could think was how to get to the girls as soon as I could. My mind went blank from rage. I don't even know what I said. I nearly ran past them all, and I couldn't get Jerry to turn the carriage around fast enough. My nephews—even Willie and Richard Mentor— my brothers John T and Henry," a sob stuck in his throat, and he shook his head, "I am so deathly sick of them all."

Despite her anger, she wanted to console him; never had she seen him in such pain. "Richard, don't torment yourself. It's just your nature to expect the best of people."

"You're too kind to me, Jewel, especially after the way I treated you this morning. I cannot forgive myself. I'd hand you my pistol except I'm partly afraid you might use it."

"Two hours ago, I would have!" As they stepped into the house, Richard wiped his face clean of dust, sweat and tears with his handkerchief, then took her hand and kissed it tenderly. Despite her impulse never to forgive him, a bit of her heart pieced back together. He shyly picked a few stray flower petals from the bodice of her dress before pulling her to him. She held herself stiffly; he bowed his head and let her go.

They stood together in awkward silence until he thought of something he hoped would soften her heart. "One redeeming event came of this morning, though. Tommy Scott? The one who bought Adi's favorite yearling? Well, he rode over to our carriage on that very same pony and gave Adi his flag."

"A very brave and foolish thing to do, under the circumstances, God love him. And what did Adi do?"

"She waved it in his face so it tickled his nose."

Julia laughed softly. The image was so clearly like a thousand others of Adi. "Well, we were both wrong about today."

"How? I mean, in what way were you wrong?" he asked.

"About Adi. It sounds like she was everything I thought only Genie was turning out to be." Julia untied her straw bonnet, then remembered her scissors. She headed toward the door, but Richard stopped her.

"I'm going to give you a birthday present you should've gotten a long time ago." Julia offered him a weak smile, but it held a promise of forgiveness. It was all he needed to propel him forward. "Nevertheless." He led her to his study. "Sit here while I do this." He nodded to the chair where he had first seen Imogene at her breast thirteen years ago.

The faint echo of James's words *Know, whenever you need to know it...* still clung to the walls. Oh, how she needed to know she was loved, really loved. "I need to get my scissors."

"They can wait. What, you think it's going to rain?" he said absent-mindedly. She watched uneasily as his hand raced across the beautiful white paper, scarring it with his angular scrawl. After blotting it, he crossed the room and handed it to her.

Despite his old and poorly healed wounds, he knelt by her side as she read it. She knew what the gesture cost him in pain.

"What I did to you this morning was unpardonable. I ought to be horsewhipped. You were looking after our girls, and I was just plain inexcusably thoughtless."

Julia finally looked into his eyes, turquoise with fresh tears.

"In my mind, you've always been free, but this makes it binding once I get it to the courthouse. And I will not subject you to my temper again, that's a promise I vowed to God on the way home, and that I make to you. But you have to forgive me."

He put his head in her lap and cried.

Chapter 17
White Sulfur Spring
July 20, 1833. White Sulfur Spring Farm

Julia rushed down the stairs and out the door to meet Theobald. She ran alongside him, yelling up to him until he reined in his horse. "I can't make it stop!"

In all the years of working together, Theobald had never heard panic in Julia's voice. He heard it now. "Did you give him the calomel?"

"Yes, but I've run short of mercury. We've used up nearly everything treating Jacob, Lucy and Kate. We lost Granny Ann and Mary this morning, but thank God Jerry's been spared. It's spread to the school. There's twenty that are down! Hephzibah and Rose!" she sobbed. When he dismounted, they walked together quickly toward the house.

Theobald put his arm around her for support. Her simple work shift stank of sickroom. Her hair fell into her face, her eyes stared and mouth drooped; she walked in a zigzag from exhaustion. "Who has been helping you?"

"Hephzibah, until she fell sick last night. Daphne and Phoebe are still alright, but they're working on the schoolboys. Charlotte's daughter just left to get some more compounds from her mother—she's been nursing Rose and Hephzibah in their cabin."

Julia struggled for breath as they mounted the stairs. When they reached the spare bedroom where Richard lay curled in a tight ball, the doctor stopped. The smell of vomit and diarrhea outdid the strong lye wash Julia had applied to the walls and floor.

Theobald rolled Richard over onto his back. Richard drew his legs up and groaned as he discharged a volume of off-color water from his bowels. It was the first time he had been conscious in hours. He grimaced and struggled to answer. "Haven't thrown up in a while. Held a little water down just now."

Theobald clenched his jaw, breathed quickly through his mouth before attempting to reply. "It's beyond belief you're still alive, you're so dehydrated. But not decimated like others I've seen today. Perhaps you received the calomel in time."

Working together with speed and agility, Theobald and Julia turned Richard from side to side, stripping away soiled garments and bed clothes and replacing them with clean ones. "Make sure you let none of the fluids touch you in any way," Theobald warned Julia as she stuffed the ruined linens into a canvas sack.

A sudden fear gripped him as he watched her; he turned away and took a small muslin bag from his valise. "Can you make this tea for him? Good and strong. It wouldn't hurt you to have a cup, as well." When he placed the little muslin bag in her hand, he squeezed her fingers and gave her a comforting smile. Julia returned his smile with heartbreaking tenderness. He watched her tuck the tea bag under her sleeve and drag the sack of linens to the door.

A tiny strand of hair caught in her mouth as she bent over. She paused at the door to pull it off her tongue with her free hand, moistening her finger to keep the hair back.

Richard's voice startled her: "Are the girls and the babies safe?"

"They are," she answered hoarsely. "They went to Blue Spring three days ago with the Indian boys who weren't sick. Thank the

Lord, we left the old dormitory standing over there! Henderson and his whole family caught it. They're here with us."

When she turned back to answer, the blue circles beneath her eyes and the thinness of her mouth shocked him. How long had he been sick? Three days, Julia said, since the babies left. "And all this time you've had no sleep taking care of me, have you?"

"Not just you, but everybody else here at White Sulfur," Theobald answered, bending over his patient.

"Where have you been, Theo?" Richard gasped as his friend palpated his stomach and abdomen.

"More like, where hasn't he been?" Julia answered instead. "The whole county is hit hard. I'll be right back. Going to make you some tea."

Theobald quickly covered Richard with an extra sheet, then followed her out. "Isn't there anyone left to help you with him?"

"Now that he's conscious, it would mortify him to have anyone else see him like this. It doesn't matter, anyway. There are none to spare." She rested her head against the wall. It felt so cool, so solid. She needed something to lean on. "It's happened so terribly fast."

"Yes. Odd how it has passed by some farms completely, while others..."

"Like ours?"

"Yes, I'm afraid so. Your place, along with the school, seem to be taking the brunt of it."

Richard groaned, and Theo ran back to him with the basin. Fortunately, it wasn't needed. He hurried back to Julia, whom he'd left mid-sentence. Mid-thought, anyway.

"All fingers are pointing our direction, aren't they?" she asked.

He nodded self-consciously and occupied his hands with carefully rolling up his shirt sleeves. When he looked at her, he could think of nothing to comfort her. Holding her in his arms had not been possible for a long time.

"Yes, it's true, and it's not just the fools around Great Crossing. The entire country now believes it's the unrighteous who fall prey to cholera. They're calling it 'God's purge'. Their proof relies on the evidence that the dead are mainly Irish, Indians and slaves. Such damned fools."

He reached out and stroked the side of her face. Although the years had diminished the yearning for her, they had not weakened his love.

"You are better, stronger, than any woman I know," he said with finality. He returned to Richard's bedside, leaving the words hanging in the air for her to take or reject as she pleased.

Julia kept her head against the wall. Her old friend's touch awakened for a moment the memory of his caress, his kiss, on that night so long ago. How many years she had suffered the pain of that desire. They never spoke of it, letting the bond of friendship grow stronger in the silence.

She heard the echo of his voice: "Know, when you need to know it, that I adore you." Then Richard's "you have to forgive me." And she had, as he made every effort to care for her, the girls, their grandchildren, as he freed Milly and Patience.

Within minutes, Julia returned with the nasty-smelling infusion. "Cures smell almost as bad as sickness," she mumbled.

Theobald propped Richard's head up with one lean, elegant hand, taking the cup from Julia with his other hand. He held it to Richard's lips. "Rest a couple of hours, Julia. I want to observe him."

"But you must have a dozen more families to—the linens will need changing. It would be even more..." she stammered.

"Nonsense. You've seen him through the crisis. Besides, this is nothing compared to the state he was in at the Thames. Go on, now."

As she reached the door to leave, she paused and watched the two men she had loved in such entirely different ways. She looked into Richard's eyes, and he held her gaze for several seconds. When she smiled to reassure him, he managed to smile back despite his pain.

"Jewel," he said, in a husky voice, "rest up, now. We've got a lot to do before we can let our grandchildren back in the house. Including the next one."

"I didn't know you knew!"

"When has Adi ever been able to keep a secret from me?" He grinned like his old self for a moment. She knew then he was going to be alright.

A thousand images of his face wearing that teasing smile passed before her as she collapsed on her bed. Within seconds, she fell asleep.

Chapter 18

Greatest Crossing

July 24, 1833. Great Crossing Baptist Church

Imogene waited with her husband, Daniel, and Adaline with her husband, Thomas, in a carriage on the crest of the hill overlooking the cemetery. When they saw Sandy's huge figure sitting atop the approaching wagon, they descended the hill rapidly, wanting to be in place for their father. He followed behind the wagon that held Julia, laid in her hastily made coffin. Old Hickory walked in a beleaguered step that fit the wretched appearance of his rider.

Sandy drove to the edge of a small cemetery outlined by pale marble squares. The white stone looked frail next to the dark slate that trimmed most of Great Crossing. This was the place where Julia returned to Jemima.

The burial mounds of Jemima's husband and sons had been flattened by nature long ago, proof that their family had been spared death for too many years. The pile of earth in the corner at Jemima's feet looked obscenely fresh, a black disturbance against the summer grass that covered the rest of the burial ground.

Daniel and Thomas stood awkwardly by as their wives clung to their father and wept. Richard shook with sobs, but he choked them back when he heard the scraping noise of Sandy pulling the coffin across the dropped gate of the wagon.

"I must do this, girls," he told them. Richard steadied himself with a cane and stepped toward the wagon.

"Sons, you come along, too." Daniel and Thomas stepped behind him. They helped Sandy steady the box; it gave off the sweet smell of freshly sanded ash. The hysteria of cholera forced everyone to bury the dead without time to mourn. Julia had been gone mere hours.

When Daniel and Thomas leveraged themselves to catch the weight, they gasped. The coffin felt empty, and they stared at each other in alarm. Richard understood the look on their faces. He clenched the bridle strap Sandy had tied around the box at the last moment. The four men walked the few feet to the waiting sexton, who slipped the lowering ropes around the head and foot of the coffin.

"It's as light as a child," the man sighed. "All the coffins feel that way if it's the cholera that got 'em."

Imogene held back an urge to slap him. She had to remind herself that he was used to death, but at his words, Adaline fell to her knees and began to sob, calling out for their mother. Thomas knelt by her, helpless to stop her.

Richard knelt with difficulty on her other side, and pushed her head onto his chest, shushing her like a baby. "You know what I dressed her in, honey?"

Adi continued to wail, unable to answer him.

"What, Papa?" Imogene answered instead, coaxing him to continue.

"It was the pretty pink dress with the big ruffles that you and Genie loved so much when you were little girls."

Weeping openly, Richard could not push away the image of Julia so horrible, so fresh, in his mind. He had taken her from Theobald, washed her, and put her in the dress he'd bought in Alexandria for her trousseau. So shrunken was her body by the devastation of cholera, the gown had draped in deep folds over her sunken torso.

"Why didn't you let us dress her, Daddy? We never got to say goodbye, to tell her we love her..." Adi cried.

"The sickness—it's so highly contagious—we were all afraid that just breathing the air in the same room with her..." Richard choked on the words. "And you know, you've got to think about your child just like Genie has to protect Rich and Amanda. But I put some roses in her hands and told her they were from her girls."

He stopped and sucked in a little air before he finished. "They were from the bushes you planted for her last year. They looked so lovely. Same color as her dress..."

He would never tell them no trace had been left of the tall, beautiful woman they had known as their mother. He would never forget the look of terror on Sandy's face when he nailed down the coffin lid, trembling with fear that Hephzibah and Rose might meet this fate.

On the short ride to the cemetery, Imogene had asked her husband to read her mother's favorite text. It was from the Book of Ruth. Now as Daniel read, Richard glanced over at Imogene, acknowledging her choice by wiping away the tears from his eyes and giving her a heartbreaking smile.

Then Thomas took a step forward. "Thank you, dear Lord, in this time of sore trial come upon so many of us, for your Son and the hope of the resurrection. Thank you for your daughter Julia. She brings back to you a life filled with kind words and deeds. She never thought of herself, but always thought about others. She never stopped encouraging us to be better than we thought we could be. We pray your grace will be upon us, so that we will not grieve, but be comforted. In Jesus name we pray, amen."

Adaline clung to him as he prayed, muffling her tears so that her husband's words could be heard. They had barely pronounced "amen" when the sexton and Sandy began pouring dirt over the coffin. They worked furiously. So many more had to be buried that day. Julia was the first, laid in the ground just as the sun rose.

"I wish we'd buried her at Blue Spring, Daddy, by Little George," Adi said. The sounds of the dirt clots grew muffled as the coffin at last became covered with soil.

"Putting her here is the last gesture I can make in her honor, honey," Richard said. He looked at Imogene. "She's a Johnson, and this is where she belongs. And I want to be buried right here beside her when the time comes, alright?"

Imogene and Adaline braced themselves against their father; the three of them wept together as the sexton tamped down the last of the soil. The doves began their mourning calls from the rooftop of the new church, making them all aware of the ordinary sounds of a new day beginning—a boy fussing at a herd of cattle, a wagon hitting a rut in the road.

"It's time to go, now." Richard straightened, wiped his face and pulled on his hat.

"Come home with us, Papa," Adi begged.

"I need to go back. All of Henderson's family and too many Indian boys are still down—we're so short of able-bodied men—they need me, and I don't think it can get me sick again. But all you, stay away, hear me? Taking care of me, that's what killed your mother. And if you came, thinking you'd help spare me the work, it might take you off, too. Or worse, one of the babies. None of us could bear going through this again, could we?"

Another group began to gather at the larger cemetery for members of the church congregation. Reverend Silas Noel led them, glanced toward the Johnson's gated plot, and met Richard's eye. But, despite the righteous indignation in his soul, Richard felt helpless, like a man with the ground giving way beneath his feet.

JAMES THEOBALD STAGGERED up the wooded hill overlooking the churchyard. He hid in a grove of young trees thick with foliage and watched the little procession leave Julia behind. Richard survived because Julia had willed it so, had sacrificed her own life to make it happen. How else explain his own inability to save her despite his skills and devotion?

With each hour over the past three days, Richard had grown stronger, Julia weaker. And at the end when she couldn't speak, when she did not know who was holding her, bathing her, willing her to stay please stay, Richard knew, and let her die in his arms, rocking her body in one final attempt to make her live.

Chapter 19
Remnants
Inauguration Day 1837. Washington, DC

The sunlight shifted; the dust settled. The castle remained on its cliff, no closer to the waves than it had been a quarter century ago. Must be getting old, he mumbled, wiping the tears from his face on the corner of the sheet.

Lydia lay there, not moving. Playing possum, he'd bet, though why she couldn't bestir herself to help him on this, of all days, he could not understand. The inflammation in his old war wounds left him crippled on mornings this cold. She knew even the act of buttoning his shirt was an ordeal and tying his cravat an impossibility. Lifting his hand to run a brush through his hair had become such a challenge that he usually left it to the winds to arrange it on his walk to the Capitol.

What he needed was a valet, but he could not bear the thought of having another man in the house and run the risk of losing Lydia like he had her older sister. Lettie had succumbed to the charms of that Indian boy when they'd gone back to Kentucky. Why was it that he never gave these girls any credit for imagination? Because Julia hadn't had any?

What Julia had was old-fashion honor, never letting herself sit idle. This new generation had too much time on their hands, and what else could they do except daydream about some young buck or going on some crazy escapade? It was a constant dance, like an old Virginia reel. The pretty young gals liked the old men for their wealth and power. They liked the young men because they were tall and hard.

Lettie—how he missed her. There had been no love on his part, but after Julia died, he had let his rage over her loss devolve into lust. Lettie was not as fair as Julia, but he found her gold skin captivating. Her agate eyes glared with a fearlessness that Julia would never have dared to show.

She proved to be just like her mother, Lily: greedy in her eagerness for presents and carriage rides to town, and generous in expressing her appreciation. Even now he shook his head in wonder and in loss. He discovered too late where she had learned such things, and he was grateful he hadn't caught the clap, or worse. But she had made him feel like a man, and in gratitude he let her have her way in the house, in the shops and in his bed, doing that which he never would have attempted to do with Julia, whom he had loved too deeply.

His housekeeper. He was stuck with it, the accepted euphemism in Washington for her other role. Lettie had put on a good show in his drawing room here on Maryland Avenue. Imogene wanted her out of White Sulfur, not that Daniel would have succumbed to Lettie's wiles. And the girl had shone here in ways that Kentucky would not have allowed. She knew how to dress and style her hair, pour tea and sit upright on the end of a settee, as if Lily had stuck around to teach her.

He sighed and looked across the bed at Lydia. If only this younger sister would turn out as entertaining to the callers who came here to hash it out with him.

He still felt badly about having to sell Lettie off when she ran away with that Indian boy. What woman, any color, wouldn't have desired him, a half-breed with the best features of both races? He had to give them credit for their audacity, running away in broad daylight in his enormous barouche, with his best horses and fifteen hundred dollars of his cash.

Patience had gotten dragged along, pretending to be Lettie's servant. Now that had hurt him. He had freed Milly after Curtis died, just months before the cholera, to work for a dress shop. And when they'd asked to come back home to live with him, he'd treated Patience like a daughter, so how she could betray him like that, he couldn't tell.

For a moment he saw Julia coming to him in the moonlight and felt her pressed against him as they fled on Pegasus. At least they'd had the sense to elope in the middle of the night. But then, they had been older. Seventeen-year-olds like Lettie and her Indian didn't have much sense, and that was a fact.

He hadn't been all that sure about his son-in-law Daniel until then. All the Pences were a quiet lot who had kept to themselves, worked hard, and slowly taken over a bit of Scott County that everybody, including himself, had coveted. Daniel had taken care of the whole filthy mess with Lettie for him, when he hadn't had the heart to see it through, selling her to a widow in Tennessee who vowed to keep a strict eye on her. The Indian boy he had to keep on at the school another year, for the revenue he brought in.

At least he got to come back to Washington, to try to forget about it all. He hoped his daughter didn't know about his goings-on with Lettie.

After Julia left him, he didn't have the heart to live in his big new house at White Sulfur Spring alone. The place was vast enough to make a comfortable inn, and the thought had occurred to him on a couple of occasions to turn it into one. But for now, it was an ideal place for his daughter and her family.

And one of these days, he'd have to close down the Choctaw Academy. Henderson was getting along in years, and keeping an eye on a hundred boys was more than the man and his assistants could handle. He certainly didn't want Genie and Daniel to have to deal with them.

With a moan, he pushed himself up from the edge of the bed, heaved a sigh through puffed-out cheeks, and dug his toes into the lamb's wool slippers to get his balance. At least Lydia had remembered to put them there. She was alright, sometimes.

He reached for his goat hair housecoat, a ratty old thing Lucy had made for him out of gratitude for getting her and Jacob over to Blue Spring. It was a comfort to him, a reminder of twenty years back, the best time of his life. Cholera had taken Lucy off the day before Julia. Then Kate, leaving poor Jacob to die last.

He hated to shave in the housecoat because the water dribbled down into the sleeves and up his arm, but he needed it this morning for an extra layer of warmth. Shuffling to the door, he looked back at Lydia, who had hidden her head under a pillow.

The sun had found her, and she didn't like being found. She burrowed into the bed covers. He wanted to yank them off and swat her good, but didn't even have to fight the impulse; it required too much energy, which he needed for the hours to come. Still, the thought of such a prank made him chuckle to himself.

He wished he could jump in the White Sulfur pool right now. He found such solace in its water. He had gotten accustomed to the gassy smell quickly enough. Julia had hated it, but that was more on account of her attachment to Blue Spring. The only reason she agreed to move to the new place was because he'd promised to give Blue Spring to Adi and Thomas for a wedding present.

It had been quite a coup for one of the high and mighty Scott boys to marry his Adi. When she died after bringing little Rob into the world, he and Thomas both nearly lost their minds. He loved his grandson, but his heart still broke every time he looked at that little face so like Adi's.

He wished Lydia would get up, but he had spoiled her over the past few months in an attempt to take her mind off her sister. More likely, she had been happy to upstage her. He let her have her way most of the time, but she knew not to push him too far. What had happened to Lettie could happen to her, and he enjoyed having that power over her when she got too smart. He had little power over her, otherwise, unable to play the part of lover to anyone. Not since Adi died.

He'd become ashamed of his carryings-on, he supposed. The girl was content to share his bed only for the night-long warmth of his body, which, he was loath to admit, had started to take on the round shape of an actual bed-warmer of the copper variety. Sometimes she seemed fond of him.

But today, right now, he needed to shave, to dress and have his cravat tied, and tied properly. He peeked down at the floor outside his bedroom. No wash water. He hollered down the staircase.

"Malvina!" Lydia let out a sigh so loud he heard it through the pillow. Selfish girl, he thought, beginning to lose his temper.

"Mallie!" He wanted to swear, but breathed deep and said calmly, "Lydia, get up, now. It may be just another day to you, girl, but I am about to become yours, Mallie's and the entire nation's vice-president. The least I could ask for is some hot water for a proper shave."

Before Lydia had the pillow off her head, the noise of Malvina's feet and the sloshing of the water came up the stairs.

"Good girl," he told her as she poured the steaming water into his basin. It splashed onto the coverlet, and Malvina glanced sheepishly at the ball under the blanket that was Lydia. Richard gathered from that look it was time to talk to Lydia again about being kind to her underlings.

Malvina was a good girl, big for an eight-year-old. She looked twelve, so people expected more out of her than she was old enough or smart enough to give. Well, maybe she was smarter than most children her age. She must have sensed that she was going to be a beauty, that it already stirred jealousy in the likes of Lydia. She kept a dour expression on her otherwise pretty face most of the time, and instead of wearing her long hair in a braid down her back, she pinned it to the nape of her neck like a spinster.

The image of the girl and her mother, standing apart on that auction platform in Alexandria, flashed across his mind. Thank God, his father saved Henrietta and Julia from such a fate. Thank God, he was able to save this child and Elvira.

"Tell your mama my dyspepsia's real bad this morning," Richard told Malvina before he pressed a hot rag on his whiskers. "Just a bowl of warm milk with a raw egg, maybe a couple a biscuits without butter should do for my breakfast."

"Yessir," Malvina replied, happy in the thought she'd get to have some of that breakfast he didn't want. Mama had already fixed up most of it. The girl turned around swiftly when she heard something fall to the floor.

"This blasted cold, I can't hold onto anything!" Malvina heard the Colonel curse, but ran toward him anyway and swooped up the razor he had dropped.

"Careful!" he admonished as he tried to back away. But he lost his balance and stumbled toward the bed, landing face down.

Lydia threw off the coverlet and came around to his side of the bed, pushing the girl away. "Stupid," she hissed at Malvina, who came back toward her master despite the shove. With Lydia on one side, herself on the other, they managed to roll and push him upright. Lydia snatched her robe quickly and tied it close around her, then sat next to Richard, rubbing his hands between her own to warm them.

Malvina found the slippers that had come off his feet and knelt to put them back on him.

"An inauspicious start for a vice-president!" he said, shaking his head, trying to laugh away a sense of foreboding. He did not like reading too much into things, and he did not want to believe in premonitions, but he believed in them, anyway. He cursed his old wounds for making him stiff and clumsy, but knew that without them, he would not have gotten where he was.

Had the indignant spirit of Tecumseh pushed him down to humble him? Or saved him from cutting his own throat? The thought made him chuckle and the girls looked at each other, in that look that often passed between them, in which he read, "he's a little crazy, but what else can we do?"

Lydia was fully awake now; her voice, far too husky and controlled for a sixteen-year-old, took command.

"Alright, Colonel, just see what you get for leaving bed an hour too soon. What's the whole mess of senators gonna do anyway if you don't get there on time? They have to wait for *you*, remember? Mallie, get him his stick from downstairs and you better be faster than a fox or I'll lay it across your backside. Colonel, you stay right where you are, and let me get the fire going before you move another muscle."

She spoke crossly, like a worn-out mother, and yanked the cover off the bed as he had so wanted to do earlier. After she draped it roughly around him, he sat as meek as a scolded child on the edge of the mattress.

Lydia ranted on as she stoked the fire. "You don't give me credit for nothing, you know that? Don't you see I had your shaving kit all set out for you? And your waistcoat and overcoat nice and brushed, and your cravat new-pressed? And what about all this kindling and firewood I brought up last night to make sure you would get a nice warm room to wake up to, but no, you couldn't wait till it was the right time to get up."

He chuckled nervously. She was right; he was up earlier than anyone expected him to be. He looked around the room that was now filling with light. He saw his toilet set, his coat and cravat, the pile of firewood, for the first time.

"I know this is a special day for you. I'm not stupid!"

Richard listened, mesmerized by the cadence in her voice. She leaned on every other word with heavy emphasis. What a preacher she would have made, had she been a man.

"Elvira and Mallie and me've been thinking about nothing else for a whole month now, and we've got the whole house ready for all the callers you're going to have piling in here for the rest of the week. But no, you can't let Lydia or poor little Malvina get an extra hour sleep!"

The word 'sleep' came hurdling towards him like a horseshoe thrown at his head.

Soon the fire crackled loudly and radiated warmth across the small room. Within moments, he tossed off the bed cover and, as Mallie came clomping up the stairs (he could tell she was playing mountain climber with his stick, the way Adi did at that age) he moved to push himself up to his feet.

"Don't you be getting up now, Colonel. You fall on that head of yours and crack open your skull, folks'll be sayin' they got some kind a drunkard for their vice-president, and you wouldn't want that in the papers back home now, would you?"

Lydia was wound up now; the cultured accent she used as his hostess downstairs transformed into the sound of the laundry girls back home. It tickled him, delighted him. He longed for her to sit on his knee, kiss his cheek and tell him how handsome he was for an old grandpa.

But no; that was Adi, and it repulsed him that he could entertain the thought of Lydia being affectionate with him in so genuine and sweet a way. Adi could be bossy and kind at the same time. Lydia was not kind. She was ambitious for praise, and the only way she would earn that is if he behaved himself and made a decent show at his inauguration and got a line or two in the *Gazette* about how dignified he looked.

He set his mind to that, and pushed away the memory of his child, and refused to hear that cruel voice always puncturing his thoughts with the main one. *Your daughter is dead at twenty-two, and you're still alive. Just like Jackson, the Fates granted your wish but demanded the thing you loved most as payment for the favor.*

Malvina put his hickory cane under his right hand. "I'm alright, now, child," he smiled sadly at her. "Just needed to get the circulation going is all." She gave him one of her rare smiles in return, and it touched him. He patted her shoulder gently, before leaning on it to get to his feet. Malvina bent under his weight for a moment then steadied him.

"Mallie, bring the Colonel over here so I can shave him." He sat down obediently in the low-backed armchair he used for reading. "Fetch some more hot water. This has gotten cold." Malvina ran off to follow her orders. Lydia wrapped a wrung-out cloth around his face. He found it more than sufficiently warm, but there was no crossing his little housekeeper over the fact right now.

"You just sit there and let those old whiskers soften up. I'm going to go get a cup of coffee. Want some, too?" she asked in an impertinent huff.

"Unh-unh. Stomach upset," he mumbled from under his face wrap.

He hated for her to leave. He did not want to be alone with his thoughts. They were all so sad, so full of longing for Julia and Adi, and the reminder that as much as Imogene and her family wished to be here for this glorious moment in his life, they were not welcome by society.

He hoped Lydia could get him turned out well enough this morning. She had a way with sow's ears like him. But no one could spruce him up like Adi could. Where had she learned such things? Not from Julia, nor Imogene. Julia had always respected his manhood and never fussed over him; he thought it was because they'd both had enough mothering from the same woman. And Genie thought he was perfect just the way he was.

He felt his mind giving way to the inevitable force of his most painful thoughts, despite his best efforts to bar them. His memories were like marshlands surrounding what was left of his heart, and it took too much courage to wade through them. How had he managed to survive the cholera and not Julia?

He knew the answer well enough. She had worn herself out taking care of him and their people, the Indian boys, and Henderson's family. She had never been a woman to hold anything back, but gave herself completely over to whatever anyone needed from her. And he had been as needy, as greedy and heedless as Lydia or Lettie.

Why, why had he sought comfort in these girls? For nigh on three decades, he'd been faithful enough to Julia, although the ladies in Washington paid no heed to his protestations and continually sought to make a match for him. "Oh, the gift the giftie gie us to see ourselves as others...' He felt like Burns's "Louse". The poet may have been thinking of this very thing—old men with young women. He tried to look at himself as others might see him, but he'd given up long ago caring what others thought.

Lydia was finally back. He could smell the coffee despite the cloth covering his face and decided it was his turn to play possum. She put down the tray on the little table in front of the fireplace. Malvina followed close behind with fresh hot water for his shave.

He kept his eyes closed tight while Lydia removed the stale towel. She replaced it with one so hot it took his breath away before making him relinquish a sigh of complete satisfaction. Then she massaged his face and scalp through the cloth, letting her hands dig between the folds of skin until they reached the bone.

He could hear the clicking sound of brush against jar as Malvina mixed the shaving soap. With one eye, he saw Lydia frown as she prepared the razor for his face. How easy it would be for her to dispatch him with one swift move!

The thought was not altogether unpleasant, and an easier way to go than by the slow death that batch of cutthroats in the Senate no doubt had in store for his political career. He chuckled.

"Be still!" Lydia commanded.

"Mmph," he grunted in agreement to her will. He wanted to laugh outright thinking about what Marty had said, how being vice-president was like dying and being buried for four years. But it had gone well for Marty who would be president in a few hours. They'd already talked about being running mates for the next round.

Mama, can you look after your boy for another eight years?

He felt so tired, so very, very old. Could he even keep going for eight more years?

You have to go on, son. Or would you rather be entirely forgotten?

AFTERWORD

ANDREW JACKSON'S POLICIES, which Martin Van Buren vowed to carry out, began to unravel soon after the inauguration. The collapse of American finance known as the Panic of 1837 doomed the eighth president and Richard Johnson to one term in office.

After their defeat in 1840, Richard returned to Kentucky, served as a state legislator, and turned White Sulfur Spring into an inn and health spa. He died on November 19, 1850, one month after his seventieth birthday, while serving in the Kentucky Legislature. Records of the time make mention of stroke and dementia, making it "painful to see him on the floor [of the state legislature] attempting to discharge [his] duties". He is buried at the Frankfort cemetery instead of the family plot at Great Crossing Baptist Church.

Dr. Theobald moved his family to Frankfort. His son became a respected physician.

Betsey Johnson and her husband, Gen. John Payne, lived and died on land at Great Crossing and were the parents of thirteen children. Betsey died April 16, 1846.

Col. James Johnson and his wife Nancy Payne had twelve children, their ninth Richard Mentor's namesake. James died August 13, 1826, during his term as a member of the United States Congress.

William Johnson married Betsey Payne, a relative of John Payne's. They raised five sons. William died in 1814 from effects of the war. Ward Hall stands on land originally settled by William.

Sallie Johnson and her husband, Gen. William Ward, had eight children. Sallie died August 25, 1846. Ward Hall, with its Greek Revival architecture, is a Georgetown, Kentucky landmark.

Judge Benjamin Johnson married Matilda Williams. He moved his family to Arkansas where he served as a federal district judge.

Their son Robert served in Congress for fourteen years. Benjamin died October 2, 1849.

Robert Johnson died at age twenty-six on August 5, 1812, in the War of 1812.

Rev. John Telemachus Johnson married Sophia Lewis. He was active in the Kentucky legislature and served in the United States Congress. His search for meaning led him to join the Campbellite movement. He became a leader of the Reforming Baptists. He died December 17, 1856.

Joel Johnson married Verlinda Clagett Offut in 1817. They settled in Arkansas. He took no interest in public service. He died June 16, 1846.

George Washington Johnson died May 17, 1810, age seventeen, at Great Crossing, cause unknown.

Capt. Henry Johnson married Elizabeth Flournoy whose family were political rivals of the Johnsons. Henry became a partner with John T in building the Reforming Baptist Church. He died April 2, 1862. His youngest daughter, Margaret, broke with him over her support of Richard and Julia. Margaret freed her slaves in 1858. She is the subject of *Like a Green Laurel* by John Erwin.

Of Richard's ten siblings, only John Telemachus and Henry survived him. As a final blow to Imogene and her family, the two men signed a vindictive affidavit filed in Scott County after her father's death, testifying that their brother "left no...children."

Imogene Malvina Johnson and Daniel Brown Pence were married by Reverend Silas Noel in 1830. They had seven children—Richard M J (died young), Amanda Malvina, Mary Jane, Daniel Franklin, Albert, Grace Maria and Edward Herndon—and lived at White Sulfur Spring. The house is now privately owned and renovated, standing today as a beautiful example of neo-classical architecture. Fortunately, Imogene's uncles were powerless to take away the property deeded to her and Daniel by her father. She died in 1883 at the age of seventy-one and is buried at the Pence cemetery in Great Crossing.

Adaline Chinn Johnson (also seen as Adelaide) married Thomas W Scott in 1832. They had one son, Robert Johnson Scott, who became a doctor. Richard wrote that she "was a source of inexhaustible happiness and comfort to me".

Only a few ruins stand at the Blue Spring Farm and the original Choctaw Academy. The land is privately owned and inaccessible to the public.

Richard freed some of his slaves. Records in Scott County include deeds of emancipation for Phoebe, along with the family of Thomas Miller which included Patsy and daughter Frances, in 1828. Thomas had earned enough money on his hire-outs to buy his wife and daughter's freedom. Milly Chinn was freed in 1832. Her relationship to Julia as aunt is speculative. Milly and Patience Chinn's names appear on the census records of 1850. Patience was born about 1810 instead of 1819, the date used in the book.

The 1820 and 1830 censuses, which list only the name Richard M. Johnson as "Head of Household," show no indication that Julia and her daughters were considered free at that time. All females are categorized only by age, have the slave column checked, without names.

Shortly before Richard died, the 1850 census lists him living with an enslaved woman named Malvina, described as mulatto, age 21, along with two children named Adelaide and Theodore, ages six and five. The census taker used an abbreviated form of the name Johnson, which indexers interpreted as 'Jusan' instead of Jnson.

Significantly, Theodore Johnson received an education in Indiana at a private school that was paid for out of a Johnson bank account. In 1862, Theodore died fighting for the Union.

AUTHOR'S NOTE
BOOK ONE: Great Crossing

C hapter 1, Inauguration. Details about the inauguration of Martin Van Buren and Richard Mentor Johnson, as well as references to Jackson's administration, such as Indian removal and Peg O'Neale, center of the "Petticoat Affair," are based on fact. Richard kept a young housekeeper at his residence on Maryland Avenue; she was rumored to have been his mistress.

Chapter 2, First Run. All Johnson family members' names and ages used throughout the book are based on genealogical research. Jacob Chase and Lucy's names are taken from the Baptist church's death records of enslaved people at Blue Spring. Robert "Robin" Johnson traveled at the behest of President Washington to the Democratic Society Convention in Louisville in the fall of 1794 to stop aggression between Americans and Spanish troops and severe economic damage to western enterprises. The account of teenage Richard accompanying his father, although possible, is fictionalized. The Marshall family and their rivalry with the Johnsons is factual, although the interchange on the barge is fictitious. The Leclercs are fictitious.

Chapter 3, Fire. The Chinns of Louisville and the acquisition of much of their estate as described are fictitious, as are Jasper and Jamie. Henrietta Chinn's name was found in research; Milly Chinn's name appears in records although the exact relationship is not clear.

Sandy Miller's name appears on Johnson church records as an enslaved person.

Chapter 4, Distractions. Robin Johnson lost bids for lieutenant governor, but he served in many high-ranking state committees throughout his years as a Kentucky founder. Suzanne Bayton is fictitious, although based on lore that Richard's plans to marry a local seamstress and teacher were disrupted by his parents' strong disapproval. Rittenhouse Academy is an early church-sponsored school Robin Johnson helped establish. Hemp, grown as a cash crop in the making of rope used for shipping, was a main source of income for Kentucky at this time. Ropewalks, where fibers were twisted into rope of different thicknesses, could be over a thousand feet long. Jemima is said to have had a close bond with Julia. The quote from Richard's Independence Day speech on that day is authentic. Slavery, though fading, still existed in the northern states.

Chapter 5, No Contest. The Scotts, for whom Scott County, Kentucky is named, are factual, although Aurelia is fictitious. It is true that Richard ran uncontested for state legislator after his opponents dropped out. He advocated for education of marginalized groups, eventually opening the government-supported Choctaw Academy for Indian boys. His daughters, nieces and nephews, and neighbors attended classes there, as well.

Chapter 6, Defeat. Richard quickly became a member of a high-ranking state committee in the Kentucky Legislature. New Orleans was a center of culture and economic prosperity where women were known to own their own businesses. Keelboats were a popular form of transportation on the great western rivers.

Chapter 7, Election. Election dates and session schedules of the US Congress are based on records and adhered to throughout the book. Lewis Marshall's attack on Julia is fictitious. No evidence exists that Richard visited New Orleans, but the plaçage ball is yet another example of institutionalized abuse of enslaved women and girls. Etienne Delamar is fictitious, as are the Balls, although it is a revered Virginia ancestral name; Lee, Chinn and Markham are colonial Virginia names.

Chapter 8, Return. Doctor James Theobald is factual; his romantic relationship with Julia is not. Henrietta's death is unknown, although ectopic pregnancies account for two percent of today's pregnancies and can lead to fatality even with modern medicine. It was included as another example of tragic circumstances women faced. The books by Dr. DeGraaf and the Dutch school of anatomists are factual. The Napoleonic wars raging at this time led surgeons to develop techniques and write about their observations. Samuel is fictitious.

Chapter 9, Arrival. All congressmen and related references throughout the book are factual. Where Richard's speeches are quoted, they are excerpts from official records, as is the president's letter to Richard. The White House, known then as the Presidential Mansion, was gray until after the War of 1812 when it was repaired and painted white to cover the scars. His private interview with Jefferson is fictitious, although references to the president's ideas are based on historical information. Most people accept that Jefferson fathered Sally Hemings's children; some feel the vow he made to his dying wife to never marry again extended to any relationship with another woman, and that the children were his nephew's.

Chapter 10, Escape. Reverend Retting and the Great Crossing Baptist Church are based on fact. No proof exists that Richard and Julia legally married, due to the constraints of the law and the church during their lifetimes. He stated she was his wife in the eyes of God; the book developed the possibility of a literal meaning, which would have entailed a marriage on free soil.

Chapter 11, Crossing. References to place names such as Gaines Tavern, Kottmyer Ferry, Great Lickings, and Bullskin Trace are historic, along with Cincinatti's early names. Reverend Dennison and the small Baptist church are factual. Emma, Mrs. Turner and Jonah are fictitious. Richard fought to end debtors' prisons for many years.

Chapter 12, Exchange. According to the 1820 and 1830 census records, Julia was considered enslaved. At some point, Robin would have transferred ownership to Richard.

Book Two: Blue Spring

Chapter 1, A Tour. The description of Blue Spring Farm is fictitious. Patsy is the only one of the house servants in this chapter based on a factual name found in records.

Chapter 2/3 First Sabbath/Callers. The church and Reverend Retting, along with family members' names are factual. The tradition and formalities as described were typical of the times. Sallie Johnson Ward and her children had moved in with Richard at Blue Spring for a year and was the closest to him of all his siblings.

Chapter 4, Expectations. Congressmen, Franklin Inn and the O'Neale family are factual; Kentucky members of Congress and others boarded there, although there is no proof Richard was one of them. Letters are fictitious, but interwoven with facts about people and events.

Chapter 5/6 A Friend/Preparations. Miscarriages today occur in an estimated one out of ten (or higher) pregnancies, while late miscarriages occur in about one out of 50. These were a common heartbreak for women before modern medicine, just as they are today. Phoebe is fictitious, but an enslaved woman named Daphne is found on church records as a Johnson farm worker. The miscarriage of little George is fictitious. George Johnson died at seventeen.

Chapter 7, Prophecy. Historical events discussed by Richard and his colleagues are factual.

Chapter 8, Imogene. The Marshall and Johnson feud escalated; the attack on Johnson family members is factual, as was the duel challenge and its resolution. Imogene's birthdate is known from

Pence family records. Quotes from the newspaper about Richard as read in the Payne Farm scene are factual.

Chapter 9, Hephzibah. Challenges of nursing, weaning and binding were common; treatments such as pokeroot were often used. Hephzibah is fictitious. Early place names and people of the War of 1812 are factual, as are their relationship to Richard. He became known after the War of 1812 as the father of the American cavalry for his insistence on the use of mounted militia, which he admired in Napoleon's campaigns.

Chapter 10, Tecumseh. All names and events are taken from factual records. Over time, Richard's supporters' claim that he was the slayer of the great Indian warrior gave way to testimony on behalf of another soldier's claim. Nevertheless, heroics became an important factor in getting men elected to high office at that time. The story of the white mare comes from a soldier's first-hand account of the battle. The Johnsons and Suggetts were heavily represented in this campaign. Richard sustained injuries that affected his health and mobility the rest of his life. He and others were taken by boat to Ft. Detroit. Dr. Mitchell was Governor Shelby's surgeon and attended Richard. Ft. Miegs was probably not used as a waystation, but it was familiar to Richard from the previous year's campaign.

Chapter 11, Adaline. Adaline's birthdate is not known. Richard's daughter is sometimes confused with Adelaide Johnson, daughter of James, who was born 1806 and died in childhood. James named his sixth child after Richard.

Chapter 12, Jemima. Jemima died February 23, 1814 and was buried at the Great Crossing Baptist Church in the Johnson plot. The plot is still there, but the alabaster headstones have deteriorated. Richard boarded with Congressional Chaplain Obadiah Brown and his family.

Chapter 13, Robin. His death date is found on records. Some have placed his marriage to Fanny Bledsoe before his marriage to

Jemima. However, I believe the stronger case is for his marriage to her in his advanced years. She was the daughter of a Baptist minister; Robin founded the town of Fredericksburg. Richard and most of the Johnson, Suggett and Payne men were Freemasons. John Telemachus struggled with issues of faith. He served successfully in the state then federal legislatures throughout his life and later became a Campbellite leader.

Chapter 14, Survival. The Tambura eruption in Indonesia on April 15, 1815, created what was known at the time as "the year without a summer." Because it was the greatest volcanic disturbance in human history, the ruination created across America and the world has many first-hand accounts. James's plans for a steamboat fleet came to fruition. He and Richard sank their personal fortunes into the Yellow Stone project. The failure of government bonds during the Panic of 1819 led to the Johnson brothers' near bankruptcy.

Chapter 15, Lily. Lily is fictitious. President Monroe and his entourage stayed overnight at Blue Spring during Independence Day week. Blue Spring hosted many dignitaries over the years with Julia's hospitality making it a popular stop for celebrities touring the western reaches of America. The *Calhoun* launched from Leestown, Kentucky, the first of six in the Johnson steamboat line. Reverend Henderson served as headmaster of the Choctaw Academy throughout its twenty-year charter.

Chapter 16, Independence Day. General Lafayette (Gilbert du Motier) of Revolutionary War fame toured America in 1824–25. He stayed at Blue Spring in late June and was feted by thousands at the property. Imogene and Adaline's performance before their guests was written about, as was the affectionate display of their Johnson relatives. The rejection of the girls at Richard's traditional Independence Day speech is based on a true event. Obadiah Brown and Richard became close friends in Washington; Mary Brown, though factual, was not a romantic interest. Her sister-in-law, a widow, may have been. The two census listings give no names for Julia and her daughters since they are included with the enslaved; historians may assume Julia knew herself to be an enslaved woman. For the arc of the story, I had her believe she was free.

Chapter 17, White Sulfur Spring. This was Richard and Julia's second home. The cholera epidemic of 1833 hit the state of Kentucky particularly hard. The Choctaw Academy, with over 100 students, as well as Reverend Henderson and his family, were affected, and killed Julia along with several other members of the Johnson household. Miraculously, Richard survived and worked to save the lives of many on his farm, despite his weakened condition. Because the cause of cholera was not understood, treatments such as mercury pills were used.

Chapter 18, Greatest Crossing. Julia's death and burial information are on Great Crossing Baptist Church records. Daniel Pence and Thomas Scott, along with their children's names, are based on records. Reverend Silas Noel's name is also from church records of the time; he performed the marriage of Daniel and Imogene.

Chapter 19, Remnants. Though not named Lettie, Richard's housekeeper did elope with one of the Choctaw Academy students and soon after was sold off as retribution. Her sister then became hostess and housekeeper at his home on Maryland Avenue. I used the fictitious names of Leticia and Lydia, daughters of Lily, to fill these factual roles. An enslaved woman named Malvina appears with Richard on the 1850 census along with that of two young children. Her appearance here is fictitious, but her age is based on that of the Malvina in the census. Her mother, Elvira, is fictitious. President Jackson's beloved wife, Rachel, died shortly after his election just as Richard's beloved daughter, Adi, died immediately after the election of 1836.

Acknowledgements

In the Fall of 2009, after visiting my daughter at her college in Virginia and with her encouragement, I drove to Georgetown, Kentucky. Strangers answered my questions with warmth and genuine kindness, even driving me to see the Johnson cemetery, the site of Blue Spring, and the home at White Sulfur Spring. I would like to thank Ken Wright, Jean Jeffords, Gene Childress, Richard Drean, Andrew Green, Lindsey Apple and most particularly, Ann Bolton Bevins, for their assistance all those years ago. I also wish to thank those descendants of Robin and Jemima Johnson who answered my letters and emails so graciously. Many researchers have come and gone, and some have published books about the Vice President, Julia Chinn and their descendants since then.

Deep, heartfelt thanks to my husband, children, family and friends who wouldn't let me give up on completing this book, to name a few: Stevie Ray, Cherie, Polly, Aunt Faye; Diane Bennett, Deb Bonafede, Peg McCay, Lloyd and Lura Campbell. Readers of the 2013 version, author Bruce McAllister, and my brother S.A. Gilbert, encouraged me as well as offered valuable advice on deep cuts and changes. After critically important suggestions from Cynthia M. Williams and Debra Thorpe, the version you are now reading came together during the 2020 "year we stayed home."

Lightning Source UK Ltd.
Milton Keynes UK
UKHW041526200622
404687UK00002B/647